Praise for Minister Faust's *The Al*

"It was only a matter of time before the hip hop culture would invade the literary world. With *The Alchemists of Kush*, Minister Faust is leading the invasion. His novel is possibly the first hip hop epic. Hip hop has a short attention span on most occasions. The *Alchemists of Kush* gives it gravitas."

—Ishmael Reed, author of *Mumbo Jumbo*

"Minister Faust's first two books broke new ground in the SF field. His latest, *The Alchemists of Kush*, not only breaks new ground; with the story-telling skills of a modern jali, the Minister creates new vistas of history, mythology, erudition, uplift, tragedy, triumph, and contemporary community activism. Once you start the first page of this book, you won't be able to put it down until you've finished the last one."

—Charles R. Saunders, author of *Imaro*

"A hell of a story. A hell of a book. A hell of a style. A frenetic novel and voice—very enjoyable. Minister Faust knows how to write about male relationships, brotherhoods, and getting into the hearts of men, and about boys turning into men. *The Alchemists of Kush* is a triumph, not just for Minister Faust, but for Edmonton and the community of Kush."

—Wayne Arthurson, author of *Fall From Grace*

"In *The Alchemists of Kush*, Minister Faust risks telling stories that threaten the empire-builders, that encourage us all to become agents of action. Such a novel demands a truthful response. I've been thinking we need prayers for right now. Advertising jingles and gangsta rhymes split our souls, jangle our spirits a thousand times a day. Minister Faust is a technician of the sacred, getting the geometry, the dance of our humanity into his words. Buy *The Alchemists of Kush* for yourself and a friend. Read it and then give it away. Give it away a lot."

—Andrea Hairston, author of *Redwood and Wildfire* and winner of the James Tiptree, Jr Award

"Minister Faust presents a fierce piece of fiction in a way that only he can. I was entertained, educated and fascinated with his alchemy. *The Alchemists of Kush* has to be one of the best books I've read this year."
—Milton John Davis, author of *Meji*

"I started *The Alchemists of Kush* and kept reading until I finished. Minister Faust has the most electrifying and true voice I've read in years. *The Alchemists of Kush* is brilliant."
—Sparkle Hayter, author of *What's a Girl Gotta Do?*

"The first modern Pan-Africanist coming-of-age story, bringing together the traditional components of the Hero's Tale with a rich understanding of Ancient Egypt and contemporary realities for diasporal youth. The characters jump off of the page as Minister Faust, one of the best black male writers of my generation, deftly moves back and forth between Ancient KMT and contemporary Edmonton."
—Lester K. Spence, author of *Stare Into the Darkness: The Limits of Hip Hop and Black Politics*:

"*The Alchemists of Kush* is its own kind of alchemy: ancient past, gritty present, mythic fantasy, social activism, it's how Minister Faust blends it all that gives the book its rare power. Reflecting the brilliance of his earlier novels, Minister Faust again strikes the perfect balance between eloquence and entertainment. Within the first twenty pages, I could (and did) imagine *The Alchemists of Kush* on the big screen. It's got that epic sweep to it. More importantly, I kept reading (and reading, and reading) because Minister Faust knows it's all about creating characters you'll love. I wept at the end."
—Mark Kozub, author of *The Uptown Browns*

"*The Alchemists of Kush* is both a powerful and vital contribution to Canadian literature that looks at contemporary Edmonton from an African-Canadian perspective. The characters reflect the true diversity of African-Canadians living in Edmonton. Hopefully this is the beginning of more great novels from people in Edmonton that look like us that tell stories about us."
—Arlo Maverick, MC/Producer, *Politic Live*

Also by Minister Faust

The Coyote Kings, Book One: Space-Age Bachelor Pad
Shrinking the Heroes
War & Mir, Volume I: Ascension
War & Mir, Volume II: The Darkold

A Bad Bad Beat Was Brewing
Journey to Mecha
E-Force: Sixteen Stories of Ultra-Freaking Awesomeness

THE ALCHEMISTS OF KUSH

The Alchemists of Kush

By
Minister Faust

INSPIRED BY TRUE STORIES

ARCHE PRESS

This is A005, and it has an ISBN of 978-1-63023-051-7.

Library of Congress Control Number: 2017936088

This book was printed in the United States of America, and it is published by Arche Press, an imprint of Resurrection House (Sumner, WA).

I gained my gold from the heart of an exploded star . . .

Cover Design by Gentle Robot

First trade paperback Arche Press edition: April, 2017.

www.archepress.com
www.resurrectionhouse.com

I dedicate this novel
to four community organizers
of diverse skills and singular spirit
who've spent decadeds of committment.
integrity. intelligence. and compassion
building social justice
in E-Town and elsewhere:

Laurence Frederick
Junetta Jamerson
Jennifer Kelly
and
Henry Carlo Service

DELTA

EMERALDS AND MAIDENS AT THE MILLSTONE

ASSAULT ON THE GOLDEN FORTRESS

APPENDICES

Author's Note

The Alchemists of Kush is composed of three stories. Each one is ten chapters long: "The Book of Then," "The Book of Now," and "The Book of the Golden Falcon."

Certainly, feel free to read the novel in the path it's printed (Chapter 1: "Then" + "Now," all the way to Chapter 10: "Then" + "Now," followed by all ten chapters of "The Book of the Golden Falcon").

But you could also read all the "Then"s as a group, followed by all the "Now"s together, ending with "The Book of the Golden Falcon" . . . or read the first chapters of every "Falcon," "Then," and "Now," all the way through to each one's tenth chapter.

Whichever path you choose, I'd be delighted to hear from you about how your order affected the way you experienced the stories and their characters.

Nub, wmet, ānkh,

Minister Faust

THE ALCHEMISTS OF KUSH

BY
MINISTER FAUST

DELTA

One
Resurrection

The Book of Then

1.

You're asking me . . . the earliest thing I remember?

Haven't I told you this story before? Many times?

Where are your brothers?

No, no, son, I'll tell you. Of course.

Sit down here with me. Water? No? There are ripe dates and bananas in the basket, there.

Isn't this a beautiful sunset? And the river . . . it looks as soft as skin.

The first thing I remember . . .

Waking up to our entire camp on fire.

Smoke-hands, choking me by the throat. And the flames so bright in the darkness I could barely see what was happening.

But I could hear it all: our men howling and fighting and dying, being butchered like goats.

Then I saw . . . enemy soldiers knocking them to the ground, kneeling on their backs, grabbing them by their hair and slitting their throats—just like that, all in one motion—and then they were thrashing in the sand, like crabs boiling in pots. And then they just stopped moving.

"Mum!" I screamed. "Mum!"

Some of our other men, I saw them running, and then they'd go down, arrows through their knees, or through their throats.

They didn't even have the chance to howl. They just choked and gurgled and tried to drag themselves for help and died before they got any.

"*Duam!*"

Duam, our strongest soldier, the tallest in the ranks. I saw him clutching his gashed-open belly, failing to keep in all his guts slithering out like white eels.

Maybe he didn't hear me, but he didn't even look at me. He was staggering, tilting, then lurching into a tree to keep from falling, but suddenly flame swept up the trunk. It cooked half his face.

Even to this day, whenever I smell a campfire, the stench of Duam as burning meat stabs fingers up my nostrils. If I'm tired or my defenses are down when I smell smoke, I have to fight not to vomit.

I don't remember if I was screaming. I must've been—I wasn't even ten yet. But I don't remember it. What I remember is that suddenly all the other kids in our camp were.

Then Shai—he was the second-oldest kid after me—was yanking on my arm.

"Who are they?" he kept saying. He was crying, shaking, clawing my arm enough to hurt it. Snot slimed all over his lip, glistening back to me from the fence of flame.

Who was attacking us? Were they even human? The cliffs on the west bank of the Holy River were infested by devils—

I screeched again for my mum, I don't know for how long. But she didn't come.

I couldn't see any of the women. And all the men were running, pouring blood or dead.

I turned, saw scream-faced kids, heard the raiders yelling to get us, kill us all, except—

They were running towards me with nets.

My heart pounded in my chest so hard I could feel my ribs shaking, but my head gonged with the only words-of-power my mum'd taught me.

"Everybody!" I shouted, readying the words in my mind. "Run to the river! Now!"

When the kids ran past me, I touched their heads or backs, spoke the words my mother gave, and each kid transformed into shadow.

When the last one was racing out of the burning grove, slipping past the raiders like smoke, I rushed along to find them at the eastern bank.

But our feet were still stamping footprints in the sand—

"All of you—quiet! Stop crying right now! We've got to wade to that island there without making a sound! All you bigger kids, hang onto the smaller ones! I mean it—stop that crying or they're going to kill us!"

They followed my orders.

When we got to the island we slipped up the beach through the palm trees over to the rocks, and then inside a cave. A bunch of rabbits bolted when they heard us and smelled us, but even they couldn't see us, because we were still shadows.

2.

Eventually, after they stopped crying, almost all the kids fell asleep nestled together like a pile of puppies. I kept guard with Shai until dawn, when the cave's bats came home like a black sandstorm.

Shai and I had to throw our bodies over the kids to keep them from seeing and running and screaming.

But when sunrise came, I could tell it still wasn't safe. I told everyone we had to wait.

So we waited two more days. We drank water dripping off the cave's walls. But we didn't have anything to eat at all.

3.

On the third morning, everyone was so hungry, even me, that I thought we didn't have any choice. It was either take our chances outside the cave, or die there from starvation. And the other kids were terrified of the bats.

We walked out together. And in all that shining sun, none of us could remain as shadows.

Across the river we saw a camp. Blackened. Smashed. A few embers glowing red. Smoke still lifting into the sky.

All of it stank from the meat of our people burned to death.

And hyenas and vultures and rats and dogs, ripping into the bodies of our slaughtered families, howling and gorging themselves like they were having a party.

I wanted to yell. I even would've, but my throat hurt like I'd been swallowing rocks and sand.

The kids started crying again. I couldn't take it.

"Shut up, you idiots! You want them to come murder us? You want devils coming here and sticking claws in your eyes and ripping your ribs out one at a time? No? Then shut your mouths!"

I knew why they were crying. I wanted to cry, too. I didn't know where my mum was. For all I knew, all the adults were dead.

But my mum . . . she must've been training me for something like this all along, because I took command of those kids without even thinking about it.

I knew what to do. And that meant making them focus on me instead of whoever or whatever had orphaned us all.

We moved out, hiding wherever we could. Sometimes Shai and I scouted ahead to make sure we weren't being tracked.

We ate whatever we could find: snails, beetles, and when we were really lucky, fruit.

4.

Weeks of walking. Past whole villages that'd been torched. Their crops, too. Animals, their legs broken and their heads half-hacked off.

And skulls. Sometimes with the eyes still in them.

When I wasn't thinking about food, or a place to hide, or where my mum'd gone and why hadn't she found us already, all I could think of was, who would do this? Why would anyone do this?

It's strange, but . . . I can't remember anything before that raid of fire. It's as if . . . as if I were born that night.

The Book of Now

1.

THERE HE WAS, SKINNY AND SEVENTEEN, ALONE ON THE SATURDAY NIGHT STREET.

The night, the darkness itself: electrical. Hummed like the neon above him did. He felt it. Intense. Violent. Almost sexual. Made his skin tingle. Made his teeth feel like he was chewing on aluminum foil.

To be young, to be a man, to be a young Black man, to be a young Black man in the shadows between streetlights on a night when clouds smothered the stars and the air seeped thick and hot like when he stepped out of the shower.

To feel the threat of some sinister somebody who could fall in step behind him trying to mess him up and take his shit, to feel that and be excited by it, because that threat was what transformed putty boys into iron men, because that transformation was what made girls' eyes stop seeing past him to focus on him like magnets on metal, because no knife-handle ever shone as brightly as the blade, *that* was what it was to walk the streets of Kush ozn a Saturday midnight with summer's hotness trickling from his pits and barely enough money for bus fare in his pocket and no girlfriend and no real friends and believing himself when he told himself he just didn't give a fuck.

Raphael Deng Garang. Bony. Skin the colour of the night and just as blue. Had a cheap XS Cargo sell-off mp3 player shaped like a thumb drive, under five gigs and under ten bucks, enough to pack a thousand songs and half of them hip hop.

The rest: Jamaican reggae, Somali ballads, Cubano-Congolese numbers, South African *kwaito*, Algerian *rai* and Kenyan *taarabu* and dozens of Nigerian Afrobeat joints.

But right then: Orchestre Baobab's "Dée Moo Wóor." Song swaggering with power, stomping its drum beats and punching its bass like Tyson hitting somebody's liver. And somewhere on back-up Youssou Ndour singing high nasal notes like an Eazy E free of madness.

Loved it. Cuz it strolled with colossus steps like he wished he could, invincible like a black hole and felt as ancient, as if he'd always known that song, as if it'd been sung for ten thousand years, as if its passion could decode all the secrets of his loneliness and pain.

But he couldn't understand a single word of it. A Senegalese song, probably sung in Wolof, and his family hailed as far from Senegal as England was from Russia.

Half of him: Sudanese. Twinned to a Somali half that didn't show on face or skin. Hadn't seen Sudan since he was a child with his mother on the run from all its screaming and looting and burning and men with guns.

And now: seventeen, lanky, alone, on 118th Avenue in the hood and in the night, and telling himself he could do anything.

Freestyling:

> *You braggin about the places*
> *Where the bullets fly like birds*
> *Ima tell y'about the spaces*
> *Where blood flows more than words . . .*

Bass-throbbing, rumbling: a sick, slick car, hyperviolet lights burning underneath its gleaming cream body . . .

. . . slowing down . . .

Stopped. In front of him.

But the traffic light was green.

Rims, spinning like roulette wheels in the movies. Except these chromes were strobing streetlights.

Swallowed thickly. Who the hell could it be? Was this it?

His hand. Flapped to his back pocket and its butterfly knife. Hovered there, not as casually as he tried to will it to.

The engine, growling. Window sliding down an electric hum.

"Yo, Rap, zat you?"

2.

Raphael didn't know the voice.

Took a step forward. Carefully.

Passenger side: kid his age, typical teenage Somali baby-face, but draped with junior dreadlocks. Like thin, black pinecones.

The kid: "Dude, it's me, Jackie Chan."

They were in the same English class. Guy sat on the opposite side of the room. And weird. Earmuff headphones practically welded onto his ears, him always bopping to beats no one else could hear, smiling too much, laughing when no one else heard the joke.

Real name was Jamal Abdi—Rap'd heard that at the beginning of the semester before the kid asked the teacher to call him "JC."

"Right," said Rap, rising above the ride's belching bass. "Hey."

"What the hell you doing out here, bwoi?" laughed Jackie Chan. "You slangin?"

Kid was always joking about something.

Rap scowled. "You got the wrong man. I was just, y'know . . ."

"Chillin? Kickin it?"

"Basically."

"Well, you gonna chill out here by yourself all night?"

"Naw, naw, I was just about to, uh . . . . "

"—ride with us?" He laughed his Jackie Chan laugh: half Flavor Flav, half Bart Simpson. "We're just cruising. Sweetly! In this *fine* whip."

Rap checked downstreet. Over his shoulder. Peered inside the vehicle like there coulda been a wolverine in there.

Didn't know the driver, but it was another kid, maybe a year older.

"Nuke, Rap. Rap, Nuke," said JC. "Rap's all right, Nuke."

Nuke. Guy was actually wearing a Kangol cap. Backwards. Smoking a cigarillo. Looked like a goof. He was wearing gloves, despite the heat. Midnight, plus-thirty, and wet-hot.

Rap didn't like it.

"Sall good," drawled Nuke. Also Somali. And like half the Somali boys his age Rap knew, Nuke spun his syllables like the blood bank'd given him a transfusion of Compton.

Then Nuke switched to Jamaican, maybe trying to make his own hat feel at home. "Respek, maan."

One of those, thought Rap. "Hey."

"Well?" said JC, head-tilting towards the back seat, an invitation. "Look, man, at least you need a ride home'r suh'm, right?"

It was true. And he didn't want to look like a wuss, either. So when the door swung open he got in. What the hell else was he gonna do?

But taking that step off the curb'd made his stomach flip, like he'd failed a jump between rooftops and was plummeting to an asphalt death.

"Yeah. Let's see what's crackin," said Rap, sampling a phrase he'd heard someone else use. Maybe somebody on Youtube or something.

3.

Pulled away. The purple blare of blacklights burned the car's interior into a nightclub, or what Rap thought clubs probably looked like.

They U-turned it east, rumbled past the old church and a porn shop and a Wee Book Inn and a Burger Baron, over cracked streets and beside cracked-out, kneecap-bony prostitutes, turned north beside the Coliseum.

The CD—some kinda techno DJ mix—had been skipping all over hell. Nuke hit EJECT and dumped it out the window. He hit a bunch of radio preselects, rejecting every one of them and finally shutting it off.

"Yo, Rap, whatcha listnin to?" asked Jackie Chan, breaking the new silence. This was the first time Rap'd ever seen JC without his headphones on. He knew what JC wanted, though—to hook his mp3 player up to the stereo in-jack.

He clicked away from the "Dée Moo Wóor" song he was listening to, over to something he figured would keep the peace with Nuke. Handed it to JC, who plugged it in.

A thunder-beat struck the car. Jackie Chan smiled. Nuke grinned.

A Dre-sampled guitar riff tore up the air like lightning. JC pumped the sound way too high, enough to dent Rap's ear drums. Dre took the mic, handed it off to MC Ren, the Ruthless Villain. Track was older than any of them, from 1991, but classics didn't ask permission.

The ghost of Eazy-E rhymed through its nose. And just before the chorus hit, JC and Nuke leapt in with the band: "Real niggers don't *DIE!*"

They'd turned a few times along the way, and were rolling west on 111ᵗʰ Ave past the Stadium. They slowed across from Frank's Pizza and beside a place called "Hyper-Market" with an "OPENING SOON" sign in the window, stopping in front of a hip hop clothing joint named Bootays.

It was still Kush, but this was a nicer part. Fewer hoes. No condoms on the street. Nobody stabbing or shooting anybody. Not that he could see, anyway.

Half-past midnight. Store was open. Through a plate-glass window he saw Somalis—staff, or owners?—chatting at the till with two guys whose backs were turned.

Nuke killed the engine.

"C'mon," said Jackie Chan.

Rap didn't like it. Yeah, he was half-Somali, but to Somalis he looked full Sudanese, true Dinka, and definitely darker than most Somalis. Even though he could speak Somali because of his mother and didn't know fifty words of his father's language, to Somalis, he was an outsider, an infidel, if not a barbarian.

Now he was sposta go into some weird dive, way past closing time, with two guys he barely knew, hopping out of a car that—and why he didn't force himself to think of it earlier, he couldn't say—was *way* too expensive for any Somali in E-Town to afford.

Shit. But what was he sposta do—wait in the car like some little kid?

4.

Inside. Figured maybe it was gonna be okay after all.

The two Somali owners, Hassan and Ahmed, were having a late-night planning session with a couple of Sudanese guys, Deng and Juk, for a mega-jam they were hoping to throw featuring K'Naan, Talib Kweli, K-Os and KRS-One.

Gonna call it the KKKK Rally. Hassan thought the name was hilarious. Rap thought it couldn't get any stupider.

And then two more Somalis showed up.

Marley. Slim beard. His partner Lexus, smooth-domed. Both reeked of ganja and *qat*. Night was so hot it was sweat-popping, but Marley, built like a middle-weight boxer, floated in his knee-length leather jacket.

Rap's gut burned as soon as the new Somalis appeared. His gut was always on fire, but Marley and Lexus were barrels of kerosene.

Yeah, the store owners knew them and there were daps all round, but when Lexus passed around a spliff—practically a ganja donair—Rap ached to get up and get out.

And if he had, if he'd just kot-tam listened to his instincts chirping madly in his ears, he wouldn't've gotten gut-punched and dropped, then stomped and had his feet and hands duct-taped.

5.

Ahmed bolted out the back door one second before Marley slipped the shotgun from his coat like an extra arm.

"Get that muthafucka!" Marley'd ordered Lexus, but the partner gave up the chase after only seconds in the alley, came back and helped Marley usher Rap, Jackie Chan, Nuke, Deng and Juk to the back room and put beatings on them all.

Rap was face down, his knife stuck uselessly inside his back pocket above his ass.

Out of his peripheral vision, Rap caught Marley, leering, blunt in his left hand and shotgun in his right. "Where's my fuckin stuff, Hass?"

"Mar, man, it aint my fault!" whined Hassan, face-down on the floor and taped like Rap. "Ahmed, he, he, he *used* it. I told him not to, but, but—"

Lexus stomped Hassan's skull into the cracked lino.

"I aint fuckin kiddin around, Hass!" yelled Marley. "Lex!"

Lexus stepped around the men on the floor.

Rap's gut burned hotter, twisting even harder. He hated Jackie Chan for getting him killed. He'd been on the run since he was a baby, if being carried by your mother counted as running. Sudan. Chad. Ethiopia. Kenya. Here.

To go through all that, only to die in a rinky-dink store surrounded by racks of giant pants and shitty, puffy jackets gaudied over with ultra-busy platinum designs—

Thunder—

Jackie Chan screamed, and so did Hassan and Rap and Deng and Juk—

Rap's face was hot and wet on one side.

Cracked open an eye in that direction.

Nuke's head was half gone.

Rap saw white bone and a piece of eye sticking out of red and black mash.

"Now, Hass, you know I'm serious," rumbled Marley. "You only got four more human shields till I get to you. So unless I get my fuckin product—"

"*Bismillah*, Marley, I ain' *got* it—"

Thunder—

"Three more. Runnin outta chances, Hass."

Rap was quivering, shaking, his teeth chattering in the heat. He couldn't tell who was the new death.

"Please, please, Mar, I'm serious! I don't—"

THUNDER—

And then there was chaos Rap couldn't see—someone got knocked over, and someone else took a hit and went down screaming. Rap shut his eyes so hard he saw flares.

Shouting and swearing and that gut-puckering sound of a joint being dislocated, a sound that'd puked itself out of his own shoulder in a refugee camp in Chad and there'd been no doctor—now, *now*, the same sound, four times: *POP-POP-POP-POP—*

6.

Sirens screamed.

Someone.

Kneeling beside Rap.

Tugging at his wrists.

Jailing the scream behind his clamped jaws, Rap slit open his eyes:

A man, grunting while he sawed through the tape, sweating, a black-and-gold skullcap above black kinks and grey wisps, matching the mix in the long goatee with no moustache. Black t-shirt. Biceps bulged under skin of trim arms working the duct tape, skin lighter than either Rap's or Jackie Chan's, halfway between chocolate and milk.

Rap strained to swivel his neck, scoped the murderers broken in wrong angles all over floor, screaming the pain of a dozen bones snapped like balsa under ballpeen.

Couldn't see a gun, bat or even pipe. Which meant this man'd taken out the killers with nothing but his empty hands.

And then Rap scoped the bloody, cratered carcasses of what used to be four men.

Tape was off. Rap and JC jumped up to split.

"What the hell you two doing?" demanded the goateed man. His widely-spaced eyes glared like a goat's. If the man'd had horns, he would've charged. "You can't leave now—you're witnesses!"

Jackie Chan's eyes whipped wildly. "That's why we're leaving!" He grabbed Rap and Rap's legs moved before Rap gave them the order.

"Hey!" shouted the man. "Hey, you freakin little creeps—you can't just—"

Outside, through the front door swinging loose like an invitation, the boys bolted past Nuke's car, sprinted across the street and ducked into the space between two stores just as the cops landed past the diagonal of where 111th Ave start bent into 112th.

"Get down!" hissed JC under wailing sirens.

"What the hell?"

"They'll see us running, dude!"

Three cruisers flaring the night into red-blue-red-blue seized the storefront's street. Red-blue smeared into purple over Bootays' roof, painting the second storey of the next-door Hyper-Market.

Goatee-but-no-moustache man, skullcap raked to the side, took position at the door, hands-up, said something to the cops leaping from their cars and plunging for cover at the sight of him.

"No," he shouted, "I'm the one who put the call in!"

"GET THE FUCK DOWN ON THE GROUND!"

Halfway to kneeling, he had just enough time to raise his forearm against the beating the cops hurled on him like boulders from a cliff.

"We can't just let them do him like that!" said Rap. "We gotta *do* something!"

JC shook his head. "Dude—Nuke's car, like, it's not Nuke's."

"You *stole* it?"

"Not me—Nuke! Just a little joy-riding, man—he wasn't gon fence it! But there's *dead people* in there now! Think they'll believe us?"

On the ground, Mr. Goatee cock-punched one cop and put him down. Then another lit him up with a Taser. Years later Rap would swear he smelled burning skin and hair.

With cops fully focused on cuffing and hauling away the man who'd just saved Raphael Garang's and Jamal Abdi's young lives, the two youths hunched down the space between two stores like rats chasing through sewers.

7.

Thirty minutes of tearing through alleys and side-streets, thirty hours of jumping behind trash cans at every distant siren, thirty days of gasping for breath and failing to stifle the gasps—

And suddenly Rap realised Jackie Chan was gone, and he was alone.

8.

At last, back at the front door of his crib. Rap's key, trembling against the lock: *clicketty-ticketty-clinketty*—

Two hands. Shoving the key. In.

The clock's angry red LEDs burned 2:03.

Shoes off. Tip-toed past his mother's room, even though she probably wasn't even in.

A scream.

He froze.

The phone rang again.

He bolted to his bedroom.

Third ring, and still his mother wasn't picking up. Was it the police? Or—

Fourth ring and the answering machine got it, two o'clock in the fucking morning and after the robot voice said nobody was home, that stupid, angry voice sloshed out of the speaker like stomach acid, and calling tonight of all nights, Rap just wished that muthafuckas *would*—

Tried pulling off the sweat-drenched shirt sticking to his back like a snake failing at shedding skin. Finally, off, and saw shirt the red spatters and small grey chunks .

Ran to the toilet, puked until he hacked up nothing but acrid yellow stripes. Briefly considered burning his shirt until he remembered the smoke alarm.

Instead he cut the old t-shirt into pieces, put them inside an empty 4L Lucerne Neapolitan ice cream tub from the recycling bin, and drowned them in bleach.

Only bruises were on his chest and thighs.

Washed somebody stranger's memories and life off his face.

Shivered himself to sleep on that hot summer night.

Dreaming: falling from the clouds till he crashed through the street, and down through the earth until he plunged into magma.

Two
Revolution

The Book of Then

1.

I WAS IN CHARGE OF OUR CHILD ARMY OUT IN THE DESERT, A BUNCH OF chubby-cheeked soldiers feasting from gourds full of mushrooms, snails and beetles during the long nights I trained them to kill.

The kids—all two hundred of them including stragglers we'd picked up along the way—did like I told them. Shai, he was the next oldest after me, was my second-in-command. We were the ones who planned the counter-attack on the night-raiders.

That's what led to every last one of us but me being hunted down and killed . . . or worse. Because there is always something worse.

By the time we'd spent three months out in the desert, sleeping in caves or in burnt-out homes by day and changing location every night, the kids started toughening up.

That's what constant fear and struggling just to live does to you. You just hope you don't shatter.

Back then I dreamed every night that my mother was looking for me, and that just when she picked me up, the night-raiders hacked us both to pieces.

I'd wake up crying, hoping no one had heard me. But whoever was sleeping next to me would be shivering.

The kids were hardly even crying any more, except when they were asleep. That's when it was worst. Like dogs howling in the distance. No—like puppies. Whimpering in a mound.

But still, they got cleverer every day, scrambling through all the wrecked places we found, digging through the ashes and the skulls, finding cups, tools, knives, anything we could use to survive.

The kids even got good at night-fishing, which is extremely tough, because the water's black and if the Moon is shining, then all you can see is its reflection broken into a thousand shining stars.

So you had to keep your eyes open and a sharpened stick in your hand, and then when you saw any movement, strike like a scream of lightning, and hope you didn't stab your friend's foot next to you.

But the fish never saw our fishers, because by then I'd taught almost all of them how to turn *themselves* into shadows.

The best fisher we had was Jedu. He was a year younger than Shai, and he taught the others. On good nights, Jedu made sure every one of us ate.

"You're the best fisher I've ever seen," Shai always told him. Shai made sure to praise the kids whenever they did their chores right. Me, I thought he was spoiling them.

We cooked over coals, the remains of covered fires. We kept small fires so we didn't attract bandits, devils or the murderers who'd slaughtered our people.

2.

"Shai," I told him the night we began planning our revolt, "you know that if we don't find a way to kill all the raiders, eventually they'll kill all of us, right?"

"I know," he said, nodding like he'd been thinking the same thing but'd been too afraid to say the words out loud.

But we were both full of shit. We were just kids. We didn't really know anything.

The truth is, the best thing would've been if we'd just kept running. Found an oasis or some deep caves. The Blackland is huge, and the Destroyer would never've found us.

That's what we called him. We didn't know who the raiders' leader was, but we knew they had to have one. The kind who turned whole villages into smoking graveyards.

So Shai and I had the kids scavenge for all the farm tools they could get, especially anything with a blade. We didn't have swords or bows, and even if we did, we were all too small to use them.

But if you sharpened a spade enough, you had a dagger. A rake we could turn into a trident or pike. And a hatchet, that was the best find of all.

I didn't know much about fighting except for how to use a dagger, which Duam, the biggest soldier, had taught me. But Shai knew how to wrestle.

So when we weren't searching for food, that's what we did. It was the only real fun we had during that season of survival, practicing with short sticks or long rock chips for knives and throwing each other around.

"Get im! Throw im! Smash im!" they'd scream, getting so riled up watching a match that Shai and I had to hiss at them to shut up just so every bandit, enemy ranger or devil in the world wouldn't come butchering.

But we had two boys, Gab and Ashgaga. Always fooling around. Slacking and straggling. Amazing they lasted as long as they did.

They were supposed to be gathering fruit, since neither one could fish worth a damn.

But it was my fault. I was in charge. I knew they were stupid and untrustworthy, but I started letting them go out unsupervised.

Those idiots came back to camp singing—actually *singing*—under the starlight.

We were all absorbed by a wrestling match, when suddenly nets like finger-thick spiderwebs were strangling almost all of us. Three of our best fighters ducked, grabbed their pikes and plunged them through the murderers—I saw eyes bulging on those bastards maybe more from shock than the agony that sent their souls to incineration.

I dipped my knife into every adult leg I could and yanked back hard and sideways. But there were too many of them—

"Run!" I ordered, everyone dashing for the river, hoping to escape like we did on the night of fire.

Back then I'd had to turn them all into shadows myself. This time I didn't because I'd taught them all how to do it themselves. But they were so panicked, they either forgot to do it or forgot how to, and nets took some and arrows took others.

The rest of us got to the river, chased by slaughterers splashing after us, who suddenly stopped terrified and ran out of the water screaming.

I looked up and saw why just before a wave knocked me down.

A giant mouth.

Rising from the water, taller than a palm tree, skinning back and revealing a thousand stalactite teeth.

Smoke stinking like puke and shit shot out of the maw, and half the kids instantly dropped into the water. The monster sucked their floating bodies in with a raging roar, sounding like the sky being ripped to shreds.

I tried running, but the monster rose and slammed into the water, and the swell lifted me off my feet.

I rammed face-first into the mud, then the water sucked me back, and I was falling into its mouth—

The abomination my mother named the Devourer of Millions of Souls.

3.

Even inside its belly, there were teeth.

They gave us our only light, those murderous grinders, shining like devil-shattered pieces of the moon.

We were crushed in upon each other down there, stacked five and even ten bodies high. Trapped. Suckers on its bellywalls clutching us in place on top of each other, no food, no water but the stinking filth in the thing's stomach, pissing and shitting all over each other because we couldn't move.

Crying there was even worse than back in the cave. It echoed more. It mixed with the Devourer's rage and came back sounding like our bodies being knackered at the joints.

The only thing I could do to keep from going insane was to hold onto the fang closest to me.

"Shai!"

21

He was pinned right on top of me.

"Grab hold of this tooth."

"What? Why?"

"See that crack? Maybe if we can cause this monster some pain, it'll open its mouth."

"And drown us? Or just chew us up?"

"How long do you think we can survive like this? I'd rather die trying to escape, if that's what it takes."

He shut up. Grabbed on. So did the boys above him and below me.

"Everyone, pull!" I said. "Now push!"

We went back and forth, pulling and then pushing. First we could wiggle the tooth. Eventually we could move it. And then the crack split wider.

And when we broke the tooth, the Devourer howled enough to pierce our eardrums to bleeding.

Suddenly we were shooting up its throat and exploding from its mouth, falling and splashing in scum and mud and slime.

I held my breath, splashing, swimming blindly with muck in my eyes and my mouth and nostrils, until I felt rocks and mud underneath my feet.

Dragging myself out on the shore in the darkness, I collapsed gasping on a bog of reeds and mush, watching the monster submerge and a wave bulging up and crashing a bunch of kids down on top of me.

4.

I dragged out everyone else I could see. They were scattered all over the scummy long-grass, hacking up brine.

I found a shard of the Devourer's shattered fang, the length of my forearm and still shining like lightning. I tucked it through my sopping waist-sash.

On my left, Shai, face-down, unconscious. I flipped him over.

A shard of tooth stood up from his belly. Blood seeped around the base, pulsing, bubbling. And then stopped.

I ordered the survivors to call out their names. They choked them out spluttering and snuffling.

We were once over two hundred.

We were down to two dozen.

In dim light, we huddled together, shivering and crying.

5.

Above the skeleton trees—at last—

The Sun.

You could look right at it without hurting your eyes. Pus-white, a pale circle, hovering beyond the fog. Fog as thick as milk. Like grey blood.

"Everyone! Listen up!" I said. "It's morning. We don't know if the monster's coming back, or if the raiders followed us. Before sunset, we've got to get food, water, and a place to hide—hey!"

Some of the kids were drinking the scum-slicked water.

Four of them, the ones who'd gulped the most, suddenly puked. Blood shot out of their mouths and noses, burst from their ears and eyes. They keeled over, plunged into the swamps, sank like rocks.

The others, the ones who'd just been slurping, started keening like hyenas. Yipping and laughing and howling and screeching. Then jumping, staggering, thrashing.

I ordered them all not to drink the water, but then I saw it in their faces, their terror when they realised it the moment I did: all of them had sucked in water when we'd plunged into the swamps in the first place.

It started in their fingers. Twitching. Then in their hands and arms. Then they were flailing, screaming and dancing.

When they stopped, the black from their eyes had drowned to white.

And they all began slogging away to nowhere.

"Where are you going? Come back here!"

They ignored me, or maybe they didn't hear me . . . I couldn't tell which.

I tried grabbing them, punching them, kicking them, knocking them down. It didn't make a difference. This entire land, this ugly, horrible, shit-stinking bog as far as I could see, these swamps of death, had murdered all us kids who'd survived the night of fire more than three months before.

Everyone but me.

So I was alone.

6.

I ran. As best as I could. In the mud.

Sometimes it sucked its way up my legs as far as my ass, like it was trying to eat me. I pulled my way out with branches, vines, anything I could reach.

When night came, I climbed a tree, hid up in one like a bird, hoping there weren't any lions or devils that'd find me sleeping and rip the meat off my face.

I was shaking with fear up in those branches. I could even hear the leaves rattling. I clutched my fang-shard so hard my hand bled.

But finally I couldn't keep my eyes open, and I fell asleep dreaming I was falling. Falling into my mother's arms. Before some horrible thing crawled out of the darkness to rip us into meat and blood.

The Book of Now

1.

RAP'S LEGS: JOLTING UNDER HIS COVERS.

Feet, aching from breaking through the street after falling a millionth time in his dreams.

The shell of Sunday morning cracked open.

Sweating. Dry throat. Tongue like sandpaper.

Sleep'd sucked. But even it was better than the shakes and cold he'd had the night before. When he'd been lying literally one footstep away from having had a shotgun paint his brains across the linoleum of a hip hop clothing store in Kush.

Had to take a whiz. Fought it. Finally went, then back to his room.

Terrified the phone would ring.

Or that the door would knock.

And that cops would Taser him and haul him away just like they did the goateed man in the skullcap—or worse, the men busting in would be friends of the killers that the goateed man had crushed.

Rap hauled out comics. Tried to read.

When lunch came and he'd been in his room the whole time, his mother knocked on his door. He told her he was sick. She didn't push it—just insisted he get his homework done.

He skipped dinner, too, at which time she finally came inside his room to check on him.

Smelled the ice cream pail full of bleach, saw the cut-up cloth soaking in it.

"What's this?" Suspicious.

"Science project," he said immediately. He hoped not *too* immediately. To sell it better: "I asked you for help with it three times already. I couldn't wait forever—"

"Well, I'm sorry, butt I'ff been busy tryingk to pay the bills around here," she said instantly. Bingo.

To keep her reeling. "That's where you were last night?"

"Yes, as a mutter of factt."

"Cuz I thought maybe you were over at—"

"I wass workingk."

A breath. "Are you planning to go to school tomorrow?"

Sure as hell *felt* sick, so he figured he must've looked it to her. She left and returned with a glass of water. "Probably just the flu," she said.

He drank it down, the water filling the cracks in his lips, driving out their pain. "Sleep it off," she said, closing the door behind her.

He'd barely slept the night before, but his mind ached like he'd been sleeping for a day. For a life.

When he didn't look better on Monday morning, she gave him permission to stay home from school and asked him if he wanted Jell-O. When he said no, she frowned and told him she'd call home to check up on him.

While flipping frantically through papers in her satchel, she verbally uploaded her schedule to him: a 9 AM meeting with the Multicultural Health Brokers Coop, a 10:30 at EISA to help some new Rwandan family . . . By the time she recited her 1 PM with a Nuer woman trying to find work, he was lost.

"There're *sambusas* from Mebrat's in the fridge if you gett hungry," she said, kissing his forehead. She returned with a tube of skin cream and said. "You're ashy."

Told him what she'd left in the fridge for him. Maybe twice to set up that she really was busy. And then running around frantically looking for something (papers? Always papers).

Heard the apartment door click shut. Closed his eyes. Tried to sleep.

Thunder.

And his eyes opened.

2.

Tuesday. Rap went to school, but in first period he was a zombie and must've looked it, because people were avoiding eye contact with him even more than usual.

No wonder. At the class break, saw his face in the bathroom mirror: stoned-looking, crazy eyes. Groggy and angry at the same time.

Math class. Supposed to be doing trig. Couldn't focus. Half of every minute: sketching action poses of Static, Adam Warlock, King Peacock, 'Pac, Lupe, NWA's original five.

The other half of every minute: sweating, staring at the door, bracing for the constable to charge into the classroom and cuff-haul him out to a waiting cruiser.

Lunch. Wasn't hungry. Went to the school library to check the newspapers. No mention in Sunday's, of course, but Monday's front page hefted

Four shot dead in store
Three suspects in custody, police suspect Somali drug gangs

Hustled the paper over to a carrel, heart punching his throat, thinking the store had to've had a security camera, pleading

Don't let my photo be in there . . .

Photos, yeah, but none of them his.

Family-supplied shots of the victims, mug shots of the two shooters. The story cited a third man in police custody charged with aggravated assault—

"Hey!"

Rap jumped back, sent his chair crashing—

—but it was only Jackie Chan standing there in his mini-dreads.

"Dude, chill," he whispered. Everyone was staring. He picked up Rap's chair.

His ever-present headphones were absent. Which is maybe why he wasn't bopping, and his pine-cone locks weren't keeping a beat.

"Have you seen this?" whispered Rap, nodding towards the paper.

"Yeah."

"They charged the guy who saved us with aggravated assault! He's in jail right now!"

"Really?"

"I thought you said you saw this!"

"I didn't read it—I just saw it." He picked up the paper, scanned it. "Damn."

"What're we gonna do?" said Rap, grabbing JC's upper arm. "He saved our lives—we can't just leave him in jail!"

JC jerked his arm back. "Dude, I already told you about the car! We go to the police . . . look, you already saw what they did to a guy who stopped a coupla killers. Whaddaya think they'll do to us?"

Rap: caught like a moth on a pin.

"Well, we gotta do something. Maybe call one of those anonymous tip lines or something. Like Crimestoppers."

"I'ont know. Maybe. Just don't get us caught, aiight? You know they record those calls, know who's calling—"

"No they don't—"

"They say they don't."

Rap nodded, scowled.

JC said, "Funeral's tomorrow. Up at the CIC. You wanna come with me?"

Rap was used to the burn—that was his name for it—the buzzing, the tightness, the wincing-stab between his eyes, the heat that bit his skin like a lit match. He walked with it, slept with it, ate with it, showered with it, brushed his teeth with it, went to school and went home with it.

But this was worse. Now it was someone'd yanked open his collar and dumped glowing coals down his neck and back, burning the meat right off his shoulder blades and ribs.

Almost fascinated him, it was so intense, until the pain spiked and he thought for just a second he was having a heart attack or a stroke. Then he remembered from Bio class that if he were having cardiac arrest his left arm would be tingling, and since he could remember the digits of his own telephone number, it couldn't be a stroke, either.

Grade 11 was less than a month from being done. Term essays and projects were due and final exams were rolling toward him like a line of tanks, followed by two months of nothingness until his final year.

And bass to that treble, here was this nut JC expecting him to go to the funeral of strangers butchered on a store's killing floor right next to him.

He'd lived. They hadn't. Because of a stranger that he'd let police club like an animal.

A stench, like someone'd taken a shit behind the carrel a week ago and no one'd cleaned it up yet.

But it was only JC, standing there in front of him, unwrapping the foil on an oily-onion-dripping burger. Reaching into one of the pockets on his mega-jeans, he pulled out three Kraft slices so creased they'd've crumbled without their plastic wrap. Then he un-bunned the top of the burger, laid down his cheese.

"God," said Rap.

"What?" said JC, slobbering. "Sjust a cheeseburger."

"'Sdisgusting."

"What're you talking about?"

"All that cheese. How can you load up a burger like that with all that congealed cow lactate?"

"What're you, Jewish? No mixing your meat and milk?"

"If they don't do that, then I'll convert."

"No food in the library!" snapped the librarian from across the room at his checkout desk. "Take it outside!"

"Well?" said JC, rewrapping and pocketing his burger, nodding for them to leave.

"Well what?"

"You coming with me to this memorial service or what?"

"Fine," said Rap as they cleared the book-scanning gate just when the bell rang the end of lunch. "Fine."

English class, five minutes later.

Thinking about the memorial service.

Knowing he had a duty to get this man out of jail but not knowing how without maybe going away himself.

Knowing he had a duty to thank this man who'd saved his brains from getting pizzaed.

From across the room, hearing and smelling JC finishing his cheese-monster.

Made it as far as the trash can before puking up the tuna sandwich and apple his mother'd packed him.

"Oh, *shi-i-it!*" razzed Matej, the skinhead-looking Croatian kid who thought he was the White Tupac. "Dawg, thass *nasty*. Don't be killin forties at lunch no more, yo."

"Matej, enough," said the teacher. "Rap, can you make it to the office?"

Evening. Mum wasn't in yet, as usual. In front of their glacial-speed computer, sipping Lipton's Chicken Cup of Soup broth just so he didn't starve.

An email popped up. Which was weird, since he never got email from anyone. But the school insisted everyone have an email account linked to their and their parents' home accounts.

It was that fool JC with a link to Somal-E-Town.com, a video story posted from the CBC news site, with still photos and footage doubling up on the reporter's narration:

> *Part Good Samaritan, part Bruce Lee, Mr. Yimunhotep Ani is a Kush-area store-owner who intervened on Saturday night's multiple homicide while it was unfolding next door to his own store, as this stunning security footage leaked to YouTube demonstrates.*

Freaking *ama*zing! Rap'd been face-down—there he was, that was him, nothing to ID him, thank god—so he never actually saw what'd happened.

This old man, Yim-something-something, smashed through the two killers like an axe through dry branches.

Rap jabbed the spacebar, rewound, watched it again. And again. And again.

According to the video file clock, the whole combat lasted two less than two seconds.

Clicking, frame by frame:

Killers in long coats standing over victims.

Black blur slipping from the back.

Hand chop into neck of Killer #2.

Rushing leg takes out #1's feet.

#1 spinning mid-air, as if his hips were on an axle.

#1 on floor, blur moving towards Killer #2 turning round.

#2 hefting shot gun.

Blur's left hand intercepting barrel, gripping, yanking forward.

Rotating trunk, right hand spearing into #2's throat.

Right hand raking #2's eyes and face, right foot puncturing #2's groin.

#2 on the floor.

Blur slowing into a man, stomping #1's knees.

Then #2's.

Finally Rap let the rest of the video roll:

> *Crippling the two assailants, Ani saved the lives of two unidentified teenage boys who escaped immediately after.*

But when police arrived, instead of thanking Ani, they arrested him. And, says Mr. Ani, they brutalised him.

Although police initially denied any wrong-doing, the leaked security footage has gone viral, becoming an internet sensation and racking over a hundred thousand hits in two days.

The resulting public outcry has forced police to change their story, release Ani and issue an apology.

Meanwhile, the reluctant internet icon has issued no statement of his own, but is now widely known online as "Blackbelt Jones," "the Bulletproof Monk" and "Morpheus."

Thousands of adoring comments from a range including pro-gun groups and inner-city-renewal activists have claimed Ani as a hero.

In regard to a civil suit against the police and the City, Ani's lawyer, Bamba Diabate, says "all options are on the table." Ben Coxworth, CBC News, Edmonton.

Was this guy for real? Had Rap actually been inside the same room as this superhero?

Hoped when he finally went to apologise to him, the man would shake his hand and not rip it off.

3.

The next day Rap and JC were busing it up 127ᵗʰ Street, a traffic-clogged lane of stout, drab businesses that city planners must've forgotten during extended lunch breaks, or maybe designed while sniping at each other.

Rap tried spacing out through his music, a One Self track called "Fear the Labour" with a strings like a Russian folk song (he knew the sound from a documentary he'd seen on the USSR in Social Studies).

Jolting him back to reality was the sight of Jackie Chan on the opposite seat drinking chocolate milk out of a Tupperware soup container.

JC caught his look.

"I buy the, like, *big* cartons, the two litre ones," said JC between slurps, embarrassed. "I usually, you know, fill my water bottle with it for school. But, uh, I lost it."

"What happened to your i-Pod?"

"Huh?" Slurp.

"You always usedta have your DJ headphones on. Even in class. You're not wearing em."

JC came over next to Rap, spoke softly. "I, uh, lost it . . . on Saturday night. At WEM. When Nuke was, like . . . *finding* a car."

Rap didn't even try keeping his voice disapproval-free. Too tired, and the burn was smoking his patience into ashes. "Why you do that, anyway?"

Jackie Chan looked out the window, probably for reasons.

"I'ont know. Wasn't really my thing, to be honest. Nuke . . . we grew up together. Usedta go biking together. Even bowling when we were in grade six. Now . . ." Shrugged.

"You're taking this pretty well," said Rap. "If you guys were really so roped."

"We go back, true dat." Long drink, then back-of-hand mouth wipe. Then he sealed the lid on his drink-tub and slid it into his knapsack. "He was like an old t-shirt. Fulla holes, got Old Spice-crusty armpits, but you still can't throw it out."

He was trying to be funny, but he looked like he wanted to cry.

4.

They rode in silence, got off on 132nd Avenue and took a transfer over to 113th and the single minaret that stood in front of the CIC.

Building's front had onion-peak arches built over the doors, and a white exterior aging into perpetual dirtiness. Above was a dome with a crescent-and-star glinting the high sunlight of a late afternoon in June.

The parking lot was jammed with cars, and so were the streets. People streamed towards the CIC, Somali men either in blazers or flowing white *jalabeeyahs* or sometimes both, men with short hair and men wearing embroidered fezzes, and *muhajabaat* in long iridescent skirts and black blouses floating down the sidewalk like a rainbow of swans.

Cop cars, four of them, up and down the block, and a few jive plainclothes White men with short mustaches joining the marchers who looked like the only time they'd ever seen the inside of a mosque was from surveillance photos.

Rap and Jackie Chan slipped inside a throng of mourners, hoping like hell the cops wouldn't see them or connect them to the security camera footage up on YouTube—maybe there'd been more that hadn't made it onto the news that showed their faces. Who'd posted it, anyway? Wasn't that Morpheus guy still in jail?

Burn was bad as ever, sizzling his legs and arms and forehead. He thought he was going to pass out on the way inside, but JC caught him.

"You okay?"

"Yeah," he said. "Just tripped. Thanks."

5.

Found two empty chairs together near the back of the auditorium. Jackie Chan went to make *wudu*.

When he came back his face was still wet from washing.

Rap didn't practice his mother's family's Islam or his father's Christianity. So he didn't make *wudu* or genuflect or look in vain for holy water or anything else.

What he did do was sit raging to himself how JC could walk around the CIC with Somalis by the boatload nodding to him like he was a cousin, but him, looking Dinka right down to the facial scarification, might's well've been invisible.

To these people his mother's side was invisible or didn't count, and it didn't matter that he could speak Somali or that he almost got murdered on the same floor as the two Somalis who got shot did.

And that's who this funeral was for. The service for the two murdered Sudanese was going on at the same time somewhere else, which he knew because his mother, in her morning briefing to him, said that's where she was going to be.

She still had no idea about his connection, and so he didn't say word-one about heading to any funeral.

"Our commoonity has suffered another loss," said Mr. Bashir.

Fifty-ish, a community organiser. Chubby-cheeked and happy-faced, Bashir man looked sadder than his facial anatomy should've made possible.

Every second he spoke, the room got muggier and hotter. Rap wished he had some of JC's cold chocolate milk, even if it did come out of a Tupperware.

Bashir shifted back-and-forth from Somali into English, English for the benefit of the reporters who came for the blood and didn't care about Black people unless they were shooting, crying, rapping, singing, running or throwing a ball.

"How many uff our young people haff we lost in the laast few years?"

Shouts and wails.

"Yes, you're right—nutt only young people. Our braather driving cab, Mr. Yussef, who wuss left to die inside his own traank?"

Murmuring engorging into shouting, a grass fire turning inferno.

Mr. Bashir waved it down with his hands and a few *insha'Allahs*.

"The young men at the, the . . . Foolton Place party?" Grumbles from somewhere up front. "Yes, that too—the drive-by shooting at the lounge. How many more haff there been? And, and how many more will there be?

"Some uff our young men, they haff lost. Lost their baliefs. Lost their sense of right and wrong. Lost their hope that they can *do* something or *be* something . . . something more than a conflicted prisoner or a, a, a jaankie. That they could be fathers. With careers . . ."

Mr. Bashir eulogised the dead Somalis: Hassan the store owner. Hard-working businessman. Loved to discuss the news. Committed soccer player. Twenty-eight. Had a twenty-three year-old wife. Two sons, one three, other only three months. Both orphaned by a shotgun shell that permanently interrupted their father's attention.

6.

Then it finally came time to talk about eighteen-year-old Dawud Abdi.

Mr. Bashir must've microscoped that boy's life to find something, anything to say that wouldn't shame his ghost: about his loving parents, great smile, sense of humour, his dream of owning a restaurant or a record store or his own music label.

Didn't mention that the streets knew him as Nuke, a long-time car-thief guaranteed to die by steel one way or another.

And didn't tell the mourners any time that afternoon that drug-related assaults were plaguing the Somali community so much that a whole lotta people didn't even bother reporting them to the police.

But quadruple-homicides, yeah, those still filitered through to the cops, and to the news.

Mr. Bashir's speech ended with thanks to the people who'd come up from Calgary and all the way from Vancouver, Winnipeg, T.O. and even the States. Rap wasn't surprised—Somali families (other than his) were always big and tight enough to form their own FIFA divisions.

And then there was an appeal from another speaker to join some local Somali group with the name "Brotherhood" in it, and someone else asking on the imam's behalf for everyone to come for prayer at the front.

Rap moved aside for Jackie Chan, stayed by himself.

7.

After prayer, with the congregation breaking up, Jackie Chan scrambled back from the lobby, shoving a folded-over newspaper at him.

"That guy who rescued us?" whispered JC. "Paper says the police only let him go after his lawyer got involved. Betcha Mr. Lawyer-Man's the dude who YouTubed that *kung fu* tape."

Screen-caps from the tape blared up on the page.

Rap shook his head. "What if the cops've got our faces off that tape?"

"Cops can't tell us apart, man," said JC, actually smiling. "Otherwise they woulda grabbed us on the way inside here."

"Unless they didn't to want cause a riot and're waiting until we leave. To follow us home—"

"Kinda paranoid, fuh real."

"Don't 'paranoid' me! I wouldn'even be *in* this mess except for you!"

Jackie Chan looked down, chewed his lip. "Thought you'd be happy. Cuz the guy's out."

Rap hit JC's shoulder. "That him?"

JC looked over. Shuffling out with the rest of the mourners was a moustacheless man with a goatee, a black-and-gold skullcap and Band-Aids marring his neck and face.

The boys tried getting to him, but the crowd crushed them back while they wedged their way with *excuse me*s and *sorry*s.

They almost caught him near the door, until several old men in white jalabeeyahs stopped in front of them as if the doorway were the most natural place in the world to have a conversation.

Over the shoulder of an old man with a beard red from henna, the boys saw their saviour descend the stairs and disappear.

By the time they cleared the blocking-line of seniors, Morpheus was gone.

And Rap didn't feel like tearing all over the place looking for him to thank him and beg forgiveness for abandoning him, just in case the cops *could* tell Sudanese apart from Somalis. He had more to lose than JC did.

"Now what?" said Jackie Chan.

"I don't know," said Rap. "Wait. What's his name again?" He scanned the paper. "Yimunhotep Ani . . . and get this, you know why he was even there that night? He owns the store next door, the one—"

"The one with the 'opening soon' sign?"

"Yeah!"

"Okay!" said Jackie Chan. "Let's go!"

Even though he'd just been chasing the man, hearing JC's words dropped Rap's stomach like he'd stepped into an open elevator shaft.

8.

An hour's bus ride later and the sun still hot and high in the June sky, the boys were back in Kush, walking along 111th Avenue over to 96th Street.

Passing pawn shops, a Burger Baron, Norwood School, the rainbow-flagged Pride Centre, a car wash with a dozen bays, a run-down body shop.

From the south bank of 111th they saw the yellow police tape on Bootays, a ribbon wrapped around the worst birthday present the community'd gotten in years.

Dodging cabs, cars and buses, they landed in front of the Hyper-Market and its OPENING SOON sign.

"Well?" asked JC. "Aren't we going in?"

Rap glared at him. "Don't rush me. Wanna think what I'm gonna say, first."

JC pushed on the glass door, but it was locked. He knocked loud and long.

Finally the forty-something man in the goatee and black-and-gold skullcap came to the door.

"Hello?"

Up close they saw what the Band-Aids failed to cover: bruises, scrapes, and the gut-puckering purple-brown ghost from a fading black eye.

"Uh . . . we're . . . we're the, uh," fumbled Rap.

The man stepped forward into the doorway, blocking it.

"Kot-*tam!*" he snapped. "You're those two kids!"

"Yeah," said JC. "Look, our bad, the other night—f'real. But man, the way you absolutely Bruce Lee'd them boys. You went Abu Ghraib on they asses! Think you could teach us that shit?"

"Jamal!" snapped Rap. This wasn't in the plan. And jazzing about a mass murder that almost included all of them, as if it were a movie trailer or something—was he nuts?

"You got a hell of a nerve," growled the man.

Rap glared at JC.

"Look, look, look, man," spluttered JC, "I know, I know we shoulda—"

"'*Man?*'" he spat. "I took a beating and an arrest from the cops and stayed in jail overnight because I stepped in to save your lives! And you two little shits ran off and didn't say word-*one* which coulda saved me from all that.

"And now you show up here expecting me to train you like I owe *you* something . . . and you call me '*man*'?"

Rap: "*Sir*. Sir, we're—we're sorry. But honest, we were just terrified!"

"*You* were terrified? How do you think I felt when the police had their guns out and were kicking the shit outta me?"

Jackie Chan: "We thought we were gonna die—"

"I thought *I* was gonna die! Thanks to you! Now get the hell outta here!"

Shoved himself back inside, leaned on the glass door's metal frame till the hydraulic hissed shut. Then he latched all three clanking latches and stormed off to the back room.

Music blasted to life: extremely loud jazz. Battering cymbals and sobbing saxophones, like someone using a wrench to beat a robot to death.

Standing on the street, Jackie Chan had already given up. "Dude *hates* us, man."

Rap's burn: as bad as ever.

9.

The next day during a lull in their English class's review of *To Kill a Mockingbird*, Rap argued in whispers to convince JC (who'd begun sitting next to him) to go back to the man's store.

The way Rap figured it, his burn'd gone up fifty degrees from guilt alone. Maybe if he could apologise proper . . .

"After your brilliant 'Train us in your Snake-and-Crane style, dude,' now we owe the man *two* apologies. And this time, let me do the talking?"

"Aiight," conceded JC. "My bad, my bad . . ."

"Oh, god," said the man at 4:33 PM on Thursday afternoon, the day after the funeral. "You two *again?*"

"Look, Mr. Ani," said Rap, "I know we screwed up. And my friend here shouldn't've come around asking for any favours. But seriously—"

"We just wanna say thank you," said JC, oblivious to Rap's immediate glare. "And, like, we'll work here."

Rap: "What?"

"You expect me to *hire* you?" he laughed. Angrily.

"He means—"

"—we'll volunteer, y'know?" said JC. Sounded thrilled with his own improv. "You can work us like slaves!"

"'*Slaves*,'" sneered the man. "Do you even hear yourself?"

Rap: "We owe you our lives, Mr. Ani. At least let us try to pay you back a little."

"Like I'm gonna let two carjackers into my business!"

"We aint carjackers—we just car thieves!"

"Jackie Chan, would you let me—! We're not car thieves. He's a joy-rider. His friend, the one who died, was the thief. And this idiot, look, I just know him from school. He offered me a ride and didn't bother telling me the car was stolen—"

"That's true!" enthused Jackie Chan, as if he were helping.

"So you're saying," said the man, as if he were laying out the plot of a particularly bad movie, "that I should let a joy-rider . . . and a kid who climbs into cars with sketchy almost-strangers . . . inside my business, handle my cash, learn the intimate details of how I make a living, and have access to all my equipment and merchandise? Have I, have I got that right?"

JC: "Well, when yall put it like that—"

"Okay," said Rap, his shoulders falling, "I get it. But."

The man shook his head. "Stand there." He pointed at a tile on the sidewalk. "No. Not there. *There.*" They moved over two steps. "*There!*"

They moved back one step.

He retreated into his store.

Through the window they saw him sitting at his computer, typing for a furious sixty seconds hard enough to break most keyboards.

Stood up, grabbed something out of the printer, marched back to the door. "Here!"

They each took a sheet. Rap scanned it quickly:

World's Great Men of Colour by J.A. Rogers
The Autobiography of Malcolm X
Always Outnumbered, Always Outgunned by Walter Mosley
Allah is Not Obliged by Ahmoudou Kourouma
Live from Death Row by Mumia Abu Jamal
An Autobiography by Angela Davis
Brown Girl in the Ring by Nalo Hopkinson
Black Girl Talk by The Black Girls
Thomas Sankara Speaks
Black Spark, White Fire by Richard Poe

Rap looked up at him with eyes that must've said, *What.*

"Read," he sighed. "All you hafta do is read *one* of them. And you," he said, glaring at Jackie Chan, "read a different one. Then teach em to each other so between the two of you, you know two books. Do that, and *then* come talk to me.

"And if you don't," he said, his lower lip a receding drawbridge, his hand forming a fist whose fingers actually crackled as they closed, "don't ever come back here again. And I freaking mean it!"

10.

The door jangled as the man leaned on the door to shut it.

Click.

Jackie Chan: "Damn, bwoi, we just got *served*."

"No, we just got *owned*."

"That guy for real? Expects us to read a book just so we have permission to say sorry?"

"Look, JC, he saved our lives. What, we gonna just drip away? I mean, obviously it matters to this guy that we do this. You can't even read one lousy book? What's it gonna hurt? What're you afraid of?"

"What're you, Oprah? Analysin me an shit?"

"Naw, I'm Dr. Phil. 'Joy-riding. How's that working for ya?' How much worse could one book be than almost getting killed for kicks?"

"Where we even gonna *get* all these? Ten books or whatever? That'd cost like fifty bucks!"

"You don't hafta get em all. Just one. And ever hear of a library?"

"Library?" The word blasted out of JC's mouth like Rap'd just said they should get advanced plastic surgery to turn themselves into fully operational Transformers.

"Yeah. The library."

"Man, what's he care what books we're readin? Got enough reading to do for school, an I aint even doin that *To Cook a Mockingbird* an whatever."

"Well, look at this list. Look at these titles. You ever have a teacher get you to read books with these kinda names? There's even a Muslim one here."

JC glanced at the list, then eyed him.

"Well I'ont even have a library card anymore. I owed like two hunnid dollars for some CDs my lil brother destroyed."

Rap tried shaking the disgust out of his head. Couldn't *imagine* not having an active card—the library was his best and only source for DVDs, and he couldn't afford renting them at five bucks a piece.

If he ran up a bill like JC's he'd never get to watch anything. And his mother'd lecture him about irresponsibility and money-wasting until two weeks after he died of old age.

Rap: "You done making excuses?"

"Nope."

"Then *I'll* take em out."

"F'real?"

"Yeah."

"Well, get me suh'm unner a hunnid pages, aiight? I got things t'do."

"No you don't."

"Dude, figure of speech. *Damn*."

"And you're coming with me."

Jackie Chan put his palms up, shoulders high, horrified. "Man!"

Rap walked away. JC drooped his head and followed him like they were hoofing it to the electric chair.

But that would've been too short a walk. Instead they soled it ten blocks south to downtown and the biggest library in the city where, without realising it, they were about to begin their revolution.

11.

Exactly one week later, the two boys stood at the front door of the Hyper-Market.

The man glared back at them through the glass silently. The look on his face suggested he was waiting for a tornado to suck them into the sky and be rid of them permanently.

When they didn't step off (and when JC's toothy smile didn't budge one tooth), the man opened the door and swept them with his eyes.

Each youth was holding a book.

"You kids just don't give up, do you?"

"Nope," they both said.

"You actually each read a book?"

"Yeah!" cheered Jackie Chan, shocking Rap.

"Prove it."

Rap took a breath to start but JC beat him to it.

"I read this one," said JC, pointing to his book and its cover: beneath a crude-ly-drawn red star, a young man in silhouette hefting an AK-47.

"It's about, like, this child soldier," said JC. "Boy's name is Birahima. Starts off as this little kid in like Ivory Coast, and gets y'know recruited into fighting in a civil war in like Sierra Leone. And these adults, right? They give these kids drugs to make em kill their parents or other kids just so they can like totally mess with their heads and basically own them.

"An you think, right, he's gon become good or improve or suh'm but he doesn't. He just fights in a bunch of wars and gets like *seriously* corrupt.

"It's depressing, but great, y'know? Like *The Wire* or *Menace II Society* or, or, or a NWA song."

"*You* listen to NWA?" said the man. "Those songs're older'n you are."

"A man has got to know the classics!" said JC. And then, without any irony, "How'd I do?"

The man chewed his lip, nodded once. Then he turned to Rap. "So'd he teach you about his book?"

"Yeah," said Rap. "Anyway, I already knew about that kinda stuff."

"Really? You read about it?"

" . . . Yeah. The kid, Birahima—pretty much got screwed over by everyone, just cuz it wasn't safe where he was born and so he got sent to live in Liberia. That's why it all happened."

"How so?"

"Liberia's full of stupid and vicious people," said Rap.

He felt Jackie Chan take a step away from him.

The older man's eyebrow: a round being jacked into a chamber.

"There's lead-headed people everywhere, making violence everywhere," said the man. "But we can't be making generalizations like that about one county. Especially not about our own people."

Rap shrugged.

"Anyway," said the man, "what about *your* book?"

Rap held his up. The cover: close-up of a man's huge hands, gripping a towel tightly enough to strangle somebody. Or maybe holding onto it that hard so he wouldn't.

"Mine was about an ex-convict. He was a murderer. You think, you know, if it's like all the other clichéd stories—"

(When Rap said the word *clichéd*, the man's eyes flickered, like he was suddenly paying attention to them for the first time. Rap smiled to himself.)

"—that the man went to prison 'for a crime he didn't commit.' But he *did* commit crimes. Appalling ones. Even heinous ones. Killed his friend when he was drunk, and then raped his friend's girlfriend, and killed her.

"When the story opens, it's twenty-seven years later, and he's angrier than ever. His name's Socrates, just like the philosopher, and he's always asking everybody questions in the story so he can figure out or even teach them right and wrong. You know, the *Socratic method*, right—the use of questions to get a student to learn, instead of just lecturing? So the book's basically his quest for redemption."

He'd worked on that closer all day, and it'd paid off: the man was *double*-eyebrow impressed.

And to prove he wasn't just sucking up, Rap added a criticism: "But there was one chapter where I just couldn't buy the whole premise."

"Oh really?" said the man, leaning against his doorjamb while the two youth stood in the street below him like Mormon missionaries on the porch of an agnostic.

Rap felt his own internal smile growing. He used to talk books with his mother, but that was years ago. Sometimes he used to talk comics with the smartest guy at the comic store, a university student, but that guy hadn't been around in a while. But no English teacher'd ever given him anything interesting to read or asked him real questions, anyway.

So under this true attention, Rap's senses crackled open like flowers anticipating bees:

The afternoon air. Hot. No dust. Smooth. Scrubbed clean by a mid-afternoon shower. Tasted sweet, like a block away someone'd torn open an orange and the breeze had blessed it over to his nose.

The chrome of a sideview mirror on a black sports car. On a storefront, a window trim mosaic made of quartz and copper. The green glass of a bottle of Ting in the gutter, refracting rainbows.

In that moment, everything on 111th Ave sparkled.

"Yeah, in this one chapter," said Rap, gleaming inside and for the first time neither ashamed nor afraid to face the moustacheless man in the goatee, "Socrates brought this injured dog to a White woman who was a vet. And she even offered to let Socrates stay with her. In her actual *house*. I mean, he's this huge Black guy, an ex-con. He scares everyone, not just White people. No way would any White woman ever do that!"

The man shifted in his door frame, chewing his lip. "Well, you know, there are women who go for bad boys."

"Yeah, but come on, I mean, he's gotta be thirty years older than she is."

"There are even women," said the man, his mouth smudging into an almost detectable grin, "who write to prisoners, lifers, death row convicts, even serial killers, trying to convince these guys to *marry em. Cuz they wanna save* em. And there are men like that, too. Lots of em. Trying to rescue women who ultimately drag em down to drown in the swamps of death."

The swamps of death?

Sounded like he was quoting from something. *Sampling.* From some unknown, unfound, unbound, underground wax pressed back in the golden age of righteous lyricalising and thunderous 88-beats. Rap liked the phrase, the echo on it. The reverb.

"Never," said the man to Rap's silent consideration, "underestimate the stupidity of anybody who wants to be a saviour."

"You underestimated *us,* didn't you?"

The man glowered. Rap's burn increased.

But then Rap realised the man was actually working double-time just not to smirk.

He stepped aside.

The boys walked in slowly past him, flashing each other smiles reading *Mission Accomplished.*

12.

"Okay, you wanna make it up to me?" he said.

Wasn't really a question, so they shut up waiting for the catch.

"Clean up. Then help paint. Then help move furniture and put up the decorations. You come every day after school for a couple of weeks, a few hours on the weekends, we'll be done."

Looked at each other neutrally, picked up broom and mop and got to work.

After sorting through a box of busted electronics including iPods, Zunes and digital cameras, the man went into the back. Hadn't exactly been chatty.

Jackie Chan whispered, "Man, this is some serious *wax on, wax off*-type shit, isn't it?"

"I don'know. Maybe."

"When you think he's gon lay summa them whip-whap moves on us?" He threw down a decent Bruce Lee *wa-aa!* and Rap laughed. "Cuz if a sucker MC make a move on me," he rhymed, "I'ma lay im out for the E-M-T!" Rap laughed again.

They worked for three hours until Mr. Yimunhotep Ani told them to go home.

But when they came back the next day, Friday, Mr. Ani looked like he hadn't forgiven them one bit. Like they'd lost all the ground they'd gained by book-re-porting.

"So you're back," he said. "Fine. Mops are over there."

When he was out of the room, Jackie Chan muttered, "More wax on. More wax off."

Rap gestured, whispered, "'Sand the floor. And don't forget to breathe.'"

After three hours Mr. Ani told them to go home.

On the third day, Saturday, Mr. Ani "greeted" them at the door again: "Hm. You two again."

He pointed them to cleaning out the garbage in the back.

There was a newspaper open to the City section, with a story about how the police were getting bad press all over the world for beating and Tasering their rescuer.

"Damn," said Jackie Chan. "Looks like Brotherman been YouTubed into an *international* celebrity. Like Nelson Mandela with nunchuks."

Rap laughed again until the old man poked his head in long enough to glower at them.

When he was gone, Rap folded up the news story into his pocket.

On the fourth day, Mr. Ani said at the door, "You two just don't quit, do you?"

The boys spent two hours washing the walls. When the first wall was dry, they primed it. Mr. Ani sent them home after four hours.

On the fifth day, all Mr. Ani said at the door was "Hmph."

When he was out of the room, the two boys quickly got bored and tired moving the ladder, going up the ladder, taping the corners of the walls, coming down the ladder, moving the ladder again, blah-blah-blah.

JC: "Dude, fuh real, how long we gotta keep coming here?"

"I'm not the boss of you," said Rap. "Who's making you come here?"

On the sixth day, Mr. Ani just shook his head when the boys arrived, then pointed at the paint cans.

They left after five hours.

On the seventh day, neither one of them showed.

13.

On the eighth day, when they appeared on time, Mr. Ani blocked the door.

"You were supposed to be here yesterday!" His eyes lasered them to pieces. "Not only did you not show up, you didn't even call!"

"I'm, I'm . . . we're sorry, Mr. Ani," said Rap, "but, but we don't even have your number, and—"

"There're two types of people in the world. Those who do what they say they're gonna do, and everybody else. What I wanna know right now is, are you like everybody else? Because if you are, you should stop wasting my time!"

"Look, Mr. Ani, we read those books, just like you asked us to," said Jackie Chan. "We even read more. I read another one, and Rap's read two!"

"Actually three!"

"And you never even asked us about em," said JC. "I thought you were gon teach us some martial arts or culture or history or suh'm. And then, we come here, we work for you, for free. And, okay, we said we'd do it, outta of respect for you, you saving our lives, but—"

"But what you're saying is," said Mr. Ani, "you want me to say I excuse you from ever having to come back here, right? That your debt's over and your guilt's excused?"

"No! We're just sayin, we're just sayin . . . it'd be nice if you didn't, y'know, act like you hate us an shit. Excuse my language. That's all *I'm* saying."

Five seconds. Ten.

Fifteen.

Mr. Ani cleared his throat.

"Well for your information . . . I had a whole meal here for you two knuckleheads yesterday! Goat, *sabaayat, injera,* chicken *suqaar, ater kik wot,*" he said, rattling off Somali and Ethiopian delish-dishes until Rap's and JC's stomachs went even-Steven in a squawk-off.

"Fuh real?" said Jackie Chan.

"*Which* I ended up eating by myself. So if I get fat, that's on you two."

"Damn," said Jamal. He looked up quickly. "I mean, 'darn.' Mr. Ani."

An eyebrow put a nail through the *darn.*

41

"Martial arts takes discipline, smart ass. You can't expect me to train people who don't even show up."

"We had to study for finals yesterday, Mr. Ani, sir," said Rap, laying on the guilt extra thick with the *sir*. "We were here all weekend, every day after school . . . but we still have school responsibilities."

"Yeah," said JC.

"Well," said the old man. "School is important."

"Yes sir, it is."

" . . . C'mon in."

Inside, everything was painted. A gold wall elbowed a red one. The third wall was a fresh white. Mr. Ani chaired the boys, then opened his fridge and toaster oven and came back with bottles and a plate of *sambusas*. "This's all that's left from yesterday."

"Thanks!" they said, tearing into the palm-sized crisp pastry triangles of curried ground beef, peas and potato. Steam rose out of the innards, and the boys they laid into them.

"You ever try this?" asked Mr. Ani.

They looked confused. The man was offering them beer?

"Nothing *haram*," said Mr. Ani to Jackie Chan specifically.

He doesn't know JC very well, thought Rap. To him, *everything's* halal. He was eating a bacon cheeseburger just two days ago.

"It's Ting, a Jamaican pop. Unless you prefer ginger beer. I have that, too."

"No, this's great!" said JC, munching sambusa.

All three men ate together, and then Mr. Ani put on some jazz, this time below the ear-splitting volume he'd played it the other day to screen them out. "Pharoah Sanders," he explained.

There was a woman's voice in it, welcoming the audience, inviting her listeners to dance and sing and rejoice with the band, accompanied by jangling xylophone and sand-shaker percussion that felt like warm remembrance. It wasn't a party as much as a joyful prayer.

Rap's mind fireworked while listening to it. He vowed to seek it out at the library—Mr. Ani said the album was simply called *Rejoice*.

Together they all painted the back room and talked about books.

When it was time to go, Mr. Ani reached into his pocket. Rap's heart leapt: money? Was he revoking their volunteer-slave status and now actually paying them?

But it wasn't money. It was joints.

What the hell? thought Rap. Thought *this* guy was . . .

But the small white roll-ups in each hand weren't twisted shut at each end.

The boys realised it at the same moment: they were scrolls.

They looked up for permission. Mr. Ani nodded it.

They read tiny, laser-printed figures in an 8-point font:

ALPHABETICAL ALCHEMY

A Africentric
B Build
C Create
D Divine
E Evolve
F Family
G Geometry
H Hero
I Individuality/ Intelligence
J Justice
K Knowledge
L Liberate
M Minister
N Nature
O Orbit
P Power
Q Question
R Revolution
S Simultaneous
T Truth/Transform
U Unite/Universal
V Victory
W Wisdom
X X-ray
Y Yam
Z Zenith

NUMERICAL ALCHEMY

1 Resurrection
2 Revolution
3 Triumph
4 Ancestor~I
5 Mother~Sister~Daughter
6 Father~Brother~Son
7 Replace~Elevate
8 Righteousness & Mastery
9 Create~Supreme
0 Peace~Life~Eternal

☞

At the door, Mr. Ani actually put a hand on each boy's shoulder, although at six feet, he wasn't much taller than either of them.

Rap flinched and stepped back. Mr. Ani let go of both of them to gesticulate through his points.

"I'm giving you a few days off to study and finish your exams. Work hard and do a good job. Come back to me when you know all the power-words from the Resurrection Scroll, in order, by heart," he said. "Then we'll talk about that martial arts training."

Instead of saying goodbye, he said, *"Nub-Wmet-Ānkh."*

More mysteries.

Out in the street, a block away, Jackie Chan exploded his best Bruce Lee wail and a jabbing, kicking, seizure-style dance.

Rap laughed. He didn't care about martial arts one way or the other.

But that list—two codes, one of letters and one of numbers, each composed of *power-words,* each a chamber of mystery he was about to unlock. To explore.

Felt the weight of it: that "scroll" was a whole world rolled up inside his palm.

14.

That night, after an hour studying the French Revolution for his Social final, Rap devoted another hour to running the mysterious list of numbers, letters and names in his head, testing himself against the scroll.

Two days later, after proving himself a fifth time with a perfect score, he realised something that snapped his attention like an elastic band against his neck.

Whenever he ran the code aloud or silently in his mind, the burn across his body . . . disappeared.

Three
Triumph

The Book of Then

1.

I WOKE UP, BARELY . . .

And for almost an entire breath, I didn't remember.

I didn't feel magnificent or soaring or glorious, but because memory hadn't choked me yet, I felt the simple calm of being not-hunted, not-miserable, not-terrified, and not even realising it.

Didn't remember I was a lone child lost in the Savage Lands. That I'd lost my mum, all our adults, and then all the kids I'd saved. That my best friend Shai'd gotten impaled on a monster's tusk. That our fishing-chief Jedu, the kid who'd kept us all fed, had drunk the water from the Swamps of Death and become a burnt-eyed corpse that kept on walking.

The breath ended, and I was awake.

My body ached from having slept all night in that tree.

White mist clutched everything. Made everything look like it wasn't there. Dead trees with their bare branches drowning in the fog, like huge black spiders boiled in pots of milk.

I climbed down.

I had to eat. I needed a camp. Something I could hide in and defend.

But I couldn't find a cave. So on top of a low hill at the base of the biggest tree, where the soil had pulled free of the roots, I found a hole. I took some vines and made a curtain over the entrance.

My home.

I was starving. I found slugs and centipedes. The first meal I'd had in a week, and the slugs were so moist and juicy I almost forgot how thirsty I was. But the centipedes were dry and salty.

I tried conjuring a plan, how to rescue the kids who'd slogged away with dead-alive eyes, a plan for how to smash the curse of the swamp water, a plan for how to find my mum. But my head was buzzing from thirst, my stomach was still aching, and I could barely think. So I tried sleeping in my hole.

2.

The sound of kids screaming woke me up.

Night. I couldn't tell where it was coming from. I grabbed the fang-shard I'd torn from the monster's mouth, turned myself into a shadow, and tried to find the source.

Down at the Swamps of Death, the sludge-water was the yellow-beige of puke, but glowing.

A pack of kids. Six of them were mine, and there was maybe another dozen I'd never seen before. All of them were kneeling around the edge of the Swamp, leaning down and lapping up water like dogs.

And then the biggest one stopped drinking, stood up and looked down at the second biggest kid who was right there next to him, and kicked him in the face.

That kid rolled away from him, and his attacker howled like a monkey. His teeth—I could see his teeth from the white-yellow glow of the Swamp—were green and rotten, nubby. Half his teeth were missing, and his gums had gone white. The cratered skin on his neck and back was oozing pus, white over brown.

The biggest kids joined him howling, turning on the smaller kids and beating them till they were sobbing and pissing and shitting from the pain.

And they dumped them into the Swamps to drown.

"Stop it, you assholes!" I shouted, and they all turned their burnt-out eyes on me.

My shadow was gone and I couldn't bring it back—was I too hungry?

Shoving my fang-shard in my vine-belt, I jumped into the evil water and jammed shut my mouth. I grabbed the little kid closest to me, pulled him to the edge, threw him on the shore and went back for the next one.

All the while, the Swamp-drinking monkeys on the shore were screaming and howling, stamping their feet, shaking their fists and baring their scummed-over, nubby teeth at me.

And then they all backed way the hell off, and I knew I was in massive danger.

White crocodiles, a dozen of them, cut into the Swamp like daggers and headed straight at me.

I reached the edge, released the kid I'd pulled with me, and then bracing my feet against a rock on the swamp's slimy bottom, I shot forward.

Ripping the arm-long fang-shard from my belt, I sliced downward through the lead crocodile's snout just before it could open.

It cracked open all the way into its brains, like a pot left in the fire far too long. Hot gore sprayed all over and burned me, sizzling where it hit the water.

The two halves of the monster's head dipped in death. Bowing to me.

I had no idea I could do that.

In that stone-still moment of shock, the crocodile's angry brothers ripped the other kids in the water into bloody mash. One swept up beside me, clamping onto the left arm of the kid I'd just pulled out of danger. He screamed and I grabbed his right arm to pull him away, but the crocodile was too strong, and I lost him.

I scrambled out of the water, turned back to see the Swamp boiling with blood and bone and thrashing tails and claws and rows of jagged teeth.

There were no kids left to save.

And the god-damned drunken monkeys were gone. I would've taken my arm-length fang to their throats if they hadn't run away. Run away leaving me to deal with those monsters alone.

I couldn't stay, not with the crocodiles raging to make me their dessert.

I ran from the white-yellow glow of the Swamps of Death to find my nest.

Down in my hole, I failed to fall asleep. Too much howling and screeching and the sight of the smallest kid being ripped to bloody chunks.

3.

I woke up exhausted. Again.

I didn't know how long it'd taken me to fall asleep or how long I'd been down. Starving so much my gut hurt.

My head ached from thirst, like a knife in both eyes.

And no slugs around for a quick snack and slurp.

So I went out foraging.

I found a mound of dropped fruit in the mud, which almost made me cry I was so happy. But when I reached for the mangoes I pulled my hand back from a lagoon of orange slime, maggots throbbing over the island pits.

Slugs and centipedes, fine. But even starving, I couldn't make myself eat maggots.

That's when I heard the marching.

Sounded like a whole army, the clanking of a thousand weapons.

I tried turning myself into shadow, but in the white-fogged daylight, weak as I was, I couldn't. So I hid behind tree trunks, massive stones, mounds of earth, looking for a place to spy on who was out there while hoping with hammering heart they weren't after me.

I scrambled up a hill, hid inside a knot of trees, peered down. I saw them.

Kids. Hundreds. Maybe thousands.

Chained.

Not moving their heads. Not talking or crying. Just marching.

Maybe they'd been drinking swamp water… but then why the chains? To keep them from killing each other? Or themselves?

And then I saw the brutes leading them.

Even at a distance I could see their markings—tattoos and body paint of an anteater-man with squared-off ears.

The night-raiders.

I waited for them to pass, then trailed them for a distance.

When the raiders stopped to eat, they fed the kids just enough to keep them marching—crusts from bread sacks the kids themselves were hauling.

When they were gone, I scrounged whatever shreds and crumbs I could. Bread'd never tasted like this before. Sweet. Rich. Almost meaty.

But it left me thirstier than ever, and with a mouth full of glue that took me forever to swallow.

4.

I tracked them until dusk, every step of it strangling my gut.

These kids had no fight left in them at all, but if any of them stumbled or fell, the shackles took down a whole bunch with him, and then the soldiers beat them raw.

Broken bones hardly made them march faster. But they never even screamed.

If there were just one or two of those bastards guarding the kids, I could've sunk Fang right through their bellies. But there were dozens. They would've beaten or hacked me to death, and for what?

Finally we entered a grove of caves, where the soldiers detached a few hundred kids from the chain-line and sent them down inside. Other kids were climbing out from the cave-mouths, girls and boys hauling basketsful of rocks and dumping them in piles. Yellow hunks glinted under the torchlight.

The guards orderd the kids to lie down. They piled together like puppies and fell asleep immediately. That was the only time they made a sound, wheezing and whimpering in their sleep.

I found the camp guards' provisions, stole whatever food I could carry, then found a hiding place.

Roasted rat—delicious! Sucked the blood out of three oranges! Ripped the guts out of a watermelon! First time I hadn't felt hungry or thirsty in weeks. And my headache finally went away.

I turned myself to shadow, and slept.

Somewhere in the night, my mother lay dead, her head hacked off from her body.

In the morning until high-sun I tracked the chain-line until it arrived at a field.

A farm. I'd seen a few before. But this one was huge. And here, there was screaming.

Thousands of kids were there already, bending and digging and grabbing and hauling and sweating and struggling, while soldiers in the fields whipped them, and other soldiers sat in the shade gorging themselves on fruit, bread, and meat.

By evening they wrangled the kids inside a corral with cisterns of water reeking like the Swamps of Death.

After unchaining the kids from the line, they re-shackled them in pairs and gave the kids as much Swamp water to drink as they could take before their bellies burst.

Then the soldiers hauled two pairs at a time into a central pen, backed out, and threw each pair one hatchet and one dagger.

Without even being told to, the kids in the pen butchered each other.

When the soldiers stopped cheering and passing each other glinting yellow metal nuggets, a guard unchained the surviving fighter and dragged out the three corpses. Teeth and an ear lay in the bloody sand. I don't know which boy lost which.

The guards threw the dead boys to their dogs who ripped the bodies apart in seconds.

Then they chained the winner to a fresh kid. And they kept repeating this until they'd cut the numbers by three-quarters.

They split the remaining quarter in halves, lined them up, gave them pikes.

Then they were down to an eighth.

Bruised, sliced, bleeding, raging and howling—

The soldiers threatened the biggest ones, told them they'd kick them down and piss into their gashes unless they shut up, got back in their chains and went to sleep.

And so they all backed down and lied down in a pile.

I felt my mind splintering. Everything I looked at looked like fire. Living children looked like rotting corpses. My mother's body was severed and strewn across the shadowed jungles of the Savage Lands. And children killed each other in front of me, and I did nothing, and I felt nothing any more.

I found a hiding place and slept and dreamt of ripping open oranges and gorging myself on roasted rat.

5.

I woke up and immediately said to myself, out loud, "Nothing I can do for any of them."

I was spending too much time alone.

At least I understood better how the Destroyer's soldiers operated, and the size of his empire. It was time to go back to my nest.

Hours into my careful march and hungrier with every step, I found a bunch of eggs on the ground, mostly broken. The insides of the half-shells were cleaned out, probably by rats.

But there was one unbroken egg there, so I took it with me for a snack, or my whole meal if I couldn't find anything else.

When I thought of the roasted rat, oranges and watermelon, my belly let out a moan so loud it actually scared me, like an animal'd crawled inside my gut and was eating its way out.

Then the egg cracked open.

A chick wriggled slowly, painful inside. A falcon chick!

It squawked at me: *Hroo-hroo, hroo-hroo . . .*

Beautiful, this tiny little bird. Without thinking I started to pet it, and the little bastard bit me. I dropped it in the peat, lifted my foot to stomp it—

But it kept calling out, *Hroo-hroo, hroo-hroo* . . .

Was it cursing me for dropping him? Ordering me to feed him? Or crying for his mum?

Just thinking about those choices almost made me cry. Not seeing all those kids murder each other at the soldiers' command, no—but this little chick that'd just bitten me.

I picked him back up. He tilted his head back squawking, beak way open. I pressed my thumb against the wound he'd torn in my finger, squeezed out a few drops of blood into his mouth, just like a mama bird feeding puked-up worms to her baby.

"There you go, buddy," I cooed to him. "C'mon. Eat your breakfast. More where that came from—"

"Who the hell are *you* supposed to be?"

I spun around, jumped up—

Grinning at me was this crazy-looking kid, my size, hair mudded and twisted up and into two tall ears.

Ringing him was a squad of jackals, big, deadly-looking black ones, each one like night on four legs, with moons for eyes.

With Fang I could've probably gutted two of them, maybe blinded a couple of others, but the rest of them would've turned my face into dinner and kept my balls for breakfast.

"Who the hell am I?" I threw back. "Who the hell are *you?*"

"I'll tell you who I am, asshole. I'm Yinepu! The Hunter! And I aint no masterless kid, neither. I work for the Sorceress of the whole Savage Lands. Anything I hunt, I kill. And nobody hunts me."

He pointed at the ground with his rock dagger. "This is *my* territory. So I suggest you stay the hell out of here before I let my friends here do my convincing for me, understand, chick-boy?"

Right on cue, the falcon squawked, *Hroo-hroo.*

"You really wanna know who I am?" I said, suddenly crazy. I mean, I actually started laughing out loud, like I'd completely cracked. "I'm . . . I'm *Hru!*"

Me laughing like that while I was outnumbered by him and his jackals, that stopped him. Probably made him shit himself. Good. That's what he probably used to mud his hair.

"So you work for a witch, huh? Big deal. I fought a whole platoon of soldiers—at night! I got swallowed by the Devourer of Millions of Souls and I ripped out his tooth and caused him so much pain he had to spit me out! I've still got it right here—see this? The deadliest sword anywhere in the Blackland *or* the Savage Lands! I rescued a bunch of kids in the Swamps of Death by splitting a whole army of gods-damned crocodiles' heads in half! Think I'm afraid of some damn mud-head weirdo whose only friends are dogs? Try me! And try Fang!"

"Oh yeah?"

"Yeah."

We stared each other down for I don't know how long.

Finally we each backed away.

When I was far enough away I turned around and started running, chick in one hand and Fang in the other.

"Don't be coming back here, you got me?" he shouted, pretty faint at that distance.

"Don't *you* be coming back here, you got *me?*"

I needed to work on my come-backs.

By the time I got back to my nest it was dark. I fed my falcon chick again, again with my blood, and sang him the only song I remembered, one my mother'd taught me about how lonely it felt to wander, and then we both went to sleep.

The Book of Now

1.

JACKIE CHAN—SCREAMING—FACE DOWN ON THE FLOOR OF THE BASEMENT.

Mr. Ani's knee jammed against his spine.

Twisting JC's arm. At that angle, only two more pounds of pressure and it'd snap at the elbow like a chicken bone in a pit-bull's jaws.

Couldn't speak—just *slap-spap-snappetty-slap-slapped* the floor—

Mr. Ani helped him up.

"Dude!" big-smiled JC to Rap, rubbing his shoulder and arm. "You've *got* to try that! It's insane! It's crack-happy!"

Rap looked at his friend brushing dust from his cheeks and missing all the dust coating his mini-dreads. Grey hair. Looked like the oldest teenager in the world.

"Yeah, looks fun," said Rap. His shoulders and neck were burning.

The Hyper-Market was less than two weeks from being open for business. Signs declaring *DATA RECOVERY, iPOD + SMALL ELECTRONICS REPAIRS, OVERSEAS MONEY TRANSFERS* yapped at pedestrians from the window.

But Raphael Garang, Jamal "Jackie Chan" Abdi and Mr. Yimunhotep Ani weren't on the main floor. They were in the basement on gym mats under the low ceiling in the midst of their first lesson in *jujutsu*.

"Your turn," said *Sbai* Ani to Rap, beckoning with both hands and all ten fingers curling in: two crabs struggling on their backs.

"Reach for me," said the man in the long goatee and the black-and-gold skullcap. "Hockey-fight style—that's what any knucklehead in the street's gonna throw."

Rap held back. "I don'know, Mr. Ani. I . . . I'm feeling sick."

"Well don't barf on me," said Mr. Ani. "C'mon. JC's already done the move five times now. Gonna hafta do it some time."

"I'm telling you, man," JC told Rap. "Fuhgeddaboudit!"

Rap scowled at him. This week it was *Donnie Brasco*. Last week *Scarface*. Next week probably *Dolemite*.

"I'll go slow," said their teacher. "Don't worry. I won't hurtcha."

Rap sucked down a breath, sniffed, tried running the Numerical Alchemy in his head. Fire ripped down his back. Loosely held the right lapel of the man's *gi* with his left hand, then slow-mo punched his right fist forward.

"Hang on," said the *Sbai*.

Clutching Rap's left hand against his own chest.

Bringing up his right arm, fist face high.

Rotating at his hips and sinking into a deep stance.

Jamming his right forearm into the elbow of Rap's grabbing arm—

—Rap buckling and shooting forward chest-first like a toboggan on ice—

Mr. Ani cranking Rap's left hand and sliding his own right hand down along Rap's arm, like strangling a snake at two ends, jamming his hand between Rap's shoulder and shoulder blade until Rap was face-in-the-floor with Ani's knee was in his back.

"Get off me! GET OFFA ME!"

Mr. Ani jumped off of him. Tried to help him up

Rap scrambled up, back, his belly-skin crawling and his back, neck and scalp rippling flame.

"Whoah, whoah—you okay? Did I hurt you?" asked the older man, eyes wide, hands up high in *I surrender.*

Rap shook his head, tried to form words, failed.

Ani: "Okay . . . . Maybe we should take a break upstairs."

Rap sniffed. Looked at the floor. Glanced glares at his elder and his peer. Hating him and JC and himself.

Upstairs he shoved his feet in his sneakers and split without saying goodbye.

2.

Three days later. A hot, dry late afternoon.

Rap came back.

Mr. Ani met him at the door.

"I was worried about you," said the old man. "I left messages. You didn't call."

Rap shrugged, looked up and down 111th Avenue broiling in the heat and the dust.

He took a big breath. "The other day." Sniffed. "I blew up."

Mr. Ani nodded.

"I don'know what happened—I just—"

"Young brother," said Mr. Ani, "it was *my* fault. It was stupid of me!"

He chinned towards the store next door. No more police tape, but the place was closed without even a FOR LEASE sign.

"You two, face-down in the store next door on a midnight multiple homicide. And then twenty metres away, genius me, planting you like petunias. Okay, maybe . . . maybe we switch you to *wing chun*. Close-combat, but no ground-fighting." Cleared his throat. "Think about it, anyway. Okay?"

Rap. Forcing himself.

"I'm just . . . . " Shrugged. "Just not maybe into martial arts."

55

"Important to be able to defend yourself. As you well know."

"Yeah, but—"

"But yeah, maybe it *is* too soon—"

"I just, you know, enjoy talking with you about books. And learning the scrolls."

Mr. Ani nodded, smiled. He held out his hand. Rap shook it.

Rap reached into his backpack, handed over a cardboard tube. His elder shook out the contents.

A pen-and-ink of Wesley Snipes, motion-blurred, swords and limbs swinging.

"Blade!" said Ani. "You did this?"

Rap nodded.

"Damn, that's excellent!" Lots of teeth. Eyes sparkling like black quartz. "This is for me?"

Rap nodded.

Ani held his fist over Rap's hand, dropped a dap.

"Golden, bruh. C'mon in."

Inside they sat drinking Ethiopian tea and listening to Mr. Ani's speakers spitting hip hop. Cloves made the inside of Rap's mouth pucker, so he ripped open a half-dozen sugar packets and pocketed the other half-dozen.

Mr. Ani returned from the other room and handed him a lender, an oversize trade paperback with no picture on the cover, just text: *World's Great Men of Colour* by J.A. Rogers.

Flipped through over names that didn't mean anything to him: Imhotep, Akhenaton, Aesop, Pushkin . . .

"Keep learning your scrolls," said Mr. Ani, while the two of them waited for JC, "and maybe one day you can write a book like that. Or," he winked, "be in one."

Rap chuckled. At the joke, yeah, but more at the wink. Mr. Ani was the only person Rap'd ever met who winked. Something about winking seemed so . . . undignified.

All the more fun coming from the most dignified man he'd ever met.

Rap's eyes drifted over the names on Mr. Ani's latest reading list, which he said was also a playlist: Mazisi Kunene, Ngugi wa Thiong'o, LKJ, the Last Poets, Gil Scott Heron, Mzwakhe Mbuli . . .

Suddenly the lyrics out of the speakers crystallised inside Rap's brain—he knew this song, this verse by Mr. Lif about how poor people taught their kids to work so they die from stress, but the rich taught theirs to invest.

"Man!" said Rap, his guard not just dropped, but shattered. "You listen to the Perceptionists? I thought you were only into PE and Kris or whatever—"

"Oh, you mean, old-timers?"

Caught. Rap could feel his own eyes form an *oops*.

"Well . . . yeah."

Ani walked behind a counter, reached into a drawer. "Boy, I've been listening to hip hop longer'n you've been a *live*. I *am* hip hop."

Pulled out some tacks and pinned up Rap's Blade picture. Right where all the customers would see it.

Grinding his teeth so hard they almost hurt, Rap suppressed his smile down to a smirk.

3.

Two days later. Mr. Ani's training basement.

Mr. Ani, standing back, surveying the boys' *wing chun* skills. Arms sliding back-and-forth in punches and blocks as if magnetically attached. Whenever the boys lost contact, Mr. Ani nudged their form.

"Not about strength," said Mr. Ani. "It's about the *U-T of N.*"

"*Universal Truth of Nature,*" said both boys, arms still clockworking.

"It's about the *P* of *P*-physics and *P*-physiology."

"*Power,*" they said.

"The application of *P* along the correct *G.*"

"*Power-Geometry . . .*"

"Good. Now, JC, you and me, let's try that take-down I showed you a few days ago. I'll do it to you, and then you try to do it to me. Then we'll stretch out."

JC tried the technique once, butchering it.

Mr. Ani told him, "Not bad. We'll fix it later."

Switched to stretching. At each stretch, it being their third lesson, Mr. Ani recited the question for each line of the third chapter of *The Book of the Golden Falcon.*

"After the first battle of the Swamps," said Ani, on question #6, "where did the boy go?"

Straining lower back muscles for forward stretches on the floor, trying to hiss out the pain. Teeth gritted. Rap and JC recited.

"*And the boy . . . abandoned and alone . . . fled the Swamps of Death . . . and returned to his nest in darkness.*"

The seventh question: "What did the boy find on his first foray?"

"*When next rose the sun . . . the boy emerged to forage and to range . . . and from a distance spied the lifeless march . . . of bound and fettered children . . . by the thousand.*"

They got up for wall stretches.

Standing with his back to the exposed brick, JC lifted his right leg. Mr. Ani ducked under, caught JC's foot on his left shoulder and slowly rose. JC winced when his toes got to eye-level, tapped out. Mr. Ani held position.

"Who led the lifeless children, and to where, first?" The eighth question.

"*Witnessing their damnable . . . procession from cover,*" said both boys, "*he saw their brutal guardians . . . break the bones of some for grim amusement . . . before casting dozens into mines . . . of lead and pyrite.*"

"Where was the second group of lifeless children taken?" Ani raised JC's leg again until the tap. JC's toe was now above his head.

"Still others," said the teens, "chainsmen led to fields . . . so as to join . . . the sun-whipped toil . . . of ten thousand others . . . digging, planting, pulling . . . in the rock and sand and soil."

Continued through each line of the "Triumph" chapter of *The Book of the Golden Falcon*, repeating the entire cycle until Rap and JC had stretched each leg front and side, including bent-leg extensions for roundhouse kicks.

Breakfalls and rolls again and again until Mr. Ani was satisfied, and then he flattened JC with a fist-catch/arm-bar/takedown. Showed Rap three times. Didn't touch him, but broke it down so Rap could repeat it on JC. Then vice-versa.

Ani'd shown them this takedown at the beginning of class. That was his method: show them the best part first, then make them sweat and strain for it. "Shining Eyes on the golden prize," he'd say.

4.

At the end. Sitting on mats in the centre of the room. Mr. Ani, at the side, activating his docked iPod.

Music, cosmic and spectral, Saturn-ring strings and meteoric horns. Rap and JC knew the artist well, now: Alice Coltrane.

Mr. Ani didn't call it jazz. He called it *supreme*. Said jazz was old slang for sex, the "exotic, forbidden sex wealthy White men slumming in Black music halls went looking for with poor Black women."

Supreme, he said, "wasn't about degrading the body, but elevating the mind and the soul."

"Galaxy Around Oludumare" was the song. Ominous. Drum rumbling. Soundtrack for Judgement Day. Rap loved it. Suited his personal sense of drama.

Mr. Ani returned from the side. Wooden case in his hands.

"Focus now," whispered Mr. Ani below the music. He whispered whenever he wanted to teach the most important thing for the day. Whispering forced the boys to listen with extreme care, because Mr. Ani refused to repeat himself—which also meant the boys were on the hook for teaching each other whatever the other one missed.

Quietly: "You both know the Resurrection Scroll. You're making great progress in *The Book of the Golden Falcon*—you already know the third *arit*.

Now, what I'm about to show you," said Mr. Ani, gesturing towards his wooden case, "is the secret to understanding society, history and even the future.

The boys leaned forward, elbows on knees, chins on fists.

"Like imagine you've been walking through a dark forest your whole life," said the man in the black-and-gold skullcap, "and then suddenly the sun rises, and you look around and see for the first time what was in fact always all around you, and where the wolves are, and where the food is, and where there's a way out."

Mr. Ani opened his wooden case. Removed and held up a hunk of dark grey rock.

"*Lead,*" he said.

He handed it to Rap. It was smooth and cold.

"Eighty percent of people on this planet are made of this," said *Sbai* Ani. "It's dense. Heavy. Doesn't conduct electricity. Blocks X-rays. It's dull and unreflective. Transformed?"

Rap: "Yeah."

Jackie Chan: "Uh-huh."

JC handed him back the lead. Mr. Ani held up a jagged, glittering, metallic yellow-grey block. Looked like a bunch of iron dice welded together.

"*Pyrite.*"

"Fool's gold?" asked Jackie Chan.

"Very good. Shiny. Pretty, even." He handed it over to JC.

"A hundred years ago just north of here, during the gold rush, down in the darkness of mines and caves, there were desperate men who dug this up. Thought they'd found their salvation. Thought they were rich.

"But only out in the sun could they see how wrong they were. Because pyrite's worthless.

"Ten percent of humanity is made of this. Transformed?"

Jackie Chan, nodding, squinting to show his focus: "Ri-i-i-i-ght."

Rap: "Yeah."

Rap handed back the pyrite. Mr. Ani held up a small pendant dangling from a fine chain, a flattened oval with a tangent on the bottom. Raised characters sang something mysterious.

"*Gold,*" said Mr. Ani.

He didn't hand it over.

The amulet glittered hypnotically.

"The final ten percent of humanity is made of this," whispered Mr. Ani.

"Gold's highly conductive. Beautiful. Precious. Whole nations used to measure their wealth based on how much of this they possessed. And it's formed inside the hearts of supernovas. You know what supernovas are?"

"Yeah," said JC. "Like, super-duper huge mega-stars. That explode."

"That's right, young brother. Where'd you learn that?"

"*Star Trek*," he said.

"Good," chuckled Mr. Ani. "Me too, probably. In the olden days. So let's transform all this.

"People are born lead, and most people stay that way their whole lives. They're the Leadites.

"And they're easily *led* astray by those who're turned into—or who turn themselves into—the Pyrites. The Pyrites are like *pirates* because they hijack people, keep em hostage, steal their treasure, and prevent them from ever getting where they're supposed to get to, even dumping them on islands in the middle of nowhere or drowning them at sea.

"And any gold they find, they steal it and hoard it, and even bury it in chests under the sand."

The boys nodded, grasping fragments, knowing that others were just beyond their fingertips.

"So who's left? Gold. From supernovas, light-sources so powerful they can outshine entire galaxies. Gold is knowledge: the most precious thing in the universe.

"If you have everything and don't have knowledge, you can't use what you do have or appreciate how much it's worth, so to you, it's actually worthless.

"If you don't have true gold, you spend your whole life chasing after and stock-piling pyrite thinking it's worth something, when actually, it's worth nothing."

Mr. Ani's eyes were slits. To Rap, the pendant was shining as brilliantly as the sun.

Mr. Ani: "Now on the other hand, if you had nothing or'd lost everything *except* knowledge, you could deploy that knowledge to acquire and use and appreciate everything else you were missing.

"The Ancient Egyptians called gold *nub*. The land of gold was *Nubia*. And so the people who achieve the state of true and living gold are *Nubians.*"

"Mr. Ani?" said Rap. "Uh, I'm half-Sudanese."

"Yes, brother. Clearly."

"Yeah, but, y'know . . . on my father's side, I'm Dinka and Nubian."

"Words have multiple meanings, brother," said Mr. Ani. "We're talking symbols here. Symbols have power, power enough to change the world. Look at em: cross, star-and-crescent, Star of David, sickle-and-hammer, swastika, dollar sign, *E* equals *em-cee-squared*—symbols.

"Just like The Book of the Golden Falcon. That's not history. It's myth. History is about facts—this happened here at that time because of so-and-so. Myth *never* happened—but it's always *true*. Transformed?"

Rap nodded. He thought he did.

"So what I'm teaching both of you right now is *alchemy*," said Mr. Ani. "Again, a symbol. I *know* you know what alchemy is."

At last for Rap, the rotating puzzle pieces slid into beautiful geometry so their connected picture emerged from chaos. He whispered, awe-ignited. "It's the mystic art of turning lead into gold."

"Exactly. We're all born as lead. If we're lucky, or if we have the right teachers at the right time, we start our own transformation into gold. Into *Nubians*. But *having* isn't the ultimate state of righteousness and mastery. We need to be *B-ing*, and *M-C-ing*."

"*Building*," said the boys, leaping on the cues, "*ministering*, and *creating*."

"That's right. So remember those proportions: eighty, ten and ten. Symmetry. Alchemists and Pyrites are even-Steven for numbers. But because the Pyrites've shackled the bodies, minds and spirits of four-fifths of the human race—the Leadites—they have power and wealth way beyond their numbers.

"So the Alchemists are locked in a . . . in an asymmetrical war with the Pyrites, who're trying to keep the Leadites asleep, dull, unreflective, unconductive, while the Alchemists are trying to wake them up, alchemise them, and change the whole world forever."

Leaning forward, he bore his eyes into each of them.

"I'm an Alchemist," he whispered. "My duty is simple: turn lead into gold. Stop the lead-poisoning. Guide Leadites from the piracy and thievery and chains of the Pyrites right here in the Swamps of Death and the Savage Lands . . . and help them transform themselves into Nubians," said Mr. Ani. "Into true and living *gold*."

5.

"Hope you're not in a rush, bruh," said Mr. Ani, U-turning on 107th Avenue at 108th Street back towards the cemetery where they'd just dropped Rap's friend. "Forgot something I was gonna give JC."

"No problem," said Rap. Really, Mr. Ani'd been driving him the long home way anyway, just for kicks and conversation.

Mr. Ani swerved his spotless, shining 2002 gold-and-black Pontiac Sunfire back west along the southern pipeline of Kush.

9 PM on the final night of June. With the window open, Rap breathed in air: hot and dry and magnificently mosquito-free. Sound system smooth with Main Source's "Just Hangin' Out," flying violins and a down-escalator bassline. Even sitting down, felt like he was strutting.

The sun wasn't even close to dipping its toes on the horizon, but it was igniting everything it touched and everything Rap saw: the dark chocolate faces of Somali girls in silk headscarves and black ankle-length skirts . . . the blue jeans and mango-satin blouses of the Ethiopian women, straightened hair spilling over their shoulders . . . across the street, the red short-shorts and lipstick on a way-too-skinny, way-too-young hooker of indeterminate race.

And the music must've been an extendamix, with the breakbeat rolling on like waves, and inside, Rap raised a sail without fail:

I melted lead from my head
And channeled lightning, I'm frightening
The Pyrites will try to drain my charge, but I enlarge
I got my gold from the heart-of-a-supernova
Righteousness is never over, moreover
I'm not dying, or crying
Cuz finally I started flying . . .

. . . the mural outside the tiny South Sudanese youth club, the one Rap'd never been inside. Glowing in the late-sun's amber.

Downstreet, Eritrean taxi drivers on break-time, standing together in the 7-11 parking lot sipping coffee from styrocups, smoking packs down to empty.

In that same parking lot, two fifteen-year-old Sudanese boys loping past a Rwandese kid standing next to mum who was filling the kid's bicycle tire. The Sudanese teens were rocking red bandanas and giant jeans drooping off their pimp-limping asses.

Rap shook his head at the pair, wondering how long it'd take Kush's Lil Wayne and Lil Bow Wow to quit trying to out-Lil each other.

Mr. Ani pulled around the block, stopped his Sunfire in front of JC's apartment, one of many facing the two sections of cemetery on either side of 107th Avenue.

"You know what JC's buzz-number is?" asked Mr. Ani.

Rap shook his head. "I've never even been to JC's place. Not inside, I mean."

"Really?"

"Yeah . . . before the night we met you, we really weren't even friends."

"I can never seem to remember that. You two seem so . . . hm."

"And plus, he seems funny about his place."

"What do you mean?"

"Well, one time he and I were busing home and he was getting off, and I told him I needed to use the bathroom, so he took me to that *halal* pizza place across the street."

Mr. Ani frowned.

The three-story walk-up was typical for the area. Ten-year-old vinyl siding that originally beautified the place had aged faster and uglier than the contractors had promised the landlords, who'd lost their shot at going condo when the economy'd had a stroke.

And no matter what, siding couldn't hide the building's forty-plus years of being squat, ugly and crumbling.

Mr. Ani checked the door registry for *Abdi*, the Somali *Smith*, and found three. The buzzer was busted. And since the lock was, too, they walked in.

A couple of Somali teens did a double-take on Moon. "Sup, man!" said the tall one. "Aintchu that Morpheus guy? From YouTube?"

The shorter one: "Yo, like Morpheus X, fuh real."

"That's me." Dropping them each a dap, he said, "Make sure you take the red pill."

Last thing Rap heard one of them say when they were upstairs: "Who-o-oah, *shit!* That was really *him!*"

6.

The third *Abdi* was the third door of the third floor. Behind it, two voices battled: a woman's and a screaming child's.

Mr. Ani's knock shattered the woman's yelling.

After shuffling towards the door, she yelled in Somali that Rap translated: "Who is it?" When she didn't get an answer, she repeated it in English.

"Ma'am, it's Yimunhotep Ani, your son's . . . uh . . ." He glanced at Rap with question marks in his eyes.

Rap shrugged, offered, "Martial arts teacher?"

Mr. Ani called through the door, "Martial arts teacher."

The door cracked open to the length of its chain. A vertical slice of a *muhajabah's* face stared across the gap.

"You!" she snapped. "The famous hero. What do you want?"

He raised his voice over the screaming, kicking child in the hallway behind the kitchen. "I, uh . . . have something for your son."

Rap was embarrassed. The woman should be showing his *sbai* some respect. He shrugged an apology for the situation towards Mr. Ani while the door shut and reopened without the chain.

The woman had a round face, but with her tent-like abaya, Rap couldn't tell if she were chubby all the way down her 5'2" frame.

The woman's glare, the loud TV, the sound of five or more other kids arguing, the same child screaming and banging—the burn spread across Rap's shoulders and down his back.

A, Africentric . . . B, Build . . . C, Create. . .

Kept reciting internally, trying to suffocate the fire . . . .

"Well?" sneered the woman. "You sett you have somethingk for my son? What? More traable? Or *draaks* to sell?"

Mr. Ani's eyebrows dashed towards each other for support.

"Ma'am, I don't even drink or smoke. I definitely don't have anything to do with drugs."

"That's why you were fighting those men who entted up dett in that store, isn't it? Over draaks? That's why you're teaching my son your k'roddy, isn't it? To be one of your gang-a-sters?"

"Actually, ma'am, I teach *jujutsu* and *kung fu*. And—"

BANGING.

The screaming kid?

The woman yelled at her other kids in Somali to take care of their little brother.

Would she be swearing like that if she knew I could understand her?

Looked past him. He was just wallpaper.

A seven-year-old cyclone with legs screamed over, eyes wild, nose running, and started banging his head against the wall.

She yanked him away, him kicking her and squealing and keening, a trapped animal. Made Rap want to puke.

Then Mr. Ani freaked out Rap by stepping inside. Rap followed as if chained.

"What are you doing?" said Mrs. Abdi while her son kicked her and screamed.

7.

At the kitchen sink, Mr. Ani grabbed a glass from the dish strainer, filled it half-way with water, grabbed the bottle of Joy and spurted a long green stripe into it.

"Who do you think you are, breakingk into my house—"

Grabbed a sheet of paper from his pocket, unfolded it, rolled it into a tube.

Crouched a metre out of kicking range from the Tasmanian Devil.

Began blowing bubbles straight up in the air.

The boy, howling, for thirty seconds, but with each second, glances got longer, transformed into staring . . .

And the boy quit screaming as if Mr. Ani'd thrown a switch.

Mrs. Abdi de-clamped her son's arms. Same switch.

The man in the black-and-gold skullcap kept blowing bubbles while the boy stood with a tear-tracked and snot-nosed face, staring at him, eyes like twin moons.

Mr. Ani, slowly: Dip. Raise. Puff. Release.

Offered the cup and the tube to the boy, silently.

The boy took the offering. Dipped the tube. Put the correct end to his mouth.

Made a bubble.

The boy squealed with delight.

"Bubbles," whispered Mr. Ani. *"Bubbles."*

"Buh," said the seven-year-old. "Buh!"

And then JC walked in

Looked like he'd just come back to his hideout after a bank robbery, and two sheriffs and a deputy were there waiting for him.

8.

"Where were you?" demanded his mother in Somali. "Thiss man has been here for half an hour waitingk for you!"

In English: "Just went to the store, Mum, after Mr. Ani dropped me off."

"I was just about to tell your mother here," said Mr. Ani immediately, "how well you're doing at *jujutsu*, and how impressed I am by your understanding of all the books you're reading."

"Thiss is Ibrahim," said Mrs. Abdi. She nodded towards her youngest child, but she was talking to Mr. Ani for the first time without hostility. "Please, please, come in."

Hot milk, black tea, sugar, spice, white ceramic cups. Mr. Ani, Rap and Jamal Abdi sat sipping, while Mrs. Abdi couldn't help but stare at her littlest one playing with bubbles, silent except for happy chirps of "buh!"

Six other Abdi children stood staring, too.

"When was your son diagnosed?" asked Mr. Ani.

Mrs. Abdi's face twitched, like someone'd just jabbed her with scissors.

JC, even more mortified than when he'd walked in, motionless, knees together, eyes scanning for anything buried inside the ancient orange shag rug to justify his attention.

"Three years ago," she said. A sigh. Hissing out of her.

"I didn't even know what wass wrong with him at firrust. He wass learning his words like any boy, but then he just stoppit. He wouldn't look at me in the eyes anymore. And . . . sometimes he, he would spit at me, or if I took him outside, he'd spit at others."

She looked at Mr. Ani. Rap saw her eyes. Wounded.

"A neighbour said he had it. I didn't even know the word . . . so I askid a neighbour to look it up on the computer." Bit her lip. "I hated anyone who even said the wordt. Andt all the people who triedt to give me advices, saying, 'You shouldn't take him outside! You shouldn't let people see him!'

"I'm supposit to keep him in a p'rison? And there's supposit to be help and treatment, but at the school, there's almossit nothingk. No help. And I have seven other children, including this one!" Stabbing a hand at JC across the room. JC shifting, dodging the motherly shank.

"And their father worruks around the clock, drivingk cab. And I am here alone while Ibrahim is like a bomb who can expalode at any time! I keep hoping, *insha'Allah*, for relief—"

"This is actually a big problem where I was living the last fifteen years, in Minnesota," whispered Mr. Ani.

She nodded, catching it: Minnesota, AKA New Mogadishu.

Mr. Ani: "Somali children are suffering from autism—"

(Mrs. Abdi's left eye flinching again at the word.)

"—in above-average numbers there. And apparently in also Stockholm and a few other places. That's what I've read."

"Back home," she said, "no one ever heard of it! No one! Now here, so many of our children . . . it's a curse, because our other children are runningk wild!" She eye-blasted her JC, but he kept scanning the carpet.

"Ma'am," said Mr. Ani, "I just want to assure you that Jamal is a good young man. Demonstrating a lot of discipline."

She ignored the comment. "How do you know about working with these children?"

"You mean like Ibrahim?"

"Yes!"

"I used to . . . in my neighbourhood in Minneapolis I saw a lot of parents struggling. Some figured out a few things that worked. You just pick stuff up, you know?"

"But I am *amayzid!*

Ibrahim, he'll scream for half an hour or more some-a-times. I worry we'll lose our apartiment! And you, a stranger, walk in here, and ten seconds later . . ."

Rap, trying to decode her: dazzled . . . or jealous?

"I hope I didn't offend you by being too forward," said Mr. Ani, "cuz I probably just got lucky . . . but if you want, I'd be happy to go over with you some of the techniques that the parents I knew used."

"Yes, yes, yes!" Her eyes were wet. Even covered by her tent-dress, the woman's chest was visibly shuddering.

Glancing at Mr. Ani's black-and-gold skullcap, Mrs. Abdi asked, "Are you Muslim?"

Mr. Ani shrugged, "No, ma'am, afraid not."

She smiled a *That's okay—you're still a good boy* smile and went to the kitchen to return with a plate of Dad's Oatmeal Cookies.

9.

Time to go, and Mr. Ani pulled JC into the hallway.

"Young bruh, whole reason we came up here was cuz I forgot I had something for you. And, uh, sorry for getting you in Dutch with your mom."

"It's okay, Mr. A," said JC.

Rap, surprised. Thought Mr. Ani was gonna *wing chun* JC into pieces for getting a ride and then turning into smoke.

But maybe seeing JC's home chaos, how mortified he was to have his autistic brother freaking out in front of him and Mr. Ani . . . maybe that's all their teacher needed to give JC a pity-pass this time.

Mr. Ani reached into his jacket pocket and took out a Zune.

"It's not new," he said. "But I refurbished it. Rap told me how you lost your iPod."

"Really? For me? I can keep this?" whispered Jamal. "Man! Thanks!"

"Yeah," he said, slapping a hand on the boy's shoulder. "You earned it."

Now it was Jamal's turn for wet eyes. He jabbered a thank you and a goodbye and scrambled back into his home.

10.

"Are you sure you're not gonna be in trouble? Cuz I can talk with your folks if you like. I mean, I'm getting you here forty minutes late."

Mr. Ani and Rap were stopped at the intersection of 118th Ave and 141st Street, around the corner from where Hamdi's had been (where a neighbour used to take him for goat and beef *suqaar*), down the street from Lee Garden, whose sign announced that it had the best Chinese food in town. But Rap had no idea if that were true. He'd never eaten there.

"No, it's fine," said Rap. "She's probably still working."

"At ten o'clock at night?"

"She works on a lotta cultural committees."

"Your dad?"

Rap looked out the window. "He's dead."

Mr. Ani paused. "Sorry, bruh. I didn't know." Another pause. "Did your mother remarry?"

Rap, subtle as a prison shank: "Definitely not. No."

"Anyway . . . " said the older man, reaching to the back seat. "Well . . . look, I didn't want you thinking I had something for Jamal and nothing for you."

He handed Rap a CD, not in a jewel box but in a printed cardboard sleeve: Leon Thomas, *Spirits Unknown*.

Rap flipped over the album, scanned: "The Creator Has a Master Plan (Peace)", "Song for My Father" and "Malcolm's Gone."

"This brother," said Mr. Ani, "also performs *supreme*. And he does this crazy yodeling—it's his signature sound. Weird when you first hear it, and then you think, 'Wow. Wow.'"

Rap felt almost a giggle poking his gut. Other than his old school principal, the neighbour who took him out for goat, and his mother at Eid and on his birthday, which was also Christmas, no one'd ever given him a gift.

"And I can, I can *keep* this?" Just to be sure.

"Course," said Mr. Ani. "You two've been working hard, and I never could've gotten the Hyper-Market ready to open without you two. So thank you. Now you go home and rest. And don't forget to study your scrolls! Especially *The Book of the Golden Falcon!*"

"*Nub-Wmet-Ānkh, Sbai!*" said Rap, soul-shaking Mr. Ani's hand and hopping out of the Sunfire.

"Raise the Shining Place, bruh."

Rap walked away from the car in the orange and blue of dusk, and up into his empty apartment. He wouldn't be lonely. He had new music, the scrolls and the *World's Great Men of Colour* to keep him company.

11.

"Hello, Mrs. Abdi," said Rap in Somali.

The next day. She was standing at the door of the Hyper-Market, trooped with eight Somali mothers and their children standing on 111th Ave in the noonday sunshine.

She smiled broadly, answering him in English. "Oh, you speak some Somali?"

"I'm half-Somali," he said in Somali.

"Really?" she said in English. "You don't look it."

He wanted to curse. He didn't do it. "You're looking for Jamal?"

"No. I'm here to speak with your Mr. *'Ani.'* " Said *Ani* with an *'ayn,* like *'Ali,* the jabbed-in-the-throat *a*-sound that Arabic had in spades.

Rap stepped aside and eight women and their twenty children ranging from age eight to twelve marched inside.

Hot inside the Hyper-Market, maybe ten degrees more than outside, and no breeze. The day before opening, and the AC was blown. Rap was dust-patchy, and his armpits were dripping—last few days of cleaning and readying the place before it opened.

The women were serene in their scarves and long dresses, like it could've been a spring morning.

Mr. Ani straightened up from behind the carrels where he and JC were installing the cyber-café's PCs.

Glanced at the group: entourage, or army?

Mr. Ani: "Whoah."

"But Mrs. Abdi, I'm not really a teacher," said Mr. Ani. "I mean, not a Special-Ed teacher. I just know a few techniques for helping kids with . . . who're like your youngest son."

"I know that, Mr. 'Ani," she said, sitting in one of the twelve chairs. Eleven women and children used the others. Everyone else stood or sat on the floor. Some of the toddlers sat colouring; others played with action figures, dolls or cars.

"But listen to me," said Mrs. Abdi. "There are many families in the commoonity who neet your help. You caan't abandon them!"

Rap ground his teeth, tried eyeing JC to say something, but his friend wouldn't even look at him.

"I'm not abandoning anybody," said Mr. Ani. "I'm trying to start a business here. We open in three days—"

"You could just offer a woorik-shop," she said, "for some techaniques—"

"Look, I'd like to help, really, but—"

"My son Jamal is working for you for free! And you can't help us even a little?"

Even the toddlers stopped moving at that.

Mr. Ani frowned. Took a breath.

"Mum, jeez! He saved my life. You know that. And he's—"

"Jamal."

"—he's teaching us martial arts and culture and stuff, and you're making it sound—"

"Jamal—"

"—like he's sweatshoppin us or suh'm! That's totally—"

"Jamal!" she snapped, holding up a finger.

She turned to the man.

"I shouldn't have said that." Gave a bow that was closer to a nod. Mr. Ani didn't move.

"I'm just . . . like many of my sisters in the commoonity, I'm very busy all the time, and so are our husbundts. We can never ressit here. We've come to this caantry—"

Mr. Ani: "I understand." Nodded his thanks at Jamal, who sub-smiled back at him before neutralising his face for his mother's inspection.

"If you caan't woorik with our kids who have the, the, the *condition*, then at least woorik with our older boys."

"I already am, ma'am."

"No," she said. "I mean, more of them."

"How many more?"

"All of them," she said.

JC, aghast: "Mum, c'mon—"

"As many as will come, then." She leaned forward, sighed like she was trying to put down heavy packages.

"Their fathers are woorikingk all the time. The boys don't want to go to the mosque. Some of them don't even go to school. What are we supposit to do? Jamal looks up to you. So does this one."

Nice: *This one.*

"Who can we turn to? The schools? They don't care. Right next to your own store, you saw what happened when these boys are corruptedt."

"Listen, Mrs. Abdi," said the man, stepping towards the door with *I'm about show you out* body language, "I'm just a small businessman. Not a social service agency. Try the Mennonite Centre, or Catholic Social Services, or the Boys and Girls Club, or CCACH—"

She stood up.

"No."

"What?"

Stepped towards him. "Jamal is right. You saved his life and his friendt's life and you didn't even know them. You're not a man who walks away when you see people in neet."

He put a hand on the door's lock-toggle.

"Help our sons," she said. No longer ordering him. Voice, shaking. "Many are far worse than he is!"

"Jamal's a good young man."

"Help him be a better one, then," she said. "And the others, too. Our commoonity will be grateful. And we'll bring our business here, to you."

Mr. Ani chewed the inside of his cheek, shook his head.

"What?" she said. "You think we won't bringk our business to a non-Somali?"

"It's been said. And frankly, I see it right here in this neighbourhood. Ethiopian restaurants, Nigerian shops, Vietnamese drugstores, but the Somalis aren't shopping there unless they have to."

She turned to the other women, then back to him. "Just watch," she said. The rest nodded. So did their toddlers, and they didn't know what the hell was going on.

Rap, freestyling on the mental mic:

> *Would Somalis let Ani sing in their chorus?*
> *And if Ani should fall inside a Somali forest*
> *Would any Somali hear him? Go near him?*
> *Or fear him? Or up and try to smear him?*

12.

Everyone was about to converge on Mr. Ani's place. But for just forty-five minutes, Rap and JC were the only guests.

Rap's skin singeing while he watched the clock tick down. JC was quiet, too, but he was helping in the kitchen.

They'd tripped out seeing the inside of Mr. Ani's crib for the first time, this hidden place directly above the Hyper-Market. No, "crib" didn't seem right. His nest? His aerie?

Both boys, stunned at the size and scope of his archives: two walls of books, milk crates full of LPs, framed portraits of Cheikh Anta Diop, Thomas Sankara, Wangari Maathai . . .

But what sent them into orbit was the force of knowing they were going to sit in a *shenu*—a circle—with all the fighters from back in the day, legends Mr. Ani'd told them about from when he was a fiery young university student and whose *sbai* had inducted him and his friends into the knowledge of lead, pyrite and gold.

Crackled through Rap's mind. Like picking up a DC after three years of reading nothing but Marvel: exploring this alternate, mysterious realm, this cosmic continuity, a glittering, unknown history of heroes, villains, victories and powers supreme.

The burn, down his throat, like lit kerosene on the walls of a well.

Distracted himself by touring Mr. Ani's archive. Ancient Sudan . . . Ancient Egypt . . . Axum . . . Mali and Timbuktu . . . African religions . . . the *Maafa*. Liberation movements, the Caribbean, the Americas, Canada. Women's liberation . . . scientists, inventors, entrepreneurs . . . novels . . . poetry . . . plays . . .

And DVDs, too. Here was everything, not just Africentric titles. Three DVDs on somebody named Tesla. Chuckled to himself at the sight of comedies such as *Mystery Men, The Royal Tennenbaums,* and *Anchorman.* Mr. Ani, fuh real? Just didn't seem like him. And yet there they were.

Jacob's Ladder?

Jumped at the sight of Mr. Ani coming back from the kitchen, carafes of tea and coffee in each hand. "What? You look spooked. Oh, *Jacob's Ladder?* Yeah, great film. Scary. American vets going crazy—"

"Oh," he said, finally breathing out. "It's something else, then."

"What'd you think it was about?"

JC joined them, hefting a tray of diced cheese and fruit.

"Well," said Rap, "when I was ten I lived in a refugee camp in Kenya, and there was this group of *mzungus* who came in—"

"Like, an NGO? A charity or something like that?"

"Yeah, well, that's what they'd say, anyway. Yeah."

"Called Jacob's Ladder?"

"Yeah."

"Think I heard something about them in the news a few years back. Didn't they—"

Knocking. The guests.

Mr. Ani flicked on the stairwell light, and with it, Rap's destiny.

"So that's the situation, and that's what I wanna do," said Mr. Ani, two days later. "Are you down?"

Ten of Mr. Ani's old friends, six men and four women, looked back at him.

The remaining *sambusas*, cool by then, sat on platter on a table in the centre of the living room. JC glanced, having waited long enough, and piled the remaining ones on his napkin.

Rap grabbed a *sambusa*, crunched it, dropping pastry flakes all over his collared black shirt. JC suppressed a laugh.

"You called this an emergency in your email," said Martin Joseph. The man had *pipes*. Rap figured he'd have to go to the gym five days a week for twenty years to get arms like that. "Where's the emergency?"

"Maybe you just *don'wanna* see it, Martin," said Sister Seshat, the social worker. Her braids were coiled up on top of her head so she looked like one of Mr. Ani's ebony statuettes. "I see it every day out there. And not just the Somali kids, either. Rwandans, Congolese, Sudanese kids—"

"That's what I'm saying," said Martin, arms crossed, like a cop. "You see it every day . . . so why now? What you're talking about, Moon, we've gone down this road before. And it's nothing but heartbreak in the end. You *know* that!"

Rap and JC eyed each other. *Moon?*

Mr. Ani: "Look, if we give up just because it's difficult—"

"Big difference between difficult and impossible," said Martin. "And we all paid the price to learn that."

Sister Seshat said, "That was twenty years ago, Martin."

"And Imhotep built the Step Pyramid forty-six hundred years years ago. Doesn't make it less true."

"I'm afraid I have to agree with Martin," said Kojo, the brother with cufflinks and sleek glasses with tiny diamonds set into the arms. "Everybody knows there's a need, Moon. But there's what we want, and then there's what we can actually do."

71

"I can't believe I'm hearing this," said Mr. Ani, shaking his head. "So we just sit back—"

"Do you actually have a plan, Moon?" asked Bamba Diabate, the lawyer who'd gotten Mr. Ani out of police custody after the Somali store massacre. Bamba kept his tie tight, and he, too, wore cufflinks. But his jacket was off. "Because what you're talking about means resources: time and money. And nobody here has much of either."

"Aren't you a lawyer?" asked Martin.

"C'mon, now," said Sister Seshat.

"We've got enough gold in this one room," said Mr. Ani, "to build a fortress."

"The Golden Fortress?" said Sister Seshat. "Moon, you didn't say anything in your message about—"

"Yimun, where'd the Fortress get us back in the day, huh?" said Martin Joseph, standing. "And where d'you expect to take us now? If Bamba hadn't sprung you, you'd still be in the Remand Centre right now. And you chose to walk in on some Somali gangsters? I mean, I'm sorry—that's crazy. I ain'down for any suicide missions, man. Not again. Hell no!"

Martin straightened his glasses and left the circle, eye-smacking everyone in it.

"We aren't kids anymore. I have a family. I don't have time for fairy tales or saving the world."

"Wait a second," said Bamba. "Don't be—"

"You all wanna do this? Fine. But listen to me," he said, holding up a warning finger, "it cost us then—all of us. And it'll cost *you* now." He backed over to the stairwell. "I can show myself out. And Moon—"

Mr. Ani didn't look at him.

"Moon, goddamn. Same old Moon. Take my advice. Forget all this shit so *you* don't end up dead, too."

The stairwell made his every step echo. They heard the door close below.

Mr. Ani scanned the room, saying nothing except for the *Who else wants to abandon me?* look in his eyes.

13.

"Boys," said Sister Seshat. "Let me ask you. How many of your friends do you think would actually come, if we helped Brother Moon set up a programme?"

They looked at each other. Rap had exactly one friend, and he was already in "the programme."

JC said, "I know a bunch. A lot of my cousins. And my mum's friends' kids."

"But how many will stick around?" asked Sister Seshat.

JC didn't answer. He seemed to understand he hadn't thought things that far through.

"So maybe, Brother Moon," she said, "you need to re-scope this. Maybe you're better off just working with these two, just doing a mini-programme or something.

72

But honestly, brother, the Golden Fortress? For kids who haven't even gone to university? Or completed high school? Hell, some of em are practically on the street—I don't mean you two young brothers. Aren't you expecting a bit much?"

"I'm not talking about making them *Shemsu-Hru*," said Mr. Ani.

"But you just *said* the *Golden Fortress*," protested Kojo. He pushed his glasses back up his nose by pushing on the diamonds in their arms.

"Yeah," said Mr. Ani, "but I'm talking about opening the gates. A whole new approach. If we're keeping all the gold locked up and letting the Leadites wander in the Savage Lands, you know what that makes us?"

Seshat said, "So what are you suggesting?"

"We *open* the Fortress. Like I did with Raphael and Jamal, here. They've been learning the scrolls a month now. Lemme show you. Brother Jamal."

JC straightened up, wiping *sambusa* crumbs from his mouth with as much dignity as he could scrounge.

Mr. Ani: "'What did the two rangers find while searching for food?'"

JC licked his lips to be sure they were fleck-free, stood up and recited,

"During forage for their daily meals, the rangers found abandoned children wandering, mad from drinking water from the Swamps of Death, and they brought them to the Master, who chased the poisons from their bodies with his herbs and fruits and healing words.'"

Adult smiles sparkled like Christmas lights around the circle. "Raphael. '*Who raised the Master's compound?*'"

"'So the Rangers and their juniors grew their walls and inside them raised their garden," said Rap, also standing. *"The Master counted bricks and time to make and cure them, and counted children as they came inside the garden for their labours, and counted days and nights and lessons yet to teach, measuring all so that it would be right and true.'"*

"*THASS* right!" said Sister Seshat, testifying, finger-snapping, then sliding palms with three others smiling as much as she was. "Just like in *The Blues Brothers!* We're putting the band back together. And we're on a mission from God. Scuze me. From *gold.*"

Others scratched chins. Shook heads. Glanced at each other. Grimly.

"This is what I'm talking about," said Mr. Ani. "So I'm proposing some reforms."

"Proposing?" said Bamba. "How much more are you proposing than what you've already done?'"

Caught, Mr. Ani smiled.

"You're right. Okay. Number one, no dress code. We all went to university. Was a lot cheaper back then—first year was what, eleven hundred dollars? Now it's five, six grand? Might as well be a million for these kids. Most of em come from huge families—Somalis, you know. Six, eight kids isn't uncommon. They rent, and in *this* market. So they're all broke. And most of them don't even own a single piece of continental clothing, let alone enough to last a week."

"What else?" asked Bamba.

"No dues."

"Obviously," said the lawyer, loosening his tie, then sliding it off his neck and scrolling it up. "What else?"

"No selling any newspapers. Besides, everything's online these days, and I'd rather have these kids do something more productive with their time."

"I never liked selling that thing anyway," said Seshat. "Took forever, and mostly I ended up shoving the ones I couldn't sell in my closet. Go on."

"They know the Resurrection Scroll. But we use it every day, together. To go over their issues, set goals, reflect on what matters. I call it the Daily Alchemy. And they're both pretty good at it."

"Really?" said Bamba. "Raphael, could I ask you to demonstrate that?"

"Uh, yes," said Rap. "Well . . . today is June 29. I can break down June as Justice, Unite, Nature, Evolution. So I'd say . . . for instance, that for us to get any justice, we need to unite. That it's our nature to evolve.

"And we need to reflect on that because, because, well, sometimes people get stuck in a rut. They stop growing. All they can do is, y'know, focus on what's wrong, and not imagine ways to make it right. And if you're defying your nature, you can't be happy or complete."

"That's good," said Bamba, smiling and nodding. "And what about the twenty-ninth?"

JC piped up. "Two is, like, revolution, and nine is peace-life-eternal, right? So a revolution is an overturning. An so many kids out there are seriously messed up. They think right's wrong and wrong's right.

"So they need to revolve their perspective, which is the only way they'll even think about looking way over on the other side of the numerals, to peace, instead of all this fighting and drugging and craziness. Which is maybe how they'll keep their lives.

"And if they have kids and raise them right, it all keeps revolving . . . eternally."

Four of the adults broke into applause.

14.

"I don't like it," said Kevin Burns.

Burns was the tallest man in the room, six-four, and Mr. Ani'd whispered to Rap that the brother was so good-looking that when he went out for a walk, straight women and gay men crashed their cars.

"What don't you like?" said Seshat. She turned to the Rap and JC. "And you, young brothers, let me say how impressed I am. Gives me goose bumps just hearing you do the Alchemy like that. Been ten years since I've been in a room with my peoples and heard anyone recite *The Book of the Golden Falcon!*"

"That's exactly what I don't like," said Burns. "Hearing just *anyone* recite our teachings. Professor Xaasongaxango didn't cut corners or trade on principles. He didn't 'make it easy' and go around lowering the bar because he thought Black folks couldn't step over."

Even across the room, Rap felt the man's spit. He ground his teeth and tried to unfist his hands while Burns kept unloading.

"The Professor didn't *pity* us," said Burns, "thinking the best we could do was dumb down a noble tradition so a bunch of hip-hopping street kids could start 'rapping' our scrolls!"

"Kevin!" said Seshat.

Rap stood up. So did Jamal. Mr. Ani eyed them gravitically. Kevin Burns glared at them from his perfect eyes in his perfect face.

"Rap . . . ."

"It's okay, Mr. Ani. You taught us. Hru escaped the night-raiders. He clawed his way out of the Devourer's mouth. He even tracked and avoided the chainsmen.

"And when the time came, he baked bricks and built the compound for the children of the Savage Lands. He knew the Destroyer was out there, waiting for him, to kill him. But that didn't make him stop. It made him get ready."

"Listen, kid," sneered the gorgeous man, "you're no Hru. And if you think *I'm* the Destroyer, you are *ser*iously deluded about how tough life can be."

"*I'm* deluded?" said Rap. He stabbed his finger into his palm. "My mother and I escaped Sudan *on foot*. We survived a refugee camp in Chad." (Stab.) "And came all the way here and started over, from scratch." (Stabbed again.)

"Maybe, Mr. Beautiful Burns, you've seen some refugee camps? *On TV?* How long do you think you could last in one? They don't give manicures there, you know."

Eyes popped wide around the *shenu*. JC whispered, "Oh, snuh-*ap!*"

"Knock yourself out, Moon," said Kevin Burns, de-chairing himself up and reaching the stairwell in three strides. "I'm not having any part of you debasing our teachings or the Professor's legacy."

15.

When they heard the door close downstairs, Rap looked at Mr. Ani. Rap'd just told off an elder, his teacher's old friend, made him so angry he'd stormed out.

Seshat leaned over to Rap and gently rubbed his wrist. "He always was a prissy asshole."

Several adults laughed. But not Sandy the businesswoman or Kojo the deacon.

And not Rap, either. He'd never met Burns before, but he knew the type. So did his mother. Too goddamned well.

Mr. Ani got up, walked to the fridge and got an ice cream sandwich. Back at the circle he leaned over Rap from behind to give it to him. Rap suppressed his shudder.

"He had it coming, young bruh," said Mr. Ani. "You defended yourself. It was geometrical."

Sandy and Kojo eyed each other and got up together. Sandy said to everyone, "I'd really like to help, honestly, but I just don't have time. I'm really sorry. If you get something going, maybe I can make a donation. Or something. Sorry."

People called out their goodbyes as she left. Rap thought she looked genuine, but relieved to be gone, too.

Then Kojo with his bright round glasses with the diamond studs said, "Listen, everyone, this just . . . it just isn't the way to go. Back in university, I mean, I was really wild back then. But things have changed for me since Jesus opened my heart—"

"Oh, Kojo!" said Seshat. "You up and got Jesus?"

Bamba gave her a look. "Sister, c'mon."

"Don't get me wrong, brother. I've been in a church choir my whole life," she said. "But Jesus doesn't tell me to stop helping my peoples. He and I don't have that kind of relationship."

"When you're ready to hear the Good News," said Kojo, "without mockery in your voice and violence in your mind, you're always welcome at the Fellowship. We're on 142nd and—"

"Thanks, bruh," said Mr. Ani. "We know where it is. We all went to the funeral there. Remember?"

He looked down. "Of course."

Kojo tried explaining himself and then finally gave up and left.

"If anybody else wants to leave . . . ?"

Mr. Ani let the question hang. People eyed each other. It hurt Rap, like ice down his neck, to see Mr. Ani's old friends leaving the room one by one, some enraged, some lost... even that asshole, Mr. Beautiful. Hoped to god nobody else would abandon him.

16.

"Like we were taught," said Mr. Ani, "Know your righteousness by what you choose to do, and by what you refuse to do." He took a breath.

"Okay. Professor Xaaso helped make us what we are. And the *Shemsu-Hru* was a brilliant institution. But these kids out here . . . they're suffering. And who gave us the right to hoard our gold? And even if we did have the right, what good's it done?

"Where's the *Shemsu-Hru* now? A bunch of old men and women scattered around the world. Dusty books and a few barely-functional websites. No public action. Just rituals based on myths. Like an old temple. A tourist attraction. A place you sit still and be quiet while somebody in charge tells you what to think and do.

"Look at the word: *shemsu* means 'followers.' That what we should be? How many of you really wanna fit that mold? Me, I'm too profane. Rap, Jamal, what'd I teach you about *profane?*"

Jamal said, "Latin?"

"Mm-hm. What else?"

"*Pro-*. It means 'in front of.' And *fanum* means 'temple.'"

"Right. So what'd it mean back in olden times to be profane?"

"It meant you took the temple treasures outside the temple," said Rap.

"Yessir. The holiest of holies. From inside lockdown to outside where all the common people could see them. Reveal the secrets. Shouldn't we be doing that? *'Make stand those who weep . . .'*"

Rap and JC joined in, and then, like the sun cleaving the horizon, Sister Seshat the social worker, Brother Bamba the lawyer, Brother Chekandino the programmer, Sister Sekhem the journalist, Brother Dedan the community educator, and Sister Yeyemo'oja the graduate student, all joined in:

"*. . .reveal those who hide their faces, and lift up those who sink down. In doing so, we will all rise nearer to the Supreme.'*"

Mr. Ani continued, "'*By the sunrise . . .*'"

And the boys and Mr. Ani's peers rang it in: "'*. . . I serve the cause of peace and cause of life. So may we raise the Shining Place eternally.'*"

It was lightning, and the charge in the air remained. Rap felt the hairs on his arms standing up.

And then he saw her, and the electricity went running back up his spine:

Sister Seshat, glancing down, dabbing her eyes, looking back around the circle, nodding and smiling.

"Damn," she said, sniffing. "Y'all *remembered*."

Emeralds and Maidens
at the Millstone

Four
Ancestor-I

The Book of Then

1.

FOR ABOUT A MONTH IT GOT HARDER AND HARDER TO SLEEP BECAUSE I KNEW that crazy mud-headed bastard was stalking me, him and his damn jackals.

But he didn't know I could turn into a shadow. So I started stalking him, just to figure out how he operated and get his weaknesses so I could form an attack plan. If it came to that.

A couple of times on night-patrol I stepped on a branch, snapping it, and all those jackals stood stone-still, except for their eyes and ears probing the darkness, trying to find me.

Idiot!

For all I knew, those jackals might've been able to see through my shadow. But I was more worried about them smelling me.

Then I'd get scared and not quiver a finger for a thousand breaths if that's what it took for them to finally march on out. Or on the times I didn't blow my own cover, sometimes I just got bored. So then I'd leave, dig up some grubs and bring them back to Falcon for breakfast. Or I'd check my rat-traps.

But I knew eventually Mud-Head and I were going to have a showdown.

I hated him. Guy wouldn't leave me alone. Thought he owned the whole Savage Lands. My only chance was to lure him up a tree where his jackals couldn't go. Then I'd gut him, or slit his throat like a goat's.

I fell asleep, dreaming my mother'd never died, but was just pretending so the Destroyer couldn't find her. And that she was still looking for me.

2.

"Hey! Asshole!"

It was him.

So much for my plan. Night, full moon, and I was stuck out in the open, no shadow on. Lost in my head, refighting all my old battles, re-losing all those kids, re-watching Shai die and the kid get shredded by crocodiles, all the while my hands did the work of strapping Fang to a long broken branch for use as a spear. I'd done such a good a job strapping Fang on I couldn't rip it off, so now it was useless against those jackals in close-up defense.

And they had me surrounded. Them and all their teeth.

So we charged each other.

"STOP IT!"

We both stopped totally. The jackals, too.

There was a man standing there in silhouette.

Moon right behind his head, like it was balanced there.

Beside him was a tall bird, up to his hip, with a curved beak. I didn't know what they were called, but I'd seen plenty of them. But this one was different. It was black. With gold eyes.

I tried moving, but it was like I was made out of rock.

My enemy's eyes were whirling, but his mouth was grimaced like he was straining to use it and couldn't. The jackals just stood like stumps, whining and panting through their noses.

"You're defiling this land, attacking each other here!" said the moon-blackened man. "You think this is what the gods want? What the gods won't punish?"

Great. One of those religious weirdos. "Gods this" and "punish that." At least in my mum's camp, I didn't have to listen to that crap. She used to laugh at people like that. "What good are the gods?" she'd say. "Don't be thanking them. I'm the one who got you this food."

But this crazy old man with his big black bird out here in the Savage Lands at night, with his own words-of-power stilling us like stone, that was a bad combination. Probably some warlock who got chased out of his village for too much dancing, or babbling full-blast in the middle of the night, or for turning people into goats. Warlocks do that, you know. Just for laughs.

"Follow me, you two," he grumbled. "And your puppies, also."

I loved that. Chuckled, even though I couldn't move my mouth. I could just imagine Mud-Head choking on it: *Puppies?*

3.

We marched stiffly. I still couldn't budge my raised spear-arm, and it was throbbing. Finally the old man noticed and told me to put it down, and my arm went down on its own, and we went up a hill in the darkness.

At the top, he ordered us to sit. All of us except the black bird did, even the dogs.

"Behold," he whispered, maybe to himself.

He lifted his arms to the horizon, the moon still perched above his head.

And the sun came up, just like that.

Blinding gold.

I shielded my eyes. Took me a minute to realise I could move again.

My enemy was figuring out the same thing.

He flinched.

I leapt up with my spear—

—and stopped, because we were surrounded by about forty gods-damned baboons, with gougers bigger than the jackals'.

The old man's gang.

My enemy and I got the message, and we both sat back down.

"That's better," said the old man. "Now be quiet and listen and hopefully you'll learn something."

He waved his hand in front of the baboons, and they all started singing.

I've seen crazy things. Devils boiling out of a sink-hole and dragging a man to his screaming death. Cows with eyes so beautiful they nearly made me cry. Veils of stars transforming into my mother's face in the night sky.

But baboons singing? That was new.

And their song was beautiful. Like gongs and chimes and the sound of the River Eternal where I came from back in the Blackland.

We listened silently while the sun rose. Even the jackals were still.

When the baboons stopped, the old man came over and crouched on his haunches.

"Now you two listen to me. I've been watching you both for quite some time. You're both resourceful. You've survived the death-traps out here all on your own. You were each smart enough not to drink the Swamp water. And you're excellent rangers.

"But for smart kids, you're both pretty stupid.

"I've seen you both spoiling for a showdown. More times than you can dream, I led one or both of you off course at the last moment."

He snorted, spat, then went on. "But I can't be everywhere in the Savage Lands, and I won't always be able to stop you two little brutes from ripping each other into bloody bits. And you'll both die. You know it and I know it."

Then he pointed out to the horizon and whispered.

White mountains appeared there, tall enough to scrape the sky's skin, with sides as straight as sunrays.

The Savage Lands were gone.

No horror-jungles filled with bandits, slavers, soldiers and murderers. No Swamps of Death clogged with crocodiles and clotted over with scum. No children marching or farming in chains, and no burnt-eyed kids gripping hatchets or drowning each other or beating each other to death.

Instead I—we, because I saw my enemy seeing what I saw, and his face looked warped and bizarre to me, and then I realised what it was, *that he was happy*, and I hadn't seen a happy face in longer than I could remember—we looked out onto the purified Blackland of lotus flowers and straight paths banked by trees all exactly the same height, and saw people by the millions, baking bread, carving statues, reciting poems, painting walls, setting broken bones, cuddling babies, sailing boats, sewing clothes, lifting stone, sleeping soundly without a fear . . .

"If you two can forget about your little war, when out in the Savage Lands it's nothing *but* war," said the old man who'd turned the horizon into the most beautiful thing I'd ever seen, "I'll teach you both what I know. So you can make our brutal world die and bring *that* one," he gestured, "to life."

We looked at each other, my enemy and me. For the first time, without glaring. Just looking.

We nodded at the same time.

"Good," said the old man. "Then come back with me to my house. I've got food and clean water that won't poison you."

"Sir?" said my enemy.

I glanced at him. So polite, all of a sudden. Like maybe underneath all that mud, he wasn't a born savage.

"I work for this sorceress, and, uh, I don't think . . . y'know . . . that I should just quit like that. She wouldn't—"

"Trust me," he said. "It'll be fine."

"Uncle?" I said, because back in my day, that's how you showed respect to an old man if you didn't know what his title was. And "warlock" didn't sound appropriate. "I have this animal I take care of. A falcon. I, I need to get him."

"You mean this one?" said the man.

Right there on his shoulder—I don't know how I missed it, but there was Falcon. Perched there as happy as could be. The old man gave him a nut, which he crunched and swallowed. "*Hroo-hroo*," said Falcon.

"Um, all right, then," I said, impressed. I didn't know Falcon knew how to fly. How did this old man . . . ?

We moved out.

4.

His place wasn't much. A hut. But it was dry. And he wasn't lying about the food and water—he had plenty of each. Even enough for the jackals, Falcon, his own big black bird, and the occasional baboon who came around.

I finally realised the baboons were just like the bird: black with gold eyes.

The Savage Lands was like that. Everything was weird.

The Master—that's what we ended up calling him—taught us a bunch of stuff neither of us knew about, like how to make bread and how to make bricks.

When he tried my first bread, he said, "We'll use this for bricks," and laughed. I must've looked hurt, because he said, "I was just kidding."

"I wonder why he's got that big old bird with him all the time," I said to Yinepu one day when we were drying bricks. "The one with the curved beak."

"It's called an *ibis*, stupid," he spat, shaking his head and laying a line of bricks. "Don't you know anything?"

Maybe we weren't enemies anymore, but he was still a jerk.

5.

We were building a wall.

It was to surround the Master's hut and storage areas. While we built it, he taught us about numbers and measurement.

"What's all this for?" I asked him.

"You've seen all those children out there."

"Yeah? I mean, yes, Master?"

"You've seen how they're being treated."

I felt my heart pounding. My neck went hot. I felt the cold anger of my blade Fang in my hand even though I'd left it back in the hut. I heard Falcon make the cry he makes when we go hunting.

I almost said the words, *Are we going to rescue them?*

Yinepu looked like he was thinking the same thing.

The Master said, "'*The ancestors scatter their wisdom like a sower his seeds, and those who would feast must first sweat beneath the sun.*'"

I didn't get it. By his face, neither did Yinepu.

It definitely wasn't what I wanted to hear: a battle plan.

We went back to laying bricks.

6.

So we didn't mount any rescue missions. No storming the mines or the farms, me with Fang and Falcon, Yinepu with his gang of jackals, and the Master with his army of rip-teeth baboons, gutting chainsmen and taking their ears for our necklaces.

But when we were foraging for supplies or checking our traps, sometimes we'd find stragglers who'd run away or gotten lost.

They were always sick and hungry and looked like hell. We'd try to convince them to come with us, but you can't always talk sense to people. And some of them were still crazy from Swamp water.

The Master took in whoever we brought back, and I was glad we'd done all that work on that wall. We had a defensible area with enough space for sleeping, and on papyrus reed mats—we didn't have to sleep in piles like dogs.

We had food trees inside the wall, and the Master ground up seeds and boiled leaves and bark and made all kinds of medicine to make these kids we found right again.

7.

A lot can change in three years.

I got strong. Became a good fighter. So did Yin. We'd stopped being idiots, for the most part, anyway. Really, him and me, we were good partners. We never talked about it or anything, but we worked well together and laughed a lot about whatever.

But we never talked about our parents.

I knew my mum was dead. If she weren't, she would've found me. She had her own words-of-power, plenty of them. And she loved me. She'd never abandon me. So she had to be dead.

And like I said, I never asked Yin about his folks.

But some of the kids we brought in stayed pretty savage. You could take their heads out of the lead mines, but you couldn't take the lead out of their heads.

One day I saw Yin whistle to his jackals and take off like he was really angry.

I grabbed one of the older kids (Yin and I were the oldest), a girl named Nef. "What's wrong with him? What happened?"

"I don'know," she said.

"Don't tell me 'I don'know.' I saw you over there with him. What happened?"

"Aw, he's just mad again. He's always mad."

"That's not true. He's great with you kids. The good kids, anyway. You say something to him?"

"No. It wasn't me. It was the other kids. Baq and them."

"Stop making me drag this out of you! What happened?"

"Well, Yinny was saying something about his witch, and, well, none of us had ever seen her, and—"

This again. I'd tried to gently tell Yin to shut up about his "sorceress," but I didn't want to hurt his feelings, so . . .

"Great. Great work, Nef."

"It wasn't me, Hru! It was Baq!"

"Did you tell him to stop? Gods! Yin's your older brother. You kids are supposed to treat him with respect. And after everything he does for you!"

She started crying.

"Well, maybe you *should* cry," I said, but I didn't mean it. I probably should've apologised or given her a hug, but instead I went to yell at Baq and his little pack of creeps.

Yin was going to be gone for a while. He was sometimes gone for a couple of days at a time, but the Master always said it was fine, that he had work to do and lessons to learn. But this felt different this time. It felt wrong.

8.

That night, after I'd put the little kids to sleep, I sat up with the Master, two of his baboons and his black bird watching the camp fire.

Inside the walls, the light didn't carry, so we didn't have to worry about bandits or raiders. And devils only came for bonfires, not campfires.

After he and his animals finished a quiet song, I asked him, "Master, why are you bothering with all these kids, anyway?"

I was still mad about Nef and Baq, and I'd told him all about it over dinner.

He looked sad. "Well, Hru . . . they're just kids. You and your partner were both pretty rough when you first came here. I know you remember that."

"Yeah. I mean, yes, Master."

"And we've both seen a lot worse than that behaviour."

He stared into his hands, like he held secrets there.

"But as for me . . . I was just like any of these kids, when I was small. Lost out there, alone, no parents. Hunted. And then my Master found me. And he was the same, you understand?

"And that's the chain of us, the golden chain going all the way back to when the First Mountain pushed its way out of the ocean." (He'd told me about the First Times already, so he didn't need to explain.) "When our ancestors want us to know something, they send somebody to teach us. My Masters are me, now. And I'm them."

I tried to absorb all that. I figured it would take me a while, so I just said, "I will understand, Master."

He smiled. Gold glinted in his black eyes from the campfire.

All the kids by then were asleep, not just the little ones, so I felt safe asking him something else.

"Master, why did the Destroyer attack us in my camp when I was little? Why'd he kill my mother—"

"And your father."

I was shocked. This, I'd never heard before.

"The Destroyer killed my dad, too?"

"Yes, son. I'm sorry."

I didn't ask him how he knew. He knew things.

"Why's he doing all of this? Enslaving these kids by the thousands? Fighting this endless war? Butchering people and making us so afraid of everything and everybody that we all hate each other?"

Again he was quiet for a long time.

Finally, he said quietly, "'*The truth is like the sun: with the same rays a bringer of life and yet a champion of death. Sustainer and annihilator, it grows the one plant full and sweet, while it shrivels the other one into crackles.*'"

I shook my head without intending to. Sometimes I loved the way the Master said things in such a pretty way, with words as beautiful as a frog's eye or a snake's scales in the sunlight. Sometimes what he said was so perfect I just had to memorise it.

But other times I just wanted him to give me a straight answer because it made my head creak and crack just hearing him.

He must've seen how upset I was, because he said, "Hru, you're not ready yet. If I told you now—"

I got up. "Good night, Master."

Finally he said good night to me, too.

I marched off to my mat and lied awake for a long time, looking at three bright stars in a row, wondering about my slaughtered parents, wondering about my friend out there in the Savage Lands alone, wondering about the Destroyer whose Empire was out there, in everything, in everybody.

The Book of Now

1.

"Now you see why I told you to get here so early," whispered Brother Moon.

Seven teenagers were huddling beside him on the rooftop.

Across from them, falcon chicks were chirping at the rising sun.

Rap loved watching these peregrines. When he was six and sneaked outside the boundaries of his refugee camp in Chad, he'd gazed for what felt like a day at a hawk flying sorties back and forth to its high nest in the rocks with food for its babies.

But what stunned him even more was six teenagers other than him forklifting themselves out of bed and across town just because Brother Moon said so during their last shenu: "Be here by 6:45 tomorrow morning. I wanna share something with you. A moment of perfect beauty."

For him it was no problem. He almost always rose early. But other kids? Other kids in the *community*?

JC whispered, "Snuh-*a-a-a-p*."

On the other side of the Hyper-Market's second-floor gravel roof, next to the vent, a pair of peregrine falcons had transformed an abandoned crate into their nest.

Their four hatchlings, snowy, fluffy chicks with grey beaks and black eyes, chirped and squawked to each other while waiting for their parents to return with breakfast.

"They're so cute!" squealed Kimmy Greenfield, the niece of the social worker Seshat.

The other kids immediately shushed her to avoid scaring the birds.

"Sorry!" she giggled, then muted herself. She was a vivacious girl who'd taken the Kemetic name Ānkhur two days after perfectly memorising the Resurrection Scroll.

"Now you know why I had you do that research," whispered Brother Moon.

"What're they doing here?" asked Almeera Nur, the Somali girl who cracked up Moon by regularly wearing both hijab and a black hoodie emblazoned with a rhinestone Playboy icon. "I thought they only liked high places, or near water."

"That's why it's so strange," whispered Brother Moon. "I just found 'em up here yesterday morning because of all the noise they were making—sh!"

Everyone looked up where Moon was looking, expecting two parent falcons hurtling talons of vengeance down on them for this home invasion.

"Sorry," said the older man. "Thought it was them. Anyway, what can you tell me?"

Abdishakur "Sixpac" Jowhar, JC's Tupac-loving eighteen-year-old second- or third-cousin, said, "The chicks are called fledgings."

Ahmed Samatar, fifteen with an Afro like the planet Jupiter, said, "Naw, it's fledg-*lings*. Fledging's when they learn to fly."

"My bad," said Sixpac.

"What else? Jorrel?"

"There's about sixty cities in North America that have, like, pairs of falcons living downtown or whatever," said Jorrel. His voice had just a hint of Kingston and Brixton, like the tang of lime in a glass of ice water.

Rap, who'd never been much of a smiler, couldn't stop grinning. Moon saw, winked at him. That made him grin all the more.

In any of his high school classes, African students hardly answered even direct questions, let alone volunteered responses. Only time he could remember any of them talking was when goofs'd cut up, fool around or drop all the New Yorkisms or Jamaican patois they could sample from hip hop and dance hall downloads.

But up here on the roof . . . with traffic noise nothing more than ambient hum in the cool, sweet air of an August morning, with the sunrise transforming everything into copper, bronze and gold . . . things were different.

They were, thought Rap, the way they were supposed to be.

Crystal Bizimana, the Rwandan girl with the cute French accent, mumbled something in her perpetually quiet voice. The rooftop morning breeze sipped up her words like tea.

"What?" said JC.

She whispered slightly less imperceptibly. "Zeir diet is moostly uzzer birts, such as pidgey-ons and daafs."

"Peregrines're endangered," added Rap. He smiled even more because Crystal's accent reminded him of the nutty French woman from *Amelie*, the DVD he'd just borrowed from Seshat, along with Lumumba. "Well actually here they're just *threatened*, but that's close enough. There's only sixty pairs in the whole province."

"Why so few?" asked Brother Moon.

"Because of pesticides. All their prey'd soaked up the chemicals in their environment, so they got it in concentrated form."

"So they'd become poisoned-animal eaters."

"Yeah, exactly. Everything they ate to stay alive was killing them and their babies. Their eggshells got so soft that between 1950 and 1970," rapid-fired Rap, "they almost went extinct."

"So what happened to them?"

"People started, like, realisin'," said JC, "that if they didn't do suh'm quick, there weren't gonna be any more. So they changed laws, made DDT illegal, which was great for some birds like eagles, but that wasn't enough for peregrines. They didn'recover much."

"So?"

Rap: "So scientists had to make special habitats for them on skyscrapers. And they fed them using falcon-puppets."

"Get outta here!" said Ānkhur. "Is that true?"

"Yeah," said JC. "Otherwise they'd, like, what's that called? *Bond or imprint* or whatever on the humans an not be able t'take care of emselves."

"Then they 'hack back to the wild," said Almeera. "That's what you call it when they finally learn their natural ways."

"To survive and thrive," said Ahmed.

"And when they live in the city," said JC, "they call em 'street peregrines.' But I call em 'street falcons.' Sounds more gangsta."

"Street falcons!" squealed Ānkhur. "That's what we are! That's what we should be called!"

Frightened, the fluffy chicks squawked their beaks open wide enough to swallow squirrels. Everybody shushed Ānkhur.

"Sorry!" she whispered. "Seriously, we should call ourselves that. We could get t-shirts. Or jackets! With big crests!"

Moon smiled in the sun. Rap winked at him.

2.

10 AM. 107th Avenue, Kush's southern cataract. Across the street from the All Nations Café, while parents and children and teenagers strolled along, the seven youth formed a *shenu* in a parking lot to perform their Daily Alchemy.

"Today is August first, the day Lord Usir revealed himself to Hru," said Rap. Except for JC, the others were still new to the Daily Alchemy, so Rap took the lead, making eye contact with everyone in the shenu like Brother Moon had taught him.

"That way," his *sbai* had told him earlier, "if people are feeling weird or whatever out in the street, they can focus on you and not how self-conscious they feel."

Rap said to Jorrel, "August begins with A, Africentric, and it's the first letter in the Alphabetical Alchemy. And one is Resurrection."

"And the first pledge of the *Nub-Wmet- Ānkh*," he said to Sixpac, "is '*By the sunrise, I choose to resurrect myself, purifying my body, my mind and my spirit. I choose to drink from the River of Life and I refuse to drown in the Swamps of Death.*' Am I right?"

He'd learned call-and-response from Moon. As everyone threw in nods, *mm-hms, yeses, true dats* or *Speak, brother!* (that one came from Ānkhur), Rap grew bolder, and projected his voice so that pedestrians could hear him. Deepened it, too. ("You always do that when you're spitting game with Ānkhur," JC bugged him later.)

"Now, Lord and Usir are four letters each," said Rap to Crystal, who nodded, "and Lord Usir being the ultimate ancestor, I think of pledge four: '*By the sunrise, I praise my ancestors and their struggles to bequeath me my legacy, not for me to*

93

bury or squander my gold, but to create justice today and forever. My ancestors and I are one, for their gold and the marrow of the pharaoh are in me.'

"So to me," said Rap to a smiling Sixpac, "that means that to be Africentric I need to remember my ancestors, which is the way to resurrect myself."

To Almeera, he said, "Resurrection, meaning waking up from the illusions and the lies of the Savage Lands." To Ahmed, "Which I can do, so long as I *refuse* to drink from the Swamps of Death, and *choose* to drink from the River of Life."

And to Ãnkhur, "That way, I'll have the strength to share my gold—my knowledge—so together we can raise the Shining Place."

After JC's turn, Sixpac threw down, and Rap was impressed. Crystal passed, and so did Almeera, but Ahmed and Ãnkhur also raised gold.

When they broke before postering around Kush to advertise the Hyper-Market, Rap told Ãnkhur he was impressed by how she raised in the shenu. JC stood behind her, shifting foot-to-foot slinkily and making what he called his "smooth Denzel love-daddy face" at Rap.

When Ãnkhur glanced behind her, JC turned statue.

It took everything Rap had not to crack up.

At the South Sudanese youth drop in centre—so tiny it was barely a hallway fronted by a door—JC started heading inside, then noticed Rap wasn't going with him.

"Dude, what's up?"

Rap shrugged, looking up and down 107ᵗʰ Ave. His rough white cotton shirt chafed his shoulders and neck on the thirty-plus morning. Was gonna be a scorcher.

"I just don'wanna get bogged down in there. Most of them don't speak enough English for us to really do any Alchemy with em. An we got a lotta posters to put up."

"Aiight," said JC, doubtfully. "Lemme just drop off a poster inside."

3.

South of Kush. Downtown. Noon.

While postering along Jasper Ave, Rap and JC were talking hip hop: the new beats JC was producing with Fruity Loops at Sixpac's house, and Rap's plan to write a song about Jehutmose III, the Alexander *before* Alexander, after ripping through *World's Great Men of Colour*.

But they stopped at Beaver Hills House Park. Not because of the park's parasol-trees dotting its small hills, or its cascading waterfall, or its mini-creek gurgling with life inside downtown's concrete greys.

But because of the crowd and what they were gawking at: a group of ultra-fit, white-clad, White twenty-somethings, tumbling and spinning.

"Dude, your lucky day," said JC, nudging him in the ribs. Across the park from them was Ãnkhur.

"Thanks!" said Rap. "I mean, shut up."

"Careful, bruh," said JC. He chinned towards her partners: Ahmed and Sixpac. A three-person postering crew. Rap felt his heart creasing at how much she was smiling at them, and without him.

He almost jetted right then, but JC stopped him, saying, "Can't score if you don't play."

After a quick *Nub-Wmet-Ānkh*—not the pledge, but just the phrase—all of them but Rap stood staring at the show.

Gyrating, dancing and round-house kicking, the capoeristas kept time to the bass-twangy *berimbau*, the bow-string/gourd combo their instructor was playing to drive the performance. Sounded like a jaw-harp.

Rap had no eyes for *capoeira*. Too busy sneaking glances at Ānkhur. Anyway, he knew enough about *capoeira*; once during *kung fu* class, Brother Moon'd said it came from Brazil, a martial art that West Africans developed to fight back against their oppressors.

These capoeristas didn't look like they'd ever worn chains or like they'd ever been West Africans. Except for the instructor, who looked like Taye Diggs but with hair, they were all White. All of them were ripped, and they flew through the air in white flowing pants and tight t-shirts. More than half were women. A couple had deadlocks.

Rap snickered. "Looks like a bunch of crumpers dressed for yoga class."

"Yeah," chirped Ānkhur. "They're like *The Matrix* dressed by lululemon."

Rap didn't know what that was, or even if it was a compliment or an insult.

"Look at that!" she squealed, even more excited when the instructor handed off his *berimbau* so he could "spar" with a student.

Taking off his shirt, he revealed a chest and abs that a welder would've taken all week to make out of steel.

Ānkhur's eyes sparkled. Rap's heart didn't just crease, it folded.

After the instructor finished dazzling all the applauding women and an eighth of the men, one of his students addressed the crowd with a microphone.

"Thank you. Thank you very much," said the young White man. Sharp rectangular specs and chiseled jaw—guy looked like he modelled eyewear. Or maybe underwear.

"*Capoeira*'s great cardio, and if you love dancing, it's awesome," he said, panting and smiling.

The other students nodded and smiled back. Two of them bounced their blonde deadlocks when they did.

"It's a martial art," he went on, "that comes from African slaves in Brazil who needed a way to defend themselves while shackled . . ."

Rap instantly ran mental simulations of how he'd use *wing chun kung fu* against the guy in the glasses. Figured he'd hafta learn jujutsu, too, since with all that spinning and hip-rotation, the *capoeristas* looked like they probably knew ground-fighting.

Imagined what it'd be like to split those glasses in two. Just one single punch to the bridge of the guy's nose.

"Carla's got pamphlets, and you can talk to me if you have any questions," said Mr. Sharp Glasses. His teacher shot him a concerned look.

"Oh, or like, of course, you can talk to Professor Nascimento, too. So anyway you can find us here every Wednesday afternoon, if it's sunny, for the rest of the summer."

"Let's go," said Rap to JC.

He had a plan.

Clasping hands in the Throne salute with the other Street Falcons (as baptised by Ānkhur), Rap hauled JC off so they could finish their job.

4.

"If you *hafta* fight a grappler and you're not trained as a grappler, then advice-one is, don't fight im," Brother Moon said to Rap.

The man handed a slip of paper to an Ethiopian teenager— the login for web carrel #4. "Enjoy, bruh. You've got until two-thirty-three."

The Hyper-Market wasn't bustling, but it felt busy. Five of eight carrels were in use, and all the customers were buying coffee.

But even Rap, with zero business experience, knew it was just dimes for the dollars Mr. Ani was spending every day to keep his doors open.

If the place felt busy, it was more because the Hyper-Market was overstuffed with continental and Caribbean products and Africentric books and merchandise.

"If you've got no choice, advice-two is," said Moon, continuing to answer Rap's question, "use a weapon from a distance, like a gun or a bow-and-arrow or an F-16." Rap chuckled.

"Advice-three is attack him in a group. Ground-fighting is all about going after one guy. If you're head-locking and arm-barring a guy on the ground, you can't be fighting off the guy's two friends."

"Uh huh," said Rap. The advice wasn't helping. He fiddled with some sugar packets at the coffee station.

"And advice four is always remember advice-zero: avoid fighting. Avoid places where people are likely to fight. And avoid places that make you feel like fighting. That's how you keep from drowning in the Swamps, by fighting *isfet* and serving the cause of *Maāt*."

"Okay," said Rap, slipping a dozen sugar packets into the pockets of his giant shorts. Not noticing, Mr. Ani kept pouring coffee for the Somali undergrad standing in front of the till. "You brought your own mug, so it's only one-fifty," he told her.

"And if you do *absolutely* hafta fight," he whispered to Rap when she'd paid and was back at her carrel, "never fight for some bullshit reason, like trying to impress a girl."

Rap looked up at him, his eyebrows almost jumping off his forehead.

"Nice try, lil brother. Mouth open, got your hands up in 'shock.' I was your age too, once, about a million years ago."

"No, but I—"

"Don't shit a shitter."

"Yeah, but honest—"

"You gotta be more subtle. Girl like Ānkhur doesn't wanna be chased. She wants to *be* the chaser. Just like her aunt, and you know Sister Seshat's tougher'n iron knuckles. You dig?"

Rap turned his hands palms up, put his wrists together, like he was surrendering to cuffs. Mr. Ani laughed.

"Yeah, okay, okay. But, but how'm I . . . y'know . . . . "

"Supposed to make a girl chase you?"

"Yeah."

"You can't," he said. "Either she wants to or she doesn't want to. But trying won't make it happen, and it'll just drive you crazy trying to."

Rap's shoulders fell.

"I know it's not what you wanted to hear, brother," said Mr. Ani. He handed Rap a *sambusa* from the tray he'd just taken out of the toaster oven. "But women aren't like, like . . . computers or suh'm. You can't just get an access code and then programme em to do what you want em to. Trust me. About three billion guys've had to learn the same lesson."

"Yeah."

"You hear me?"

"Uh-huh," he said. "But, y'know, you think I could, maybe, try with the *jujutsu* again?"

"Rap, c'mon."

"No, really, I just wanna learn."

Moon looked at him, shook his head, raised an eyebrow. "Okay." He changed gears. "You ever ask your mum how she and your dad got together? Who was doing the chasing?"

Rap's eyes probed the ceiling. It'd never even occurred to him to think about his mother *dating* his dad, romancing and all that, falling in love. The idea of his mother and father laughing or flirting or dancing or actually—

His father was barely a ghost to him. A couple of honeymoon shots at the Meroë pyramids, a slim book he'd written on the South Sudanese independence movement based on his master's thesis, a gold chain wrapped inside a carved wooden box. The box was stained with henna, rubbed with amber. It felt and smelled like memories.

He knew they'd met at the University of Khartoum. His mother was one of the many Somali women there, and according to her, more than half of all students there were female. Maybe she *had* had to chase his dad.

"I don'know," said Rap, wonderingly.

"Ask," said Moon. "Maybe your mum knows something you can use, y'know? Something in your DNA."

Moon went to make coffee. Rap grabbed another *sambusa* and wrapped it in a couple of napkins, then stuffed it in one of his cargo pockets.

He wanted to talk with Mr. Ani about the *capoeira* demonstration. To tell him about the nearly all-White group of performers who looked like runway models. To quote him the line from Mr. Fashion Glasses about how *capoeira* was "created by African slaves." But he didn't.

Nor did he know why thinking about it all made his shoulders burn.

5.

Grabbed an internet station, set up a Facebook group for the Street Falcons, then grabbed a stack of handbill-coupons advertising the Hyper-Market and went walking into the bright, hot August afternoon.

Ānkhur.

Every time she giggled, Rap felt giddy. Every time she smiled and nodded at something he said, he felt the top of his head pop open, like the sight of her teeth could wind him up like a jack-in-the-box.

But so what? Couldn't compete with guys like Ahmed or Sixpac. And definitely not with that *capoeira* master.

Didn't even know how you asked a girl out. Or what you did *after* you did.

He wasn't a fool. Or a monk. Wasn't like he'd never seen porn. But he didn't like that shit, didn't like how they treated those girls. And he wasn't trying to bone Ānkhur, anyway. What he wanted . . . .

Yeah, like that movie *Amelie.*

All of it was great where she was having fun and wondering and yearning and waiting and trying to meet somebody she was crazy about. But then at the end, after all that build-up, when she finally meets the guy, she just up and insta-bones him.

There were guys who did nothing but *blah-blah-blah* in school bathrooms about getting some, or how the pussy was so good, or how much they wannid to get summa *that.*

And even he—he, who'd never gone on a date—knew that almost all of them were bullshit vendors who'd never made a single sale.

On 97th Street in front of the Chinese Lucky 97 Market, he injected handbills into the palms of a group of Rwandan teenagers, chatting them up and pointing the four blocks up and one-over to the Hyper-Market. They were all nods and smiles and saying how they'd check it out, and he felt good about it.

So if he *did* ask her out and she said yes, what would he wear? What about his teeth? He had better teeth than most kids who'd grown up in refugee camps, but still. Every time these days he saw himself in the mirror brushing his teeth he winced at his snaggles.

107th Ave. Dropped in on one African-owned business after another, except the Somali internet café down there (the competition), talking to the owners like Mr.

Ani'd taught him to. Liked getting so many smiles from adults, treating him like he had legit business. With respect.

When it came to dealing with authority figures, what with all his recitation and interpretation of the Scrolls and *The Book of the Golden Falcon*, and titrating the Daily Alchemy, he was ten times more confident than he'd ever been in his life.

But dealing with girls? Nope.

Read this one book he'd found in the library, *Malcolm X: The Man and His Times*. There was this one part where Malcolm used to take his wife Betty to the beach and read her poetry. Man, you had to be smooth with a capital *oo* to pull off shit like that. Otherwise you'd get called corny, which was like having a girl shove you into the guillotine and have all her friends pull the lever.

But if you *could* do it, man, she'd be talking to her friends about you forever, until they were all jealous or sick of hearing about it. That'd be nice.

But get real. Plus, he was too skinny. And he had facial scarification. Sure it was way subtler than it was with most South Sudanese, but still. And what if she didn't like dark guys?

Make sure you ask her about herself, said Mr. Ani. *Don't be like some knuckleheads and just start blabbing about stuff she doesn't care about, like PS3 games or some action movie or Tupac trivia whatever.*

Maybe he should ask Sister Seshat? Get a woman's . . . nah. Ānkhur was her niece. She'd tell her everything.

And he didn't have a car, and neither did his mother, and he couldn't even borrow Brother Moon's cuz he didn't know how to drive.

And pay attention, cuz if she starts telling you stuff about herself and you're not interested—

I know, I know—make sure I'm listening so I can ask her about it anyway—

No, brother, no. The opposite. If you're not interested in what young sister's saying, it means you're not interested in HER. In which case, you gotta fly on. Listen. L: Liberate. Transformed?

On the avenue, dapping flyers in hand after hand.

Tried imagining her hand. Putting his fingers on it. Wrapping them around and looming through hers. They'd be cool, slender and soft. Piano-playing fingers. She'd giggle when he took it.

Figured after a few minutes of that, he could level up and check out her eyes.

6.

"So Moon, you *want* this store to fail?"

Sister Seshat. Man, she could rock and shock Rap at will. Even Brother Moon scratched his head.

But he didn't look angry. Just leaning against his till, wearing a *my fly's down* smirk and looking over his cramped Hyper-Market.

Then he switched tactics.

"*What?*" he said, as in, *Aren't you seeing what I'm seeing?*

Place was full, on a Wednesday night, and everyone was drinking coffee."

Seshat: "You got people paying, what, a crummy five bucks an hour—"

"Well, four—"

"You're making my case for me, brother," she said. The lawyer, Brother Bamba, smiled. "And coffee's going for?"

"Uh," said Moon. As if he were inserting his head into a noose. "Buck-seventy five. Buck-fifty if you bring your own mug."

Bamba laughed. Like Seshat was just about to roast Moon's beans.

But sitting at carrel #4 and managing their Facebook group, Rap was shocked. He knew Brother Moon's business wasn't raking cash, but never thought it could actually go under.

"There are 'net cafés on Jasper Ave charging five bucks for one coffee," said Seshat. "One coffee! How you sposta to keep your doors open when you're clearing eight bucks a night after expenses?"

"Eight bucks and twelve cents," smirked Bamba. "To be fair."

She smiled. "You've got no focus here. You're selling *everything*. People coming by for data recovery wanna know you can handle super-sensitive material! Them walking in and seeing money transfer, phone cards, Yoruba statuettes—" (those she did from memory; then she scanned and pointed and blasted) "coconut oil, prayer mats, mango juice, Black baby dolls, Zapp CDs? You're selling *Zapp*? Some raggedy-ass copies of *Jet* and *Final Call*, mouse traps, dashikis, fishing rods, *hair*-extensions—"

She was making up the last few, but she had Moon and Bamba laughing. Rap was still amazed at the sight of Moon with his peers. Whole different man when he wasn't forced to be in command, keeping everything moving and everyone safe.

Not that he wasn't nice to him and JC and the other Street Falcons. But here, with his old friends, the colossus got to power-down to human scale.

Wished he got to see his mother do that. Not when she sat on ten committees a week and did fifty home visits a month, independently contracting for Catholic Social Services, Mennonite Centre for Newcomers and every other NGO she constantly had to hustle for work.

She didn't have a man, not a *real* man, not all to herself—except for the one in the honeymoon shots in front of those Sudanese pyramids. Wasn't like other Somali mothers, getting to take off her *hijab* with her husband and kids. Yeah, she didn't wear *hijab*, but all that meant was she didn't have one to take off. No man around to laugh with and lean next to on the couch while debating the news or weep with over sappy TV shows or movies. No man to come with to parent-teacher interviews with or the school play. And she was too busy to've gone to those by herself anyway.

Seshat said, "This menagerie bursting your seams here isn't doing any favours to your business cred."

"Look, I do the data recovery upstairs," protested Moon.

"Doesn'matter! People coming in here and smelling patties and seeing people spill Ting all over themselves are not thinking, 'This place should be entrusted with my hard drives.'"

Seshat triangle-snapped on that, and Bamba did a Jamaican flick. Moon shook his head, smiling.

Rap finished his Facebook letter to Sixpac and JC and hit REPLY.

"Why not add printing and photocopying?" said Seshat. "Print-on-demand? Hell, just go into publishing. And add a driving school. And more groceries, of course—"

"Okay, okay! I surrender! So what're you suggesting?"

"About time," she said. "Can I have a coffee?"

He chuckled and poured for her.

"Thank you. Now," she said, sipping. "Damn, that's nice. Ethiopian?"

"Tanzanian."

"Right. I can taste the Kilimanjaro. Anyway, Bamba and I were thinking. Place next door is still empty, right? After those shootings, people aren't exactly lining up to rent it."

"Yeah . . . ?"

"Why don't you divide the Hyper-Market in two? Keep the cyber café here, put almost everything else next door?"

"You just said I couldn't earn enough profit to keep one place open, and now you're saying lease two?"

"Tweak your rates," said Bamba. "A bit more for coffee, a bit more per hour. Not much. Add more net stations with the freed-up space. Next door, put all your goods."

"How'm I supposed to afford that? Not to mention extra computers?"

"Where'd you get these?" asked the lawyer.

"Venezuela."

"Chavez PCs?" Bamba laughed. "My man Brother Moon does not change. I love it."

Rap checked out his PC, never having thought about where they'd been made. If someone'd asked him he'd've said China. *But if they could make them in Venezuela, why not in Nigeria or Uganda or Sudan? They have oil, too.*

Knew about Venezuela from Mr. Ani, always talking about the revolutionary president with African ancestry and wiry hair, calling him "our Bolivarian brother."

"Don't worry about the money," said Bamba. "Sister and I will come in with you."

Moon's head rocked back. A smile slid open, curious. Then it clicked off. "You . . . serious?"

"I'm a lawyer," said Bamba. "I'm always looking for a good place to launder my money."

Moon laughed. Seshat said, "And I've been in Social Services fifteen years. That's more heartbreak than anyone should have to take. Plus I have years of experience with my parents' store."

"That's right!" said Moon. "I forgot . . . they took over, uh—Caribe's Soul Shack on Whyte Ave?"

"Yeah. Turned it into Miss Thang's. Still going strong—even selling our own line of Miss Thang fashions. I was general manager my first four years as a social worker. And I still do the books."

"Well," said Moon, "I can't lie. That would really . . . pull my ass outta the Swamps. And if I could make enough money to maybe hire a coupla these kids to do the dailies—" (Rap's heart started pounding like a drum-and-bass beat track) "—I could spend more time—"

Seshat: "Building up the Laboratory."

Moon: "'Laboratory'?"

"Bamba's word," said Seshat. "I like it."

"Cuz we're Alchemists?" asked Moon.

"And," said Bamba, "because we're not the *Shemsu-Heru* anymore. We're something new."

"We need an HQ," said Seshat. "I've been talking to my City Councillor, Mohinder Bhatia. He thinks he can get us a storefront cheap, or even free, 'specially in this area, cuz we're doing youth outreach. Say it's a lock if we can do some tutoring and get some drop-outs."

"Sister . . . you . . . you're a miracle-worker!"

"Think about it, Moon—they're on crocodile-backs down at City Hall, terrified you're gonna sue the police department, the mayor, everyone, for police brutality. City'll throw grants, facilities, whatever atcha just to avoid a lawsuit they know YouTube'll make them lose."

Bamba said, "And if we get the storefront, there're federal grants through Multiculturalism and Citizenship."

"And we should be leveraging your fame as a crime-fighter, Moon," said Seshat. "Using that Youtube of you, putting together all those news stories—"

"Oh, you mean the stories claiming I was a drug dealer?"

"No, the ones saying you were a heroic entrepreneur intervening in a deadly situation to save a couple of kids. We market *that* properly, tie it in with the video? You're suddenly the hottest martial arts teacher in town. 'Study with the famous *Sensei* Ani!'"

"*Sbai* Ani. And I'm not famous."

"Oh yes you are. And you should be *more* famous," said Bamba. "And before you can protest, no, not for ego, but because that fame can make building the Laboratory that much easier."

"The *Street* Laboratory," said Rap, sitting at his carrel.

All three adults turned to him.

Wasn't like they hadn't been ignoring him. He hadn't even joined the conversation until that point.

They traded glances, nodded.

"I like that," said Brother Moon. "*The Street Laboratory of Kush.*"

A spark—*zap*—rippling up his spine. Like he'd just carved hieroglyphics on the wall around the Step Pyramid, lines that sunrise would kiss golden for ten thousand years.

> *So let me you tell the whole story*
> *Of the Street Lab-ra-tory*
> *The Falcons, without guns*
> *Will conquer all and take the glory . . .*

7.

11:49 PM IM response from Sixpac:

> *UR DLY ALCHMY WS ATOMIC*
> *10 AM 2MRW*

11:50 PM IM response from JC:

> *B there fo sho*
> *Got yr bk, bra*

Rap grinned, and his own grin felt like ice cubes.

Clicked off IM, back to Word. Kept refining. Kept reciting against an instrumental version of PE's "Revolution."

8.

Sixpac. Brother had magic wands for fingers.

Black magic-making, and jaw, knee and fingers came down on the final conjuring. JC, Rap, stunned.

"So," said Sixpac, smirking into their silence, "something like that?" said Sixpac.

"That was *DOPE*, kid!" said JC, rocking his mini-dreads.

"*Pacman*," said Rap, "you're like DJ Premier. Or Hi-Tek!"

JC: "Man, you're like, like, like Pete Rock or suh'm. Or the RZA! Rap, check this out. I'ma play it back with the drum track."

Sixpac got off his bed, put down his e-bass, then leaned past JC at the computer to hit SAVE on the live track he'd just fed to Fruity Loops file. *Tappetty-tap-tap*, and then merged it all, and then PLAY.

And then drums, and synth tracks, and noise FX, and the ultra-low-frequency bass blackness.

A trillion air molecules jumping, thumping, crumping on the same beat at the same time for the same rhyme in Rap's mind.

And between the megaspeakers, *thunder.*

"Thank you so, so much for this!" said Rap, leaping out of his chair. "This is gonna be amazing! Put the Pyrites on notice!"

Sixpac raised his fist, dropped a dap on Rap, took one back. JC followed.

And while the air was getting funky from three teenaged boys and three hours of constructing beats, they didn't even notice the stank. When they finally broke upstairs, they only did it outta thirst.

Sixpac. Hard to believe he was third- or fourth-cousins or whatever with JC. The brother's place was a clean, newish split-level with a driveway in front. The Jowhars were the only truly middle-class Somali family Rap'd ever seen.

Only three kids—practically childless by Somali standards. Sixpac's dad was an engineer with Stantec. His mum was a nurse. His older brother, a Commerce student at Concordia, owned his own Hyundai minivan with only one dent and just a few chips in the paint.

And Rap'd finally agreed with JC to work with Sixpac because even though he felt totally outclassed by the taller, way better-looking, carved-biceps eighteen-year-old, it turned out that Pac was actually a decent brother, and he'd leapt at the chance to help Rap out.

Back downstairs in Sixpac's room drinking Barq's and cream soda, no one bothered to open the window or even the curtains.

Sixpac's computer desk and shelves boasted their bounty: two drum machines including an 808, a *waa-waa* pedal, a patchbay, two Technics 1200 turntables, a Roland keyboard, and a sixteen-channel mixing board.

But JC went after the small. Something on the shelf, no bigger than a credit card, but clearly gear. Picked it up.

Sixpac said, "Portable scratch pad. But no inputs or outputs. So my whole thing is, I'd use . . . *that* one."

JC picked up the unit Pac was pointing at, size of a small mixer or a big external burner.

"Arc 3," said Sixpac. "Whole thing is, you got twin loop banks, pitch control. Use that and the *Ion* together, you're good to go."

"But this'll be outdoors," said Rap. "Won't the sound get eaten up in all that space?"

Sixpac smiled, pointed to the closet.

Rap slid aside the double doors.

Thing came up to his waist. Sat on its own dolly.

Had two car batteries wired into it, strapped on with bungee cords.

Sixpac hit a remote. The volume meter crackled to life: a cosine of radiant blue LEDs. The thing hummed directly into their bones.

"Me and my brother built im outta spare parts," said Sixpac. "We call im Optimus Prime."

Rap and JC, whispering like they were at mosque:

"*Awesome.*"

9.

Friday morning. Moon and Rap brushed dust off their knees, finished fiddling with the web cam, then tippy-toed off the roof.

Downstairs at carrel #12, Rap clicked on the desktop's AERIE icon.

Onscreen, four peregrine falcons chirped and squawked in silence.

"I can set up a mic if you want," said Rap. "Do you have an all-weather one?"

"Think so," said Moon.

"I can put a link in our Facebook group, so everyone can watch the falcons whenever they want to."

"You kids today are different," said Moon. "Watching chicks online aint what it usedta be."

Rap laughed. Moon put a quick squeeze on Rap's shoulder, let go. Rap didn't flinch. He actually smiled, even though Mr. Ani couldn't see it.

The door jangled and the massive Somali Mothers Crew rolled in, twenty-kids-strong, led by JC's mum.

Thanks to Rap's tutelage, Moon offered up *maalin wanaagsan*. Got some smiles and impressed mugs from the women, and *ma'a-salaama* in return.

Moon offered tea, but Mrs. Abdi was there on business. So were the other two *muhajabaat*, women Rap'd never seen before. Mrs. Abdi wanted Moon to lead some kind of something on autism for their community, starting with explaining to these other women what it was.

Rap scanned the little kids. A few seemed obviously off to him. Jackie Chan's little brother was with them, bobbing and droning.

"Well, the thing is," said Moon, "scientists have been wrong about autism for a long time."

"Whatt do you mean?"

"They used to diagnose autism just by looking at how kids behaved. But that's like looking at a car's windshield or hood to figure out what's wrong with the engine."

"So whatt are you sugg-a-jestingk?"

"The new thinking is that in up to fifty per cent of kids, they're really suffering from seizures."

Mrs. Abdi looked confused. Rap translated the concept, and when that didn't work, subtly mimed.

She reared back like she'd smelled something awful. "My son has never done that."

"No," said Moon, "but seizures can be absolutely tiny, so tiny nobody sees them. *From the outside.* But with an EEG, a brain scan, we *can* see them from the inside."

"*Brain-scan?*" Like Moon'd said they should open up her kid like a tin of anchovies.

"It's nothing dangerous. An electro-encephalogram. It's just like an X-ray, but safer. It's a way to measure electricity flowing inside the brain. Our thoughts are basically electricity."

One of the other ladies had a back-and-forth in Somali with Mrs. Abdi.

"She wants to know whatt is happeningk insidte her son's brain, if whatt you say is true."

Moon looked at the ceiling, then back to them. "Okay, see, the brain works . . . like a city's electrical grid. So a seizure is like lightning hitting the generators and the lines. Makes equipment go into overdrive in some places and knocks out power in others. Surges and blackouts, simultaneously.

"When kids have these seizures, they're overloaded. Everything's too much for them, so they can barely make sense of what's going on around them, let alone learn about their world. Sometimes not even enough to learn words, or how to behave."

Mrs. Abdi translated parts of that, then relayed another question. "So why do our kidts get these seizures or autism here, but nott back home?"

"It's probably environmental. Certain fungi, you know, like mushrooms? But right inside the soil? They can cause seizures. Toxic plants. Pesticides. Heavy metals—"

"What?"

Rap explained in Somali.

"Yess, okay. Like, mercury?"

"Exactly," said Moon. "Or chromium, or iron—they can leach right out of cutlery, cooking utensils . . . . Lead, definitely. Too much lead, or any of these other poisons, and you could end up trapped inside your own body, like a corpse. Or a zombie."

Mr. Ani opened his hands, like he was holding a body right there.

"Looking on the surface was never enough. But now we know better. Now we know that if you look inside, see what's wrong, we can get the right medicine to, well, to resurrect these children. So they can live with us. Talk with us. And love us."

Translations. Excitement.

"So," said Mrs. Abdi, "where do we gett these *ee-ee-jeez*?"

10.

Wednesday. Blue sky. Hot sun. Amped *berimbau* music twanging across Beaver Hills House Park while the *capoeristas* flipped and pivoted halfway between break-dancing and taekwon-do.

The battered Hyundai minivan pulled up next to the park. Rap, JC and Sixpac jumped out, popped open the back doors of the van, then dollied the massive Optimus Prime onto the sidewalk before rolling it into position.

Pac's brother Luqman flicked on his hazards. Red alert. As the wheel man.

JC plugged the Arc 3 portable DJ station into Optimus Prime with a single yellow RCA digital cable, then connected the mic. Sixpac clicked the remote and the mega box flickered blue.

Rap's heart was beating so hard it felt like someone punching him in the throat. JC hit the button.

Beats ripped through the crowd like IEDs.

"*ONE-TWO, ONE-TWO,*" said Rap, voice echoing against the downtown buildings of Beaver Hills park.

Repeated the one-two a few times to pull the audience from the capoeristas and give JC and Pac enough time to finish their sound check.

Rap cupped his mic. "We ready?"

Pac nodded. JC did a test-scratch on the Arc 3's wheel.

"*I'M THE EMCEE NAMED SUPREME RAPTOR,*" blared Rap, well-rehearsed, dizzy offa nerves.

Pac adjusted the volume.

"AND THIS IS MOBILE DEEJAY JACKIE CHAN ON THE WHEEL OF STEEL."

Pac finished adjusting.

"And this here is Super-Producer Pacman Prime. And we're the new crew in town.

"Called *Golden Eye.*"

Someone'd turned off the *berimbau* CD, and the *capoeristas* had stopped prancing, just standing, hands on hips or arms folded in frustration at the interruption.

JC turned up the beat and the vocals. Rap's fist tightened on the mic like he was riding lightning.

> *Cap-o-eira, cap-o-eira,*
> *Got some thoughts I wanna share ya*
> *People listenin: I'ma scare ya*
> *People listenin: I'ma dare ya*

Some kids in the crowd whooped. Probably never'd seen a diss show live. Then again, neither had Rap.

The 808 drums thumped in like a giant's footfalls, crashing through the sampled strings of the intro to Carl Douglas's "Kung fu Fighting," mashing-up into the accelerated slap bass of Cameo's "Skin I'm In."

And Rap leapt back in:

> *Why do you steal our culcha*
> *Ya vulcha, lemme insult-cha,*
> *You flip-floppin clowns*
> *Dance to me an I will mulch ya*
>
> *You're triflin, an stifling,*
> *An thiefin up our dreadlocks*
> *Lookin dreadful ... an deadful*
> *I-might just-give-ya-some headknocks*
>
> *Ya acrobatic preppies*
> *An yuppies lookin-like-guppies*

Tryin-to-fake the funk
They-step-to-me-an-say "Whassup, G?"

I aintcha homey or ya brotha
Defin-IT-ely not your lover
So back away from Black
And getcha hands up off my mother!

JC scratched dozens of chirps, even did the bird, and dozens of teens in the park crowded forward while Rap re-rhymed the opening chorus.

Rap: legs like springs on every bound and leap, lungs pumping, soaring.

Capoeira leader, Mr. Taye Diggs, standing on the cobblestones, glaring.

Three of his male students looking at each other, *What're we gonna do about this?* built into their faces.

Ya breakdancin smurfs
Are rich but worthless, and turfless
You're-callin-my ancestors "slaves"
But you savages-lived-in-caves

Up in the Savage Lands
Your savage plan I understand
You Pyrites tryinna steal
The gold of old—I will not fold

Because I'm Nu-bi-an, I'm true bein
The sun that conquers cold

On the edge of Rap's vision, Pac's brother ripped away in the minivan, escaping the #5 bus pulling in.

Rap, hoping they wouldn't hafta bug out before Luqman orbited back.

Cap-o-eira? Double-dare ya
Dancing freaks, you think we scareda

You? You freaking losers?
Boozers, probably cruisers

You're wussy wimps in white pajamas
Fightin you would be a snooza!

Capoeristas.
Into a phalanx.
And then advanced.
Rap caught JC's and Pac's eyes:
Wrap it up NOW.
Belted out his last chorus while his new teen fans howled laughter and cheers.

> *I dare ya, double-dare ya*
> *Triple-dare ya, Cap-o-eira!*
> *Aint scareda ya flare*
> *Ya cap-o-eira capybaras!*

"What the hell's your problem?" shouted the chiseled Mr. Fashion Glasses over the beat.
"No problem," said Rap into the mic. "I just don't like Pyrites stealing our culture!"
"You don't exactly look Brazilian to me!"
"Oh, like you do?" said Rap.
Pac and JC pulled on Rap's arms. JC said, "Luqman's back! Just saw a cop-mobile. Time to split!"
"Yeah, run away, ya little coward!" said Mr. Specs. "You come here, disrupt our performance and then when it's time to step up like a man, you wanna drive off in a goddamned mini-van!"
JC and Pac dollied Optimus Prime back inside the van, but Rap held his ground, his butterfly knife in his pocket, ready to spring its wings.
The instructor landed at ground zero, pecs straining beneath his t-shirt, his ultra-beautiful face a final challenge to Rap, just as the Golden Eye crew finished packing their vehicle.
"You are a verra rude young man!" said Taye Diggs. Portuguese accent, almost Frenchy to Rap. "Why you do diss to me?"
Walking backwards to get into the van, Rap kept staring down the capos and their leader, his eyes the only curse-out he needed.
Slid-slammed shut the door, and wheels-squealing, they were out.
Laughing, howling to themselves about their glorious victory and the debut of E-Town's greatest hip hop crew ever, and the origin story that would one day be written up in *Vibe* and *The Source* and *XXL* remembered forever.

11.

Night. At the Hyper-Market. Pac was at home working on beats.
But JC and Rap were there when the phone rang.
Mr. Ani answered it. Listened and talked.
Looked over at the two of them.

"Oh, lord," said Mr. Ani. "Okay. I'll deal with it."

They gulped. At the same time.

"Do you know which one?" said the man, turning back to the phone. "I see. Okay, Paolo. We're coming right over." Phone down. Walked over. Rap, in his carrel, felt tiny, caged. And the farmer had an axe.

"That was Professor Paolo Nascimento," said Mr. Ani, "instructor over at the Capoeira Academy. Good guy. Said he recognised some kids who'd been handing out my flyers last week. Said they crashed his performance today, disrespected him in fronta the whole audience."

The two sides of Rap's brain'd been at war since he'd hatched his plan. One hemisphere said Moon'd approve of him publicly schooling Leadites and melting Pyrites.

The other hemisphere said nope.

"JC," said Moon. "I know this all was Rap's idea. You're in charge of the Hyper-Market till I get back. You know the whole operation . . . I was gonna do this anyway, but as of now, you're hired."

Jackie Chan howled quietly: "Da-*a-a*-yumn!"

Rap's eyes glummed out, his head drooped, as he and Mr. Ani walked out to his car.

12.

Capoeira Institute. Mr. Ani led him. They stood at the back while the capos danced and kicked.

Felt like Robin, and Batman was hand-delivering him to Arkham Asylum as a gift to the Joker.

Moon offered his hand to the capoeira master. "I'm really sorry about my, my student here."

The man took it. "Mos' martial art school dismiss esstudent who disgrace de eschool like heem."

"That's a fact."

Rap stood burning.

Professor Paolo Nascimento glared at him.

"Diss isn't, what's daat called? In data *Karate Kid* movie?"

Moon: "Uh, Kobra Kai dojo?"

Paolo: "Yes, exactly. I am juss a hard-working immigrant, like your family. Why you come to disraapt my work? Keep me from earning a living? Should I do dat to your faader if I disagree wit him?"

Rap. Silent. Staring at the wall.

"I'm asking you a question! Why you do diss to me?"

Eyes on the man.

"Cuz it just seems like—!" Took a breath. "Here you are, taking the culture, teaching it to all these preppie, yuppy mzungus, an you're letting them call our ancestors 'slaves.' I mean, that's not right. Okay? You're selling us out!"

Paolo: "First of all, dese people pay my bills. Yes? Dey are my esstudent. I'm sure if your Mr. Ani has '*mzungu*' customers, he is not refusing their money. Am I correct?"

Moon: "You're not wrong, bruh."

Paolo: "An secondly, you tink I should wait aroun for 'our people' to take my classes? Originally dat's all I tried to do here. How long I try diss? Almost two year. I rent racquet ball court at a healt club. Could not get even one Black person to take my class. You tink it's better for me to go to work for White people as a janitor instead of taking White people's money as my customer?"

"Yeah, but they're just gonna take over *capoeira* just like they took over rock and roll. Or jazz. Or Africa!"

"If our people abandon it, we can't complain, can we?" said Paolo. "And you! You want to know how to fight. You are Sudanese, yes?"

Rap: "Half, yeah."

Paolo: "Dere's Sudanese wrestling. Why don'you know how to do dat? An Zulu combat. But I saw you take a *kung fu* pose today, no? Dat's Chinese. Are you not stealing deir culture?"

Rap's mouth opened, then closed. Not one word even peeked out between his lips.

"So? You have nutting else to say to me?"

Rap gritted his teeth. "Why're you letting your students call us slaves?"

The *cap*-master sighed, exasperated. "What?"

"Last week. That guy with the fancy glasses said African slaves invented *capoeira*. And you've got it on your website!"

The professor ground his teeth. "It's true, daat's why!"

"Yeah? Well Mr. Ani taught us better than that."

Paolo looked at Moon. Moon squirmed a bit, but didn't intervene.

Rap went on. "All peoples were enslaved at some time. But we don't talk about them all like that. In Europe they called em serfs. Same thing as slaves, but nobody calls em that! The Nazis enslaved the Jews. But nobody says, 'The Nazis went to Poland, picked up the slaves, and used em to build stuff.' Why not?

"Cuz people understand that Jews are human. That they know the Nazis didn' *civilise* them—they had history and language and culture and minds before the Nazis enslaved em.

"But Leadites don't know that about us. All of us who got taken in the first *Maafa* or hammered in the second one! Leadites've been blinded into thinking we were *al*ways slaves. Which means they think that's all we'll ever be!"

Moon. Suppressing a smile.

"I don'know whaat diss 'Leadite' is or '*Maafa*' or whatever. All I know is we got enslaved. Daat's all I said, and daat's all I meant!"

"Then why not just say that?" snapped Rap. "And say that before the Maafa we had great civilisations, like, like Mali, an, an, an Songhai, an Benin, an Egypt an Axum an Meröe! And then say the West Africans fought back against their oppressors and leave it at that and just stop calling us slaves!"

Moon cut it off, addressed the man in white.

"Brother, I've admired your work for a long time. You know that. My, my *student* here's very smart, which you can see.

"But, obviously *today* . . . he was out of line. Way out of line. He should've talked to you first, not wrecked your show and interfered with your livelihood."

"Daat's right! An he still has not apologised!"

Moon stood. Looked down. "Rap?"

Rap. Not a word. Felt smoke pouring off his back and head.

Finally choked it out.

"Sorry."

Breathed.

"I was . . . out of line. I should've . . . paid you the respect . . . of talking to you . . . before."

Glared across the room at Mr. Fancy Glasses leading the class, glaring back at him. Sneering, even.

Imagined that idiot cartwheeling around him, and when his head was upside-down, front kicking right into his face.

13.

Mr. Ani hadn't said anything for five blocks and five red lights. He'd hit every one.

Rap heard him take a breath. Finally.

"Brother is one good looking dude. You know?"

Rap, eyes forward. Where was *this* going?

Moon: "Built like Shango. Tall. Surrounded by beautiful, young, athletic, educated women. Who hang on his every word."

Rap, sideways glance. Kept his face aimed straight ahead while Jasper Avenue slid past them, west becoming east under their wheels.

This wasn't Kush. The people on the Ave weren't Kushitic. Coffee bars, hoity restaurants, a big white cathedral like a wedding cake for giants. And summer women in heels and summer men in sunglasses in the 9:30 PM sunset.

"And crowds love him," said Moon, his two hands strangling the wheel. "Why wouldn't they? He's like a breakdancing Bruce Lee. Been doing *capoeira* for fifteen years. When brother slips and falls on the ice, that shit looks better than Baryshnikov."

Moon slowed for a yellow he could've easily passed through. "Baryshnikov's—"

"—a famous dancer. Yeah, I know."

Moon: "Hm."

He put his indicator on for RIGHT, then pulled over to park. When the indicator snapped back, he put slapped it down again.

Click-tick . . . click-tick . . . click-tick . . .

"Meanwhile, you're an angry young man. With all kinds of mysteries and secrets, and hell, that's your business. But you've got a month-and-a-half of *wing chun*. And some of his students've been doing *capoeira* for years."

... Click-tick ... click-tick ... click-tick ...

"Doesn't matter if it looks like dancing to you. Just the cardio alone means they could break your ass in two and serve it to you like Kit Kat."

Green light. They rolled.

"Some rules for you, Rap. And I mean, we have got to be straight on this. Number one, never start a fight you can't win."

They turned north on Jasper, passing the comic book store with the neon Superman logo in the window and the Mountain Equipment Co-op.

"Number two, don'be going out prospecting for trouble. These are the Savage Lands. Trouble will always find you—you don't need to go out there begging and pleading for it to come snatch you up."

Up 124th Street and west on 118th, passing the Burger Baron and pawn shops and rent-to-own joints and shambling women with skirts too short for the law.

"Number three?" said Mr. Ani, turning to look at him while driving, "Don't be jeopardising other people on some bullshit. You coulda gotten your brothers JC and Sixpac messed up, or Sixpac's equipment busted up, or alla you arrested! And there you were on that same spot a week ago with *my flyers* in your hands, which means bringing it all back on me!"

They pulled up in front of Al Hambra, Rap's apartment. The older man killed the engine.

"That what you want?" said Mr. Ani.

Rap looked at the man's mouth, the sharps of his incisors.

"For all of us to get shut down? For all these Street Falcons to get tagged and bagged?"

Rap stared forward.

"Adults love to say shit like, 'You gotta think when you're in these things.' But when you're in em is too late. You *created* a circumstance in which an explosion was inevitable.

"And that happened because you had a live current running through you, and you didn't use any of the gold I've given you to ground yourself!

"We are Nubians! In the Savage Lands! Surrounded by Leadites and Pyrites, Rap! You understand me? We don't have the right to throw away our chances, especially when most of us'll never get a second one! Everything we do affects every other one of us!

"Some of us slipped into the Swamps or were born there, but today Rap, you ran up, jumped in and pulled JC and Sixpac down with you to drown."

The young man started to defend himself, but Mr. Ani told him, "Go home, Rap."

Rap unfolded himself from the car. Legs and arms were weak. Like he had the flu.

Mr. Ani's eyes: straight ahead. His hand turned the ignition.

The man drove away, with the air smelling of fast food and gasoline and flowers and too much perfume, and the night heat boiling it all together and pouring it down his throat till Rap wanted to puke.

Streetlights, pale moon and scant stars, lights warbling, phasing, strobing . . .

Not even going inside, neck on fire, and all the loneliness of the universe on him, untouchable at the centre of a hurricane.

Five
Father-Brother-Son

The Book of Then

1.

IN THE DARKNESS, WITH THE SCRATCHY MAT AGAINST MY SKIN, I WOKE UP.

I smelled her, even before I felt her hand against my cheek.

Mum . . . you're alive?

But she wasn't there. I jumped up. The moon turned a path into a silver brook. I walked and then ran for hours, because she was out there . . .

And then I found the hut and her in front of it with a small fire, with a man and a boy I'd never seen, and they didn't see me but I saw them, hugging and giving kisses and eating bread and meat and fruit.

I ran forward. "Mum? I thought you were dead! Why didn't you—"

"Get out of here," she said.

I felt like she'd put a spear between my ribs. I stayed as still as stone.

She stood and pointed and yelled: "*Get out!*"

I woke up, clutching myself in a ball on my rough mat, biting down as hard as I could so I wouldn't wake up the Master or the kids.

Yin still hadn't returned.

2.

If Yin'd been gone for a day, maybe even two or three, we wouldn't've worried. We probably wouldn't even've noticed.

But a month?

Even the Master—and he was as calm as a bird on a hot breeze—even he was getting worried.

So he sent me to look for him.

Other than Yin, I was the oldest, so it was my responsibility. But I also *wanted* to go.

Master Jehu—he'd finally revealed his name to me and Yin, and he'd told us to be careful about revealing our names and letting people name us because names are words-of-power—had been teaching me new words-of-power.

It was time to see how well I'd mastered them.

3.

At dawn I left the compound, with Falcon scouting overhead.

Thanks to the Master I was beginning to learn Falconic (I could understand it, but I could barely speak a squawk of it), so Falcon could tell me if he caught any sign of Yin.

From the ground, I was sniffing for what Master Jehu called *heart-smoke*.

Angry people, miserable people, terrified people, even joyful people, left it everywhere they went. Only people who barely felt anything went through the world without leaving a trace.

Yin's trail was strong.

But Yin had been gone a long time, so there was no way for me to know how far he'd gone. That night I slept as a shadow while Falcon kept watch, and then he'd sleep on my shoulder for a while every morning (I rigged up a pad and straps with donkey leather so he wouldn't rip my shoulder to hell with his talons).

On the second day I found a village. All the houses had been torched. The animals were hacked apart. Burned, too.

So were the people.

It was so quiet I couldn't even hear the wind.

On the third day, even after all the horrors I'd seen in my young life, I saw something I'll never forget.

"Who *is* the Destroyer?" I finally asked myself after I finished puking.

That's what I found myself saying out loud whenever I felt like crying, but couldn't. You see enough depravity and you think, that's it: it can't get any worse.

And then you see.

Hills.

Of *hands*.

On the fifth day I found Yin.

It was in an old, old place. Wrecked homes with crumbled bricks. Stone buildings, all were caved in. Must've been a hundred or so in total.

But the most amazing thing was that the city wasn't abandoned. Thousands were living there. Thousands of dogs!

Thank gods they were peaceful, though. I pulled Fang out of my belt to keep ready, and Falcon on my shoulder was spreading out his wings to make himself look even bigger than he was.

But he kept hitting my head with his wings, which let me tell you were strong.

"Cut it out!" I told him. I didn't know how to say that in Falconic, but he got the point.

Finally I found the centre of town, and the crumbling platform.

In the City of Dogs, the leader of jackals should've been king. But he didn't seem like one. He was just a lonely kid crying by himself while thousands of dogs ignored him.

"Hey, Yin," I called.

He looked up, shocked. "Hru! How'd you find me?"

"Hey, c'mon," I smiled. "It's me."

He sniffed, looked like he had almost enough energy to consider smiling, then lost it.

"Have you been here the whole time?" I asked. "The Master's worried about you. You've been gone a month, you know."

He looked out into the distance.

"You got anything to eat around here?"

It took him a while to nod, like he'd forgotten how to understand. "Sure," he said. "Come on."

4.

Falcon and Yin's jackals looked happy, like they'd missed each other. My feathered pal shared shreds of the roasted rat I was eating. The jackals ate the heads and spines—snapped them down in two-three chomps.

"So, seriously, Yin, why didn't you come back?"

Finally: "I got sick of those little punks challenging me. Talking like, like I didn't really have a sorceress."

I nodded. Maybe I took too long.

"See?" He said. "Even you don't believe me."

"No, no, I do. Really. Look, c'mon, Yin, those kids are savages. You know that. They don't believe anything until they see it."

"Anyway," he said, turning away from me, "she's had me tracking things down for her for a couple of years now. I came out here to get her latest list."

This was all news to me. "And?"

He shook his head. "She, she . . . she wasn't here. I mean, she taught me some words-of-power so I could always signal her when I was coming here, which is where we always met up. But she never showed."

He looked like he was going to cry. I'd never seen him like this. I didn't even know how to comfort him.

Then one of his jackals farted and we both tried to ignore it. But the smell was so awful even Yin started laughing, and then I couldn't help myself.

We headed back to the Master's compound, and when it got dark we made camp. I was exhausted. Falcon stayed up to guard me, but Yin and his gang went to look for food.

I woke at the jackals growling and snapping, then leapt up seeing Yin ripping past me straddling a crocodile's neck.

119

Yin plunged Fang handle-deep into the croc's brains, and the monster kept thrashing and thrashing until its tail split a small tree in half.

Then it fell down, dead, with blood and brains leaking out of its skull.

Its dagger-teeth were just a finger away from my face.

"You must've been tired," panted Yin. "You weren't shadowed? And where's Falcon?"

I glanced around. Where was Falcon?

I looked down again, saw how Yin had blinded the beast before splitting its head. If he'd come back only a moment later—

I don't know what he saw in my face, but he looked embarrassed or maybe shocked.

Finally he said, "Just don't be dying on me, all right?"

5.

When we got back the next night, Master Jehu was thrilled.

We feasted—boar roasted with mangoes, carrots and apples, and crisp bread, which soaked up the fat just beautifully. I mean, just the bread and fat alone would've been amazing, but everything together? Even the jackals were part of the party, gnawing on boar bones. So everyone was happy.

I was angry.

Why'd Falcon left me defenseless like that? I mean, yeah, I was probably shadowed when he left, but still. He and I argued in Falconic for quite some time, which the little kids thought was hilarious.

Finally Falcon, maybe irritated at the laughter, went to perch inside the sleep area. Fine. Be like that, I squawked.

Over dinner, Yin and I told the kids about our adventure, but we left out the worst stuff. Yin did a pretty good job on the crocodile story, though.

The kids'd been working hard while we'd been away, so they spent the night dancing and singing. Master Jehu said he'd use just enough words to keep the compound silent from the outside.

I hadn't even known he could do that. It must've been taxing, because he looked strained the whole night. But he must've felt everyone really needed the celebration.

When the kids finally went to sleep, he looked doubly relieved, and I could finally hear crickets and cicadas again from beyond the wall.

The Master stopped Yin and me from going to bed, even though we were both exhausted.

"I wanted to speak with you boys about something important," he said.

"Yes, Master?" said Yin.

"It's time you both learned about the Destroyer."

That had us both.

6.

"Until thirteen years ago," he said, fire flickering gold in his black eyes, "the entire Blackland south of us was ruled by the wise and compassionate Lord Usir.

"He was from far, far south, further up the River Eternal than I've ever been. Here. This is a picture of him."

He handed us the incense burner he sometimes used when he prayed to the gods (to set the mood, Yin told me). Lord Usir was in profile, sitting on a throne, with a tall crown shaped like a gourd. He was holding a flail, the kind farmers used on grain.

He took it back from us, burned some incense in it that smelled like honey-smoke, and continued.

"Actually, he'd been away in that thirteenth year, bringing his Instructions to peoples in the outside, even across the seas, to spread knowledge to create prosperity, justice and peace. He taught that it's hard to have one if you don't have the others.

"While he was away, his wife, Lady Aset, ruled, and his brother, General Set, was her second-in-command. Except . . . Set was Lord Usir's brother. He resented being number three. In fact, he even resented being number two. Resentment . . . well, boys, you hold that long enough, it could break anyone. Even enough to wound the gods.

"So when Lord Usir returned from his mission, General Set set a trap for him. His own brother.

"The second night after Lord Usir returned, the General's job was to set up the feast to honour the Lord's labours for universal peace. There were delegations from all the towns up and down the River . . . presenting gifts, seeking blessings, performing music and acrobatics, everything.

"Naturally, Set kept the greatest gift for last, his own—a chest of perfect sleep, he called it. It was decorated in reliefs of pyrite and made of sweet-smelling cedar wood all the way from Rebarna across the Great Green Sea."

I took a breath from the incense like I could smell the chest of perfect sleep myself.

"So Set asked his brother to try the chest out, and his brother obliged him.

"It was the last mistake he ever made."

7.

"The chest was cursed," said the Master.

"Once Lord Usir laid down in it, he couldn't get out. Set's men slammed a lid on it, then brought out pots of molten pyrite and sealed him in it, and took out daggers and turned them on everyone there.

"It was chaos—guests and delegations running, dogs biting and running and howling, food tables getting knocked over, Set's men stabbing everyone until the sand was red."

The fire was dying, and the darkness was creeping in around us.

"Of course Lady Aset fought back with all her strength," said Master Jehu. "No one in the Blackland could wield double short-swords with more grace and speed. She dropped four of Set's soldiers who were hauling away the chest. Took them at the knees before they even knew what was happening.

"But the chest was sealed, and before she could pry it open with her swords, dozens of Set's men rushed her.

"She killed more of them, but it was no use, there were too many of them, so she had to flee and hide while her palace turned into orange fire and its smoke bled over the stars."

He looked up as if he could smell that smoke. But above, the stars were visible, singing silently to the moon.

"Set's men spent three days and nights seeking her with murderous knives and fingers cruel," he continued. "But they couldn't find her. They had to return empty-handed to collect Set's rage. He executed the platoon leaders for failing him.

"But Lady Aset couldn't track where the soldiers had taken her husband. She figured they'd gone north to the Savage Lands. She didn't know if they'd taken Lord Usir out of the chest as prisoner, of if they'd killed him.

"But one day she found one of his hands. It still had a ring on it she'd forged for him herself.

"And a week later she found one of his feet."

He shook his head, swallowed, chewed his lip.

"So she knew that her husband was dead," he said finally. "But back then she was very devoted to the gods, and she prayed and begged them to help her find all the dismembered pieces of her husband and put them back together . . . so that with their power, she could resurrect him, and together they'd overthrow the Destroyer and his forces and once again rule the Blackland in justice and in peace."

Yin and I looked at each other. We'd never heard of anything like this before. Making deals with gods? Bringing people back to life? Was this woman crazy?

Master Jehu leaned forward, looking at me sadly. It was tough to see his face because the fire had gone down to nothing but embers, and the moon was right behind his head like it was hiding there.

"My son," said the Master, "when you were a boy, before the night-raiders came for you, what did your mother's warriors call her?"

My heart stabbed me. I was afraid of where this was going.

"I, uh . . . I think it was . . . '*Inetch.*'"

"It's an old, old word. *Avenger*. You were so young, you probably never even wondered why. That's her war-name. She's the Lady Aset. Lord Usir was your father."

He turned to Yin.

"And you, my son . . . General Set is your father."

The Book of Now

1.

RAP, BLINKING. BLINKING CRUSTY DRY EYES INTO THE DAYLIGHT. HEARING them crunch.

Clock claimed 7:47 AM. Had to full-shoulder shove his thoughts to budge through the sludge between his ears.

Get. Out.

Of bed.

Closed his eyes, looking backwards in the darkness.

No dreams last night. Again.

8:03 AM.

Pushed back the covers. Trudged to the can. But his mother was in the shower, so he slogged to their patch-job PC in the living room.

An itch: click on the nest icon for the rooftop webcam, to check on the falcon chicks. But he'd deleted that icon . . .

Hadn't seen them in four weeks. Must be getting big. Maybe even flying? He'd never know.

Brought up iTunes. Hit *Random*. Checked his Facebook. Tried to decide . . . already unFriended all the Street Falcons except JC.

Decided: finally deleted all of JC's messages.

UnFriended him, too.

Took him a minute to realise iTunes had conjured up Leon Thomas to sing—and actually yodel—his song "Echoes":

> *There is a place*
> *Where love is king*
> *It's where echoes shine*
> *And reflections ring . . .*

Sure there was.

Still, the man could sing. Double-clicked up LimeWire, searched LEON THOMAS, found something called "Song for My Father" held by exactly one user uploading at about one bit per day. Clicked it. It'd be a while.

Had to get up—he was knocking his knees together to confuse his bladder off its DefCon alert. Searched for a Public Enemy/ULLA-dub-ULLAH mash-up he'd heard about. Five users. Click. Five other PE mash-ups. *Click-click-click-click-click.*

Clicked forward on iTunes and heard that Senegalese passion-ballad "Dée Moo Wóor," the one with superstar Youssou N'Dour singing back-up. Just didn't feel like an 8 AM song.

Turned off the music, but that song kept ringing like kora strings in a bottomless crystal cavern . . .

His mother emerged from the bathroom, body in a threadbare purple bathrobe and head toweled up white. Steam pouring out behind her like a cloud, and for just one second, Rap's brain rebuilt her into a butterfly woman bursting from a chrysalis.

"Tomorrow's the big day, huh?" she said.

He frowned, looked back at the screen.

"Raphael, I askid you a question."

"'Sno big deal."

"Firrust day of grade twelve *is* a big deal," she said, stepping towards him. "It's a chance at a farresh start."

Computer clock: flicked to 8:15 AM. Hovered his cursor over it. Monday, September 5.

"Same teachers. Same school. Same kids. Same sack of shirts."

"It's up to you! My godt, you wannit things to turn out the same as last year? And the year before that? And—"

"Mum, how come you never talk to me about my father?"

His mother, hands frozen half-way from yanking down her head-towel.

Then she finished yanking. Two clumps of hair stood up on either side of her forehead, like a cow's horns.

"Where's *this* coming from? And don't change the subject—"

Phone rang. His mother grabbed it, eyes still on him. No point in telling her, anyway: 8:15 AM, September 5, five users on his search, five other mash-ups: *Father-brother-son.*

His mother caught the number on the phone, her eyes ping-ponging while she toweled her hair with her free hand.

Rap clicked back to iTunes and went headphones to overwrite her telephone conversation, but even NWA wasn't loud enough to annihilate that laugh, that AutoTuned joy.

Finally saw her covering the phone with one hand. De-headphoned half-way.

"I *saidt*, have you gotten your school supplies yet?"

Shrugged.

"That's no, then." She went to her purse, pulled out five fives, handed them to him. "And no comics."

After she was out to her latest contract with Catholic Social Services or the Mennonite Centre for Newcomers or Edmonton Immigrant Services Association or whatever she was doing, Rap did something he hadn't done since his second Christmas out of the refugee camp and in E-Town.

Back in the day, kids at Sifton Elementary'd told him that at Christmas time, parents in Canada hid presents in closets or under their beds before wrapping them. He'd searched but hadn't found anything because there'd been nothing to find.

But on the morning of September 5, he was after something way more valuable than a PSP or every season of The *Boondocks* on DVD.

Ear on high gain just in case his mum came back for something. Quick scan underneath her bed and in her chests of drawers yielded a negative. Went straight to her closet and the dozens of boxes stacked there.

Fifty-five minutes of unstacking, sifting and searching, and there it was.

A small wooden box. Opened: two withered envelopes kissed with Sudanese stamps. He could read enough Arabic to make out his mother's surname, and his father's full name in the return address rectangle, but that was it.

Three photos he'd never seen before. A shot of his mum: a Somali Muslim woman in Dinka wedding clothing, beside a man who was obviously his father, at the centre of a Dinka wedding party in what was probably the city of Juba. She was the palest one there by far, and mum wasn't pale.

Next photo: his father, standing in front of a wall of waving, golden wheat.

His father.

No crackle of the familiar. Like looking at a history book. A famous stranger.

And yet that face, with skin and eyes that cloned his own, so dazzlingly dark his scleras were amber. A smile like a supernova: radiating love at whoever was standing behind the camera.

Third photo: mum lying down and laughing on a couch, his father stethoscoping his ear against her harvest-time belly and smiling like he was listening to his favourite song.

His eyes.

His nose.

His smile.

His *future*.

Why hadn't she ever shown these to him?

2.

9:35 AM and it was already hot. Radio said it was a record Labour Day. Was gonna hit thirty-five. But biking made it cooler.

Helmetless, on his scrappy third-hand ten-speed, Rap zipped underneath 127th Street's ceiling of leaves, and smiled, imagining himself in goggles and a trench coat with the wind whipping his jacket out behind him like a cape.

Then he'd've been Static, riding his electromagnetically-levitating garbage can lid like a 'hood Silver Surfer on his Galactus-brand board. Making any problems disappear by finger-pointing ten-thousand volts at them.

But that wasn't true even for Static. Course, Static had a team, the Heroes. Rap hadn't seen any of the Street Falcons in weeks. And Static had Frieda, his sorta/maybe-not girlfriend. Rap didn't even have a girl *friend*.

107th Ave, Kush's southern border, quiet on a holiday Monday morning, and plenty of stores closed for the long weekend. Maybe most grade twelve kids really were out buying school supplies and new clothes, but with twenty-five bones, all he was gonna get was—

WHY DID THE DESTROYER
KILL MY FATHER?

—hit the brakes so quickly he damn-near crashed into a too-skinny, too-young prostitute hike-skirting across the street. Apologised, backed up, checked it out again.

Posted on a rectangular green street-lamp marked *NO POSTING ALLOWED*.

Glossy sticker, gold printing on black. No pictures. No copyright line. No url.

But no question who created these. That was the fifth question from the Revolution Scroll.

Glanced up. Damn.

105th Street.

No such thing as magic or miracles, the old man'd told him. Just the universe giving you endless chances to reflect and learn something through your Daily Alchemy. Up to you whether you actually did.

Whatever. Give him shit for telling the truth about a bunch of punks, but then let these other kids break the law putting stickers up on decorative poles?

Still.

Hadn't asked his mother anything about his father since . . . actually, had he *ever*?

Growing up in refugee camps in Kenya, and then Ethiopia, and then Chad, and finally in basement apartments here . . . to his mother, today only mattered for how it affected tomorrow. So better forget every yesterday they'd ever had.

All he knew was that his father had died in a car accident in Khartoum on the way to teach university, and then the country had gone to hell and his mum'd been running ever since.

Who was his dad? What was he like? If he'd lived, what kind of relationship would they've had? Would he've spent more time with him than his mum did? What would he think of his art? Would he've been proud of him? Would he've—

On 107th Ave, two Somali kids probably headed for grade ten slowed down and stopped to look at him.

"Oh, shit!" said the taller boy. "You're—you're—"

"You're famous!" said the other one.

Weirdos.

Shoulders and neck burning, stood up on his pedals and rolled along without looking back.

More stickers yelling at him from lamp-posts, bus-stops and building-sides, and he read them all:

WHY COULD I NOT RECOGNISE
MY OWN BROTHER IN THE SAVAGE LANDS?

HOW DID THE DESTROYER DEAL WITH ME
BEFORE I WAS READY TO FACE HIM?

WHY DID I AND MY MASTER'S CHILDREN
RAISE A GOLDEN FORTRESS?

DO NOT DROWN IN THE SWAMPS OF DEATH,
BUT DRINK FROM THE RIVER OF LIFE

Two Sudanese kids pimp-limping by in bandanas, maybe even the same Lil Wayne and Lil Bow Wow he'd seen weeks before, slowed down to whisper to each other while chin-nodding at him.

One squeaked something at him in Nuer (he knew it was Nuer, even if he didn't know what it meant). The other kid tried Dinka in which Rap was equally useless. Both kids jabbered excitedly.

What the hell was going on? Checked his fly. Nope. Didn't look like they wanted to fight, either. And they weren't *laughing* . . .

Whatever. Weird shit was in the air.

Would've be so simple to head east to 111th Ave and 96th Street and check out what everyone was doing, maybe even—

Stood on his pedals, eyes west, and pumped to 124th Street with Lil and Lil squeaking behind him.

3.

Down in the basement comic store on 122nd Street and Jasper.

Rap saw it, stopped to gawk. His heart blasting an old-school 88-beat.

A glossy bookcaser screaming *Buy Me.*

A *Static Shock* collected edition.

Wiping handlebar sweat on his pants, he reached up, cradled it, flipped pages without even breathing, glancing secrets he'd only been able to infer from the out-of-sequence issues he'd spent years collecting.

The book was twenty-three bones and then some.

When he and his mum arrived in E-Town he was twelve. They shared the basement of a house on the north side with another refugee family, and he went to school at Sifton where the only teacher he'd ever liked, the principal, Mr. Jack, used to dole out hugs to his school full of refugees, immigrants and misfits like a nurse dispensing vaccines in the UNRWA camps.

After the first time, the man never tried hugging him again. His smile shook—like Rap'd stabbed a needle in his arm. Real pain. Not something else. But every day after that, Mr. Jack always gave Rap a manly handshake and a smile that Rap finally decided he could trust, when he no longer felt the need to put a knife into the man's neck.

Back then his mum still wore *hijab*. Mr. Jack, an honest-to-god White man, used to kid around with her and the other *hijabun*, threatening to hug them, too.

These were women who expected White people to fear them, or ignore them, or condemn them. And here was a White man offering them hugs? In front of their children? Was this *mzungu* crazy? Didn't he know they could all strap on dynamite or something?

But those women thought Mr. Jack was a hero. And finally so did Rap. Especially after the man gave him two wrinkly, water-damaged *Static* comics he'd found in some desk, probably assuming little Raphael Deng Garang'd be thrilled to see a superhero kid who shared some of his skin colour. And fact was, Mr. Jack'd been right as rice in a bowl.

Rap'd heard of superheroes, but he'd never had his own comics before. Couldn't even read English. But Mr. Jack taught him how through those two comics. He could still remember the first English sentence his mind could decode from text, a line from Static: "Sorry I kept you on hold for so long."

And when his mother got them a basement apartment all to themselves at Al Hambra, they fled the north side like Muhammad skipping Mecca.

So Rap never got the chance to say goodbye to Mr. Jack, the only White man he'd ever trusted, and even actually *liked*. Lost him like he'd lost everything else in every other midnight flight and terrifying river-crossing of his life.

After that, teachers were . . . they were all like the ass-wad he had the next year in grade seven. Mr. Manna didn't know he understood English, and with him sitting right there in front of him, Manna'd told another teacher that Rap was "dumb as a sack of hammers."

Rap didn't speak because he didn't want to. And that was true now, too.

"Rap!"

He glanced up from the bins he was scrounging through.

"Shit, dude! Where you been?"

4.

The black pine-cone mini-locks, longer now.

"Hey, JC." Kept scrounging.

"Oh, man, you are *not* gonna cold me like that," said JC, standing next to him. "You don't answer my emails, my Facebooks, my phone calls for like half the summer, and when I find you, you act like you saw me two minutes ago?"

"Well . . . I've been busy."

"Really?" said JC, still standing. "Doing what, exactly?"

"Stuff. Aiight?"

"Lemme get this straight. *You* get *me* involved in some crazy shit with some *cappa-worstas* that could've blown up like a brawl, but you're treating *me* like I somehow messed *you* up? Please tell me you are not doing me like a bitch."

Rap's neck burned. "Yeah, and you got a job out of it!"

"Oh, you are not using that against me!"

JC, the kid who was always smiling, joking, head-bopping or otherwise talking it smooth-n-easy, knelt beside him in front of the bottom rows of comics and actually snarled.

"Brother Moon was ready to offer you that exact job, Rap. But you seriously coulda cost him, and you know it!" He jabbed a finger at Rap's face. Rap leaned back, fighting the urge to snap that finger off.

"Don't be mad at *him* cuzza some shit *you* pulled," said JC. "Least ways own up to it. Don't be going all bitchified at the man cuz he doesn't want everything we're working for getting smashed up fore we barely even started. Cuz that's some bullshit right there."

The hipster store attendant walked over. "There a problem here, JC?" said the White dude, his soul patch bobbing on his chin with every word.

"Naw, naw, Dave," said JC, smoothing and soothing with a smile. "Just trying to get my knucklehead friend to stop being such a knucklehead."

Dave looked at Rap for a second as if he recognised him, but didn't know from what. Then he shrugged and went back to the till.

JC dropped his whisper further, sandpaper on stone.

"Dude, I let you be for a while, cuz I figured you needed your space. But seriously, you can't be leaving me hanging like that. We boys. My Nubian. My best friend, man. Aint sposta be just cold desertin your number-one like that!"

Hit him like a fist in the ear: best friend.

Barely ever had a friend. And now, guy just drops the b.f. bomb on him? What do you say to that?

And worse, he knew he'd punked out on him.

"Let's get outta here," said Rap. He pulled out his five fives, paid for the Static book *Rebirth of the Cool*, and they hit the street baking in the strangely hot September.

5.

Biking to Rap's place in silence, the words "best friend" flapping behind them the whole way, like torn newspaper stuck in his spokes.

Had no clue what to do with a house guest. Never'd had one before. Well, not exactly. There had been one, the same and only one, off and on for two years when his mother wasn't home, which was most of the time. But that was totally different.

And now here was this guy, who by virtue of being his only friend was in fact automatically his best friend. Who was mad at him. And now for a *second* legit reason.

Wasn't until they were in Rap's room that JC stopped mad-moping, cuz in desperation Rap finally cracked open what he'd never shown anybody before.

"Da-a-a-a-yum, bwoi!" JC kept saying, flipping through Rap's art pads bursting with inked drawings of Adam Warlock, Nightcrawler, Cyborg, Hawk Man, Morpheus, Blade, Marvel's Falcon, Lupe Fiasco, Fela Kuti, Baaba Maal, the original five members of NWA, and Static riding his electro-hovering garbage can lid.

"Oh, man, this shit's the bomb! Damn, bwoi! Damn!" JC pointed at a lanky caped man with a big C on his tunic. "Zat who I think it is?"

"'Super Chappelle.'"

"What's his powers?"

"Makes you laugh till you puke."

"Snuh-*app!*"

JC grabbed Rap's newest drawing pad off the shelf: almost thirty fully-inked images straight outta *The Book of the Golden Falcon*: Hru and the children swallowed by the Devourer, Hru and Yinepu meeting Master Jehu at night, Yinepu and the Sorceress, Hru fighting Set . . . .

"Man, you got so many ink-styles! Like all these ones in the Swamps, and with the Devourer. The line work's so spooky!"

"Yeah . . . that's wood-cut style. I was really influenced by John Totleben on those. And Wrightson."

"They did, like, *Swamp Thing*, right?"

"Exactly."

"But over here," he said, flipping carefully to high contrast picture, "Hru fighting Set, that's more like Mignola."

"Definitely. Or Michael Golden."

"You old school f'real, dude!"

"Well, 'snot like I'm doing Kirby or Ditko."

"True dat, true dat. Yo!" He jabbed at the full-colour pages of the Sorceress, Master Jehu and Lord Usir at the end of the book. The pages were warped from water colour. "'Slike Mshindo . . . or Alex Ross, bruh!"

Rap could feel his own smile poking into his ears. Mshindo was a brilliant comic painter, but Ross did interiors, too. There was no higher compliment for a would-be comic artist than being compared to Ross. Like being a young martial artist and getting sized to Bruce Lee.

"How you learn to do shit on this level?"

He thought about it. "I always loved to draw. Even in the refugee camp in Kenya—there was this aid worker from Nairobi who used to give me paper and pencils after she saw me drawing in the dirt with a stick. When I got here, I started reading comics and just copied artists I liked. Then I got books outta the library."

"And this one," said JC, flipping through another book he'd grabbed off the shelf, *How to Draw Comics the Marvel Way.* "Yo, who's WW?"

Shocked, Rap glanced over JC's shoulder. He'd forgotten about the inscription. Below the weird, shitty, pen scribble of a muscle-man in a tank top were the words

Rap never forget
your powers littel dude

WW

He blinked hard several times.

Powers?

"Just some guy."

"Can't believe you held out on me!" said JC, putting back the drawing pad. "How come you never showed me these? You could be working for Marvel or DC right now!"

Rap laughed. "Naw, naw, c'mon."

"Fuh real! Hey, where's your comics, anyway?"

Rap glanced around, eared the hallway, even though he knew his mother wasn't there. Knelt. Flipped up the blankets at the foot of the bed, tugged down and slipped away the cloth that covered the box-spring.

JC goggled: half as tall as the box-spring and hidden inside was a reinforced box, wide as the bed, topped by springs so even if you sat on the bed you wouldn't feel it there.

"How the hell you build that?"

"Grade 8 Industrial Arts."

"You built that just to hide your comics?"

Shoulders and neck chafing, Rap blanked on his way to a lie. Never'd had anybody to explain the box to anybody before.

Pulled out three columns of comics in mylar bags with acid-free cardboard backings. Handed JC his treasure trove, eager to see JC cackle and snap over them.

But all JC cared about was answers.

"Why, Rap?"

"Aw, my mum threw out my comics once," he said, skin burning. "Byrne X-Men, Starlin *Warlocks* . . . probably worth three hundred bucks' worth! She just trashed em!"

"Dude, how the hell'd you afford three hundred bucks worth of comics when you were in grade eight?"

Rap froze.

Stupid—

"JC, can you translate something for me?" Flailing. Probably even more stupid than taking him to his room. But if you fire your gun once, might's well empty your clip . . . .

"Translate what?"

"Something from my mum."

"*You* speak Somali."

"Yeah," said Rap, pulling out the last contents of this stash-box. The letters he'd stolen from his mother closet that morning. "But it's written in Arabic."

"Whoah, you serious?" JC barely glanced at the first lines of the first letter he opened. "You wanna be reading your dad's love letters to your mom? Dude, you even sure they're from your dad?"

Rap's head creased down the middle. *Love* letters? And maybe *not* from his dad? Forced himself. "Yeah."

"O-*ka*-ay," sing-sang JC. Like he was about to jackhammer open a case of dynamite.

Felt like one of those dreams where you were at school naked. Having his friend invade his mother's privacy, invading the privacy of his phantom father, even invading his own privacy by letting JC know things about him seconds before JC could translate the black squiggles on crinkly blue paper into English. Assuming he'd even tell him the truth—

Naw. This was JC.

His best friend.

And since he had no other way to do this archeology on the ruins of his own family, he pressed ahead.

"'My *hilwa*'—that means, like, sweety, honey-pie, cutey, 'You're the woman . . . I dream of . . . every night.'"

Rap glanced over JC's hands, making sure he wasn't greasing the letters with cheeseburger grease or whatever. But he was holding the letters like a *Qur'an*.

"I sometimes think of you . . . when I'm teaching class . . . and supposed to be concentrating on these students. But . . . I miss you all the time . . .'"

Went on that way for a page. Rap, reeling: his mother as a young woman, maybe only twenty, before he was even born. His father at the University of Khartoum. Already a professor?

Second page: "'I worry . . . that while you're away . . . visiting your family in Somalia . . . you'll tell them about me . . . like I kept daring you to . . . and they'll disown you . . . or keep you from me, the infidel, forever . . .'"

Hardly even heard the rest of the page.

Why didn't she ever tell me any of this?

Pages turning, crackling, dragging him back.

"'I always loved it when you . . . sent me letters . . . and put a candy inside . . . and wrote, 'Kiss the envelope before you open it.' And when I ate the candy, I thought of you . . . and of kissing you. And . . . missing you. I will love you forever . . . I can't wait . . . until we are married. Your . . . husband to be . . . *Jini*.'"

JC grinned at him. "Damn, boy, your pops was smooth like Usher on Pennzoil!"

Rap laughed—

Front door thunked opened, body-checking his heart and brain.

Became a tornado, grabbing the letters and the stacks of comics and sliding them into his bed-box and replacing the box-spring cover and the blankets and then tucking art pads behind the books on the built-in wall-shelf above his bed—

"Dude, what's the deal? Zat your moms?"

Lying on the floor, *Static Shock: Rebirth of the Cool*—

Shoved it between mattress and box-spring, hauling JC into the living room—

Stopped dead.

His back burning, stomach and colon and nutsack twisting at the sight.

Wished they'd stayed in his room or sneaked out the basement window and headed to the 7-11 or the courtyard or anywhere but right there, where his mother was leaning against the wall with Dr. Liberia pushing up against her.

6.

Her eyes blaring horror at the sight of the boys, she shoved herself and the good doctor off the wall.

Dr. Liberia glanced over-shoulder, pretending he was straightening a picture with one hand and not fooling anyone that he was straightening something else.

Turned back around, adjusted his wire-frames, patted the greying kinks in his thinning hair.

His mother throat-cleared. "Raphael, you're home!" She straightened her hair and blouse, failing at faking innocence. "And you, you haff a, a *friendt* here?" Saying it like, "When did you grow all those extra arms?"

Rap, the only sound he was emitting: teeth grinding so loudly it sounded like he was chewing ice. JC's eyes went wide in his peripheral. He could practically hear him saying, "*Dude* . . ."

Then JC waved and said, "My name's JC, ma'am."

Rap, thinking, Did he just *say ma'am*?

"Hi, boys," said the doctor.

Rap's mother flustered on.

"We, we didn't, I didn't expeccit you home. Either of you! Well, I jussit met you, so of corrus I didn't expeccit you! Nice to meet you. JC. How, how do you know Raphael?"

"We were in the same English class, plus we both go to—"

Rap: "—to the same mall right across the street from school."

JC geared into reverse, floored it.

Rap's mum: "So . . . what do you two have plannedt?"

Rap: "Hang out for the rest of the day. Right here. Too hot to go anywhere. Basement's nice an cool."

"Yeah," said JC. "Juss chill, kick it."

"Both chilling *and* kicking?" said the doctor. "Sounds demanding."

Rap calculated the comment's contempt at a 4 on the 10-scale. He'd heard way worse from the old freak. Still felt it like a steel-toe kick in the tail bone.

"Don't you boys," said the man behind the wire-rims, "feel like seeing a movie or something?"

Rap, ice-crunching. JC looked at him.

"Uh, if you're short," said the doctor, reaching for his back pocket, "I could cover you."

Rap's mum cleared her throat again. The doctor's eyes rolled ceiling-ward for less than a second, but Rap caught it.

"Or, y'know . . . just," he said, pulling a ten out of his wallet. "It's on me is what I'm saying."

"It's twelve bucks just for one," said Rap. If there wasn't any more ice between his teeth, it was all in his voice.

"Raphael . . . ."

"When I first came to Canada, movies were only five dollars for adults," said the professor, emitting a twenty. "Here. Get yourself some popcorn. Or drinks. Or whatever."

When Rap didn't budge, JC took the five and the twenty from the wire-rims. "Thanks!"

Rap glared at JC and the Liberian professor, and then the two youth backed out. Like two ants escaping the anteater who'd just smashed inside their hill, leaving their queen to die.

Shoved their shoes on, down the hall, and then the man's yell muffled by the door: "You're *wel*come, Raphael!"

"Dude!"

JC, puffing and struggling to keep up, while Rap biked top-speed through leaf-shadows and sunlight on the side-road of 117th Avenue.

"You, you never told me your moms was like a total—"

Over-shoulder, Rap laid both eyes on him like the hands of UFC champion.

JC slowed down, gave himself an extra couple of metres between the two of them, apparently understanding that if the word "MILF" passed his lips, Rap'd sidekick him right off his bike.

"—a total, y'know, beautiful, like . . . fox or whatever. Respect, bruh!"

Rap sped up, banking south down to 116th avenue. JC stood on his pedals by the time he caught up, panting.

"—like Iman! I swear—even sounds like her, same kinda throaty voice—"

"Would you drop it?" Rap didn't need anybody telling him this shit. He'd heard it a million times before. Sometimes he even saw it himself.

"Sorry! So, what movie you wanna see? Hear *Black Panther 3*'s great—"

"We're not seeing any movies! And gimme that money!"

They pulled over. JC handed over the green Queen, but told Rap to wait for the blue Laurier. He whipped out a pen, scribbling a black bowl-cut and pointy ears on the dead prime minister.

He jiggled the bill at the corners. "'Fascinating, Captain! Two to beam up!'"

Rap laughed before he could stop himself. JC had powers.

"So, what's your mom's boyfriend's name, anyway?"

He let it go. "Doctor Needle. Jacob Needle. He's this geology professor. Teaches at the U of A."

"Decent dude to give us movie-money—"

"*Don't you get it?*"

JC's eyes narrowed, then went wide.

"Oh, snap, bruh. I didn't—man, and in the middle of the day, too! Oh, shi-i-i-i-t."

"Yeah."

"Yo, how often he up in there?"

Rap cranked up his eye-lasers to *Obliterate*.

"Naw, man, I mean, like at your place! All I mean is, you obviously hate the dude. I'm just . . . like, I feel you, knawm sayn? To have some seriously wrong old Skele-tor-looking freak in your house, an he's got a hold on your mom? That's, like . . . *hellacious*. That's Swamps of Death shit right there."

A minivan drove around them. Hanging out the windows, two little kids eating Revells, ice cream melting down their arms.

Rap looked at JC like he was seeing him for the first time.

Rap: "Did you smell him?"

"Huh?"

"*Booze!*"

"Oh! Thought that was bad cologne."

"Yeah. 'Old Lice.' Last year he drove us home during a snow storm from some university thing. Guy was tanked. Swerving the whole time. Thought he was gonna kill us."

"Damn, dude. Why didn't you moms, you know, tell im to, like—"

Rap hit ARM on his lasers, and JC shut his mouth.

"When she's out at night doing South Sudanese community work or her contracts or whatever, he calls, doesn't matter how late, always drunk, rambling on about whatever, yelling at *me*, saying, 'Where is she! Where is she!'"

Swallowed. Took three tries to clear his throat.

"Called her a whore once."

Looked up.

"If I . . . if I had the chance . . ."

"Damn, Rap. Fuh real."

7.

A block west of the Hyper-Market, Rap refused to give his front tire one more revolution.

"'So whatcha gon do?'" said JC, with as much bass as he could. To Rap, he sounded like the retarded brother from *The Green Mile*.

"What?"

"'So whatcha gon do?'"

"What, is that *from* something?"

"I downloaded this concert movie with Richard Pryor, right? 'So whatcha gon do?' That's what Jim Brown kept saying to Richard Pryor after he burnt himself free-basing and Rich was still messed up and wannid to keep on doing coke—"

Rap could tell JC was X-raying him.

"Yo, Richard Pryor was like this comedian, right, and Jim Brown was this football player—"

"I know who they are!"

But he didn't, and he didn't know what free-basing was, either (he heard it as free *basin*, and tried to figure out how a bowl could cause burns). But he definitely wasn't gonna ask now.

"Aiight, no worries, no worries. But still, I'm sayin, 'So whatcha gon do?'"

"About what!"

"About Brother Moon! About the Alchemy and the Street Falcons!"

JC looked up and down 111th Avenue and the sleepy holiday midday traffic. Looked back at Rap with nothing sleepy in his eyes.

"Damn, Rap, you got some Destroyer-type shit going on inside your own home, this whole last month you just ran and dove into the Swamps like they were a hot tub and y'won't even yell for help—hell, I tried throwing you a golden chain I-don'know-how-many-times, an insteada grabbin on you just let it sink in the sludge!

"And here's Brother Moon givin you a place to hang out, he's teachin you martial arts, teachin you history, the Scrolls, th'Alchemy, and you, you're shittin all over him, like, like, like . . . like a little *bitch*." Nodding, biting his lip, eyebrows way the hell up. "Aiight? I said it. Just because he got mad at you for some shit you did which almost messed up everything he was tryin to build—"

"You were there too, JC! By choice! Nobody put a knife to your nuts!"

"Yeah, you right! An I told im I was sorry! An I was!"

Rap marveled at the situation. Here was JC burning him down. And yet . . . he didn't feel any fire.

Maybe it was because of what he saw in JC's eyes.

Still. "He doesn't care about me."

"Bullshit!"

"He ever even ask about me?"

"Yes! *Constantly!*"

Rap looked back down 111th at the boarded-up Wendy's, like maybe he could hide inside it.

"Can't stay shadowed forever, dude!"

Rap looked him full on, and JC ripped him.

"You got so little forgiveness in your heart, man, you won't even talk to this brother?" JC blinked repeatedly then turned a second and palmed his eyes.

Turned back, eyes red and still blinking.

"You really that Lead-headed?"

"Don't be calling me a Leadite—"

"Then why you always drowning yourself in the Swamps?"

"What the hell're you talking about? I don'even drink!"

"Dude, Swamps aint just drugs an shit! Yeah, for *some* dudes. For another it's too much porn, or another dude it's being a super-ho. But for you? No disrespect, I'm sure you got your history and all, but you're one angry, grudge-holding mother-fucker. You grip a grudge like a anchor grippin mud! And there you are, drownin at the bottom of the Swamps an you just won'let go! Kickin with your last breath anybody who cares enough to swim down and try and drag you up!"

JC raised a finger at him, nearly wagged it. Like an angry elementary school teacher. Bared his teeth.

"Time to replace-and-elevate. Drain your Swamps. Before they drain you."

Before Rap could drop a word, JC biked the block to the Hyper-Market without looking back.

Rap watched JC hop off, lock up, disappear inside.

Finally Rap turned around and biked away.

His tires took him everywhere and nowhere.

Finally, when September's sun descended to bathe the city in indigo, Rap rolled up along 118th Avenue. At the Camel Boys Café he laid his Spock-bill on the counter and bought three ground beef sambusas and a cream soda.

A couple of Somali guys, probably a couple of years older than he was, started glancing and then staring at him, turning back and whispering to each other and smiling and glancing back again.

He took off.

On 107th Ave near the All Nations Centre, Rap slowed down at the sight of a fire hydrant shooting water into the street. A couple of city workers crouched around it doing something that didn't look like much of anything.

Instead of plowing through their super-puddle, Rap hopped up onto the sidewalk across the street, watching the churning lagoon vibrate streetlights into snapping electric arcs.

Night time and shooting water.

Before he and his mum'd moved to Al Hambra, the three-storey walk-up on 118th Avenue (to get away from all those trouble-making Somalis, she said), they'd lived in that north side basement suite. He hadn't known the expression "latch-key kid" back then, but that's what he'd been.

One cool September Saturday evening, out of curiosity, he'd twisted and twisted the hot water tap to see how far it would go, only to be cannoned by scalding water shooting straight up from the dislodged tap.

Within seconds the water was swelling around his feet.

His mum was out working and after five minutes of banging on the door to the upstairs renters he realised they weren't home and so he'd slopped high-speed down the street in his soaking long johns looking for any adult who could help him. A man he found raced back with him to the suite and turned off the hot water valve and left without any English words passing between them except his own "Thank you! Thank you! Thank you—"

The city workers turned off the water.

Hunched over his handlebars, Rap stared into the draining pond . . .

Water, water
Nuff to drown a son or daughter
Wash away a certain slaughter?
It oughta . . . it oughta . . .

8.

Midnight. Basement suite was dark.

Nearly jumped when he saw her there in the shadows.

Streetlight struck her puffy eyes.

"Where'ff you been?" she snapped. Her ever-throaty voice was scratchy. Even squeaky.

"I—" She was *never* home before he was. He didn't have any lies ready. "I was just—"

"Your little Somali friend Jamal called. We hatt a goot long talk about this, this, this *caalt* you've joined!"

God. JC again. And *Somali.*

"It's not a cult, all right? Jeez! Since when do you care what I do?"

"Whatt? How can you say that? Of corrus I care!"

"You didn't even know JC was my friend! I was hanging out with him practically the whole summer! Didn't you ever wonder what I was doing all day? Where I was going?"

"You're a youngk man! I'm your maather . . . I didn't wannit to . . . to smaather you!"

"Yeah. Yeah. Smother. That's funny."

"Don'tt you use that tone with me!"

The phone rang. His mother didn't move.

"What's wrong?" said Rap. "Not gonna answer it? It's only midnight."

"What's thatt suppossit to mean?"

"Had another fight? What'd he do this time?"

"Don'tt you talk to me like thatt! I'm not one of those White suburb yuppies raising some snotty little brat! You answer me!"

"You wanna know? You really wanna know?"

"Yes!"

Ring. Ring.

Silence.

"When you're out doing your work, your volunteering, being everywhere in the world but here, Doctor Liberia spends—"

"Don't call him that."

"—*Doctor Liberia* spends all night calling here! Drunk like some old bum in the streets, yelling—*yelling at me.* 'Where is she?' Like I know!"

Ring. Ring—

"It's why I can't even stay awake some times in class. An you don'even wanna know what kinda names he calls you!"

Ring. Ring. Ring.

Ring. Ring.

Ring.

Silence.

Streetlight in her eyes, glistening down her cheeks.

Good. Good! Not just me who has to feel it!

"All these times, you out there with him, bringing him here—the guy's married! Married, mum! How can you do that to yourself? An him taking us to his goddamned Faculty Club party and showing you off like meat and me some kinda thing he's got no choice to bring along, like goddamned Curious George, an half those people you're shaking hands with prolly know his wife *and* his kids! How you think that makes me feel, huh? Knowing what they think about you? Knowing what these Somalis everywhere in the community think about you?"

The gates had busted clean off the hinges, and now seventeen years' worth was rushing out in a torrent.

"'You little shit!' That's what he calls me every time he calls and I hafta tell him you're not here! 'Quit lying to me! Where is she? Who's she fucking? You're eating food I paid for, you little little shit! I'm the one paying half her goddamn rent, so you better tell me—'"

"No, no, Raphael, he wouldn'tt—please, tell me he doesn'tt . . . I didn'tt . . . I didn'tt know—"

"Oh, so it's okay he talks to you like that, just not to me? *You really think that?*"

"Raphy, Raphy!" Hunched over, face in her hands and looking up at him, eyes begging. "Why didn't you tell me? If I'd known, I wouldn't've—Raphy, I won't let him—"

"Oh, you knew, Mum, you knew, don't tell me—"

"—no, I didn'tt, I didn'tt—"

"—now you just can't *pretend* you didn't know!"

"*I didn'tt!*" she screamed and stood, grabbing him by the shoulders and then crush-hugging him to her chest.

The wall banged three times, rapid-fire. "Shutt up!" she yelled at it.

"Oh, so now that you know, you're sorry?" said Rap. "You're gonna pro*tect* me? Is that it? Like you've always protected me? That's hilarious!"

She pushed him back but kept his shoulders in her claws and yelled.

"How can you say thatt? I've always proteckited you! I crossid two caantries on foott proteckiting you! I crossid rivers with crocodiles proteckiting you—"

Ring. Ring. Ring—

"Mum, I swear to god—!" He stepped back from her. "There were times . . ."

He'd said it so low she craned her head forward and squinted.

"There were times when that old bastard called that I just pushed him, pushed him, just *hoping* he'd try something. Figured if he came over when you were out, tried to break in . . . I'd be justified. Even the police couldn'say anything. If he woulda just come over . . ."

—his mother's mouth, a dead gasp in it, and her eyes black moons in white skies, and he thought: At last.

"I'da slit that motherfucker's throat."

Her mouth, unhinged.

Silent sobs.

She sat. Actually *sank* into that couch. On the couch's arms, the dangling edges of the couch's throw-cloth. Shaking with her shuddering.

Priceless. She'd never cried about *him*. Only after one of her fights with Doctor Liberia, the married asshole who treated her like shit.

Shit was what was left when you took something beautiful and delicious and full of life and chewed it up and dumped it in acid and squeezed the hell out of it until it was nothing but a mess.

A school night. First night before the first day of grade twelve.

She reached out to him and he bolted out the door.

Heard her running after him, bare feet slapping grubby carpet on stairs and the concrete outside, and him scrambling to unlock his bike with her grabbing and tearing at him and him shoving her away with one arm—

Jumped on his pedals and her grabbing him again, screaming to come back home that instant, but him wrenching himself away and wobbling forward as fast as he could—over a rock or maybe a branch or maybe her foot?—and hearing her slap-slapping barefoot down 118th Avenue behind him—

Clearing the 7-11 parking lot, speeding away beneath gaunt white streetlights gazing down from halos of moths and flies.

Her sobbing and screaming echoing down the silent darkness of 118th Avenue: a man's name, again and again . . .

Six
Mother-Sister-Daughter

The Book of Then

1.

I sat alone near the embers after Master Jehu told me the truth about my martyred father, my sword-wielding mother, my betraying, murdering uncle, and his son, my cousin, Yinepu.

Me, the embers, the moon and the stars.

I couldn't talk. I wouldn't.

So they finally went to sleep and left me by myself.

He'd kept all this from me. For years.

And Yin, to think, to think that his own *father*—

Not even Falcon was there. With all his disappearances of late, who knew where he'd gone to, or when he'd return . . . if ever?

I couldn't count on anyone.

While the compound slept in the dark silence, I walked out with a water-skin slung over my shoulder.

I refused to go shadowed. Instead I raked the night with my eyes, plucked Fang from my belt, silently daring anything or anyone to come for me. My hands were too dry. They ached. They were agony. I knew I had to anoint them with a balm of blood.

2.

I walked a day.

I saw a family of black hares. Fang was in my hand. They flattened their ears when I stepped on a fallen palm frond. I took another step and they merged with the shadows of the jungle.

I saw an ibex before it saw me, but its nose twitched at my stink and leapt away.

Finally I saw the lioness whose intended ibex dinner I'd just sent running.

She chose me as substitute.

Her blood was steaming. I'd never had a hot bath before.

Fang's white glow shimmered pink.

That night I found the tallest tree I'd ever seen in the Savage Lands, as tall as the white, straight-sided mountains I'd seen in the vision that Yinepu's master had shown us on the night Yin and I had nearly killed each other.

I climbed it, found a resting space to perch. I closed my eyes, whispered words-of-power someone once had taught me, and while watching the crescent moon lift like an ibis on a hot, dry updraft, I found myself softly singing: *hroo-hroo . . . hroo-hroo . . .*

3.

I awoke to the brilliant gold of sun. The whole disc, bright like forever, perched on the horizon.

I clamped shut my eyes, shielded them with my hand.

Where there should have been fingers, there were feathers.

I stretched out what should have been my arm, but was my wing, and knocked myself off my branch, hitting others on the way down, spreading both wings to slow myself before I slammed into dirt and rocks below.

I landed, looked down.

Talons on long, curving toes.

I moved my tongue around—I had no teeth. Just a beak.

How?

Walking was awkward—the balance of it. I wobbled and fell, got up, managed a few more steps.

I tried flying, but couldn't figure out how.

I spent the rest of the day trying.

That night, my wings finally knew what to do.

I slid silently among the stars.

I bathed again, but this time inside the mind of a cloud.

When the sun again gave birth to itself and all the sky flared to life, I felt the pull, like a thirsty tongue tastes mist.

Below me was the City of Dogs.

I glided down, felt the wind's hot and rough caress, slowed and wrapped my talons round the shoulder of a fallen statue.

The dogs caroused at will, but left alone the central square of abandoned stone structures.

On a granite platform there was a black stool glistening like water beneath starlight. Someone was sitting on it, hidden behind vines like a tent-curtain.

In a wing-beat I knew it must be Yinepu's Sorceress.

She called to me—not in human words, but in Falconic:
Come to me.

My wings took me before I could even form the idea to refuse, and I perched upon her arm.

My little bird . . . she said sadly, stroking my head feathers . . . *don't you know who I am?*

And instantly I knew who she was, and I became a boy again, and fell to the ground.

"*Mum?*"

4.

"You don't look like I remember," I said.

Her hair: it was eight thick braids plastered with mud. She'd decorated the skin around her eyes with black strokes and curves—stains of berry juice?

So many years.

So disturbing.

"*You* do," she said, her voice buckling from what seemed like pride and fear at the same time. "And yet, you're so grown up. You . . . you look like your father did . . . when he was your age. So handsome!" She breathed in sharply. "You're a man now."

I didn't want to hear her shit. "Where the hell've you been?"

Her eyes said she could've wrung my neck like a chicken's.

But then she forced herself to look into the sun as if she were counting all nineteen of its rays.

Finally she smoothed her face and said, "Listen—" She said the name she'd given me when I was a baby.

I told her, "That's not my name anymore."

"What?"

"I've blacksmithed my own name. I'm Hru."

"*Hru?* What kind of a name is—oh. Of course. Well then . . . *Hru* . . . that's going to take some getting used to, isn't it? Well, Hru—"

She spun out a long story about how my father'd been murdered by my uncle, how she'd had to run for her life, how she'd hidden and ranged through foreign lands seeking support, how she'd failed out there and returned to seek out every city, village, hamlet, farm, quarry and hermitage to raise an army, how she'd been recruiting and training legions of warriors, witches and warlocks to take back the Blackland. How she'd been hunting for all the hacked-up pieces of my father's body because she'd made a deal with the gods—

And suddenly I knew. "*You* trained Yinepu."

"You know Yinepu?"

"Don't lie to me. I know he would've talked about me to you. All this time . . . you *knew* I was alive. But where were you?"

"That's not . . . . Yes, son, he talked to me about someone named Hru, but how was I supposed to've known that was you?"

"When I told you my name, you didn't say, '*You're* Hru,' like you'd just figured out who Yinepu's friend was! Did you? *Did* you?"

She leaned back, nostrils flared, but I leapt in.

"So for *years*, you've been training my *cousin*, teaching *him* your words-of-power, even though you abandoned me, your actual son!"

She breathed in quickly to answer, but I kept on.

"You know how long I dreamt about you? How much I cried and begged the gods—the gods you always told me would let us down, or didn't exist, and now I find out you're making *deals* with them?—to come back to me? To take care of me? To love and protect your own son instead of leaving me to have to kill again and again in the Savage Lands just to stay alive for one more sunrise?"

"I looked for you!" she yelled. "For months! And found nothing. For all I knew, you were dead! But I still kept—"

"Maybe you just wanted to *believe* I was dead, so you'd be free of me!"

"I didn't want to believe it was you, because I didn't want to believe again, to raise my hopes that you were alive just to have to grieve losing you all over again—"

And then I was looking down at her head, rolling beside the black throne until stopping face-down, and her topless neck and body slumping into the throne and falling forward to the dirt.

And in my hand was Fang, dripping and steaming with my mother's gore.

The Book of Now

1.

PAST 1 AM, STARS SUFFOCATED BY CLOUDS, AND THE SKY LIKE A BED SHEET with flashlights behind it.

Standing in the alley behind the Hyper-Market, Rap felt all those splintered glaciers of hail gathered way above his head, felt them like they were just about to stab his neck and back, like he was being lowered onto a bed of nails.

Must've been five minutes banging on that door. Knuckles and ego took it for five days.

Finally footfalls coming down the stairs, and the shove on the door, and the gap beaming yellow light nightward, and the silhouette of the man eclipsing it.

Moon.

Slumping when he saw Rap.

Somehow his eyes, his whole face, slumped with his body.

And Rap winced while separate burns competed for his body.

The older man's eyes mustered not even a glare. Barely a glazed gaze.

"Mr. Ani," said Rap, figuring he'd lost the right to call him Brother Moon, "I, I just . . ."

Hadn't figured out what the hell to say. It'd been a month since he'd seen his *Sbai*.

And now way past midnight, the night before the first day of his final year of school, after taking his mother's head off in the worst fight he'd ever had with her, he was here.

Finally: "Uh, can I, can I . . . ?"

Moon backed up.

2.

He'd been up in Moon's suite before, but for a month Rap'd told himself he'd never enter it or the Hyper-Market again.

But there he was, with the streets dark and the sky flaring white. His bones creaked at him that he shouldn't've been there. Eyes throbbed, too big for their sockets. Gut like a toilet.

And neither of them had said even a word yet.

Standing on the other side of the room, Mr. Ani leaned over his electric samovar to pour himself a cup of tea. Didn't offer any to Rap. Didn't offer him a chair, either.

"It's one in the morning." Mr. Ani blew steam off his tea. He didn't say, *What the hell do you want after all this time?*

But Rap heard it, anyway.

Lights flickered inside. Sky flickered outside. Wind kicked up.

Thunder hit worse than a bad neighbour's party.

Rap. Wordless. No cards to play.

"My . . . my mother . . ."

Moon jerked forward a step, his eyes snapped suddenly awake.

"We . . . had this huge fight—I was screaming at her—she was grabbing at me an I just took off an left her in the street—"

"Whoah, whoah, whoah—slow down." Moon gestured towards the couch. "Take it from the start."

Wind tidal-waved the suite again. Sky flickers, and thunder smashed sooner this time. Rap glanced at the ceiling like it was going to crush him for his sins.

Sins he listed, not in any neat order, but in a cyclone.

Screaming at his mother and abandoning her after their fight. Burning her with other people's accusations that she was a whore. Wanting to hurt her for the years of chaos—his whole life—but most of all for letting that drunk asshole Doctor Liberia into their lives. Not letting.

Bringing.

And he was in that cyclone, flying apart because his centre could no longer hold it all together. He, who never said anything to anybody about his family, here he was, scattering into the gale his poison spores.

And then the lights died inside and stayed dead.

The windows went slate-grey electric for a full four seconds.

Moon placed and lit six candles, and before the samovar went cold, drafted Rap a giant mug of tea spun with twelve spoons of sugar and half a cup of heavy cream.

He remembered.

Took the heat in his hands, blubbering into the steam while wind and thunder tried to silence him. Still in his cyclone, still blubbering that the refugee camps were sick, savage places like human zoos, where fugitives, aid workers and soldiers competed over scalping your soul. That his father was dead and he'd never known him and he'd been on the run ever since his father'd died. That his Somali mother hated Somalis as much as they hated her.

That he hated hearing the phone ring because of Doctor Liberia's telephonic terrorism whenever his mum worked at night. That his mother let the son-of-a-bitch drunk-drive them home one night on icy streets, and when he fish-tailed off the road into a snowbank he smacked his mother with the C-word twice while trying to floor them out of it. That he wished to god he had the money to get himself out of there.

That he'd told his mother he'd wanted to lure Doctor Liberia to his death. And to stab her with the truth of that.

And there were things, true things, terrible things, he'd wanted to tell Moon but couldn't, cuz it'd be summoning monsters up from the bottom of the river that he could never banish back to their netherworld once he'd loosed them. But he could finally say and did say that he was afraid all the time and angry all the time and ashamed all the time, and that, and that, and that the first time in his life he'd really deep-down felt any different—

"—was with *you*, Mr. Ani. The first time I can remember! That I didn't feel like, like I was . . . . "

Felt his lip, slick from snot, throat thickly drowning his words.

"Like I was swimming in, in, in a swamp full of shit. And going under."

Thunder: explosion. Apocalyptic bass. Lightning scorching the room like Hendrix guitar. Mr. Ani's eyes flaring like twin moons.

And then the drum solo hit: hail so total they couldn't talk.

So Rap sat drinking tea, grateful for the screaming silence stifling tears and shuddering chest, grateful for the darkness to hide his smearful face.

3.

After minutes of overhead *ratta-ta-ta-tatta-tatta*, rain joined the beat, overtook it, gentler than the icy prelude.

Finally Rap said words he'd never told anyone but his mother, except this time, nobody was forcing him to.

"I'm sorry."

Mr. Ani. Gazing at him. Chest rising and finally falling. Nodding once in the golden hush of six candles. Almost a bow.

Moon: "I didn't know what the hell was wrong. Always knew you were a hurt young brother. Obviously. Got scars like armour.

"But I gotta tell you . . . . " he said, hefting himself off the couch to pull the tap on the samovar. No steam left.

"I gotta tell you, Rap," and Rap didn't know whether to sing or cry at the sound of his name, the first time Moon had said it since he got there, whether this was the run-up to an *it's okay* or to a *get lost forever*.

"You don't just . . . you can't . . . when you get angry at people, that's . . . that's part of life, all right? Being connected to people, caring about them and then getting hurt . . . that's just paying admission to the planet. Can't have one without the other.

"In the Alphabetical Alchemy, what's *S*? *Simultaneous*. Transform that, Rap. Leadites who don't accept *S*, they try living all one way, they get so far out of balance they fall into the Swamps, or they fall off the edge of the world. Either cracked-out or dicked-out or spent-out looking for permanent joy, or depressed and suicidal.

"You still remember your scrolls?"

Rap nodded.

"*Book of the Golden Falcon*. Fourth Arit. '*What was the Master's answer to Hru's second question?*'"

Sinking hands into mental loam. Digging round cool of roots and worms.

"'*The truth is like the sun: with the same rays a bringer of life and yet a champion of death.*'" Grateful he hadn't forgotten. "'*Sustainer and annihilator, it grows the one plant full and sweet, while it shrivels the other one into crackles. The time to know will come when it is right, but it is not right yet.*'"

Moon: "So you understand. I hope. Doesn't mean the sun is *trying* to burn those crops, even though that will eventually happen. But it's up to you whether you keep on watering them."

Rap nodded.

"C'mere," said Moon, gesturing towards the mantel.

Rap came over to where Moon had brought a candle. They looked at a framed photo of a boy and a girl, probably six and ten, standing on either side of a chubbier Moon whose hair was thicker and all black. The boy's arms were at his sides, but the girl had her arm around Moon's waist.

"That's Kiya," he said, pointing to the girl. "And that's little Ptah."

"You have *kids*?" gasped Rap.

"They're not mine. Legally," he said. "Or biologically. But I raised em both since my boy was six months. Their mother, Katrina . . . we met right here in E-Town. She already had em both, had em from some idiot goof who had no idea how much gold he and Katrina had mined. Rich and stupid.

"When I met them, this little girl was already four years old. Spooky. Barely spoke a word. Probably on account of Katrina and her boyfriend Todd having named her—can you believe it?—*Toddrina*."

"That's a name?"

"Not in *my* scrolls. Name was sposta be 'a symbol of their love.' Symbol of the fact they didn't know shit about a decent name. For whatever reason they just named the boy Pete. He got off lucky. But Todd, the freaking loser, he took off after baby number two.

"I met Katrina when I was in my last year of electrical engineering at university. She was beautiful. And desperate to get man for herself and her kids.

"Me, I loved em all, and yeah, I loved being a rescuer. I was only twenty-one, and suddenly I was instant daddy. I renamed those kids. She let me, let me do that. And we got married, and moved to the States, and for a long time, it was good. But Kat . . . . "

Moon put the picture down, looked out at the dark city.

"She was always into get-rich-quick-schemes, and she finally found the best scheme of all."

Rap waited.

"I never met the dude. Just as well, cuz I'da probably killed him."

Moon cleared his throat. Twice. Then the hail went drum-rolling again, and lightning-cymbals lit up cracks in Moon's face like lunar canyons.

"Bottom line, she served me with papers, cut me off from the kids. *My* kids. I'd raised em, saved em, basically. But she had never let me legally adopt them. And Buddy Dude was a lawyer. You can guess which kind."

Moon's eyes: a mess like ten years of not-sleeping, like rustjunk stomping a lawn to death, like food shoved to the back of a fridge, rotting and dripping.

Rap hated that woman he'd never even met, that she could break the strongest man he'd ever known.

"See," croaked Moon, "cuttin somebody off, not talkin to em, not warnin em, not givin em a chance. That's . . . that's one of the worst things somebody can ever do to somebody else, Rap."

Hail sizzled the roof, rattled the window.

Rap felt something: not the burn, but a brine, like puke.

Couldn't look at Moon, even when Moon walked to the window.

"If you . . . if you wanna have your mum in your life, Rap . . . if you wanna have *me* in your life—"

The window shattered.

Rap rushed over to Moon.

"You okay?"

Moon knelt in the puddle of rain and ice chips, glass shards and dark droplets in halo round him on the worn linoleum. Wind, feeling like snow. And Moon, motionless and kneeling.

"Brother Moon!"

Moon snapped out of it. They grabbed tea towels, broom and dustpan from the kitchen, and while Rap cleaned up, Moon taped a black plastic bag round a sheet of cardboard, then duct-taped it into the window frame.

Rap held up for Moon what had smashed the glass.

A look in his eyes like he was holding the Holy Grail.

A hailstone.

The colour, shape and size of an egg.

Moon put it tenderly into a jar and then into the freezer.

He brought out sheets and a pillow, told Rap to call his mother so she wouldn't be calling police-hospital-and-morgues all night, and then went to bed.

Rap took the couch, turned on his phone long enough to text his mother that he wasn't dead and that he'd see her sometime in the future. Wasn't the first time he'd gone night-hawk.

Sometimes she even knew. She'd just hafta deal.

4.

Moon woke Rap at sunrise.

Together they recited the nine oaths of the *Nub-Wmet-Ānkh*, standing in a *shenu* of two to create their Daily Alchemy.

151

Toast and eggs, then Moon sent off Rap for his first day of Grade Twelve, but not before Rap asked for another reading list.

Moon scribbled down some names, then reached shelfward to hand him *Street Soldiers* by Joseph E. Marshall and sent him packing.

The city looked like a war zone on Rap's ride to school: shredded gardens, massive tree branches laying across roads, broken glass everywhere, even a car window smashed. Hundred-thirty kilometres-per-hour winds'd do that. Specially with hail.

First period, Day One, and within fifteen minutes Rap'd already covered borrowed paper with drawings of Static Shock, Warlock, Huey Freeman and Spawn.

Couple of Somali guys kept turning around glancing at him, then swiveling back smiling and whispering.

Ignored them and everyone else the whole morning, drawing, in classes he didn't care about with teachers who would never know him.

At lunch he found JC, and for the second time in his life, he apologized sincerely.

After telling him an eighty-percent accurate story of how he patched up with Brother Moon, he gave him a drawing.

He'd spent most of the morning penciling it, using a Sharpie for the block-blacks and a Pilot Fineliner for the detailed inks: a Starlinesque splash of Hru and Yinepu battling crocodiles and chain-wielding, slaving murderers in the Swamps of Death.

And the logo, below: *Supreme Raptor* and the *Black Jackal.*

JC: "Dude, dude, dude! This is the absolute shit!" Rap smiled. "I can really keep this?"

"Yeah. Just don't tape it up in your locker—"

"Gimme some credit! I'll obviously put up a photocopy! I'ma stash this in Mylar!"

Two girls who looked like siblings but weren't—one was Jamaican and the other was Nigerian (Rap knew from first day roll-call in his Social class)—kept sneaking peeks at him from their open lockers.

Rap snapped at JC, "What the hell's going on?"

"What? Maybe they think you're cute. Go spit some game, man."

"Yeah, right! Everywhere I go last coupla days, people're staring at me, whispering . . . I mean, what the hell?"

"Like you don'know."

"What're you talking about?"

JC's eyes went wide, followed by his grin. Then he took out his Zune and clicked through it.

On the small screen, a small Rap, JC and Sixpac moved a crowd in a shaky, hand-held universe. Hoots and applause nearly drowned out Rap's rhymes.

"Dude, you're a star! *We're* stars! There's like four thousand hits on this shit, and a coupla hundred comments!"

"Man . . . !"

"Just assumed you knew. Been on YouTube for a month! Somebody musta cell-phoned it or something."

"Why didn't you tell me?"

"Uh, excuse me? Mr. Cut-Off-and-Un-Friend-Everybody-and-Napalm-Every-Bridge? I'm sposta be telling you Golden Eye's gonna go on tour with Maestro and Politic Live when you won't even hardly talk to anyone?"

Rap took the dis. He deserved it. "Guess it's time to make some changes."

"Time to live, man. L-I-V-E: Liberate Intelligence, Victory-Evolve! Golden Eye, Do or Die! I got my own crack of Fruity Loops, dude. Me and Sixpac already got enough beats for like *two* albums!

"Shit, this video's practically the top recruiter for the Street Falcons! We're up to like a hundred people already, fuh real! You should peep the size of the *shen*-rings we build—"

JC stopped. "What, what is it? You look like you just got pantsed."

Rap sucked his teeth.

JC: "Oh, I get it. You're thinking, when you bugged out, you were like the number-two man right after me, and now you're at the back of the line?"

Rap: "Well, first off, you were the number-two man after *me*. But . . . yeah. Gonna feel weird. People I don't even know, knowing scrolls I haven't even heard of . . . . "

"Dude, don't worry. Maāt rules everything around me. Can you transform that?"

Out a month and he was already way behind on the lingo.

Over lunch JC sneak-peaked him the new Scrolls, spun him tales of the new crew and all the mad shit they were doing, and they laughed, schemed, bragged and dreamed.

And for a few minutes he even folded up his umbrella despite the forecasted hailstorm with his mother.

5.

"Supreme Raptor!" squealed Ānkhur from across the room.

Took her all of two seconds. Rap'd just stepped into the Street Laboratory, the new Street Falcon HQ a block east of the Hyper-Market—

(*Felt it*: first time there for him. But not for the Falcons he'd shut out for a month. Plus the newbies—

(Glanced round the walls: posters of Malcolm X, Wangari Maathai, Thomas Sankara, Lubna Hussein, Mo Ibrahim, and a shelf load of Africentric books and DVDs—)

—then everybody was watching Ānkhur flinging her arms around Rap's neck.

Cheeks burning, and despite his usual miserable self he couldn't help but smile.

Ānkhur: "*Hotep*, Brother Raptor! Welcome back!"

First close-up he'd ever had of those ripe-plum lips.

Really wanted to push Ānkhur away before she could detect the effects of those lips on his circulation, but she had him vised to her waist.

"Sister," he finally giggled, "you're like an unopened can of Coke."

"Huh?"

"Always bubbly."

She laughed and hugged him again. "And you're always corny! Good thing I love popcorn!"

Over her shoulder he saw Sixpac. She'd probably boyfriended up by then. Felt his heart go crusty.

Wiggled out of Ānkhur's hug to drop a Throne-clasp—left fist into right palm—on Sixpac.

Clamped his jealousy, too. Couldn't do like JC said, make Golden Eye into E-Town's hottest hip hop crew, if he was beefing with their producer over a female.

Then dropped thrones on everybody else he knew, adding in *Nub-Wmet-Ānkh*.

JC hadn't been exaggerating about recruitment. The Street Laboratory was packed. Including with kids he'd never imagined would go anywhere near Alchemy. Kids in jeans the size of potato-sacks. A kid with a yellow-metal grill, and—damn!—at the back of the room in bandanas, two little Sudanese kids . . . was that the same Dinka Lil Wayne and Lil Bow Wow from 107th Ave?

"Look at brother's eyes," laughed *Sbai* Seshat, Ānkhur's aunt, standing next to Moon. "Only 4:30 and the gang's all here. Aint nobody here running on CP time, young man."

"Well go on, newbies," said Brother Moon. "Introduce yourself to the city's most YouTubed hip hop contender!"

That was all he needed to hear to know for sure that Moon had forgiven him.

Too many new people to remember their names, and too many original Street Falcons who had new Kemetic ones: Sixpac was now *Senwusret*, after the three pharaohs who'd conquered swaths of Europe; Jorrel was now *Joser*, after the pharaoh of Imhotep who'd designed the Step Pyramid; the dark-skinned brother Ahmed was now *Kem-Ur* ("Great Black"); the Rwandan sister Crystal with the cute French accent was now *Sekhmet*, after the lion goddess.

A legion of new kids ranging from junior high to high school graduates, dressed anywhere from street to straight, skin glowing from midnight to sunrise, and faces from Cairo to Kingston and Alexandria to Amber Valley.

And to all of them he was either Raptor or Supreme Raptor, and JC, coincidentally, was exactly what he'd logoed him as on the drawing: Black Jackal.

With his prodigal-glitters dimming to gleams, Rap scanned the new scene, the new relationships, new potential rivals, and new potential burns inside the storefront of not much but tables and chairs against the walls.

Place was packed. Had to be a hundred kids, easy.

His eyes kept landing on a new sister. Must've been two inches taller than Rap. Huge smile. Glamourous weave she kept leaping from one shoulder to the other like a starlet's cat. Still went by her Leadite name, Thandie.

Brothers were orbiting her like spy satellites stealing intell before a war. That smile: sunshine, baking sand at the shore. But the eyes were ice cubes in a drink.

And then the door jangled and in ran Almeera, the Somali girl who always wore a loose *hijab* and hoodie with a rhinestone Playboy logo.

Rushing—

"Sorry I'm la—"

—and slamming into Brother Moon's chest.

Everyone laughed. Almeera, shrinking, mortified: "Sorry, Brother Moon!"

"Sallright, Sister Yibemnoot," said Moon. Rap X-rayed the name: Heart in sky? Heart of the sky?

She crinkle-smiled, slipped through the crowd to find a place in the shen-ring forming. Had a graphic novel tucked under her arm. Persepolis? He'd read the library's copy. She reads comics? Damn.

To fit everyone they formed three concentric shen-rings. Moon began the *Nub-Wmet-Ānkh*.

"By the sunrise . . ."

"*BY THE SUNRISE . . .*"

" . . . I choose to resurrect myself . . . "

" . . . *I CHOOSE TO RESURRECT MYSELF . . .*"

" . . . meaning I will purify my body, my mind and my spirit . . . "

" . . . *MEANING I WILL PURIFY . . .*"

The chorus of it, the echo, shimmered up and down Rap's spine like electro-dazzle up a Tesla coil. He'd never heard more than ten people reciting their oath, and now here that, squared.

At oath's end, Almeera, now Yibemnoot, nodded to Brother Moon and stood forward.

"Today's Alchemy. September 6. S, Simultaneous, and 6, Mother-Sister-Daughter."

Everyone hushed. Gone was the awkward girl who'd bounced off Moon's ribs. Here was somebody commanding everyone's attention, even weaved-up Thandie's.

"To me, Simultaneous/Mother-Sister-Daughter helps me understand all my roles. I'm a daughter, like all mothers are. And I'm a sister. One day I might even be a mother myself. So even though I've got rights and responsibilities in two of those roles now, I'm also preparing for the rights and responsibilities I'll have as a mother."

Rap couldn't keep from smiling, watching her alchemise. She'd just measured and poured her metals into beakers. Now she was about to fire up the furnace.

"And even if I never become, like, a real mother, I mean, literally, with my own kids and everything," said Yibemnoot, "as a mother, like Aset the Avenger, it will be my duty . . . to, to teach and lead my people in the Savage Lands. To show them how to defeat the Destroyer. And raise the Shining Place eternally."

"Transform, Sister," said Sbai Seshat, nodding, and then it was dominos: dozens of heads nodding to Yibemnoot's every phrase. "Transform," they echoed.

"Now, if I become Aset only, a warrior-mother only, then, well, then I can't live. I wouldn't even be able to drink from the River of Life, because when you're in command, all you can even do is just get ready for war. So I have to be, *simultaneously*, a sister, and a daughter. Just so I can even remember what it's like not to have all the answers or even be afraid some times."

"Thass right!" said Seshat.

"And that's what'll make me a better Aset," said Yibemnoot, "because then, I'll know why some of the young blacksmiths have dropped their hammers. Not because they don't wanna build, but because their hands aren't all callused up yet. And I can even tell them, 'No, that's okay. Don't feel bad.' You know why? 'Because only soft hands can comfort the Wanderers in the Savage Lands—'"

"*Transform!*" said Ānkhur, without even a shred of her ever-ready giggle.

"And because I can be *simultaneously* hard and soft, old and young, day and night, I can hear the cries of those who sink down, and be strong enough to lift them up. I can break the pyrite chains off of Wanderers' necks, and still place my golden chain into their hands!"

"*Transform!*"

"I can be the master teacher, who is not too proud to learn! Like Ptah-Hotep said forty-five centuries ago, 'Wisdom is more precious than emeralds, yet it is found among the maidens at the millstone.'"

"TransFORMED!" said Seshat. Applause crackled the room like hail on a tin roof. "Did young sister here grant gold to her fathers, brothers, and sons, and to her mothers, sisters and daughters?"

*True-indeed*s popped out around the rings, cymbals on Yibemnoot's sax. Her rhinestone bunnyhead sparkled on its black hoodie.

That girl had just rocked the house and he hadn't dropped so much as a single rhyme.

Damn, thought Rap, and not even a fire-ant's bite of jealousy on his neck.

6.

"So if y'all transform correctly," said *Sbai* Seshat, "you're gonna be up in that cockpit *flying* the plane your own self."

Chattering, laughing, clapping: *Sbai's* announcement rocked everyone's gyroscopes.

Seshat and somebody named *Sbai* Maāhotep had hooked up all kinds of amazing gigs through some city councillor who liked what they were doing, including free passes for bowling and movies, two grants for part-time jobs at the Hyper-Market, and even free flight lessons at the municipal airport.

But flying lessons? He was going to fly an actual plane?

Practically ran the two blocks to the Hyper-Market so he could talk to Brother Moon, who'd left to get back to work.

Hand on the door, Rap checked out the business beside the Hyper-Market: DSL – The Data Salvation Lab. Sorta remembered . . . that time when Seshat and Moon's lawyer friend, Bamba, had talked about becoming partners and splitting his business into two kingdoms they'd help govern.

Based on the DSL's sandwich board, Moon's new business had absorbed all his data recovery and electronics repair. That left the internet café and Africentric books, t-shirts, CDs, DVDs, statuettes and others goods to the Hyper-Market.

Inside the DSL, Moon was slotting a disembodied hard drive into a docking station. A twenty-something Rwandan brother was working the till and helping a customer.

"Raptor!" said Moon, glancing up and grinning. "Great to see you inside the *shenu* today. Grown, huh?"

"Yeah!"

"People've missed you, bruh. That Sister Yibemnoot's really something, isn't she?"

"Yeah, absolutely!" Stopped, afraid he was gushing. Hyperlinked to another topic. "Thanks for the props about my rapping. To be honest, I thought you might still be—"

"Look, bruh, quality is quality. Can't deny that. *Don'*want to. I mean, NWA's lyrics might be evil, but nobody can deny their rhyme skills or Dre's production."

"—so, so you're really not mad anymore?"

Moon tapped his keyboard after checking the drive-analysis.

"Raptor, you saw how crowded the Street Laboratory was today. That's partly cuz of you. You're our online emblem now."

"Our mascot?"

"Our cyber-*icon*. See all those roughnecks there today?"

He nodded, thinking more about Ãnkhur, Yibemnoot, and the girl with the big eyes and the weave. Thandie.

"Back when I was a young Alchemist," said Moon, "we were all university students. Middle class families or trying to be." Moon placed the hard drive inside a Mylar envelope and then into a multi-tiered inbox marked *Deep Recovery*.

"But you," said Moon, "you're giving street cred to the Street Laboratory for these wanderers who've been drinking swamp water their whole lives. They'da never come here cuz of me or Sister Seshat or Brother Maãhotep—"

"Who?"

"My lawyer friend, you know, Bamba."

"Oh."

"Yeah, he's using his Hru-name again. Seshat never stopped using her Aset-name. Anyway, yeah. Your YouTube's helping young brothers and sisters who've been needing serious attention for lead poisoning."

The twenty-something Rwandan technician politely broke in to ask Moon a question about recovery times. Moon introduced him: Hakizimana, a comp-tech student at NAIT. Family bills—always, always family bills—meant Hakizimana'd been ten bucks away from having to drop out of school.

But swooping in at the last second was *Sbai* Seshat, STEP grants in hand, for him to get hooked up with Data Salvation.

The brother barely spoke—truly, he whispered. Rap remembered that until he himself came on with Moon, he'd been the same, never speaking up unless he was forced to. When the quiet cat whispered, "Pleased to meet you," Rap figured that compared to Hakizimana, he was practically Chris Rock.

When Hakizimana ghosted away to the back room, Moon said, "Here with his aunt's family." Lower voiced: "Lost everybody else during the genocide."

Felt like descending a staircase and missing a stair. Just one sentence about a brother he'd been dismissing, and suddenly he felt more in common with him than almost anyone he knew.

"He a Falcon, too?"

"No," said Moon, shaking his head. "Be a long time before he's gonna wanna join anything. If ever."

Moon in the back, and Rap, alone, finally turned on his cell.

Seventeen voice-mails and thirty-one texts.

All from his mother.

Live coals in his gut.

Moon returned with a small tool and cracked open a busted iPod lying in the FIX inbox. Rap slipped his phone back into his too-big pants.

"Look," said Moon, glancing around the iPod's open guts. "About what you said, me being angry about that video of you . . . I was once a young hot-head too. I totally get why you tried to bring revolution to those *capoeristas* in the park. Truly.

"But when you live long enough, you gain a new power. Suddenly surfaces aren't like lead shields, anymore. You can X-ray things all the way through till you perceive the simultaneity, dig? Perk of getting older. I look back at all the times I was dropping matches into gas tanks, and no matter how much water I hauled *after* the fact —"

Moon's eyes scrambled back and forth, like they were decrypting a password.

"Professor Xaasongaxango," he said, apparently having decided. "He was *our sbai* , the one who brought Alchemy to E-Town back when we were at university. He'd studied under Cheikh Anta Diop himself, the founder of Alchemy."

Moon looked back up from the mechanical body he was dissecting. His eyes were soft.

"I thought the world of Professor X—all of us did. The strongest elder any of us'd ever met. And when it came to African histories, Kemetic history, Yoruba civilisation, all of it, he had a mind like a computer."

Moon's eyes and fingers focused on the iPod's entrails.

"But I got upset at him over some stupid shit. Doesn't matter what. Convinced myself I was right and wouldn't hear otherwise from anybody. And this was right at the same time the university was putting whips on Professor X's back, bullshit crazy accusations he was leading a cult or training terrorists or whatever." He put his tools down.

"So when the end came, I wasn't there."

Rap: "The end?"

"Professor Xaaso," he said, "died of a heart attack. Wasn't even fifty. And we were estranged at the time."

Moon moved to the DSL's hospitality carrel to pour two black-and-gold cups of tea from a stainless steel carafe. Rap accepted his with thanks, glancing at his cup's hieroglyphics and its painting of the god Jehutí writing on his palette.

Blowing away steam, Moon finally continued.

"Here in the Savage Lands, our men disproportionately suffer heart disease. Guess you could say we're exceptional." Shook his head. "Lifetime of lead poisoning and the weight of all those chains and ancestors' chains and a hundred million links of ghost chains.

"Now, you try telling a *doctor* about ghost chains, buddy'll probably try shoving pills down your throat or lighting you up like in *Cuckoo's Nest*. Or he'll say the problem's in your genes, or you eat too much soul food or some bullshit like that, even when you don't eat pig. You know—it's all *our* fault."

Rap sipped his tea, trying to calculate Moon's orbit.

"You know what that does to your heart and brain," said the man, "all those decades of being doubted, patronised, overlooked, passed over for jobs, having people that you trained get promoted over you, being called oversensitive or accused of being paranoid? While time and again you watch lesser men climb on board the elevator and they're shoving your desk and you in it out the window?"

Rap swallowed. Tea was bitter—seriously needed sugar. Wasn't the right time to get it.

"Whether it's lead poisoning or a million cuts from pyrite blades," said Moon, "a broken heart's how it ends for way too many of us."

Rap knew he was expected to say something. Knew what Moon taught him: if all you've got is dumb answers, ask a smart question.

"So, well," said Raptor, "how do we not die like that, then? Me, like . . . when I get really angry . . . it's like you said, it's like fire outta control. Like my whole body's on fire. I can't stop it! How'm I supposed to, to, to *control* that?"

Heard the begging in his own voice. Desperate for Moon to understood how much he wanted to know how to forgive. But he had no practice at it, and nobody who'd modeled it for him until now.

And unless he planned on moving in with Moon, there was a battle gathering on his horizon like thunderheads—

"Gold-minding," said Moon, ushering them back to the desk so he could work on the iPod.

"Gold-minding? What's that?"

"It's about using breath. Breath is power. It's transforming your own mind."

"You mean, like . . . *mental* alchemy?"

"Indeed, bruh." Moon finished removing a damaged component. "When you're in the middle of a crisis, breath is a weapon, or a tool—and if you don't use it right, it gets taken away and used against you.

"But if you're trained, you can be like Hru ripping out one of the Devourer's fangs and making it into his spear-head.

"When you're in a revolution against your own pyrite mind—that's an actual brain region called the reptilian brain or the limbic system—you've got to wield your own breath to restore leadership to the frontal lobe. The gold mind."

Replacing the damaged part he'd removed, Moon continued, "And once you learn to inhabit the gold mind at will, it becomes your command-and-control centre to accomplish everything you want in life. It's your *internal* Golden Fortress."

Moon clicked the iPod's guts back inside its body. Rap imagined Moon as a pharaonic priest, preparing the king's body for eternity.

"So, how'd you, uh . . . I mean, after your teacher died and everything," muddled Rap, "how'd you, uh . . . . "

"Forgive myself?"

"Yeah."

"Our Golden Fortress burned down the day Professor X died, Rap. So if I do ever figure out how to forgive myself," said Moon, "I'll let you know."

Didn't know how much was metaphor and how much was matter. So Rap just *hmph*ed.

"Meantime, we all gotta Replace-Elevate. Can you transform that?"

"Drain the Swamps. Build the Shining Place on the elevated land."

"True indeed." Moon smiled at him.

But Rap knew from way back, from his days in the refugee camps, that smiles were often just mirages for a man dying of thirst: lying about water and serving sand.

7.

"It's gon be like Dave Chappelle's *Block Party*, dude!" said JC the Black Jackal. Raptor'd just gotten back to the Street Laboratory, walked into the tail end of a planning session.

"When?"

"Next summer!" Jackal's locks swayed, now longer than pine-cones, making him look like a young Bob Marley.

"You're telling me these new Falcons are laying out plans for something ten months away?"

"Damn skippy," said Jackal, slurping from a carton of chocolate milk. "But you know what we actually gon do?"

A street party the northern drag of Kush, 118th Avenue, which they were calling *Khair-em-Sokar* ("Road of Sokar"—and 107th Ave was *Khair-em-Nubt*. Without the map of Ancient Kemet on the wall, Rap would've been lost on the original names for Saqqara, Luxor and Waset). Multiple bands—including Golden Eye, of course.

(Good thing they had ten months to get ready. Sure, he had notebooks full of lyrics, but they had music for exactly one song, and no stage show. Jacking a show from some *capoerista* show-offs in the park was one thing, but rocking the mic when everyone *expected* you to rock the mic was another.)

"But dude, it aint just a party! We're recruiting! Plus, we gon have like booths and shit set up all along Khair-em-Sokar, an tables, with information for the community, on services and stuff. Get all them social agencies, mosques, churches, whatever.

"And the Falcons'll be selling shirts, books, DVDs, whatever. And then just like in old-old-old-old-*Old* School Kemet, we gon raise an obelisk!"

"What?"

"Seriously! An obelisk! Brother Maāhotep usedta build sets and stuff for plays, right? He's gon make an obelisk, just like in the ancient temples, and we'll raise it up just to show what we can do! It's gon be insane! Geo*met*rically insane!"

Jackal pushed an eyebrow up so high it disappeared behind his locks, like a signal for conspiracy.

"And Sister Yibemnoot," he said, leaning in, "you should really work on her. Get her to sing. Cuz trust me, she can sing!"

"What makes you think *I* can—"

"Dude, you blind?"

Rap went open-lipped, like he'd just found something weird in his mouth. "Get outta here."

"You didn'notice?"

"What makes you think I even—"

"Reading you when you like a girl is like reading *sky*-writing—"

Rap shushed him and yanked him to the inside of an alcove formed by two book shelves. "Whatever."

"Don't sleep on this. 'Because a grind is a terrible thing to waste.'"

"That girl wears *hijab*!" he whispered. "Seriously doubt she grinds. And I'm not some pig who's just tryinna, y'know . . . . "

"You so hung up on Ānkhur you can't even—"

"Would you shut up? Besides—"

"Besides nothing—"

"*Besides*, like I said, she wears *hijab*. So even if she does, y'know—"

"Grind?"

"No!"

"Like you?"

"Yeah, basically. Even *if*, it's not like she can date or whatever. Plus she's Somali. Don'want her whole clan coming down on me with AKs, rigging my cell phone with an IED."

"You *should* be thinking about an IUD. Think you'd be the first brother in history to date a Somali girl and not get caught?"

"What, like you have?"

JC opened his palms and grinned. "You like her, right?"

Rap opened up remote-surveillance on her from across the room.

Two months ago when they met she was Almeera. Now she was Yibemnoot. *Sky-Heart*. But still that same loose *hijab* draped down her black hoodie with the rhinestone Playboy bunny logo. Still as intense with that too-too-rare smile.

There she was, talking with two other muhajabaat, excitedly showing them the guts of the *Persepolis* graphic novel she was carrying.

Pointing with those hands. Typical Somali girl hands: like a child's.

A hot morning, sun already ironing his neck, and her eyes glinting like dark amber. Birds and birds and birds, like a canopy of leaves ranging overhead, strobing them with shade. Eight years old and ripping into an actual mango together, one his mother'd somehow finagled him in the refugee camp. And then howling at the sight of each other, faces mango-smeared and dripping . . .

And then a stench: curdling milk, puddles of puke—

"Yo, Earth to Raptor."

Rap shook his head.

"So, you gon—"

"*No*."

Jackal scowled, kissing his teeth. "You're cracked. Throwing away a perfectly good girl like that!"

Biking nowhere for half an hour. Then finally landing at the Sprucewood library on 95th Street and 115th Ave, just south of, what was it?

Khair-em-Sokar.

Ignored his cell-phone. Begged scrap paper from the librarian. In a quiet corner, tore out a bunch of small squares, scribbled out ten words and quick icons on each. Orbiting them round their central star for the divine geometry, replacing and elevating the system again and again . . .

7 PM. Couldn't pretend any more that people weren't turning around to look at him. Stomach'd been growling louder than a horny pit bull.

Grabbed his cell-phone, texted his mother.

8.

A couple of pretty young Somali *muhajabah* sat smoking sheesha at the back of the restaurant. Never saw that before. Rebels, but not in the good way. Not Street

Falcons, he knew that for damn sure. Headscarves and tight clothes. Things were changing.

Another couple of Somali girls sat leaning into each other at the ear, sharing white earbuds and audio lines going into one mp3 player. Looked like they were both flesh on the ends of a giant white wishbone.

And rowdies on more *sheesha* pipes: a mixed group of Somali and Dinka teens, ball caps and giant pants, too loud and swearing.

The owner, an Ethiopian brother who looked like Rakim, swung over and told them to settle down or leave. They started back-talking, and then Rap's mother walked in, and Rap didn't know who to be more afraid for.

The owner brought them a combo platter for two: gravied meat and vegetarian dishes in small bowls on a sheet of white pancake *injera*. The rowdies were gone.

No hugs when she'd landed at his table. Skull-faced. Sunglasses. *Inside.* Which she never did. Sure, she'd strut outta the house in a shiny red shirt or show too much neck or arms, but sunglasses *inside*?

Finally she took them off. Her eyes: large, red, accusatory.

Not like he'd expected bruises. Doctor Liberia didn't use his fists. Didn't have to.

Sat.

Awkwardly.

Glancing at his mother.

Her, staring out the window.

As if, maybe spray-painted on the drug-store mural across the street, she could read instructions for how to hack inside her son's mind.

For "a dialogue," like guidance counsellors and other corny adults loved saying.

Looked around, dodging her glare. Classy joint, this Habesha. Ethiopian paintings, white tile floor, rich brown wood and high ceilings. Hovering in the air, incense like honeyed ginger, waiting like a promised kiss.

Rap'd never been there before, but he hadn't been to many restaurants, period. They never had money for eating out.

The food sat between them, pieces on a chess board, straining for either him or his mother to start.

"Since you won'tt come home," she said finally, "I guess we haff no choice but to take our biss-nuss out in public."

Not *that* public, but just like she liked it. No Somalis. Not anymore.

He said, "How can we even afford this?"

"How can we *afforrad* it? I helped the owner with some publicity when he started this place. We met through the Africa Centre. *He's* always loyal to people who help him." Eyes, window-ward. "But we are nutt here to discuss the family foodt budget, Raphael—"

"'Raptor.'"

Eyes flicked onto him. "Excuse me?"

"*Raptor.*"

"Aren't you getting a little oldt for dinosaur nicknames? Or, or, or is it the basketball team? You don't even play basketball!"

How would you know?

Sucked down as big a breath as far as he could, then released it s-s-s-lowly like Jackal'd told him (advance intell on Brother Moon's promised gold-minding).

"No. Like a bird of prey," he said, clearly as possible, trying not to sound patronising. "Like a falcon."

She shook her head, chewing her lip.

He gave himself a 39% on voice control.

"So since when are you calledt—"

"Since a long time."

"Fine. R-*r-r*-ap-tor."

That rolled *r*.

Since he was a kid. Like being hit rapid-fire with a rolled-up newspaper.

And he wasn't down with letting anyone hit him with anything anymore.

Raptor: "I'm moving out."

"*What?*"

Diners, the owner, a waitress: looking.

She lowered her voice, leaned over the table.

"Stop talking such nonsense!"

"I'm sick of dealing with Doctor Liberia—"

"Don't call him that—"

"—and how you let him treat you like some—"

Swallowed, searching for a word. Any word but *that* word. Her large eyes now larger.

"—like somebody who doesn't deserve respect."

His mother unfurled a roll of injera, tore it into shreds for picking up *doro wat* and *gomen* and *atekilt aletcha wot.*

But then she put the pancake bread down, without scooping any chicken, spinach or curried potatoes and cabbage.

"Thank you," said Raptor, "for not insulting my intelligence by claiming he respects you when you know he doesn't."

"My silence," she whispered, "has naathing to do your manipulative talk. And you are nutt the adult, here. You don't give me *ultimata*—" (even coldly furious, his mother insisted on the correct Latinate plurals, something he hadn't even understood until Brother Moon began teaching him etymology) "—about who I can have a, a *friend* ship with—"

"It's not an ultimatum. I'm not threatening to move out. I *am* moving out."

"You dun't even have a job! Are you planningk to live on the street?"

"I'm moving in with my friend Jackal," he lied. *Improvised.* "His family's nice and they already—"

"Jackal? Jackal? You're staking your future on a boy named *Jackal*?"

"I don't care whether you like his name. It's a done deal. And I'm not sticking around anymore for when that drunk old bastard drives you both head-first into a truck or off a bridge!"

"What do you want me to do, Raphael?" she hissed. "To gett you to stupp this insanity?"

Knew he had her on the ropes.

Ten seconds. Staring.

Twenty.

"You're tearing this family apart with these threats!" she said finally. "Your, your father . . . his last words to me, his last words to me were to hold onto you—"

(The sidekick she'd never even tried throwing before, that's how desperate she was, how bad things must've gone between her and the Destroyer, that she was lying on her side in the octagon and'd fired her last good one and was completely defenseless—)

"My *father*!" he said. "How many times in my life have you mentioned his name, ever? And now you think you can just, like, *invoke* it? Like a word-of-power? Like that's all it takes to stop me? You really think you have that much magic left?"

"*Whatt* are you even talkingk about?"

"My whole life you've been locking-down information on him like a refugee hoarding food!"

He'd come up with that line three hours before. Gave himself full credit on the writing, and a 90% on delivery.

But his mother was educated. Emotion alone wasn't going to take her out. He had to brandish his intelligence in front of her like a sword beneath a skyful of lightning.

"Why is that, mum? Why have you refused to pay me the *respect* of teaching me about my own father?"

She didn't even try denying it.

Reaching down, picking up her crumbled injera, scooping a shred of chicken into her mouth and swallowing like she was taking cancer meds.

His mother: "Whatt do you wantt to know?"

Didn't smile. Didn't even smirk.

"*Everything.*"

9.

"My family ran very successful businesses in Somalia before the government collapsid."

Been a minute of lip-licking and false starts before his mother'd opened with that.

"Mining equipment, computers, satellite dishes . . . after the government fell in 1991, all of us endedt up across East Africa. My parents, my aancles and aunts, set up businesses wherever they wentt."

At last he was eating, but he could barely taste the food from straining to imagine his mother's—*his own*—vast, wealthy family flung across Somalia, Kenya, Tanzania . . . who knew where else? With faces that didn't look anything like his.

"We endedt up in Sudan," she said, damming a cascade of hair behind her ear. "Because I was oldt enough, I went to the University of Khartoum. Forget everything you see on the TV about Muslim countries. That campus was full of female students in every field. My parents wanted me to become a doctor."

She snorted at that.

"I was in my thirdt year of Journalism, the firrist time I saw your father. He was speaking at a studentt eventt. And he was dressed very conservatively, in a narrow suit and a tie. I thought maybe he was one of those Christianists. The evangelicals, you know." She shook her head.

"He was talking about engineering, using engineering skills in the rural areas, employing local people, nutt falling for those Western 'aid' programmes where they fly in and house one or two rich foreigners when they could've hired ten local doctors or engineers or technicians for the same money."

She sighed, blinking, and her eyes went wet and sparkling.

"I was excitedt by every wordt outt of his mouth. Talking about studentt brigades, taking our skills to the countryside, making a peaceful revolution in poor people's lives.

"Now, my parents were business people. They hadt no idea their crazy rebel daughter was in the Sudanese Communistt Party for a year already, which was illegal then, but it was also the mostt progressive party for women, and had a lot of women leaders, like my hero Niemat Kheir. Anyway, hearing this young, beautiful man talk about revolution . . . it fired me up.

"I guess I imagined myself wearing a beret and a couple of bandoliers, except filledt with pens instead of bullets, getting rural people to tell their life stories of struggle, teaching them how to write, empowering everyone . . . . "

She chuckled. "This rich Somali girl-communist telling Sudanese women how to—well, I was young."

For the first time, she smiled at him.

"And so I signedt up to help however I couldt. And I started workingk with your father.

"He was so serious when he was giving thatt speech. Yes, he was passionate, but I wondered if he knew how, how to be *fun*. If he knew how to *laugh*."

The owner, the Rakim-looking brother, brought them a pot of spiced tea. His mother poured for both of them.

"Once we were on a planningk committee together," she said, "he started slowly showing his charm, like putting a litter of puppies out in the yard, one at a time. He could make any ordinary story about simple things seem amazingk, like, like if was tellingk you about gettingk groceries at the outdoor market, he'd talk about how a big man haulingk sacks talkedt with a lisp, or the way a chicken hangingk from a hook lookedt like a guilty husband hidingk from his wife. He'd have everyone in the room laughingk.

"He was skinny, just like you. If he were carrying two sacks of rice, he might haff weighedt seventy kilos. But he hadt broad shoulders. Beautiful, blue-black skin thatt was like . . . like polishid ebony. Eyes like that looked right into you and crinkled every time he smiledt or laughedt. Which was mostt of the time."

Smiled, shaking her head. Arranging salt and pepper shakers, napkin holder and water glasses.

"When we'd been working together for a couple of months on figuring out a development project, I managedt to slide into the conversation that I could never marry a smoker."

"My father smoked?" The words'd jumped Raptor's turnstiles before he could tackle them to the floor.

"Oh, yes! Like a factory! He hadt long, slender fingers, and he usedt to holdt his cigarettes out like this—"

Demonstrated: holding a rolled-up napkin at its base, its tip pointing straight up. Raptor could almost see the smoke rising to stroke the ceiling.

"—and anyway, that's all I said on the subjeccit, and aboutt a week later, thatt was the only time I ever saw him graampy. Just a little short-temperedt with everyone." Smiled. "Tryingk to quitt. I mean, he *hadt* quitt. *For me.*"

Eyes glimmering, wetter still. Blinked and blinked.

Raptor remembered it all, everything he'd never seen and had never heard.

His mum, still, after all that time.

In love.

"He was stylish, you know." She smirked. "Very suave."

She looked up and around, as if she could see his dad strutting around the restaurant. A head-turner, even in death.

"He had some few beautiful shirts from Nigeria with all that embroidery they do on top of batik. Especially yellow. Oh, my godt—with *his* skin? He would glow! He was glorious! And he had a black, silk Vietnamese jackett, too. I lovedt thatt one. It had a golden phoenix on the back—I never learned where he gott it. He was so . . . so cosmopolitan!

"But mostly he wore thatt narrow suit of his. To think I'd thoughtt he was an evangelical. But really, he just lovedt Sam Cooke."

Raptor laughed. "My dad loved Sam Cooke?"

"Oh, yes. When we were working alone he used to sing me 'Chain Gang' and 'Cupid.' And he loved 'Change Gonna Come.' And he lovedt Sam and Dave, too, and all those 'sixties rhythm-and-blues artists. So he dressedt just like them. It was his 'schtick.'"

His old man. The Sudanese styler.

"Now, even in a large city like Khartoum, even att the university, women were conservative, so they didn't, you know, they weren't throwingk themsellevs at him. But they talkid to each aather. They all talkid about him, the beautiful golden man."

"Huh?"

"His name."

"I don't get it."

"*Jini.*"

He stared back at the explanation that wasn't one.

"His name! Your last name, Garang, it's like . . . for the Dinka, Garang is like Adam. The original man. And Jini means 'gold.' You didn't know that?"

Gold. Amazing. "No," he said.

"My fault," she said, "that you don't know more Dinka."

No kidding. And your fault I'm only finding out about my own father now.

He sucked cool air down as far as he could, trying to drown the burn.

"So all these women, they used to gossip about me. I was too 'aggressive.' So they called me Araweelo."

Raptor blinked hard. "What do you mean, *they* called you that? You mean, like, it's rude to call you by your first name or something, there?"

She showed him her driver's license: *Kaultom Farah.*

"Your name isn't even Araweelo?"

"Not legally," she said. The name came from "the morality police," she said: jealous female Dinka students angry at her for "stealing" a good Dinka man, jealous Muslim women who called her a whore for working unchaperoned with a man (angry because she had the guts to go after him), or the Somalis who accused her of slumming with a Dinka.

"I didn't wear *hijab*, so I was a badt woman. *Loose.*"

Raptor chuckled. He knew the old-school meaning of the word, knew his mum didn't know kids today used it to mean something anatomical. Same difference, really.

She snorted, oblivious. "And pushy, and talkid too much, and thoughtt I was a queen. *That's* why Araweelo," she said. Told him, when he still didn't get it, about the ancient Somali queen who ruled at the time of Christ and was one of the most powerful women in history.

By legend, she'd hanged enemies by their balls.

His mother smiled at his reaction—like he'd been slapped. Obviously liked that she could still shock her son.

Tried imagining Doctor Liberia punished with an Araweelo Special.

"To them," said his mother, again oblivious to the reason for his smile, "'Araweelo' was the ultimate insult. But I lovedt it. I startedt introducing myself as that, which droffe them crazy! And your father lovedt it, too."

"So . . . did you, like, date? Or, how long did it take you to get married?"

Her smile vanished.

"There were," she said, wiping the condensation off her glass, "complications."

10.

"I knew my family wouldn't approve," she said. "Yes, they'd travelledt, they were educated. Yes, they'd never forcedt me to wear *hijab* and so I never didt unless we went somewhere extreme. They were consideredt liberal. Maybe a little too Western.

"But one of my older brothers who'd gone to Italy was married to an Italian woman. They never forgave him. So for me, a daughter, to marry a Dinka, a non-Muslim . . . thatt was *haram*. He wasn'tt even a Christian!"

"Really?"

"No. To them he was *kafir*. That's the kind of slur they use against animists. But he was Dinka. He believedt in *Nhialic*. Dinka are monotheistic, you know. Not pagans, like ignorantt people say." She laughed. "Look at me! I'm an atheist, and I'm defendingk . . . the point is—"

"Did your parents know? That you were an atheist?"

"Are you crazy? They didn'tt even know I was a communistt. Not thatt they really caredt about religion, but who wants a wild daughter ruining the family reputation?"

"So how'd you get married?"

"*Masaafo*," she said. He didn't react. "Your Somali's so good, I justt thought you'd know thatt word. We *elopid*."

Eloped. Amazing. He chuckled. Happily or un-, he didn't know. How many more secrets could there be?

She spun out the tale of how they waited to finish their studies, then fled for the southern city of Juba where his family lived.

To a Dinka girlfriend headed for studies in Berlin, she gave eight letters dated across the following calendar year, to be mailed on those dates, which wove a fiction of how she was seeking a reporting job with *Der Spiegel*, but she'd take any news work she could get.

Since she'd always been the wild child, she knew they'd believe her fiction—hell, she actually did freelance a couple of stories from southern Sudan to the German daily, and had her friend send clippings of her bylined pieces to her parents.

"We likedt living in Juba," she said. "It was smaller then. Just a dusty town with red soil and hills on the horizon. A hundredt thousand people—barely bigger than Red Deer."

Since he'd never been to Red Deer, that didn't help him.

"And your father's family, they embracedt me like their own daughter," she said, "which overjoyedt me. But it also made me ashamedt because I knew my family would never give my husbandt the same treatimentt."

While his father's brothers were helping them build a house next to his parents' home, Araweelo and Jini built a cross-disciplinary team of students at the University of Juba. Bringing pre-natal and neo-natal care to rural people, building water purifiers and teaching them how to make their own, helping them create small businesses and set up international sales contacts.

His mother led another project: not teaching just literacy, but Dinka literature and creative writing.

"It wasn'tt just the North-South war we were dealing with in Juba," she said. "Thingks had always been harder in the south.

"Outside Juba, schools were even worse than they were inside. Maybe two kids in a hundredt finishedt school. Girls almost never didt. Andt the authorities didn't emphasise or even respeckit the Dinka culture.

"But we helpedt people change thatt. We taught parents and grandparents and children. They put on plays and wrote stories and learnedt debating . . . we even publishedt a small book of poems, and another one of legends and songs and elegies, because everyone there hadt lost so many people in the war.

"But I have to tell you, Raphael—sorry, R-*r-r*-aptor—I mean, to you it may sound crazy, but those were the most exciting times of my life!

"I had a handsome, brave, brilliantt husband, I was free of my family and their bourgeois attitudes and backwardt inhibitions, I had justice-work I caredt about with beautiful, kind rural people who treated me like a goodt granddaughter who'd come back home.

"And I was young and foolish enough to think it wouldt lastt."

Hung so long on the words that Raptor had to finally lean forward and ask her, "But?"

"But butchers came and murdered your father."

"Murdered?" sputtered Raptor. "You told me he died in a car accident! You, you . . . why would you lie about that? My god—"

"Don't *rush* me, Raphael!"

"What would *possess* you to—"

"Don't you dare talk to me about 'possess!' You haffn't hadt to wander in the wilderness with the misery I haff! You haffn't hadt to suffer the knives I have, plungedt into my heart again and again, every time I look at your face and see—"

Everyone in the restaurant silence, looking at them.

Then turning back around.

She stood up. Marched to the washroom.

He sat.

Wondering if she were going to turn off the tap for another seventeen years of his life.

Neck and shoulders burning, brain cranking triple-speed for the words to apologise.

Her talking to the owner, confirming their tab was zero.

Deep-breathing. Deep-breathing.

That panic to apologise cracked into shards, plunged into the waters, dissolved.

11.

9 PM on 118th Avenue (*Khair-em-Sokar*, he reminded himself). Air was cool while they walked west, and the sky was charging itself into an electric violet so intense it hummed.

Been talking an hour. Couldn't remember the last time he'd had his mother's attention that long. Breathless, like hauling ass across a river by jumping from one crocodile's back to another: discovery, terror, exhilaration.

"When the army came to Juba," she whispered at the three stars piercing night's veil, "they arrestedt everyone workingk with us. Said we were all workingk with the SPLA. That's the—"

"—the Sudanese People's Liberation Army. I know what it is."

Glared at him. Him, catching her eyebrow, armed.

They crossed the street. A turning taxi stopped to let them pass. His mother waved to the South Sudanese driver—yet another person she'd probably helped.

"I'm guessing," said Raptor, clawing for more credit, "the fact his last name was Garang didn't help."

"It's a common name," she said, then nodded anyway. "But haffingk the same surname as the rebel leader doesn't endear you to the gunmen tryingk to kill him."

But as she explained, neither she nor his father had been in the SPLA or its political wing, the SPLM. His mother already had a party, and his father didn't trust large organisations, especially ones with guns.

"Your father was always more of an anarchist." She shook her head. "We'dt be up all night arguingk, listening to Sam Cooke and debating Marx versus Kropotkin . . . nott thatt the soldiers caredt."

"So what happened? I mean, after everyone got arrested?"

Her smile: like a blossom, losing its petals in one strong wind. "Months of misery."

No visitations for prisoners in the camp, but if there had been, they'd've arrested her, too. She'd been outside Juba on business when the army took the city. A poor family in the countryside took her in.

For "a forever," she didn't know if her man were dead, tortured or maimed. But when the SPLA retook the city, everyone was freed. Sort of.

"Your father wass a typical Dinka. Tall and skinny." They crossed 97th Street, passing the statue of a giant baseball bat his mother had always called the Freud statue.

"But after jail, he wass a skeleton. He'dt lossit his right pinky finger. He never toldt me how. He looked twenty years older."

Nearly all his father's fellow prisoners immediately joined the SPLA, especially after seeing how the national army had murdered its way across Juba, forcing kids to become soldiers.

"Nott thatt the SPLA didn't haff child soldiers," she said. "Some were only eleven years oldt. Turning children into killers . . . it's the worst abuse there is. And then these children, they twistt them, destroy their souls, and so they go out, and they, they, they infeccit everyone they meett like a virus."

Panicking that they'd have no choice but to join the war or be killed by one side of it, she and Jini decided to flee Sudan.

But she was five months pregnant.

He stopped walking. "You didn't *know*?"

"I was young. And I'dt always, well, I'd always . . . I hadt an uneven, you know— cycle." She stopped, turned to him.

"You know whatt thatt—"

"Yes, I know what that is!"

"Well, I don't know! I'm justt . . . !"

She resumed walking west. He sped up to catch her.

"Anyway, I didn'tt *show* much for the longestt time. I'dt been sick when your father wass in jail, so I thoughtt it wass just nerves.

"But by then I was so sick I could barely standt up half the time. I was throwingk up constantly. I'dt lost weight even though I was pregganant. How couldt we leave Sudan then? We didn'tt know whatt to do, so we hidt out in the countryside, switching homes among people we'dt worked with.

"And then it was Christmas, when you were born. And from thatt moment onwards," she said, "we were like birdts. Birdts who never foundt a branch to landt on."

For the government, Jini Garang was a marked man.

All it took was his letter-writing. He'd spent two years trying to build international business contacts so Dinka and other poor people could sell art and handcrafted goods and maybe attract an investor for small manufacturing.

To the men in the shadows, that made him look like a foreign agent.

After months in hiding, with horrible stories about what the army had done to his family, Jini Garang hacked a last desperate gambit to get them out of the country.

Fifty kilometres south of Juba, a contact stashed a motorboat. Given the poverty in the south, that boat might's well've been a yacht.

The plan was to hide by day and motor upriver by night, aiming for Uganda, but otherwise foot-crossing the border to meet another church-group contact who'd get them to Kampala or over into Kenya.

"Your father hadt me reciting every step of the plan," she said, "all the contaccit information, all the locations—he even hadt me drawingk outt a map by memory, again andt again."

But none of it mattered.

Somebody had tipped off somebody else.

"The nightt we were supposit to escape, we were bangingk around on dirt roads in your grandfather's car, racingk to get to the Nile. But then we saw somebody chasingk us, somebody in a vehicle thatt *wasn't* thirty years old and fallingk aparrit.

"And we knew, we didn'tt even haff to talk, we understoodt: we'dt never make itt as far as the river before they caughtt us and killedt us.

"I was holdingk you in my arms and your father was screamingk at me to repeat the plan, repeat the plan, *repeat the plan!* And I was so scaredt I was cryingk because I knew whatt he was goingk to do.

"He toldt me I hadt to keep goingk without him and he pulledt over and kissedt me and you andt jumpedt out and saidt, 'Hangk onto him, no matter whatt!' And then he ran straightt for thatt car thatt was followingk us.

"And I never saw him again."

In the shadows between two streetlamps, she turned away from him. The insides of her wrists, up against the sides of her cheeks, once, twice.

From television, he knew that that was the moment he was supposed to hug her.

But he hadn't watched that channel since he was a kid.

"So whatt couldt I do?" she said. "Whatt couldt I do?"

Was she actually asking him?

She'd raced to the motorboat in the darkness, threw in their four bags of food and belongings, set her swaddled baby on the boat's floor, and somehow started the motor on the first try before dodging crocodiles and hippopotami on their long trip up the Nile.

Her story, his story, their story dwelt in nights, past and present beneath a dome of blossoming lights, her words slipping round his skin in harsh caress like a coarse blanket, as if he'd lived her tale with more than just an infant's bewildered perceptions, when he'd been baby-pressed against his mother's back or breast or belly, when his mother's body might as well have been the sky stretched out and wrapped in glinting golden chains of stars from horizon-fingertips to horizon-toes.

Her voice. Hollowing against concrete, mosquitoes humming like a violin section: a time warp echoing a phantom-life nearly two decades gone and half-a-planet away.

Never even got close to Uganda. A hippopotamus destroyed their boat and almost took them with it.

"They're nott cute, like in the cartoons, you know!" she said. "They're monsters, with mouths bigk enough to swallow you whole. They kill more people than any other animal in Africa!"

They'd joined up with dozens and then hundreds of displaced Dinka marching across southern Sudan, eventually re-routing thousands of kilometres off-course to refugee camps in Ethiopia, and later to Kenya, back to Sudan and then to Chad and back to Kenya again as countries changed governments and governments changed whims and lives.

"I remember," she said, "how birdts would be standingk by the thousandts over dusty fields, and then suddenly—*whoosh!*—they'dt all be scuttered and flyingk. That meantt raiders were comingk."

"Raiders?"

"Gun men. Men who plannedt to kill us or rape us or sell us into slavery, or rape us and *then* kill us—"

"Who were they? I mean, which side were they on?"

"Men with guns are always on the same side," she said. "Whoever paidt for the guns."

And she and the few women who still possessed white clothes agonised that they couldn't wear the colour of mourning for their butchered men and sisters and parents and children, "because then the bombers could've seen us while we were walking."

Flooding over Raptor like the rushing Nile: a month of marching from Sudan to Ethiopia . . . terror when gun men confronted them . . . relief and tears when it was SPLA, there to protect their raggedy convoy . . . running out of food and then water, and only UNHCR caches dropped along their paths to keep them alive . . . some wanderers so hungry they ate leaves, some dying from eating poisonous ones . . . his mother fording a river with him floating beside her in a handmade basket, and crocodiles would have massacred them both except the monsters were too busy ripping spines from ribs from four other people while she fled to the opposite riverbank to scramble up a tree with him, later strapped to her back, to stay there all day and all night . . . and one cataclysmic day in Ethiopia, when something like eighteen thousand people tried crossing a river to escape murder-by-militia, hundreds of them drowned after their boats overloaded capsized or hundreds others were killed by unknown gunmen.

And finally, after years of running and being run out of one land and into the next, they left their camp in Kenya for Canada.

He'd asked her about his father, and the story had taken them all the way here. He wanted—he needed—to ask her about Kenya. About Jacob's Ladder.

But how much could either of them take? All this misery from their past. Like diving into the Swamps of Death to rescue children drowning there: how long could you fight off the crocodiles or hold your breath before you died in the depths?

Another time.

Maybe next decade.

But one final question.

"Why'd you name me Raphael?"

Figured it had to be heavy. Probably not the painter. Obviously not the ninja turtle. A grandfather's name? Some radical?

She smiled. "Your father wantedt to call you Samuel, after Sam Cooke. But I hatedt the name Sam, so I saidt why nott the *new* Sam Cooke, Raphael Saadiq?"

"Get outta here! That retro guy? Are you serious? I'm named after *him*?"

"I don't expect you kidts today to appreciate good music—"

"'Kids today'? My mp3 player's got Sam Cooke on it! *And* Fela! And King Sunny Ade! And Hugh Masekela! And Harry Belafonte—you coulda named me after any of them—"

"Well, it doesn'tt matter anyway, since now you're a Raptor, Raptor."

Stopped walking. Facing each other. Next to the municipal airport on Kingsway Avenue at 117th Street, the road lined with sodium lamps gleaming like the eyes of a promenade of sphinxes.

"Mum." Invoking her title for the first time that night. "Why didn't you ever tell me all this?"

Her, looking above the airport and up into the vast darkness of space. A single helicopter slicing the night with its search beams.

"What were you afraid of?"

Her eyes, on that helicopter.

She swallowed. "I don'tt know. I justt . . . I wasn't raisedt here, Rapha—*R-r-raptor*. With *Oprah* and *Maury* and people goingk on national television and tellingk all their secrets—"

"We're not on TV. And I'm your son."

Closed her mouth.

Did she even know why she hadn't told him?

Her: "Are you really goingk to liff with this wolf-man friendt of yours?"

"His name's Jackal, Mum."

"Jackal, then. Are you? Can'tt we talk aboutt this in the morningk? Couldn't you jussit . . . wait a few days, and, and talk together aboutt this?"

He looked up. The helicopter, heading north.

"So, does that mean we're gonna talk about you and Doctor Liberia, too?"

Both of them, standing in silence. Watching the chopper sliding slowly beyond the dark buildings of the NAIT campus before finally diappearing.

12.

Two days later. 3:30 PM in the afternoon at the Street Laboratory.

Raptor disclosed it all to Moon. The conversation. His own confusion.

"People hang onto all kinds of shit for what they think is all kinds of reasons," said Moon, sorting through Falcon registration files, making a call-back list to track Falcons who hadn't been round in a while.

"But those reasons are all pyrite," said Moon. "There's just one real reason."

"They think hanging on'll help them survive—live longer, be happier, be safer. 'Don't give away that food! Don't share that friend! Don't say "I love you."' They figure if they give away their stash, they're vulnerable. Can you transform that?"

"Transformed," said Raptor. He'd double-timed it by bicycle to get there after school before the *shenu* for the Daily Alchemy.

But already other Street Falcons from closer high schools such as Vic and St. Joe's were trickling in and trading Throne-clasps and *Nub-Wmet-Ānkhs*.

A whole squad of Falcons was ooing and awing over the Street Laboratory's newest poster: a digitally-coloured blow-up of the picture Raptor'd done for Jackal, the one of Hru and Yinepu battling monsters in the Savage Lands.

Raptor smiled at their admiration, then asked, "Hey, who coloured that?"

"Sister Yibemnoot. She's got skills."

"Man, she could colour for Dark Horse!"

"Indeed," said Brother Moon. "But let's focus. Look at Hru and the *Mesnitu*, his legion of Blacksmiths. What'd they do because of all the pain and misery they were suffering? Did they hole up in the Savage Lands, hoarding their gold? No. One, because they knew there was no way that'd work: the Destroyer was coming for them no matter what, and their mud-brick fortress was gonna fall. So what *did* they do?"

"Revolution?"

"That's right. And . . . ?"

"Replace-Elevate?"

"Transformed, bruh!" Moon smiled and offered him a Throne-clasp. The man never clapped him on the shoulder like he did other Falcons, not since he'd freaked out during that first *jiu-jitsu* lesson.

"They went across the Savage Lands," said Moon, "to all the sweatfields and mines and cells and harems where people were chained and tortured and terrified, and they made stand those who wept, they revealed those hid their faces and they lifted up those who sank down."

Already a couple of dozen Falcons had arrived, forming two concentric rings.

"They didn't hoard their alchemy," said Moon. "They *taught* it. So everyone could rise nearer to the supreme.

"If you *keep* your gold, it just devolves into lead. Whole tombs full of it. It's only by giving it away that you truly become rich . . . . Transform that?"

Raptor looked at him a while. "Yes."

"Good. Now let's join the *shenu*."

"Whatcha working on?" said Yibemnoot. Clutching her rolled-up waiver like a scroll. She'd cornered Raptor at his table at the back of the Lab.

5:38 PM. Most of the Falcons were heading home for dinner and a parental signature on the waivers for the free flight lessons *Sbai* Seshat had arranged.

Raptor'd already forged his mother's signature on his.

"Uh—"

"C'mon," she said, reaching for his stack of ink drawings. He had to fight the urge to stop her.

She glued her eyes to the top one, a falcon with triumphant wings, silhouetted against a sunburst, orbited by a series of Kemetic hieroglyphs.

"Supreme!" she said, bright eyes and teeth. "What's this for?"

"I'm . . . uh . . . I'm trying to come up with, like, a logo or a flag or something, for the, y'know—"

"The Street Falcons!"

"Exactly—"

Tried not to stare at her staring at his art, pointedly staring at some posters even when he saw her staring at him.

"So, brother, did you even see what I did with your Hru and Yinepu poster? The digital painting?"

Looked away and nodded. Glanced back.

Her smile flatlined.

"Oh. Well . . . did you . . . uh . . . like it?"

Chewed the inside of his mouth. "It was, uh, y'know . . . I just didn't expect . . . I mean, I've never worked with anybody on art before. I mean, you did stuff I, uh, I just wouldn't've done."

She put his art back on the table.

"Oh."

Great job, genius.

Raptor: "But, but it was good. I mean, really."

She backed a step away from the table, glanced out the door towards the bus stop.

"Muh-maybe, sister, we could, y'know . . . do some *more* art or something."

She glanced back at him.

"I gotta catch my bus, Raptor," she said.

Walk her to the bus stop, moron.

Stayed sitting. Watched her walk out. The door, jangling open, hissing closed.

Looking down, shuffling his papers, uncapping his pens.

13.

"You two kill me!" said Moon that same night at the Hyper-Market. "I'm really disappointed with you!"

Raptor and Jackal, staring at feet, floor, walls, anything.

"Well?" pressed the older man.

"Brother Moon, what difference does it make?" said Jackal. "We're still gonna get our diplomas—"

"*Worthless* diplomas," he growled. "You're taking, what do they call it now?" He glanced back at their class schedules he'd asked to inspect. "English Thirty-Two?"

"Thirty-*dash*-Two," offered Raptor.

"When I was in school they called it English 33. Remedial. Get a diploma, Do Not Pass Go, Do Not Go to University."

Both boys: "University?"

"Yes, university!"

"Brother Moon, all respect due," said Jackal, tilting his head so his locks grazed his right shoulder, "but, but, university? I mean . . . what good's that gonna do?"

"Better jobs, better money, live longer and healthier? What's not to like? Get smart or die slaving!"

"My dad has a PhD," said Jackal in a small voice.

Raptor snapped his eyes towards his brother, who never talked about his father. Moon's eyes widened.

"And he drives a taxi."

Moon paused to pour coffee for a customer and give him a login code for carrel #3.

"Okay, I transform that," said Moon. "It's true. A lot of our people from the continent are in the same pit. Pilots who aren't allowed to fly, surgeons who aren't allowed to slice, teachers who aren't allowed to teach—"

Jackal: "I can't afford fifteen-twenny grand trainin for a job they aint even gon *give* me."

"Listen," said Moon, "you two are smart. You know the Scrolls, you're masterful with words when we make our Daily Alchemy . . . we talk about books, you're both insightful. Your posts on the Street Falcons blog are excellent—"

"You *read* those?" The bright words'd bubbled out of Raptor before he could stop them.

"Course I read them! Why wouldn't I?"

Moon brought them to carrel #6, opened up their school's website course listings for English and laid out their battle plan: they were immediately to get out of Grade 12 remedial lit class—English 30-2—and *re*-register in half-year Grade 11 academic English, 20-1, so they could take 30-1 in the second semester. He'd give them any help they needed.

"But later for this 'good enough' bullshit. You two have *gold* minds. Why your teachers never saw that before—well, we know why they didn't see it. When it's our kids, getting sixty percent is supposedly the best we're capable of. No cause to worry or even call home.

"*I'd* been teaching you? I'da pushed you into advanced placement. That's what I took when I was your age, and not even half the class had your smarts. They were just there because their parents were judges, doctors, professors—ambitious people who wanted trophy kids, regardless of what they could actually do."

Jackal: "But what about a J-O-B? Even if I *got* the paper?"

"Bruh, success is like . . . like a penalty shot. You grab your stick, focus on the net, you still gotta beat that goalie, but yeah, you could score. But you skate off the ice, take your blades off, then you have zero chance of hitting the mesh.

"I can't guarantee you'll make the point, but I *do* guarantee that you'll *get* that shot, and that means being ready for it when it comes, and *staying on the ice*."

Moon asked him what he wanted to do for a career.

"I wanna be a producer, like Jay-Z."

"J-C, Jay-Z," said Raptor, and they all laughed. Jackal dropped: "He's got like two hundred million dollars—"

"You wanna be a producer? Supreme." Still at carrel #6, he image-Googled Jay-Z, brought up the boyish-looking aging rapper in a power suit.

"So you go to NAIT and study sound engineering. Get a diploma so you can work in any music studio anywhere in the world. You take some business courses so you can handle your own money—"

"Yeah, but Jay-Z never went to university, and he's super smart."

"Think about basketball, bruh," said Moon, image-searching for shots of b-ballers. He clicked on two, left them up.

"The buzzer's gonna go off in ten seconds. Do you get lazy, like this guy, don't even run, just take the shot from behind the centre line? Or do you run like this guy to take your shot from the key?"

Clicked back to Jay-Z.

"Jay-Z's one in a million. There's *maybe* a coupla dozen music producers earning his kinda money. You're damn right, he's smart. You think a lawyer's smarter than he is?"

Jackal said, "Hell, no!"

Raptor: "Maybe Brother Maāhotep."

Jackal: "Well, yeah. He's pretty smart. But he aint rich."

"Brother's doing well," said Moon. "But outta all the *un*educated but intelligent young rappers out there, how many you calculate wanna get rich, but end up poor? Maybe, ninety-nine-point-nine-nine-*nine* percent?"

"Now, what percentage of *educated* lawyers who *aren't* smart get rich? Or at least Maāhotep-comfortable?"

Raptor rolled back on his heels. Jackal eyed him sideways.

"You transform that?" said Moon. "Yes, Leadites and Pyrites buried your father's gold. That's a fact. It's serious. But you were *born* in the Savage Lands, transform? So what can *you* see, because your Shining Eye was forged here, that your father can't?"

Jackal looked at the screen, then at Moon. "I can see the traps? The pits the chainsmen dug in the ground?"

"Transformed. And what else?"

"I can track the Wanderers? Like, to build up an army?"

"Transformed. And?"

"I can train the *Mesnitu* and make my own forge?"

"Transform—"

"I can drain the Swamps of Death and master the elevated lands, and raise a Golden Fortress for the orphans of the Savage Lands—"

"Transform—"

"I can create hope, joy and justice to make stand those who weep, to reveal those who hide their faces, and to lift up those who sink down—"

And all three of them leapt in: "In doing so, we will all rise nearer to the Supreme."

Grade 7. Raptor, sitting at the back of the class. His homeroom teacher Mr. Manna, the same one who'd called him "dumb as a sack of hammers" in front of a colleague without realising he could speak English . . . he was making the class announce what career they wanted when they grew up.

Raptor spent the long wait with coals in his lungs till it was his turn, hating being forced to talk in front of the class, but telling the truth: he wanted to be an astronomer.

In front of everybody, Mr. Manna told him he should focus on something attainable.

"Do you know what 'attainable' means, Raphael? You're probably good with your hands, right? How about being a cook or something like that? Or maybe house painting. Long as there's houses, there's always gonna be money in house painting. But a scientist?" He actually goddamn *chuckled*.

"That's just not *attainable* for someone like you."

A gaping asshole. Raptor'd never doubted his own brain: when he put his mind to a task he was smarter than almost anyone he knew.

But so what? What was attainable on the open roads of the world when the pyrites posted men like Mr. Manna with swords at every gate and border?

"Earth to Raptor," said Moon.

Jackal was looking at him, too, eyes waiting. "I said, what do *you* want to do for a living?"

Reflexively, shrugging: "I'ont know."

Instantly, Moon: "I don't believe you. If you could do anything, if you could *be* anything—"

Burning, his shoulders—

And the cell phone ringing in his pocket.

Checking: his mother. Excused himself, slipped into the corner to take it.

After he motioned for Moon to step away from the cash register so they could talk in the corner.

"My, uh . . . my mother." Shook his head as if to shake away the embarrassment. "She wants to meet you."

"Based on your voice, should I be afraid?"

"Honestly, I don'know. Maybe."

"How long do I have?"

"I can stall her for maybe a week."

"Stall her? No disrespect, but how hard a woman is she to deal with when she's angry?"

"Like the Devourer of Souls."

Moon snorted. "Thanks for the heads-up. In the meantime, you get your registration changed, transform? And tomorrow I wanna X-ray your math skills."

9 PM. His and Jackal's shifts were over, and since Jackal's parents were actually letting him sleep over a second night in a row (what was one more teenager inside a Somali apartment?), they headed out together.

His mother. She was resourceful. Like a detective when she wanted to be. She knew where Moon's businesses were.

Raptor's worlds were on a collision course and there was nothing he could do to stop it. And not Static, not Master Jehu, not even Hru and all his legions armed with shining golden hammers had the might to hold back planets.

14.

Saturday. Just before noon. At the flight school off Kingsway Avenue since 8 AM, learning how to check the flaps, the ailerons, the rudder, the suspension and fuselage, and then the fuel and oil levels.

With the pilot beside him inside the Helio Courier's cockpit, Raptor checked the radio, local air traffic, weather and wind speed, and then the pilot taxied into position before lifting him, Jackal and Moon into space.

Still ten days away from witnessing his mother storm into the Falcons' Somali mosque forum on autism and yank his mentor into a side room to order him, "Stop tryingk to steal my son!"

So in that pristine moment before world rammed into world, Raptor hurtled through the sky while encased in steel, his brother and his teacher at his back, his heart hammering like a guild of blacksmiths.

The pilot yelled at him above the roar that it was time, and Raptor put his left hand on the controls, and vibrating up his arm into his heart was all the power of the engine and the wings, and by uniting the circuit with his right hand, he felt exhilaration coursing through him left to right: arm, leg, leg, arm, head. . .

. . . descending. . .

. . . banking. . .

. . . strong-arming the delicate labour of staying on course. . .

. . . and climbing . . . .

The Helio rattling in the rushing river of air, loud like swimming inside a vein of lightning, and the sky a membrane of blue so intense it was an infinity away and close enough to touch.

And for the brevity of those forty minutes suspended above the earth, and for the first time in his short, broken life . . .

Raptor felt

entirely

free.

Seven
Replace-Elevate

The Book of Then

1.

I'D ABANDONED MY MASTER, MY COUSIN-AND-BROTHER, AND MY FORTRESS OF children.

I was alone in the Savage Lands.

And I'd murdered my own mother.

I invoked my words-of-power to become a shadow. Said them again, and again, and again, *kheper-nyi em khaibt, kheper-nyi em khaibt, kheper-nyi em khaibt . . .* until the shadow became so deep that the world itself became a shadow to me. The stars darkened. The moon was snuffed out. My hands in front of my own eyes were gone.

I'd melt into the night and be done with it all forever.

No more nightmare nights of abandonment and rage. No more trying and failing to save kids from being butchered by crocodiles. No more witnessing soldiers enslaving children, beholding hills of severed hands left behind as flesh-cairn warnings. No more being lied to or denied the truth by those I trusted most.

No more.

2.

And so I stayed in the realm of shades.

How long'd I been there? Half a day? A month?

But I could still hear.

Everything was choked and thick and far away, like I was drowning at the bottom of the Swamps of Death.

Thudding of many paws on sand . . .

The flapping of wings . . .

> *. . . Yih, seseneb, ser, skhai Aset-netchit,*
> *Aset-uret-mut-Hru, Aset-Mehhit. . .*
> *maākheru em Yih . . .*

Who was there? What was happening?
Flickers of light . . . the moon smashed
on the surface of the water . . .
Real? A dream?
Was I dying?

Who are you?

I'm the Measurer.

Ah, so you're the Measurer. Your reputation flowers across Ta-Seti, the Blackland, the Savage Lands, even down to Rebarna.

Thank you.

That's not a compliment. They call you a baby-eating baboon. They say you snatch up children after ambushing their parents and slitting their throats, then "appear out of nowhere" to these wandering orphans like you're some sort of saviour. Take them to your prison and then do gods-know-what to them.

People believe whatever they want, even obviously idiotic things.

I notice you didn't deny my charge, Measurer. So how about it? Are you the one who kidnapped my son? Enslaved him? Imprisoned him? Broke his spirit to make him think I'm his enemy?

Dogs, growling, ready to attack . . .
Whispered:

Keep your legion still, my son. Don't let your belly control you. Close your Shining Eye, and dream of a lotus flower sipping from the mists of morning.

Silence.

You're wrong, milady. Yes, I recruit abandoned children, but not for the mines, not for the fields, nor for the dunes of organised murder. Others do that—you may know some. I recruit these children for my school. I teach them because no one else will. We work together to feed and house each other. And no one's enslaved, except perhaps by loyalty or love. Yes, your son's in a prison, but not one I made.

Again, silence.

I strained at the edge of my hearing,
hearing nothing, and even the shards of light died.

. . . absence, not even echo,
not even shadow, not even spark . . .

. . . simply

nothing. . .

3.

I'd forgotten I'd ever had eyes, forgotten they'd ever been open or closed.

I opened them anyway.

I was gone from the world.

Below my feet:

A vast white disk of silt and sand.

It ran to distant edge of a black dome embedded with stars.

And before me was Master Jehu.

Except his skin was even darker than usual, as black as the sky above, and his eyes were rimmed with gold.

"Master . . . where are we?"

He touched my shoulder. His hand was cool water on burned skin.

"My son," he whispered, "I've taken you to my secret abode: the Silver Desert. When all you children are asleep, this is where I go to pray and think. To become strong again."

I looked around in awe, and when I gazed up, my gut leapt as if I were looking down, as if the only thing keeping me from falling were the Master.

There, "down" in the sky, a disk of blue and green and streaked with white. Somehow I knew it was where I was from.

"Master, thank you for this blessing. But . . . why've you taken me here?"

"You . . . you don't remember . . . what you did, do you?"

What did he mean? I tried to understand, but my past was thick, wet, jade-dark, cold. I tried moving through that night-jungle, but weeds and vines wrapped round me till I couldn't move.

"My boy," said the Master sadly. We sat together on white rocks. "You sank so far into the shadow-world I took me months to find you."

Why didn't he give up after all that time? "You looked for me for *months*?"

He was surprised, and even hurt.

"Why wouldn't I?"

In his eyes: all his years, all his children saved, and all the ones he'd lost.

I hugged him. He hugged me back without hesitation.

187

We walked past jagged silver mountains, finally kneeling to drink the sparkling water from a lake of tranquility.

He told me what I'd done.

It was like the Swamps surging over me, full of shit and blood and brine and vines, and a whirlpool sucking me down—

—and the Master's hand caught me, and pulled me back.

"All this time," I whispered, panting, panting, "I've been asking, 'Who is the Destroyer?' And—"

"Yes. Well," said the Master, "there are questions we all need to ask of others, and of ourselves, forever."

He held my shoulder. "Come with me."

4.

Down we went.

Deep inside a vast bubble in the rock, the Master led me to a basin in the stone. He made me stand at the centre.

He ascended stairs hacked from the walls, stood beside a huge stalactite whose bottom was shorn off, the broken fang of a monster big enough to swallow the sun.

Whispered: words-of-power. . .

. . . echoing, echoing, *ECHOING INTO THUNDER.*

Molten silver erupted from the stalactite, flooding the basin and scalding me up to my legs, my chest, my neck—

—screaming, and the silver burning me, chewing the meat from my spine, screaming and screaming, burning, *DROWNING*—

—and as I died, they bubbled up beside me: Duam, our strongest warrior, guts boiling out of his belly—I held onto him . . . blackened, smoking skeletons—I clutched them . . . children, their hands full of roots and rocks and each other's eyes and teeth—I grabbed them . . . a woman's torso, her empty neck—I held onto it, too . . . and that woman's head, her face, her eye-sockets puddled with searing silver, reflecting my face while her mouth screamed steam—I reached for it, too—

—above, upon the stairs, Master Jehu yelling at me, echoing thunder crushing his voice—and yet—

Do not drown in the
Swamps of Death!

—but how? How could they be here?

Let go of them!

He hurled a great golden chain which unfurled all the way to me.

Hold fast!

My vision was white with agony. My hands were burning bones dripping flesh. I couldn't—

Refuse to grasp the golden chain
and die. Choose to and live!

I released the savaged corpses, wrapped my ravaged hands around the chain, and Master Jehu pulled me from the scalding cauldron, my flesh attached by agony alone to my bones, my lungs emptied of screams.

He laid me on the stairs, spoke a word-of-power and broke off a length of chain as easily as tearing leaves from maize. He looped the shining gold, a sun-ray curved upon itself, and placed it on my heart.

"Hold this talisman," he said, placing my ruined hand upon it. He whispered to me a word-of-power.

"Close your eyes. Breathe as deeply as you can. Sing inside your heart the word I've given you."

I did.

The silver swamp drained away down holes inside the rocks.

My pain was gone.

And my body was whole again.

"Master . . . what . . . *how*?"

"This is where your souls have been trapped," he whispered, but this time, the echoes scattered like dewdrops from shaken leaves.

"Whenever your souls fall to drown in the Swamps of Death," he said, "clutch this *ujat*, breathe from belly's base to the peak of your skull, speak the word I've given you, and free them."

"But . . . how can the Swamps be here?"

I saw myself, twinned and tiny, inside the Master's onyx eyes.

"The Swamps of Death," he said so quietly I almost couldn't hear him, "are every-where."

Into my spine, like an arrow, and then silver flowed scaldingly again from the stalactite, so much faster than the first time that we'd both burn and drown.

"What is it?" yelled Master.

I didn't want to say—surely that couldn't be it? "I don't know, Master!"

"Tell me, Hru!"

I choked out, "Why did Falcon leave me, Master?"

"Remember what I taught you!"

I clutched my *ujat*, breathed from my belly's base to my skull's zenith, invoked his word-of-power, did as he said, and the silver stopped spewing . . . but it remained below us in the bottom of the basin.

"All things," said Master Jehu, "meet the wind eventually."

He clutched his own *ujat* and continued.

"Since I became a man, I've found and gathered children wandering the Savage Lands. I've fed them, given them Instructions, watched them build cities, sometimes seen them burn them. And I've grieved for all of them.

"We must go back, Hru, to the world of tears. The both of us. Our compound in the Savage Lands isn't enough for all the children lost in pain. We built a wall to protect everyone inside it. Now we have to do the same for everyone *outside* of the wall.

"The compound can't last, and can't do what must be done. So you must build a Golden Fortress, one that will last forever, that will shine in the sunrise as a beacon to the universe."

"*Me?*"

"Yes, you. Not by yourself, of course, but with others. And you, because of who you are, are indispensable."

"But Master . . . with what I've done . . . how could I . . . I don't *deserve* to—"

"I've healed you because all people deserve to be healed, Hru. But I'm sending you to build a Golden Fortress because the cosmos needs it. And because of your debt and your guilt, you must be the first mason to hew and lay its stones."

"*How?*"

"Go back to the compound with me. And every place you find a rotten wooden beam or crumbling, sunbaked brick of mud, insert a stone you've cut and baptised in molten gold."

I took his hand in mine, held my *ujat* with the other.

We breathed and whispered, and the silver drained away below us.

We ascended to the Silver Desert.

Master Jehu invoked words-of-power I'd never heard before. He stood before me, a black ibis with gold-rimmed eyes, and I was a black-feathered falcon with golden talons.

We flew among the stars until we found ourselves again inside the Savage Lands at night.

I told the Master how I planned to start my labours, and he gave me benediction.

5.

Out beneath the white-fogged sun and among the dead-black trees around the Swamps of Death, I wielded Fang, the bringer of death, the agent of a son's worst crime.

Skeleton-trunks and -branches crashed where my arm made wind. I gripped their bases, hurled them, cleared a highway.

Crocodiles formed an army round me, hating me for their brother I'd killed those brutal years ago.

I held my blade towards them. It shone no longer white, nor pink, nor even silver. But now a gleaming gold.

"Find another place to haunt and hunt," I warned them. "I won't invite you a second time."

Some crawled away among the vines. Others sank into the Swamps and disappeared.

I sank Fang into the soil, cutting mud and roots and rocks, sweating and hurling rubble to the west, digging my channel to drain the Swamps of Death.

The Book of Now

1.

WELCOME IN," ECHOED MOON'S VOICE FROM THE BOTTOM OF THE STAIRWELL.

Raptor: fussing, hustling serving dishes of greens and candied yams and carved turkey from kitchen to dining table, and the steaming bean pie straight. His drum-n-bass heart skitter-scattershot on every step.

And then there she was.

Top of the landing in the suite above the Hyper-Market, putting down a bag, sliding a Saran-wrapped bowl of salad onto the counter, brushing snow from the shoulders of her coat like it was totally normal for her to be there.

Hadn't expected her to dress like *this* tonight. Sure, sometimes she got lucky at Good Will or caught a sale at Zellers. Figured she'd be formal or maybe plain, not this blue satin fitted-blouse trying to out-sheen her hair, not dark pants spotless and iron-creased.

Yeah, he'd seen her since he'd moved in with Moon, but at this moment his eyes had hit Reset. He saw her the way Jackal'd described her months ago: like Iman.

Her: left foot. Right foot. Again. Small gesture: handing him the bag she'd just put down. Nodding. Sad/resigned.

"Merry Christmas, R-r-raptor. And happy eighteenth birthday."

Took it from her.

Moon pointedly left to hang up his mother's coat.

"He really helpedt you cook all this?" Araweelo sat, admiring the remains of the wealth spread across the table. She put her napkin beside her plate. "It was all delicious."

"Your son's a very intelligent young man. Picks up things quickly. I showed him a few things in the kitchen—"

Raphael: "I love cooking!" Too quickly, too loudly. A pre-emptive strike. He was sure she was gonna say something like *How come you never cooked like this at home? Or at all?*

Then again, she herself hated cooking. Maybe she'd never regarded his lack of interest as a failure.

Been two months since she tried guilting him into coming home. Hadn't criticised him or complained once during dinner. Briefly inspected his spotless room at

Moon's loft, saying she was impressed how responsible Raptor was. But that was it: only sign she was checking up on him.

Been ready for all-out combat that night. In September she'd yelled at Moon in person and on the phone. Since then, ice replaced fire after Raptor'd finally told her he wasn't actually living with Jackal, but with Moon.

Her, then, almost pleading: "How do you know he's nott a draak dealer? Or a pedophile?"

But time rolled. And eventually so did she. Even met Moon twice for tea. To discuss terms of her surrender.

Now she was here, and nobody was yelling. Fact, she was even *smiling*.

"You big into Christmas?" asked Moon. "I mean, for a Somali?"

His mother gave *that look*, flame-sizzling Raptor's neck.

"Dependts what you mean by 'big.' For an *atheist* , yes, I guess so."

Moon chuckled. "I hear that."

And then she chuckled too, and that was that.

Conversation. Laughter. Finally Moon put on music, and Raptor and Araweelo eye-mailed each when the shuffle mix landed on "100 Yard Dash" by Raphael Saadiq, the retro rhythm-and-bluesman after whom Araweelo'd named her son.

Didn't know if it was the turkey's tryptophan, or maybe the carb-overload from the bean pie that'd steamed its vanilla-pecan cap into a lagoon, but Raptor's head, chest and limbs were humming. Like falling asleep on a bus next to the radiator after walking half-an-hour through a blizzard.

Coffee and tea stoked conversation. Araweelo told Moon how back in the camps, she'd earned the name "Madame President" because of her advocacy of fellow refugees.

"But what they didn't understandt," she chuckled, "was that I stayedt busy to keep from going 'cuckoo.'"

Moon laughed at the word, but for Raptor, that one sentence hyperlink clicked him through a gallery of his mother's committees, meetings, workshops and other busy-ness that consumed her since they'd landed.

Moon, quieter than usual. But smiling. Listening to how she co-edited an online newspaper by, for and about South Sudanese women, one of the only online papers of its type in the world, and was helping a local Dinka mother promote her PC-built CD. Smiling every time she produced a Dinka term from her word-forge. Raptor, for the first time, clutching each expression to his own spine, hammering it till it rang and echoed.

Dheeng: a mindset of dignity.

Other topics that meant little to Raptor, but crackled like popcorn between the two adults: how Moon didn't give two breaths for pseudo-revolutionaries waging online wars instead of organising in their own neighbourhoods, beret-wearers lost in rhetoric while "waiting for the Red Rapture."

Araweelo cracked up at that. She said after she got to Canada, she read Mao's Little Red Book in English for the first time, and then burnt it. Did the same with al-Qadhdhaafi's Green Book.

"Once I foundt out the truth about the 'strong men' back home, how many people they butcheredt, how many lies they toldt" (her eyes: like she was calling down lightning) "there was no way I was ever goingk to believe in 'strong men' again!"

And she and Moon ripped into bitter eulogies for a dozen fallen gods.

Raptor cleaned the table, washed the dishes. Minding and rewinding the strong man his mother'd lost while racing with her baby towards a boat on the river to nowhere. Thinking how despite her boast, she'd never stopped believing in strong men, had chained herself and her son to a brutal-mouthed adultering drunk for years.

She could brag all she wanted about destroying pyrite idols, but she was the one who'd thrown open the gates so the Destroyer could enter their land.

"Young bruh," whispered Moon, while Araweelo fussed her coat and scarf into place, "I think your mum seriously needs you to come along for the ride. It's Christmas. Come on."

For Moon—under protest.

Pulled on his coat, grabbed a sabaayat he'd pan-fried hours before, and scrolled the flatbread into his pocket.

Sat chewing it in the back seat of Moon's spotless gold-and-black Sunfire.

Rolling down *Khair-em-Sokar*—118th Avenue—Moon and Araweelo chattering. Raptor couldn't really hear them, what with Zuhura Swaleh's sweet wails and the Mombasa band's keyboards sparkling over Moon's sound system. Sat watching streetlights streak past like falling stars.

Finally pulled up in front of Al Hambra apartment across from the 7-11.

Moon leapt out of the Sunfire to open Araweelo's door, then walked her to the front entrance.

Raptor took his bitter time getting out of the back seat.

His eyes froze.

On Al Hambra's landing. The two adults hugging in the street-lit darkness. Breath misting away from each one's face as they pulled back. Raptor's stomach boiling Christmas-birthday dinner into brine soup.

Wasn't like she held him *that* long. Just *too* long.

Moon passed him on the way back to the car, giving him time for his own goodbye.

"Kinda surprised you even came," Raptor blurted at her. "Never thought Doctor Liberia'd let you. Figured he'd want you waiting for him after his family dinner ended—"

"—Jacob and I aren't seeing each other anymore, Raptor."

Stood silently staring at his mother. All out of ammo.

"I'm hoping," she whispered, "that, well . . . it's almost the new year."

She leaned in to kiss his cheek before he could pull away. Put one hand on the door before slipping inside, turning: "Let's findt a way out of this wilderness we're in, all rightt?"

Closed the door, probably so she could pre-empt whatever nasty shit was gurgling in his guts.

And she woulda been right.

2.

Raptor wanted to rush the older man.

Wanted to.

February 6, 6 PM, everything but car lights black through the window of Data Salvation Laboratories. Moon waited until the last customer hit the street and the quiet Rwandan NAIT student Hakizimana began cashing out.

Finally, finally, he opened Raptor's report card.

Raptor's lungs, like balloons, ready to pop.

Moon, eye-cannons swiveling right onto his skull.

His hammer-fist up beside his temple—

Moon: "Transformed!" And slow-mo John Henrying a dap down to Raptor's fist.

"Seventy-five percent! On your *first* stint in academic English!" shouted Moon. Brother Hakizimana worriedly peeked around the corner.

"Here," said Moon, handing him a package from below the counter. Raptor opened it, but had no idea what it was.

"It's a model rocket," explained Moon. "It actually flies—hundreds of metres, straight up. I bought myself one, too. We're gonna build em! It's a great hobby. Usedta launch these when I was your age."

Raptor thanked him. "Is this supposed to be a metaphor or something?"

"You damn right it's a metaphor!" He slow-punched at Raptor, who ducked gra-a-a-acefully.

"Next up, Grade 12 English . . . and we're gonna make sure you get an honours mark!"

And Raptor—remembering the many nights they'd worked together on his assignments and essays and how many times, when he was seven seconds away from quitting Moon said, "Just gimme seven more minutes. If you don't get it in seven, you can quit"—Raptor believed him.

3.

"On behalf of my fellow young Alchemists," said Yibemnoot onstage, looking strange without her rhinestone Playboy hoodie, "and because I even got a score of 880, I dedicate tonight's transformation to the double righteousness-and-mastery of Brother Malcolm X, who dwells eternally in peace."

She'd gotten the top score at Afro-Quiz but lost the crowd in her victory speech.

The MC, a Malawian systems analyst and community activist named Siyani, explained to the crowd why the young sister was highlighting February 21, saying how impressed he was by how educated and conscious the new generation was.

Then the crowd gave Yibemnoot her props, and Raptor struggled to keep the fireworks from his eyes.

In the basement of the Stanley Milner, outside the theatre where they'd just been doing battle, young Alchemist contestants double-armed their trophies and prizes, while families and fellow Street Falcons surged forward for bumps, daps, soul-shakes and hugs.

Jackal: "Damn, son. You see them other contestants? Jaws all hanging slack like broke jock straps?"

Raptor laughed. "They looked like we pantsed em or suh'm."

Thandie, the tall, pretty Falcon with a perpetual orbit of boys, held court in the corner. She'd gotten eliminated in the second round. The questions weren't fair: a whole category on Nelson Mandela? Sister Ãnkhur giggled compassionately, reminding her that everyone'd gotten the same study package. She backed off when Thandie unsheathed her eyes.

Raptor, who'd won second place, refocused on his mother and Brother Moon (a super-smiling Moon kept repeating, "*You lit em up!*"), excused himself to slide over to champion Yibemnoot inside a forcefield of friends.

But no family.

Dropped congrats, waited for the other Falcons to move on.

"Sister 'Noot. Um, a few months ago, I was kind of an idiot. Y'know, about—"

"—about my digital colour-job on your artwork."

For real, he was actually hoping she'd forgotten, that her silence since then was just shyness. Nope.

"Right. So, I'm sorry I didn't express myself very well. Wasn't that I didn't like what you did. Actually, if you wanna know the truth, I . . . I loved it, in fact. I'm just . . . well, honestly, I don'even know why I—"

"Maybe it's because you're so used to being alone."

That damn near knocked him over.

"Huh?"

"Drawing. You're used to doing it all yourself. I wasn't trying to steal your credit, brother."

"I know. I mean, I know that *now*." Apologised again. "But when you said I was used to being alone, I thought you meant—"

"I meant that, too."

"Whoah—"

"You don't need to deny it, Raptor," she said, twirling a finger around one of the dangles of her relaxed *hijab*. The other dangle was draped over a turtleneck and the kind of vest favoured by local Muslim girls. Looked less like chastity-armour and more like a bustier.

"Yeah, but how'd you—"

"'Like detects like.'"

Looked at her a long time before nodding.

Then he explained his proposition to her.

"Especially," he said, "you know, after tonight—"

"No, that's totally geometrical!"

"Great! So . . . when would you like to . . . y'know . . . ."

"Tomorrow? Wait, is that even too soon? Yeah, of course it's too soon! How about, no, I mean, like, when would *you* like to, y'know—"

"No, no, tomorrow's good—"

Stumbling over each other like a couple of morons for another minute until, thank god, Jackal came over and started cracking on some damn thing and babbling about Golden Eye and the Kush Party and how it was all gonna be so gold, it'd be the party of the millennium.

Raptor slipped away for a glass of pop so he didn't pass out and break his head open in front of everyone like a kot-tam punk.

4.

Raptor pressed the button. The explosive exploded.

—massive *hiss* and *whoosh*—

—and all forty-two of the young Alchemists stared at nothing.

The rocket'd shot up so quickly, none of the young Alchemists had even seen it move.

Then they all looked up, jabbing at the tiny line against the cold blue morning sky, suddenly *poof*ing a parachute like an instant mushroom for a slow, slow return to earth over the field, well inside the forest line.

Jackal: "*Da-a-a-a*-yum."

"Supreme, bruh!" said his beat-producer Senwusret.

"Geo!" giggled Ānkhur.

Raptor'd just thought the rocket was going to lift off slowly, like the space-shuttle. But it was all over before he'd had a chance to enjoy it.

But so what? Saturday sunrise, and sky like sapphire, air cold but moist and sweet. A few dozen Street Falcons outside the city, roosting at the Strathcona Wilderness Centre, Friday night till Sunday afternoon.

Launching rockets from the middle of the field, and late March with the snow just gone, and they were mudstuck on every footstep.

Moon'd said: no mp3 players. Learn to hear again. That sunrise, their only soundtrack was the chirping of birds. Wasn't a car engine in hearing distance, not even from the highway.

Sbai Seshat, always a genius at pushing the right bureaucratic buttons and getting City funding to run Falcon programmes, got them this place, a massive cabin-style fortress forty minutes out of town where three-dozen kids from Kush had come to learn Alchemy.

First time camping ever, for most of them. Except for kids such as Raptor who'd grown up in camps.

Brother Moon led the applause. "Who's next?"

Jackal leapt. Slid his rocket's launch lug onto the pad's guidance rod, then inserted the electric match into the black-powder motor.

And what a rocket. Three times the size of Raptor's—a triple stage beauty like the Saturn Vs that took Americans to the moon, except that Jackal's was so tricked out it was funkadelic.

On one side of the black body, flaming, graffiti-style logo:

Jackal Is Still Numba 1!

On the other side, Gothic Germanic script:

Lift This Mutha UP!!!

Four fins, and on each side, a colour sticker he'd digitally designed and printed. Each one a different take on his own face: scowling, sobbing, cheering, smirking and more.

Jackal: "Yo, check this out." Everyone pre-emptively looked up.

Jackal pressed the ignition button.

The rocket shot up above the trees and blew itself to fiery bits.

People didn't know what to say.

Jackal said, "Da-*a-a-a*-yum."

Everyone broke up howling, cracking wise and whip-snapping wrists.

Sbai Seshat: "I hope your rap career does what that rocket just did." More hyucks.

Raptor heard Thandie fake-whisper to her orbit of boys, "Wonder if he does that with his girlfriend." They laughed while she smiled. Jackal didn't hear it, but Raptor saw Yibemnoot scowling.

Moon questioned Jackal until they'd figured out the problem: Jackal had painted his rocket *after* it was all assembled, thereby inadvertently gluing together the vehicle's three stages.

Furious at himself for not having inspected it, Moon carefully went over the remaining fifteen rockets (all single- and two-stagers) before he cleared any for launch.

When all those were done, Moon's lawyer friend, *Sbai* Maāhotep (Raptor was still used to calling him Bamba, the name he'd met him under), unpacked their rockets out of Maāhotep's car.

Then teens *oo*-ed and *aw*-ed: Maāhotep's looked like a *real* Saturn V, as tall as he was and painted white-with-black detailing just like the NASA giant.

Moon's looked alien to everyone, so he explained that his was a rare Soviet Soyuz-style model rocket, orange accents on a green body. Both Maāhotep's and Moon's had cameras, and Moon said they'd all get to see the footage when they recovered their rockets.

The thought of little tiny cameras inside those rockets made Raptor's mind gyroscope, as if he were a Micronaut riding those rockets himself.

Raptor'd never seen a day like it.

When he was growing up in camps in four countries, it was always hot outside, there was never enough food, and danger could come from anywhere: other displaced people, raiders such as the Janjaweed gunmen outside the Sudanese camps, or in other countries, nationals who resented their presence and hunted them like coyotes.

But the Wilderness Centre's wooden fortress was clean and handsome. Friday night was a blast. First "sleep-over" he'd ever had. Crazy conversations with a dozen or more people at a time, spinning in every direction for hours. (Something called "nature walks": *way* better than marching thousands of kilometres from one camp to another.)

Saturday dawn: Daily Alchemy, then rockets with the blessing of the sun. Then pancakes and sausages and eggs and toast.

They'd branched into different laboratories over the day led by the four sbaiu: martial arts with Moon, African histories with Maāhotep, ethics shen-ring and role-playing with Seshat.

Outside, it was alternating shifts of archery and hiking led by *Sbai* Nehet. She was a Poli Sci doctoral candidate. Long braids clasped with a cowrie shell band, and cheekbones and biceps so cut she looked an *orisha*. Ānkhur said, "Half the girls wanna be her, and half the boys wanna *do* her." (Finger-snapped.) "That's *out*."

Lunch: hamburgers or vegetarian stew plus fries. Dinner: meat- and meatless gumbo and greens.

And everyone was happy.

Hit Raptor like a sweet chinook: couldn't remember ever having said those words about anybody, in any place, at any time.

In the corner, sopping up gumbo with Somali *moofo* bread, Moon whispered: "Bruh, notice all the extra-street Street Falcons staring at you all day, hanging on everything you do, listening to everything you say?"

Raptor realised: this had been going on so long that it didn't even register on him any more. *Habituated* to it, like he'd read in that Psych text.

"Know what that is?" said Brother Moon.

Raptor waited.

"That's power, bruh. And what did Spiderman say?"

Wearily: "'With great power must also come great responsibility.' Yeah, but Brother Moon, I mean, what? You expect me to be a role model to them? Is that what you're saying?"

"Yes."

"I'm just a kid!"

"Not to them, you're not. Did Hru get to say, 'I'm just a kid' when he was out there in the Savage Lands?"

"No, but—"

He nodded towards four of the streetest of the youth. Dawud, Junior, Ahmed, and Francois, ages fourteen through nineteen. They smiled back, puffed up a bit. At being noticed by Brother Moon and the Supreme Raptor.

Raptor had to admit he'd been expecting these roughnecks to break into fights any minute with themselves, with other Falcons, with wildlife. But all day they'd been acting like they'd just come from church and were heading off to mosque.

"Look at them," said Moon. "Them boys are so street they aint got asses—they got asphalt!" Raptor chuckled. "Doesn't matter you don'*wanna* be a role model. Geometrically, soon as they're looking at you like that, you are one. Transformed?"

Reluctantly: "Transformed . . . but—"

"So how do you help them cast off their lead and pyrite idols?"

"'*I grasp the golden chain to elevate myself from the Swamps of Death*,'" he recited. Then, with more conviction: "'*Where I have cast wanderers in the waters to drown, I will battle crocodiles to place my chain in their hands, so that those who have sunk down may elevate themselves.*'"

"Supreme."

Outside. Wooden deck. Cold air of sunset. Falcons chilled out sipping mugs of double-sweet, double-thick, dark hot chocolate. Specifically, fair trade hot chocolate.

In her cute French accent, Sister Sekhmet (lead name, Crystal) had presented on how more than forty per cent of the world's cocoa came from her Ivory Coast. And that there, the cocoa barons literally enslaved children to harvest it.

Falcons: stunned and furious. Tens of thousands of kids from Côte d'Ivoire and neighbouring countries lured or trafficked in, picking cocoa beans on modern plantations, chained in a modern Savage Lands.

Sekhmet explained nearly every chocolate product they'd ever eaten or drank had one secret ingredient: the slavery of their own brothers and sisters.

Falcons swore one after the other they were done with chocolate, and soon they were in chorus on the ninth verse of the *Nub-Wmet-Ānkh*:

> *By the sunrise, let us create hope, joy and justice, to make stand those who weep, to reveal those who hide their faces and to lift up those who sink down.*
>
> *In doing so, we will all rise nearer to the Supreme!*

Blushing, Sekhmet told them they didn't have to quit chocolate forever. There was fair trade. *Sbai* Seshat brought out trays of steaming mugs full of the surprise beverage, the plan all along.

But Sekhmet warned: just because they could buy something evil-free didn't mean the battle was over. They still had to drain the Swamps. They still had to transform lead into gold for the hundreds of millions who spent billions on slavery so that all the children in chains could be free.

"Yo, Jackal," said Senwusret, sipping and slurping.

Sen and his two Golden Eye partners, cold-lamping on the edge of the deck. The snow-skinned lake turning blue in the dusk.

Sen: "Still gonna drink that nasty chocolate milk outta damn Tupperware containers?"

Raptor laughed so hard he splattered hot chocolate all over himself. Then all three of them were howling. He'd never been much for laughing, least of all at himself, but hearing Sen crack on Jackal for his chocolate milk weirdness was seriously hilarious.

Got round to talking crew business, how they were gonna grow Golden Eye into something serious. Gigs. An EP. Maybe an album. And of course a tour.

Jackal'd already let Sen take over scratching so he could learn how to make beats himself. Now he wanted to step up beside Raptor on the mic.

"Dude, fuh real, I'm like totally transforming my lyricality! I'm *geo!*"

He spat a few rhymes, just enough to make them want more. Raptor and Sen applauded, magnetising the attention of other Falcons.

"Picture it, dude," Jackal said to Raptor, "you're Talib, I'm Mos, and Sen'll be Hi-Tek!"

Raptor smiled. "No, I'm Run, you can be DMC, and Sen's Jam Master Jay!"

Sen: "Naw, man, my whole thing is, you're Salt, you're Pepa . . . and I'm Rick James!"

They all laughed.

After dinner, but before the movie extravaganza of *School Daze* and *Lumumba*, Moon returned to the city for his night shift at the Hyper-Market.

So Brother Maāhotep stepped up. Other Falcons knew him well, but Raptor didn't. The man always looked put-together: even out here at the wooden fortress, he was collared in a shirt and snug sweater.

Looked almost like Raphael Saadiq in one of his retro-1962-ish videos. Ānkhur called him "a sharp-looking brother." Girls whispered and giggled about him. Boys were impressed by his lawyer-hood. One said, "Good to know we have one on *our* side for once."

Maāhotep showed them a ten-minute torrented video, a documentary about a decade-long Soviet experiment from the 'sixties or something to domesticate foxes. In the last two thousand years, it was one of the only successful attempts to domesticate generations of a species.

Onscreen: Russian lab coats handling silver fox kits (Raptor loved that word—they weren't cubs, but *kits*, like model rockets you could build).

After ten generations of selective breeding among the least aggressive kits, suddenly the little foxes erupted with a range of totally unexpected behaviour and features: floppy ears, spotted and patchy coats . . . they *barked*, they trusted humans, they could be trained to perform tricks. They began looking like dogs, dogs being far more wolf *cub* than wolf.

In *shenu*, they revolved again and again around these transformations, X-raying them on every orbit.

Raptor hung back, not out of alienation but fascination. The Falcons weren't like kids from school, clueless and clued-out. They were magnetised inside this Biological Alchemy (Maāhotep's phrase). Maybe if they weren't constantly being injection-fed MTV/MuchMusic bling and videhoes, some of them'd dream of becoming scientists instead of . . . whatever the hell it was they dreamed of (he realised he didn't know because he'd never asked them).

Maāhotep gave his own X-ray. The Soviet scientists theorised these less aggressive foxes had lower levels of adrenalin, which was itself connected to melanin and a range of other hormones, which produced all the changes including in hair colour.

"So tell me," said Maāhotep, "what the effects were: positive, negative and neither."

A bunch agreed that increased intelligence was the main benefit, but they split on whether lowered aggression was. Some said gentleness helped them get along better, but others said it made them easier to capture.

They also split on appearance. Some loved the range of beauty, but the moment someone else said, "It's like they lost their identity," eyes went neon around the room as to why Maāhotep'd shown them the video.

"Ho'd up, Brother Maāhotep," said Francois, the sixteen-year-old Rwandan street youth who'd traded his French accent for Young Jeezy's. "Are you like, like, sayin that . . . the foxes're *us*?"

"Am I?"

Ānkhur cut in slowly, doing her own geometry while she constructed her sentence: "And are you saying that, well, this old experiment was like . . . *slavery*? Because we changed colours? And learned new things?"

Yibemnoot: "You mean new tricks? Or that we even just *got* tricked? I seriously don't think Brother Maāhotep is saying slavery or colonialism was good for any of us!"

More, shooting around the *shenu*. Maāhotep, finally: "Think. Domestication hurt these foxes in certain ways, *and* in other ways it helped them. So. If the foxes could decide, which way should they go?"

Revolving, X-raying, transforming . . .

Maāhotep, near the zenith: "Now, in school, that's where you'd stop. Get you to debate whether it's good or bad for a fox to be domesticated, and leave it there.

"But we're Alchemists. We don't play that here. That kind of either/or thinking goes against our teachings. It's Leadite thinking, taught by Pyrites to keep Leadites unreflective and unconductive. So use your Alchemy."

Ten seconds passed while eyes probed the rafters.

"S," said Raptor at last. "Simultaneity."

"Geometrical, brother. A thing can be two things or even many things at the same time, even things which seem to contradict each other, or which actually *do* contradict each other.

"The foxes gain from both ways, and they lose from both ways. So what should they do?"

Yibemnoot: "Take the best. And even just lose the worst."

Jackal: "Don't just find somebody else's way. Make your own way."

"Which means we, right here in this room, need to learn where to discard a metaphor," said Maāhotep. "Because models lie. They're bigger than what they're modeling so they exaggerate, or they're smaller and ignore too much detail.

"So where does this parable of the foxes break down for us?"

"Well, my whole thing is, we were never animals," says Sen. "We were scientists. Civilisers."

"That's supreme geometry," said Maāhotep. "So in the model, it wasn't you who was the scientist. *That man* was. He captured you, ran experiments on you, caged you, either where you lived back home or took you from there to bring you here, like the Devourer of Souls swallowing you up and spitting you out in the Savage Lands, in order to make you and others believe you're animals. Savages.

"And some of them—and you can see it in some of our behaviour today, some of us—still do believe that. Is that geometrical?"

Around the room they nodded, muttering: "That's geo."

"And some of you are so used to that," said Seshat, "you're not even surprised when your own parents whip you."

Around the *shenu*: *uh-ohs* and *oh-no-she-didn't*s magnetised to guffaws and *I-hear-that*s.

Seshat: "And you'll even defend getting licks from your parents, and call White kids wusses or sissies cuz you think you're so tough because you took licks. But look at them. Look at everything they own. They're running the planet! Did they get licks? Not most of the ones in charge.

"But you, you're gonna defend getting licks in your own homes? If you like licks so much, why not just defend getting licks from the cops, too?"

"Or prison guards," said Raptor.

His street-clan took notice. Francois said, "Or security guards."

Yibemnoot threw in, "Or occupying armies."

"We're beat to the bottom and summa us wanna *brag* about it," said Seshat. "Maybe we oughta do the geometry on that!"

☙

Raptor stared at the ceiling from his second-tier bunk. Exhausted and energised.
S: Simultaneity.

Two hours of ripping on getting licks, split down the middle, no resolution and finally too late for movies. Fast clean-up. Then the bunks.

Staring up into wood in darkness.

Below him, Jackal. Snoring like a fleet of lawn-mowers.

Too bad. Out here, outta the city, inside this wooden fortress at night in the dark seclusion, maybe he could've told Jackal . . .

Drown that.

But Maãhotep, man. So what if he dressed like a preppy? The brother was gold.

5.

Sun-hewn Sunday. Final morning of their camp.

Three dozen teens hustled from bunks to wash and eat breakfast so the seven youth who'd been readying themselves for four months could stand before them to reveal their gold.

Sbai Nehet called them to speak each definition of the Alphabetical and Numerical Alchemy, and the meanings of Lead, Pyrite and Gold.

The Resurrection Scroll.

> Q: What is E?
> A: *E means to Evolve, to grow into new forms because of differences previously not perceived as advantages . . .*
>
> Q: What is H?
> A: *H is Hero, one who struggles at great risk, not for personal reward, but to defend the vulnerable and create justice . . .*
>
> Q: What is M?
> A: *M is minister, a person who ministers. To minister is to care for and serve others . . .*
>
> Q: What is X?
> A: *X is X-ray, short wavelengths of electromagnetic radiation produced when high-speed electrons strike solid targets. To X-ray is to look through opaque surfaces to see what is hidden within . . .*

Sbai Maãhotep asked each of the eighteen questions that summarised the whole of *The Book of the Golden Falcon.*

The Revolution Scroll.

Q: Where did my father travel and why?
A: *My father ranged the world to shine the light of his gold upon every eye that dared to see . . .*

Q: Why did the Destroyer kill my father?
A: *The Destroyer killed my father because he sought to own my father's lands, his scrolls, his kin and his gold . . .*

Q: Why could I not recognise my own brother in the Savage Lands?
A: *The poison of the Swamps of Death afflicts its victims with shifting bouts of madness and of blindness, so I mistook my kin for my enemy . . .*

Sbai Nehet bade them call as one the Nub-Wmet-Ānkh, and then engage the Catechism of the Birth of Gold.
The Triumph Scroll.

Q: Where did you gain your gold?
A: *I gained my gold from the heart of an exploded star.*

Q: What can "exploded star" symbolise?
A: *An exploded star is called a nova, a star too massive too contain itself, a rare place massive enough to form heavy metals such as gold.*

Q: What else can "exploded star" symbolise?
A: *Because our star is the source of all life on earth, "exploded star" can symbolise any dead parent, or any fallen scatterer of the seeds of life . . .*

At the question, "Where do you keep your gold?", they gestured to their hearts. At the question, "How do you share your gold?", they cupped their hands at their mouths, like megaphones.

Q: How did you learn to mine it?
A: *I learned to mine gold from the minds of my teachers, and my teachers' teachers, and all their teachers stretching back to* Sbai *Usir Nebertcher.*

Then each performed their Daily Alchemy.
And then as the *Sbaiu* declared them each to be Apprentice Alchemists, they met the applause of their brothers and sisters.

6.

Final surprise of their weekend at the wooden fortress: T-shirts for everyone. With a brand-new Alchemist crest designed by Raptor and Yibemnoot.

After explaining how she'd finagled yet another grant to pay for the shirts, Seshat called upon the two young artists to X-ray for everyone their months of visual experimentation.

Each element in the seal, said Raptor, represented one number in the Numerical Alchemy, and therefore one verse in the oath of *Nub-Wmet-Ānkh*. Resurrection was the nova.

"The scarab is Revolution," said Yibemnoot, "because the scarab was called *Kheper* in Kemetic, which is just even called rotation or revolution or evolution. And the sunrise there on the falcon's head? That's *maākheru*, or Triumph—"

Yibemnoot stopped, waited for Thandie and her huge eyes to quit conversating at her boys-in-orbit. After a moment, she made a show of straightening up.

The spinal-column *jed*, 'Noot went on, was an ancient symbol of Lord Usir as the Great Father and also all Ancestors. The Hru-falcon was the I, the Hru that every person became in the epic struggle of his or her own life.

Above the Hru falcon were the *sen*-eagle and *sa*-swan: Brother/Son and Sister/Daughter, with the Throne for the Great Mother, Aset the Avenger.

"We chose the god Jehutí's scribe palette to represent Replace-Elevate," said Yibemnoot, "because you can even just write right over your old scrolls, all the old lead and pyrite ideas, and replace them with golden ones."

"The Maāt feather is for justice," finished Raptor, "for Righteous-and-Mastery. The *Ujat* or Eye-of-Hru is Create-Supreme, and the *ānkhs* and *shenu* in the falcon's talons, those're Peace-Life-Eternal."

Might's well've been Christmas morning the way those kids scrambled for their shirts.

In the madness of the modelling, Jackal yanked Raptor over to the side.

"Smooth, bruh. Damn, I should be takin lessons from *you*!"

"What're you talking about?"

"Getting that girl off to the side for two months . . . 'designin shirts.'"

Raptor: cheeks burning. Tried slamming shut his grin. Teeth got in the way. "Get outta here."

Both looked over at Yibemnoot who was walking back from changing around the corner. Overtop her vest, the t-shirt's Alchemical crest. And as she passed, on her back: the word-stack *Nub-Wmet-Ānkh*, gold on black.

"Shit," whispered Jackal, "way she's all up in that tight t-shirt, I'm like, 'You wanna design something with me right now, sweet thang?'"

Raptor shoved him away, laughing.

And stuffing clothes and afropicks in knapsacks, and hauling everything onto the bus.

And the lake gone first, and the highway streaking past, and yellow prairie revealed from melting snow as far as the horizon.

And knowing he was losing something by leaving.

And the city coming back, and around them.

And even with what he'd suffered and survived in the wilderness of his childhood, he mourned going back to the concrete jungle.

Not in misery. Maybe just a stealth nostalgia, a love he'd never known he had, suddenly, suddenly remembered, like the scent of oranges after a bad cold, like sunshine after endless rain.

7.

"Yo, yo, yo, kid! Shit's not *right!*"

So said Wa-Wa, tromping out of the shop, freshly-cut heads turning to watch him bug the hell out.

The sixteen-year-old Rwandan—known to his mother as François—was so angry didn't even realise he was bunching up the flyers he had in one hand and strangling the rolled-up posters he had in the other.

Raptor, irritated: and not just at the waste of good printing, which he took away from the kid immediately.

François had totally messed up inside Duke's, the Jamaican-owned hair shop on *Khair-em-Nubt*. Worse, he'd melted down while wearing his Alchemist t-shirt on Alchemist business. Out promoting the Kush Party, only three months away.

Raptor, burning to spit it in Wa-Wa's idiot face: You fucked up in there! You came in street, you left street, and now you're in the street. And dumping mud on our name by doing it, genius!

Instead, gold-minding: three . . . extremely . . . deep . . . *breaths* . . .

Started drawing the kid out, the way Moon'd shown him, getting the kid to explain what'd happened, in the correct order, so Wa-Wa could see how he'd tripped the owner's alarms, and broken his own geometry.

"Dude was tryinna punk me, man!" railed Wa-Wa.

"Maybe he was, Wa, but X-ray that. *Punk*. Power-Unity-Nature-Knowledge. You collapsed in there. How'd you lose your Unity?"

The Rwandan's face expanded like it was going to go Hindenburg. "I—"

"Breath is power, Wa."

Wa looked into the blue sky, sucked down a breath and held it. April sun played on his closed eyes.

"Hold it in . . ."

In a minute they started again.

"I lost my, my Unity," said Wa, "cuz I, like . . . I forgot . . . my Knowledge of my own Nature . . . So I couldn't, like . . . use my Power?"

"Transformed. So show me the geometry in there."

"When the owner rolled his eyes, I wanted to like haul off an smoke im."

"Uh huh."

"An he'd already kept me waitin an hour—"

"Really? When'd we go in there?"

"Okay, okay . . . like, fifteen minutes."

Raptor raised an eyebrow, just like Moon would.

"Okay, ten. But that old bastard was lookin at me, lookin at my pants like he thinks I'm all ghetto—"

"Okay. You had the knowledge of the Kush Party. And you have the knowledge to step into a *shen* and do the Daily Alchemy in front of everyone. You can teach it like a preacher. So you're geometrical, right?"

Wa-Wa, looking down, nodded. Like he didn't believe he'd ever done anything right.

"Now, you say that man was looking at you. He owns a business. Making money offa cuttin heads like yours every day, brothers with pants so big they make yours look like Spandex."

Wa-Wa laughed, but he was still angry. Raptor thought, *Did I just say that? Sounds like something Moon would say.*

"You had the gold. But you kept it down in the mines. Next time, you wear your gold. Stand up straight. Look him in the eye. Don't mumble. Shake his hand confidently. Make your case quickly, try to up-sell him and then jet. Transform?"

Wa-Wa nodded.

"Young Falcon," pressed Raptor, straightening his own spine. "Transform?"

Wa-Wa stood up straight, looked him in the eye and announced, "Transformed."

Other Street Falcons were working *Khair-em-Ånkh-Tawy* and *Khair-em-Sokar*. Nehet was contacting NGOs and community committees, Seshat was working the City for clearances and permits and whatever else you needed for a block party in Kush, and others were trying to get the city's best reggae and hip hop bands for E-Town's first Pan-African festival.

Raptor resolved to take Wa-Wa back to Duke's the next week. They walked to the next business.

"Yo, Brother Raptor," said Wa, perking up. "I like got this idea I thought maybe you could help me with. We could both make some money . . ."

"Yeah?"

"But, uh, I don'know if Brother Moon would approve."

Took in a breath. So did Wa. Both let them out before continuing.

"I don't know either, but tell me your idea."

Wa-Wa told him.

And then continuing to seek sign-ups for the Black Pages project and sponsorships for the Kush Party, they kept on canvassing every community-owned business on *Khair-em-Nubt*.

8.

"And those, those *rhine*stones—"

From behind Senwusret's bedroom door, Thandie was practically bursting with laughter.

Raptor burst in and snapped, "What's that sposta mean?"

It was dark in Senwusret's bedroom recording studio with the curtains drawn. But reflecting the PC's light, Thandie's giant eyes were as bright as oven elements when she aimed them at Raptor.

She must've thought that look alone would finish him off. Girls as pretty and tall as she was could usually walk over anybody.

But she had no idea who he was or what he'd done to survive.

When he didn't back down, she tilted her head forward like an axe. "Excuse me?"

Jackal and Senwusret opened their mouths to defuse, but Raptor wasn't playing that.

"Think I didn't hear you? Cracking on brothers like Wa-Wa and Ahmed, saying they're 'ghetto,' laughing at Yibemnoot cuzza how she dresses—"

"I think your *girlfriend* can stand up for herself," sniffed Thandie, then turned back and tossed her hair like a White girl.

The Supreme Raptor: "Maybe that shit plays with your fan club, Thandie, but it's worthless with me. Brothers like Wa-Wa and me, sisters like 'Noot, we've escaped kot-tam *wars*. You think we're afraid of people like you? Suburban snot-nose suck-asses who think they're better'n us?"

"You'd better back off, Rappy, before I—"

Senwusret: "Whoah, whoah, whoah—"

Jackal: "My peoples, chill! Chill!"

Jackal hustled his best friend down the hall.

"She likes bad boys, Jackal," said Raptor, "or at least she thinks she does, but she's got no idea just how bad I am—"

"Yo, bruh, c'mon, she's just—like you said, she's suburbs, knawm sayn? She doesn't know any better—"

"Why'd she even tryinna join us, huh? She's no Alchemist! Never will be! She doesn't belong—"

"Yo, Raptor, c'mon. Alchemy doesn't belong to you! If she's good enough for Brother Moon and Sister Seshat—"

"She's *using* you," said Raptor. Like he was laying a gun on a table between them.

Jackal opened his palms. "Damn, Rap, that's cold. She's performing at the Kush Party and she just needs some music. That's all. Sen an I both think she can really sing—"

"So what? If this is how she talks about us! And I heard her sing when we were on the weekend camp, JC. No real voice—just all vocal tricks and sizzle, like some little wigger-girl who just started free-basing R&B!"

"Free-basing" he learned from an online urban dictionary after Jackal dropped it on him the previous summer. His best friend scowled at the dis.

"I'm telling you," Raptor continued, "she's using you, and when she gets what she wants, she aint gonna be whispering sweet nothings and draping her hair over your face. She's gonna be sinking her claws into the next brother she thinks she can get whatever she wants from."

"Look," said Jackal, flipping open his cell for the time, "her session's running late, man. We can do Golden Eye beats tomorrow. You should just—"

"And this is how it starts," said Raptor, throwing his knapsack on his shoulder and hitting the stairs.

"Rap! *Rap!*"

9.

Sunday evening, after supper. Raptor. His old bedroom at his mother's apartment. Smelled like dust and sweat.

Standing and looking through an art pad of inked drawings he'd done of Lupe Fiasco, Fela Kuti, Static, Hawk Man, Morpheus, and the original line-up of NWA.

Once, at Moon's place (usually he'd just call it his own place, too, but standing in his old bedroom . . .), he'd been blasting some NWA while studying.

It was the smooth-bumping "Always Into Something," classic Dre production from *Efil4Zaggin*, crazy-ass wails and bass as dark and sweet as Coca Cola. Moon'd said, "You're *still* down with NWA?"

"Why not?" He didn't even mess with Moon's implication. "The beats are dope. And they've got great flow. You can't deny that."

"*Hitler* had great flow, too. And way more fans."

He'd laughed at the audacity of that. Moon was an expert at, what was the phrase he'd taught him? *Reductio ad absurdum*. "Look, I'm not saying I agree with the lyrics. And besides . . . long as I don't act that way, does it matter? Fuh real, I've seen your DVDs. *Goodfellas, Pulp Fiction, Full Metal Jacket*—"

That was Moon's turn to laugh. "Transformed, bruh! I surrender!"

What else was left inside his old chamber of secrets? A half-dozen science fiction paperbacks he'd bought at Wee Book Inn, including *Imaro*, a "sword & soul" about another Earth where a warrior greater than Shaka and Imam Al-Mahdi combined scourged the unrighteous.

A couple of *manga* robot models he'd built when he was thirteen and for that stretch of six months he'd had unlimited spending money, before the incident. His bed.

He knelt down, felt for the secret lock-box he'd built into the foot of his box-spring.

Didn't need to look inside it.

Stood up and looked at the room again.

Felt the room's amputated separateness, its absence from him cool on his flesh like an autumn wind. He was a cobra marvelling at the sheath of skin it'd shed a whole version of itself ago.

Wandered back out to the kitchen where the two adults were engineering the Kush Party.

His mother glanced up at him. Her gaze: it looked *on* him, not *at* him. It didn't clutch him anymore, but let him be.

It was detached.

Not out of abandonment or a severing. More like his mother was finally disentangled from him. Like at last she had enough distance that for the first time she could see him as an actual separate being, with his own life, his own needs, his own perspective different from her own, and she could actually make room for that.

Amazing. Moving out had actually made them closer.

"We've got vendors and NGOs up to our collar-bones," said Moon. Then he nodded towards Raptor. "And some ultra-talented Street Falcons for performances." Raptor smiled. "But for the average Jane and Jamal who could go anywhere on a hot summer day and night, our main stage damn well better have some musical acts like nuclear magnets, 'Weelo.'"

'*Weelo*'? That was new.

"I can ask," she said, not reacting to the nickname at all, like it was a bracelet or necklace she always wore, "Souljah Fyah, Politic Live, Haimanot Brehanu—"

Raptor snorted.

Whoops.

She turned her eyes on him.

"Well, I'm just saying," he said as fast as he could, "you're gonna get the best reggae band, hip hop crew and Ethiopian singer in town? Just like that?"

"Why not? I know them all."

"You *know* these guys."

Araweelo chuckled, but rolled her eyes while doing it.

"Yes, Raptor. I've helpedt all of them with publicity. Even with Politic Live's annual 'Hip Hop for Hunger' concert, even though I keep telling them to change the name to '-*Against* Hunger.'"

She turned to Moon. "When he was little, he was shockutt when I didn't know something. Now he's shockutt when I know anything!"

Raptor tensed. But the laugh was gentle and open. And no slap in it.

And he found himself joining in their chuckle, marvelling at it all.

Moon at his mother's kitchen table, a mug of milk-thick sugar-shai steaming in front of him.

His mother sitting casually across the table from a man, a *real* man, laughing without even a hint of desperation's cackle cracking his eardrum. Her smile, calm and tender, her eyes soft without the panic-lights of scrambling to stall the inevitable blow-out with the man across from her.

Those two adults on either side of the rickety Formica table, leaning millimetres more towards each other every day they met, probably not even aware they were doing it.

His own shock—and joy—at feeling no burn anywhere, at *not* suspecting her of trying to take Moon away from him to wreck him and then destroy everything.

For the first time he could remember, she was actually happy.

Didn't have to picture it in his head or draw it or write about it, and it was better than any video game, movie or TV show. Because it was there, three-dimensionally in front of him. And if he wanted to, he could actually touch it.

Right there in his family home.

The phone rang.

His mother looked at the phone-screen. Eyes, flinching.

She took it in the bedroom.

Voice muffled behind the door, raised. Angry. Pleading. Trapped.

He turned away from Moon, knowing he knew, remembering 8:20 in *The Book of the Golden Falcon* and the fate of Master Jehu's wooden fortress.

10.

Two days later, evening, in the Street Laboratory, Brother Moon wrapped a long blue belt around the waist of an eight-year-old.

Mrs. Abdi and the Somali mother crew cheered, and so did everyone else.

Ibrahim Abdi bowed to his teacher, then ran over to hug his mother, his brother Jackal, and the rest of his family. Moon came over with him.

And Mrs. Abdi, in front of everybody, hugged Moon.

Jackal's face: like his mother'd practically just stripped down to a halter top and danced to Lil Kim. And Moon and the Somali mother crew had the same reaction.

Mrs. Abdi finally let go of tall Moon, wiping her eyes.

"Lastt year," she choked, "Ibrahim could nott speak ten wordts. And now . . . more than three hundredt. And this! The martial artts!"

"I'm glad I could help, Mrs. Abdi."

"Next year," she said, like she was talking about flying to Jupiter, "Ibrahim starrats gradte one!"

"I just wish," said Moon, "every child's parents could learn about this treatment when their kids were young. Before they've lost too much time."

"Now itt's supper-time!" said Mrs. Abdi. "You come!"

11.

The next day, afternoon at the back of the empty Street Laboratory.

At the PC carrels. 'Noot, singing like she was on Heaven's playlist, finally peeped over her shoulder and saw Raptor standing there.

Jumped and nearly fell out of her chair, yanked off her headphones, mortified.

"I didn't even know you were there!"

"Don't stop singing! You've got a beautiful voice!"

Straightening herself, glancing between him and the screen. Eyes flashing: *Are you "even" teasing me?* "No, no . . . . Now, Thandie, *she* can sing. I just holler and croak."

"No way, 'Noot!" Pulled a chair and sat. "I mean, she's all right in a there's-this-girl-I-know way, but you? You're ready to make a CD. Like, today!"

Waved if off, pointing at the screen. "*Any*hoo . . . "

"What song was that, anyway?"

Waved it off, and he kept pushing. Shifted into appeasing for her fastest escape. "It's *taarab* music. It's from Kenya and—"

"—and Tanzania! Sister, c'mon, think I don'know *taarab*? Zuhura Swaleh, Bi Kidude, Siti binti Saad—"

At those stars' names, she beamed a concentrated smile at him so beautiful it almost made him dizzy.

"Yes, yes! Yeah, I was singing a song by Asha Abd—"

"—Asha Abdow Saleebaan, from Somalia."

She shook her head in amazement. "Yeah! How do you know Somali singers?"

He almost said *I'm half Somali.*

"Public library. And you?"

She laughed, unjacked her headphones from the PC so Raptor could hear her *taarab* playlist. They chatted music until Raptor abruptly said, "'Noot, tell me about a movie that makes you cry." (One of Moon's X-ray questions.)

After a microsecond: "Hindi movies."

"Really?" Shock suppressed his laughter. To him, Hindi movies made the average *Avengers* comic look like Shakespeare.

"Yeah. When I first moved here I worked at grocery store/video store in Millwoods, in, y'know—"

"Little India—"

"Exactly. So I used to take out movies."

"And you could understand them?"

"Yes. I can speak Hindi, but I'm better with Punjabi."

Amazing. Add in Somali, Arabic and English, and she was practically a UN mission, which wasn't so off—her Christian grandfather had been an MP in Haile Selassie's parliament.

So *she* was a hybrid, too.

Blurted: "Why don't we do a duet at the Kush Party?"

'Noot: "What?"

"Golden Eye's performing. You knew that, right? You could join us. We'd be like the Fugees!"

"You're crazy!" she giggled. "Thandie—"

"Aw, forget Thandie. You could sing her into the Swamps! 'Noot, seriously, what good's your gold if you keep it buried in the mines?"

She swivelled her monitor towards him, showing him the graphics she'd been working on. "Do you think Wa-Wa's gonna like this?"

Blasted through that barricade. "You wanna be watching the stage from the street and thinking, 'That coulda been me?'"

"—because I could even make this flag bigger, or move the silhouette over here. And whaddaya even think about this font?"

"You could be the next Lauryn Hill, 'Noot—"

"Stop!" Laughing and smiling.

12.

Dark and hot inside that damned black bag he was wearing. Almost tripped cuzza the damned flare right in his eyes—might's well've been police headlights.

Jackal shouting . . . from somewhere out there in the darkness. His mother whistling and wailing Dinka-style, embarrassing him in the way all teenagers were embarrassed by their parents.

Squinted, saw her in the front row of the auditorium sitting next to Moon, the two of them smiling and applauding, and his embarrassment disappeared. Kept walking across the stage.

To Raptor it was 99% meaningless. Grad? A full month before they'd even written their finals? Stupid.

And anyway, even with his high English 30-1 grades, he still had to upgrade a bunch of other courses next year at the blandly named Centre High, where all kids who'd smartened up too late finally had to go.

Then there was the empty symbolism of the mortar board and the gown. What good were symbols if nobody knew what they meant?

Alchemy was all about symbols, etymology, geometry: developing your Shining Eye to see the secret science of the world surrounding you.

And why should he celebrate some school that gave him nothing but pyrite about himself and his people? The Street Laboratory was where he'd gotten real gold.

Why should he celebrate the school where, just when he was starting to shine, they called him "difficult" and "aggressive" and accused him of "recruiting for some Black Falcon gang"?

During the March 21st anti-racism school assembly, Golden Eye had performed, dazzling students and even some teachers. But then came whispers and secret complaints from secret complainers and his vice principal demanding a print-out of his lyrics and them telling him point-blank they were investigating him and even combing his online content to see if he was "violating school policy." And of course, eventually, the VP told him "someone was concerned" that his song was "racist." And no proof. Not even a solid argument. Just "someone was concerned."

Kot-tam. He'd been *concerned* about racism his whole life. No teacher or principal had ever asked him about *that*.

And his VP called in his mother and she showed the man why she was called Araweelo.

Accepted his diploma from the principal who'd never done a damn thing for him, raised his hand up like a black-gloved Olympic athlete, heard Jackal and a whole chorus yell, "Supreme Raptor!" and "Raise the Shining Place!"

Adjusted his kente scarf—Moon's grad gift—and left the stage to the applause-thunder of all the Street Falcons he'd recruited in person or by YouTube.

Far as he was concerned, his real graduation would be when he knew all ten scrolls, when he be transformed into a Master Alchemist.

13.

Khair-em-Ānkh-Tawy, what the Leadites called 111th Avenue. Hot June night. Muggy. Like the air was sweating.

A full block east of the Street Laboratory, on the south bank of the avenue, on the corner next to the Burger Baron. Raptor and Wa-Wa slanging product to a steady stream of young male Somalis. And making bank.

Two customers looked up, saw an angry skullcap coming straight at them, and split.

Wa-Wa's eyes lost their whites. Raptor froze, bills bunching out of his hands like he was harvesting spinach.

"What's in the bag?" demanded Moon.

Wa-Wa handed over the plastic shopping bag. Raptor groaned inside.

A t-shirt.

Front: against a giant field of blue and with a single white five-pointed star above his head, a silhouette-man defiantly hoisting a machine gun. In the movie poster font of *Pirates of the Caribbean* was scrawled the title "Pirates of Somalia."

Moon flipped the shirt around. Raptor knew well what was there, since Wa-Wa, 'Noot and he had designed it. The slogan *Defend Your Mother* blared overtop an ancient exchange:

Alexander the Great:
"How dare you
prey upon the seas!"

Pirate:
"I have one ship
and so am called
PIRATE.

"You have a great fleet
and so are called
EMPEROR.

"How dare you prey upon
THE WORLD?"

Choked. Was this gonna be another show-down, like after he'd called out the *capoeristas*?

They'd sold a hundred shirts already to a legion of laughing Somali teens and men. He knew that when *Blackhawk Down* came out, pirated copies got shown across Mogadishu, even inside movie theatres, with Somalis cheering the battle scenes in the way Hollywood never intended.

Moon, lasering the shirt with his eyes, his eyebrows up like Sputnik.

Even though the film was one big lie—a flick in which Somali generals dressed like Crips, a David vs. Goliath bullet-fest that fucked up which side Goliath actually was—Somalis cheered seeing even *caricatures* of their countrymen slingshot a stone right between the giant's eyes.

And those t-shirts popped-and-locked from the same culture-jamming mortar-fire as that Blackhawk-down-low.

Raptor knew he was doing with clothing what he did with rhymes and poetry: sampling. Remixing . . .

From a faked-out FOX tale
Nailing patriots as pirates
Hailing and sailing from a distant sandy ghetto
Gangbangers ship-jacking on the high seas
CNN damning them for fighting foreigners fixed on
Stealing their nation's naval food supply and
Drowning their shores in death-tides of the Pyrite Empire's radioactive
excrement.

And now Moon was gonna come down on them? For this? Because this wasn't "a positive image of the community"?

Kot-*tam*—

Moon pulled out his wallet and counted out seven fives.

"This enough for two?"

14.

Sitting inside Maähotep's law office, Raptor felt the couch trembling. It was blue and Scotch-guarded. He didn't know if it was him or Jackal making it shake.

Moon looked more angry than scared.

"How the hell can they do that?" he demanded.

Maähotep opened and closed his hands like he was letting a bird out of a cage. "They were both seventeen when they committed the crime, so under the Young Offenders Act—"

Moon: "They're kot-tam *murderers*! Murderers get to go free? I mean, I could see a coupla rich White kids going free—"

"Those dudes were only seventeen?" spat Jackal. "Seventeen? You serious? Fuh real? They looked, like, twenny-five or suh'm—"

For Raptor: the room. Tilting hard right. Clutching the couch's rough arm so he didn't keel over.

Those spliffed-out ice-blooded killers Mahamad "Marley" Moallim and Hassan "Lexus" Awale were now eighteen, and for whatever reasons their prosecution was taking too long to come to the bench, so the judge'd said they had the right to walk free until they had their week in court.

All their bones that Moon had broken had long since healed.

But the hearts of those Leadites—

"Damn, Brother Maä," said Jackal. He hadn't even opened his chocolate milk. "What the hell we sposta do now?"

Maähotep swivelled in the chair behind his desk. He sighed, pursed his lips, obviously weighing his words.

Framed behind him on the wall were two pictures. One, a signed portrait of dark-haired White man in a suit, signed *To Bamba: For Justice, Ralph.*

Two, the classic portrait of the Senegalese Sufi mystic Sheikh Ahmadou Bamba, shadow-faced and cowled, like a Jedi Knight in white. To Raptor, at that moment, he looked more like a Grim Reaper.

Finally Maähotep offered slowly, not even looking at them, "If they go anywhere near you, we can get a restraining order . . . . "

Nobody even bothered to dignify the remark.

Moon, Jackal and Raptor stumbled outside. Raptor chewed the hot, dusty June air, stenched by the smog of rush-hour traffic clogging past them.

Maãhotep's storefront office was on *Khair-em-Ãnkh-Tawy* in a terra-cotta building facing a McDonald's and Kingsway Garden Mall. Broad daylight. High visibility.

All three of them looked around, scanning for revengers with guns.

"Brother Moon," said Raptor, "I'd like to learn how to grapple."

Instead of lifting double-eyebrows, all Moon did was nod.

That night Moon changed the work schedule at Hyper-Market so he could teach two extra martial arts evening classes per week at the Street Laboratory.

"Amazing, isn't it?" said Moon, after pinning his student in a yet another *Sanuces-Ryu* floor technique.

Moon got up off him at once. Raptor leaned up instantly.

Being held, clutched, grabbed, sat on, mounted. That's what ground-fighting and grappling required, and for a year he'd avoided it. Now he forced his mouth to de-sneer, replace-elevating his face out of disgust and into "curiosity."

Brought his new face towards his teacher while he wiped sweat off his forehead with his forearm.

"Amazing," said Moon, "how being bitten by a hyena doesn't seem so bad when we're worried about being eaten by lions?"

15.

'Noot abruptly stopped singing and turned off the music.

"What is it? *Seriously*, this time." Head forward, hands on hips.

Raptor shook his head like a wet dog, like he could fling the demons out.

"And don't deny it," added 'Noot, "cuz it's outta character for Brother Supreme Raptor to be just even forgetting his own lyrics."

Saturday morning. They were the only two Falcons at the Street Laboratory, but there'd be more any minute, gearing up for their Kush Party performances.

But he wouldn't snitch on himself.

She filled the kettle, plugged it in next to the window, and hummed out her song for the three minutes until the water whistled.

Sunlight and steam and singing.

Eyes beaming the morning. Her, running and giggling while he chased her past tents and tin shacks and desperate people ignoring them or yelling at them, jumping piles of trash and thrashing through puddles, dancing and laughing and singing and never knowing there was anything more to life than hunger, fear, flight and joy.

'Noot poured the water into the pot, adding Somali tea spices from a baby food jar.

Cloves and cinnamon. He could taste them on the steam.

Sunlight and singing and steam.

"Steam"—jazz he'd learned from Moon. An Archie Shepp number, almost a hymn, a lyric explaining that few joys could equal the intensity and ineffability of the end of pain.

'Noot spooned sugar into a tumbler, poured the red mixture over it, handed it to him. "This is how they drink tea back home."

He didn't say *I know*, just took it and thanked her.

Sat down, the both of them, looking out the window at people strolling Khair-em-Ãnkh-Tawy . Looked up into that face of hers, just like Queen Hatshepsut's, and he told her everything about the killers who were free and probably after Jackal and Moon and him.

'Noot leaned forward. "So what're you gonna do?"

"I don'know." Feeling the chair wedging the metal hardness of the butterfly knife in his pocket against his leg.

Seeing her hand lift. Time fragmenting like a glass breaking in sunlight . . . .

Her hand, skittering forward. . .

Her *hijab*, drooping corners pointed at her thighs. . .

Her eyes, black and wet. . .

Her hand, passing her knee, drifting towards his hand. . .

His mind, echoing the thought: *Even with that loose* hijab, *I have never seen this sister touch any man's hand* . . . .

Her fingers, almost on top of his . . .

—and time spewing forth again full speed with Thandie busting in through the Lab's front door, smiling and cackling with Jackal in tow.

'Noot reared back.

Raptor burnt Jackal with the oldest look in the book of best-friendship: *Can't believe you're messing up my game like this*!

Jackal's grin ripped into a grimace. The brother knew he'd messed up. Before Thandie could start some shit—which he knew she would, he'd already seen those giant eyes of hers dancing all over the two of them—he told 'Noot, "Let's fly."

His heart was speed-bagging his throat. Blood throbbed in his ears, like bass overloading cheap speakers.

Raptor handed 'Noot the package.

"You do like grapes, right?"

Felt like the biggest gamble he'd ever taken. He knew from TV you were sposta buy a woman flowers if you liked her.

But if it turned out she didn't like you back, after the killer-embarrassment of giving unrequited flowers, how were you sposta stop your skull from popping like a zit? Her walking around holding some decapitated plants while you tried keeping your face from cracking off and hitting the pavement?

No. Red globe grapes were still a gamble, but smarter. Colourful as flowers, and sweet-tasting instead of sweet-smelling. And then, if she didn't like you, you could eat the evidence and pretend like nothing'd happened.

'Noot: "I *love* grapes!" she said.

That smile. The eyes. Like sunrise.

They exited the Congolese grocery on *Khair-em-Sokar* and headed over to the Camel Boys Café.

Inside the sambusa shop's lemon-yellow walls, Raptor and 'Noot snacked on sambusas, and each sat doodling cartoons on napkins to make the other laugh: sausage dogs, animé kids, exploding robots, and best of all, caricatures of other Falcons.

'Noot sketched a Jackal with dreadlocks so long and tangled they formed a net that made him trip and spill his jug of chocolate milk.

Raptor laughed so loudly he spewed crumbs. Everyone turned to look. He slammed a napkin over his mouth.

Bad enough he was in a Somali joint where Somali parents went, and sitting with this Somali *muhajabah* (even if her *hijab* was loose . . . or was that worse?), and with his Dinka face nobody was gonna think he was her brother. Or even a Muslim.

Quickly quieted himself, embarrassed.

"O-o-oh!" said 'Noot, disappointed.

"What?"

"It's just, it's just . . . you have such a great laugh, and you don't laugh very often. And when you do, you usually just even cut it off."

He felt . . . something. Not the burn. Skin wasn't crackling. But heat, all over his torso, like a hot shower. Or an actual bath.

She was keeping track of his laughter.

Deflected. Asked her what her plans were now that she'd graduated.

"With my Bio marks, my family expects me to be a surgeon. But me, I just wanna head my own graphic design firm, y'know? Plus even web development and advertising."

"You'd be great at it. You're a great artist. And you know all the software."

Put down her can of cream soda. "And owning a firm like that? I think I'd be a first."

"Yeah! Definitely. But you shouldn't rule out medicine. You're so smart you could probably discover a cure for cancer."

She chuckled. Flashed those eyes at him.

"Or something even worse," he said, seizing the moment.

"Worse than cancer? Like . . . ?"

"Like being a jerk!"

Her, laughing, and him reeling her in: "Yeah, y'know, think of how much better school'd be. Your teacher's a jerk, you just drop a pill in his coffee. Bing! Your parents aren't nice, bing! Thinka how many marriages you could save. Or if your boss is mistreating you. One pill, jerk's gone!" Her, laughing still. "And y'know what'd be the ultimate?"

"What?"

"If you went herbal for the cure. Jerk *seasoning*."

She howled, covering her own mouth in embarrassment. Now it was her turn to get everyone's attention. But this time he didn't care.

"Priceless," she said. "Jerk season? So people'd get hunting licenses or something?"

"Uh, that'd be good, too, but I was saying—"

"—and that'd be the one time of year you could *tell* em they were jerks!" She actually snorted laughs, twice, which smacked a smile right onto Raptor's face. "And they couldn't do anything about it!"

"Yeah, and in addition, it'd be jerk *seasoning*—"

She kept laughing and riffing on "jerk season," going on and on. He smiled, letting it go. So what if he didn't even say it? She thought he did.

Their conversation moved on eventually to Moon and Seshat and Maãhotep. He laughed when five minutes later, she handed him her finished napkin-doodle of a scowling face in a crosshairs. The logo:

JERK SEASON – Limit 100.

16.

"No, over *there*!" hollered Maãhotep in safety goggles. Falcons were carrying in what looked like sections of scaffolding. "And don't drop them!"

'Noot and Raptor stepped back inside the Street Laboratory. Place looked more like an Industrial Arts lab. Wood dust was choking the air, spitting out of Maãhotep's band saw, screaming like a pterodactyl.

Falcons were hauling wood boards and sheets from Maãhotep's pick-up. Maãhotep had a pick-up? Had to be his, though. Two bumper stickers: one said, "War? How's that Workin' For Ya?", and the other: "Justice or Just Us?"

Everyone lined up beside him to learn to use the band saw.

Stacked to the side were the slices. 'Noot told Raptor check out the cuts and assemblies: not squares or rectangles, but carefully measured trapezoids.

Maãhotep the lawyer. Button-downs and cufflinks and silk ties and suits that musta cost two hundred dollars. Brother was *kempt*.

And now here he was, driving a pick-up, wearing jeans and a paint-spattered T-shirt, wiping dust from his face and wielding power-tools like Imaro swinging a sword.

Brother was a lawyer, but he didn't blink at getting his hands dusty. Moon'd once told him, "Neckties've killed more good brothers than rope." Maybe so, but maybe not always. And using words for a living, to build justice? That was alchemy, right there. Gold. Geometrically Nubian.

☙

Spotting Raptor and Noot, Maãhotep sucked them into the whirlwind: sawing, painting, wiring, drilling and screwing the trapezoidal plates in place upon a framework of four-by-fours.

"Don't cut your fingers off!" snapped Maãhotep.

Raptor yanked his hands back. The *Sbai* grinned at him, and when Raptor saw he still had all his digits, he grinned back.

"Like this," said his teacher, helping guide the board two-handed into the screaming metal teeth.

With the noise of everyone's labour giving them intimacy, Maãhotep asked him how he was holding together since the news about the "alleged" killers being sprung.

He faked a tough, but Maãhotep locked eyes and asked him again. And a third time. Just like some prosecutor on *Law & Order* or *The Wire* or something.

"No shame in fear, Brother Raptor," said Maãhotep. "But there *is* danger in pretending it's not there. Like having a fire in your house and being too ashamed to put it out or flee the premises."

They cut some more boards, and then Maãhotep stopped.

"There's a million tough guys out there. Men who spent all their energy distracting themselves from their fear instead of dealing with it. Alcoholics, crack-heads, or corpses—dead by hall party, or dead by AIDS. Distraction kills, young brother."

Ten boards and twenty clouds of dust later, Raptor cracked open his vault. By one millimetre.

"When you're in the camps, the refugee camps, I mean," said the teenager, wiping his right palm on his chest like he was taking an oath, "you were always in danger. But that's life, right? I mean, the Savage Lands are everywhere, right?"

"But Raptor, Hru didn't just *accept* the Savage Lands. He used Replace-Elevate."

"But Brother Maã," he said, burning, "I'm not Hru. This is real. Real thugs with real guns who really splattered brains two inches from my head!"

Maãhotep gave him a look he'd never seen before: soft and hard, simultaneously. How was that even possible? Maã had serious alchemy.

Maãhotep: "You think *The Book of the Golden Falcon*'s just some fairy tale?"

"C'mon, you're not telling me all that stuff really happened? With magic and monsters and people turning into birds—"

"No, obviously not. *The Golden Falcon*'s not facts. It's truth. The facts are all the everyday details. The truth is forever. It's what we all share. In *The Golden Falcon*, you think, what, Hru isn't constantly overwhelmed and terrified?"

Sounded like a rhetorical question, but Maã magnetically-locked his eyes. Waiting for an actual answer.

He'd never thought about it. Yeah, it was an exciting story, yeah, and it was great to learn an African legend. And yeah, Moon'd said it was about their lives.

But still, myths about something so ancient . . . they just didn't seem . . .

But yeah . . . now that he thought of it, one *ārit* after the next was about how afraid Hru was. How he had to run and hide and how only if he got pushed hard enough, did he stand up to fight. How often he was ashamed of what he'd done.

How much he wanted to change things.

Amazing. Maā could alchemise him with a single question.

17.

"*'Tell of Master Jehu's inquest,'*" said Maāhotep. The eleventh catechismal question for the seventh ārit.

Still standing at the band saw. And Raptor, before he even began reciting the words, heard the verses chiming through the caves of his mind down through tunnels snaking the world, echoing back to his internal ear.

And him, hearing them, as if for the first time.

> *Using Moon as Eye again, the Master peered inside the shadow of Hru, and found a night of fire inside which children screamed and fled into the darkness . . .*
>
> *A swath of towns whose citizens were butchered inside blackened, smouldering homes . . .*
>
> *Countless men of murderous knives and fingers cruel he'd met and never met who wished to strip his bones of meat . . .*
>
> *And the body of a headless mother on the sands beside a throne.*

Maāhotep: "All that pain and that regret, being constantly hunted . . ."

The armpits of Maā's t-shirt were soaked. He wiped sweat off his forehead, left sawdust in his hair, like he was going grey.

"It's not just some fairy tale, young brother. It's the truth of our lives, of every African, everywhere. You, Jackal, 'Noot, Moon . . . your mother . . . me. All of us live in fear. And all of us have either already faced the threat of death, or one day will."

"Yeah, but all respect due, Brother Maā—"

"You're about to ask me, 'But what are you supposed to do now, against killers walking the street?'"

"*Yes!*"

"Obviously—"

"I mean, they don't know my name or Jackal's, but Brother Moon was all over the news, and he's still up on YouTube. He lives—I live—right next door to the crime scene!" Shook his head, eyes wild, scanning the room for something, anything.

"You're a lawyer," said Raptor finally, as if those words were keys to a safehouse. "Isn't there something you can do? Sue em or something?"

Maãhotep's eyes widened. Raptor explained: "Y'know, for psychological distress or something."

"Trigger-men usually aren't deterred by civil suits," said the man. "But you already knew that. Look, could they come after you? Yes. Will they? They're more likely to run. Or get themselves killed, because people like that are usually pretty stupid and prone to taking stupid risks. And we know they're desperate."

Raptor looked at the wood that Maã was feeding into the bandsaw. Flinched as it screamed. Felt like it was him going into those teeth.

"But how'm I supposed to protect myself if they come after me?"

"Well you know Moon and I've got your back—"

"Yeah, but—"

"—and I've seen your *kung fu*. You're good—"

"All the *kung fu* in the world can't do anything against a bullet in the back of your skull. You know *that*."

Maã nodded. Ran another board through a long cut, let the right side drop, then ran the left piece in his hands through two smaller cuts along the pencil marks across the surface.

"I'm talking to you now not just as your lawyer, but as your *sbai*," he said, leaning towards him. "Don't go hunting these men."

"I wasn't gonna—"

"Rap, c'mon. I'm from Jamaica," said Maa. "Ha ha! Look at your face—didn't know that, huh? 'Bamba Diabate' dun'soun *yahd-bwoi* nuff fi yu?"

The unexpected accent tickled Raptor enough to make him smile.

"Before I became a Sufi, even before I became an Alchemist, I had a different name and a different life back in Jamaica. And I had my own enemies. People who made it absolutely clear they were willing to kill me. Main reason I left. Back then I was right where you are right now.

"With one difference. You have allies."

He rested a strong but gentle hand on Raptor's shoulder. The teen marveled at it, even while Maã kept talking. Because he felt nothing. Didn't even flinch at it.

But who'd want to hurt Brother Maã?

"Don't go hunting these idiots, but keep your eyes open," said his elder. "Watch your back. Have your cell handy. But if these men corner you . . . you defend your life by any means necessary."

Raptor's eyes must've shown something.

Maãhotep: "You heard me." He ran more wood straight into the saw.

18.

Raptor. Evening shift. The Hyper-Market.

Pouring out dregs from a neglected coffee pot. Washing out the flask. Filling the maker with fresh water.

Mind kept running back to his talk with Brother Maã.

'Noot agreed with him: Maã was deep. And "cool like ice cream," said 'Noot.

Woulda felt jealous, but there weren't any sighs behind those eyes. Just facts. After all, brother was an attorney, an Alchemist, a Sufi, and obviously a carpenter with enough electrical skills to be prepping the wiring for their construction.

And he could do that while calmly directing Street Falcons in screwing the trapezoids onto their 4X4 cube-frames and priming the wood before applying gold paint. Said he learned how to do this kind of thing partly from his father, but he'd amped his skills considerably by constructing sets in theatre.

Taking an orbit inside the Hyper-Market, Raptor scouted empty cups, collecting a half dozen, nodding yes to the people running tabs who wanted refills, hauling the cups back to the dishwasher and running another load.

Plus brother's Alchemy was so strong that whether they were in a daily *shenu* or just in any conversation, he could stack up anything with divine geometry or show where someone else's argument was barely a Jenga tower. And all Maã had to do was tug on a single Leadite concept and the whole damn thing came crashing down.

That Congolese couple was at the till, the one that liked hanging out at the Hyper-Market every Saturday night before checking out all the community hall parties.

He signed out two consoles for them, smiled, told them he'd bring them their usuals—triple cream, triple-sugar, a Tanzanian fair trade roast called Mwalimu.

He liked watching them. They were old, in their thirties or something, but they were always affectionate and gentle with each other, touching each other's faces softly like they were wiping away fallen eye lashes.

The woman—he knew her name was Mimitah from the sign-up sheet—always wore intense colours, especially flower prints.

The man, Kanda, always wore continental shirts, which Raptor respected, since from what he could tell, in plenty of communities—Arabs, Indians, Chinese—only women wore traditional clothes.

Seemed like women were always the true guardians of culture. Lady Aset's hieroglyphic was a throne—sometimes she was even just called the Throne—like she was the centre of the Fortress itself.

'Noot loved how Maã used Sufi stories (she read a lot about Sufism) and even Christian parables when he alchemised. She said that made him extra capable of reaching all these diverse Falcons, using what they were raised with.

Plus, he was always bringing them food: pizzas, falafel, Jamaican patties, roti from former clients of his in the community, sometimes people who he'd worked for cheaply or *pro bono*. He said they were happy to help.

Plenty of these Street Falcons were so street they maybe didn't eat three squares or some days even one. How was anyone hungry all the time supposed to learn or get a job?

And these were some rough-looking brothers, too . . . head-hugging braids or bandanas, loping pimp-limps cuz they'd seen it in the videos, staring and glaring outta reflex—the kind he'd've crossed the street to avoid back in the day.

These brothers treated *Sbai* Maãhotep with geometrical respect. He even heard one talking about being, what'd he say, a *barrister* and *solicitor* one day, "just like Brother Maã."

"Brother Maã feeds them twice," 'Noot'd said.

Raptor smiled at that. Put it on the bench of his lyrical workshop:

> *Brother Maãhotep feeds the bodies*
> *And feeds the minds*
> *Dropping wisdom-in-the-schism*
> *To heal the blind . . .*

19.

9:00 PM. Shift ending. Moon asked him to update the Falcon blog with a new reading list.

"Me?"

"Yeah, you, why not?"

"You're the one who's read, like, a million books—"

Brother Moon chuckled. "So? You've read a hundred thousand."

"But I—"

"You don't get more gold by burying it, young bruh, you get it—"

"—by sharing it. Yeah, I know . . . . "

Logging in, he thought about what he'd been learning, what'd been transforming him and the Falcons recently.

He summoned seven deep breaths to relax his mind, as Moon'd taught him.

Hm . . . what was today's Alchemy? July 7 . . . seventh day of the seventh month . . . Interesting. How much, recently, he'd been sevening or at least trying to seven. *Replace-Elevate.*

The titles started coming, books from the library or Moon's own vast collection he'd finished or was part way through, and a couple 'Noot'd recommended. And every new one he got, he slotted it alphabetically . . .

> Ishmael Beah, *Long Way Gone: Memoirs of a Boy Soldier*
> Octavia Butler, *Parable of the Sower*
> Wangari Maathai, *Unbowed: My Autobiography*
> Monique Maddy, *Learning to Love Africa: My Journey from Africa to Harvard Business School and Back*
> Njabulo Ndebele, *Fools and Other Stories*

Mongane Serote, *To Every Birth Its Blood*
Bobby Seal, *Seize the Time*
Ivan Van Sertima, *Blacks in Science*

Impressed at his list, and with himself. Making this list: it was a promotion.

Made a note to go back and annotate the blog with his own comments about why he chose each book and how each book was about *sevening*.

20.

Raptor wasn't headed out for any parties. Didn't like em. Wasn't up to stepping out Saturday night-style, not even to hang with Jackal or Senwusret or . . . .

Well . . . 'Noot, maybe, but it was night and that girl was *muhajabah*. She was at home. And was gonna stay like that.

Told Moon he was clocking out and then went upstairs, to what he secretly called the Palace of the Moon.

For over a year he'd been returning to the Hyper-Market which was literally right next door to the store where someone had almost turned his skull into cherry pie. And for six months he'd been living and sleeping and eating just above it.

Wasn't there something . . . *strange* about that?

Yeah, sure, he couldn't control where Moon lived and worked, but from what he learned in Psych 20, wasn't he supposed to have Post-Traumatic Stress Disorder or something?

Climbed the stairs. Knees like putty. Hands like sponges. Throat like a boa was crushing it.

Why, for a year, had he not cared that he had brought himself back daily to Ground Zero?

Key-hand kept missing the lock: *Clicketty-tinketty-clacketty* . . .

Steadied it. Entered shadows.

Didn't matter why he'd been okay before. Denial, or whatever. And if denial'd helped him function all that time, denial was a good thing.

But at that exact moment he felt it all, smelled the burnt-meat stench of hunters, tasted them waiting for him somewhere in the gathering darkness, felt them like slime sliding over his crotch, heard the echoing screams while from the chaos came men with murderous knives, and fingers cruel.

21.

At Moon's PC, Raptor checked the blog for comments on his booklist, but there weren't any yet, so he cross-posted the list onto his Facebook page, then checked his email where he found a message from Maāhotep.

Nub-Wmet-Ānkh, *Br. Raptor,*

I've been thinking a great deal about your situation since this afternoon. I strongly urge you to cope with the stress by developing your gold-minding powers.

If you'd like help, I'd be happy to guide you. Professor X recruited me as his deputy instructor of gold-minding, and I helped Br. Moon through some difficult times with those skills.

Tonight, try gold-minding with the following in mind.

1. I've FTPed you an extra-low-frequency drone track. The drone will guide your brain into a theta-wave frequency: simply put, it'll keep your brain from racing. It's my own track, so you'll hear my voice.

2. Focus on Replace-Elevate. Inside the cave, every time khetiuta arise from the water, visualise grasping Master Jehu's golden chain.

3. If that doesn't work, breathe more deeply, use the power-word focus, and visualise any beautiful, happy experience you can, with as much detail as you can, and alternate with the power-words "I am free."

4. What about when you're on the street and feel afraid? Breathe deeply, close your eyes if it's safe, and use both repeat-phrases until you're calm again.

5. If you can't keep khetiuta out of your mind, visualise your body falling into the Swamps of Death, but picture yourself as your own ka, standing on the shore. Sigh with patient amusement at yourself and say the words, "How did It fall in the Swamps again? I just hauled It out of there!" Calling yourself "It" will help you detach from your destructive emotions and thus break the destructive positive-feedback loop.

6. If all else fails, play Tetris (or any video game). Trauma research shows that playing Tetris right after a disturbing experience helps divert the brain from ruminating on the it, which lessens future trauma. And nobody ever ODed on Tetris.

7. Finally, check out the links below before you try gold-minding tonight, in the order I gave them. Focus on what Malcolm said about prisoners, and remember that Hru lived in the South and the North, too.

Nub-Wmet-Ānkh,

Sbai Maāhotep

22.

No doubt, he was intrigued.

The first link led him to a Malcolm X YouTube video. Since entering the Golden Fortress, he'd seen plenty of Malcolm X videos that Brother Moon recommended. But this one was new to him.

Malcolm X. Slim. Tall. Short haircut. A sharp suit like something Brother Maā would wear (or maybe his own dad), punctuating every sentence with his sword-finger:

> *You and I have never seen democracy. All we've seen is hypocrisy . . . . If you go to jail, so what? If you're Black, you were born in jail. If you're Black, you were born in jail, in the North as well as the South.*

Born in jail.

Why'd Brother Maā want him to reflect on that?

The second link: trailer for a documentary. Some hoity-toity British woman:

> *Why couldn't a prison cell be just like a monk's cell? Sister Elaine was very keen to help prisoners meditate.*

An elderly White woman in black. Stooping, adjusting a White prisoner's hands. The con was sitting on the floor in one of those Buddhist postures.

A Jamaican brother. Must've been a prisoner, too—dressed just like the meditating White man. Him, nodding:

> *I guess she saw the need . . . maybe out of her divine inspiration, because it really helps. This is like the only sane moment in prison.*

This old White lady was really teaching prisoners to meditate?

Some English guy:

> *It's a gift that can not only get them through their time of incarceration, and allow them to see it for what it is, but you're giving them something to take out into life afterwards.*

She's a Catholic nun. She's also a musician. And she's also a Zen master. So she crosses religions completely.

Finally an old woman's voice—the nun's?—soft as the wind:

Your spirituality is what you do with the fires that burn within.

Clicked off the video, played a few levels of *Serious Sam*, then went to bed. Put his headphones on. Clicked on Maã's drone.

Hadn't been much good at gold-minding. His mind was practically a NASCAR track.

But Maã was a smart brother, so . . .

Lights off.

Slowed his breathing. Inhaling as deeply as he could until his lungs wanted to burst.

Then slowly . . . let . . . it . . . out . . .

And again . . . and again . . .

Turned on his mp3 player.

The drone . . . echoing inside his skull, distant and near like thunder.

Continued his breathing and descent into the cave.

Maã's voice in his ears:

I am creating a more golden mind than I ever have before . . .
   Relaxed . . . completely at ease . . .
   My body is soft, supple, like water . . . my head is soft . . . my eyes are soft . . . my jaw is soft . . .

The Voice told him to repeat internally:

I am at peace . . .
   I am relaxed and confident . . .
   I am protected by people who love me . . .
   I am strong . . .
   I know how to help myself, and how to ask for and accept help . . .
   I am balanced and at one with the universe . . .
   Whenever I need strength, I repeat my power-words, "I am free," and suddenly I am refreshed, at ease, and more powerful than I was before . . .

Back from the cave. Past 11 PM. He'd been down an hour.

He'd never been able to last more than three minutes before without distractions blasting him right out.

Stunning: when the Voice told him to, he'd visualised himself, down to the last detail, on a perfect day: confident, relaxed, happy, even charming. While visualising, he felt his cheek muscles bunching up wider and wider every minute. And whenever threat-thoughts arose, he followed Maã's instructions: visualise something that made him happy.

'Noot. Smiling at him.

Slid softly into luxurious sleep.

He pierced the sky, flew past the Moon, past Mars and the asteroids and flung himself far out to Jupiter. Gazed at its ancient hurricane, bigger than three Earths.

Hovering above it while Jupiter's moons whirled past him, the massive world's rings glittering like frost on a Christmas Eve window.

To him, the Great Red Spot looked nothing like a hurricane. It was calm. Wise. Reassuring.

It looked just like the *Ujat*.

The Eye of Hru.

23.

Sunday morning. After Daily Alchemy with Moon. Biking to Senwusret's place in Highlands to make beats with Sen and Jackal.

Sen'd Facebooked him: just got a whole new set of MIDI kora patches. Sen was on a mission to Africanise hip hop into something he was calling Imhotep-hop.

"Whole thing is, Rap," he'd said on the phone, "you got brothers in Senegal and Kenya and whatever making hip hop, but it all sounds American. They gotta do like Thomas Mapfumo. You hearda him?"

"Yeah, he—"

"Yeah, his whole thing was—in Zimbabwe, right?—to use traditional instruments, like the thumb piano, the *mbira*, in modern music—" (Couldn't stop Brother Sen when he got like that.) "—cuz before that he'd been doing Beatles songs and shit, and then he brought back the *mbira* to make spirit music, revolutionary music. *Chimurenga!*"

"Yeah, I heard about—"

"So I'm getting every kinda MIDI patch I can for African instruments: *mbira, balafon, kora, jembe, begena*, banjo—"

"Banjo? Seriously?"

"Oh, yeah! Came from West Africa, originally—"

Halfway to Sen's place he saw a pickup truck in front of a beautifully-maintained house in Norwood. Two bumper stickers: "*War? How's that Workin' For Ya?*" and "*Justice or Just Us?*"

Immediately hopped the curb and jumped off his bike so he could ring the bell and tell Maã all about gold-minding down in the cave—

The door opened. A tall brother stood there. Plush white bathrobe hanging open. Man had a hairless, chiseled chest, like a male-model's. Silk pajama bottoms draped over his feet to touch the tiled floor.

Man's left ear: a small diamond sparkling. A coffee mug hummed steam in his hand. Way behind him, a breakfast table brimming with food.

"Can I help you?"

"Oh, sorry. Wrong house. I saw, uh, my friend's truck—"

Sounds of a sink running, then stopping, and a door closing. And then coming out of the hallway, another man in a matching plush robe.

Maāhotep.

He saw Raptor, started to say hello, but the teen backed up, almost fell down the front porch, jumped on his bike and jetted.

Didn't look back at the sound of Maā calling his name down the block, didn't look to see if Maā's bathrobe was flapping in the warm Sunday morning breeze.

24.

"Why are you looking at me like that?" said Raptor. "Didn't you hear what I just said?"

Senwusret's basement recording studio. Dark. A single blade of light knifed through the curtains.

'Noot and Jackal stood staring back at him. Brother Sen sat in front of the computer with Fruity Loops open on the screen.

"Well, whole thing is," said Sen, "you sure you saw what you said you saw?"

"Yes! You ever know me to exaggerate?"

Nobody said anything to that.

Jackal went back to chewing an Egg McMuffin he'd enhanced with three cheese slices of his own. The cramped studio reeked from teen sweat and McGrease.

"Well?"

"Just sayin, is all," said Sen. "Cuz, y'know, could it've been his brother?"

Raptor *pfff*ed.

"Well . . . damn . . . . Sbai Maāhotep? I'ont even wanna *think* about that."

"What about you two?"

Jackal and 'Noot glanced at each other, waiting for the other one to start. When neither did, Raptor snapped, "You're both Muslims!"

"So?" said 'Noot.

"'So'? It's against your religion! Doesn't that make him a hypocrite?"

"Well, for one, *Sbai* Maāhotep is a Sufi," said 'Noot, "and Sufis always do things their own way. They also have a reputation for being kinda 'out there,' but they're usually pretty smart—"

"What about you, Jackal?"

Jackal saw Noot's reaction: eyes and nostrils flaring. Jackal, sighing, shoulders stooped. Waiting for someone else.

"Dude, it's a big world," he said at last. "My whole country fell apart. Yours too." Corrected himself at the first sight of Raptor getting even angrier. "Both of yours."

Jackal was the only person who ever remembered that his best friend was half Somali.

"Nunna my business, fuh real," said Jackal. "Yours neither. And don'we got bigger fish to batter?" Bit off and gobbled down some more of his extra-cheesy McMuffin, then crumpled up the wrapper.

"You gotta keep eating that disgusting McShit? You're stinking up the whole studio!"

Jackal. A raised eyebrow, just like Moon would do. "Bruh, I can see you're upset, so I'ma let that one go. But you are seriously acting like an asshole right now."

Glanced at 'Noot, but she wouldn't even look at him. Felt a tumour in his chest. Completely different from the burn. A rigid, serated mutant mass, gutting him from the inside.

Shook his head, then checked Senwusret.

"Look, my whole thing is, don't get me wrong, I don'agree with gayness, and the Qur'an forbids it. But like, on the everyday? So long as they don'mess with me, I don't mess with them."

"Sen, if something's wrong, people gotta take a stand—"

"There's this one *hadith*, Rap, where the Prophet, peace-be-upon-him, says if you find a dog dying of thirst, you should dip your shoe in the well to give him water. I mean, thing is, most Muslims think dogs are impure, and shoes are so impure you can't even be praying in em. So—"

'Noot: "Who are you to judge Brother Maä?"

Raptor: "Who do I have to be? I'm an Alchemist!"

"And he's your teacher, and he's been an Alchemist longer than you've been alive!"

Ignored her, looked at Jackal. "It's like you're not even surprised!"

"Dude, I'm surprised that *you're* surprised. Just figured you knew. Brother Maä's so sharp. *Always* sharp . . . the haircut, the suits. He's slim. I mean, that's like a whole thing on *Seinfeld*."

"I can't believe you!"

"Dude, why you always be running and throwing yourself in the Swamps?"

"I'm out!"

Senwusret: "Rap, c'mon, now—"

"Dude, what about rehearsal? Kush Party's in a week!"

He turned dramatically. "Then today, you three are on your own."

Someone gasped, but he was already out the door.

25.

"It's important!" Raptor was trying to pull Moon into the back room of the Hyper-Market.

Sunday afternoon, gorgeous weather outside, not many people were cyber-caféing it. Even so, Moon had a thing about leaving the floor unsupervised.

Raptor: "We have a Pyrite in our midst. A *khetit*."

The explosion from that bomb lifted Moon's eyebrows.

Fiend. Demon.

They went to the back room.

"I've got something really—I don't even know how to start! Something . . . disturbing to tell you. About Maãhotep."

The corners of Moon's mouth turned down. "Explain."

Shot out the details: what he saw, how he saw it.

Moon said, "And?"

"And? *And?* He's a *faggot!*"

"Young brother, number one, lower your voice!"

The glare.

Moon peeked around the corner, but the only two customers were headphoned.

"Number two," sword-finger arcing, "I don'*e-e-ever* wanna hear you talk like that again about anybody, let alone Brother Maãhotep, your teacher and your senior Alchemist!"

"Did you even hear what I just told you?"

"Oh, I heard you—"

"Well what are you gonna do about it?"

"Do? What're you talking about?"

"The Street Falcons! The Alchemists of Kush! This is a programme for young people! Some of them desperate! Vulnerable! You can't have a, a, a—"

"Gay brother?"

"I never figured you for somebody who'd get all caught up in PC vocabulary, Brother Moon!"

"PC? How about Polite Consideration? You love NWA, but I never hear you saying 'nigger.' So why should you be using the word 'faggot'?"

"You can't compare those things! We're *born* African! They're—"

"They're born gay—"

"Being 'gay' isn't a heritage or culture or a race, it's a, a, a sickness!"

Rolling his eyes. "Raptor, this is the twenty-first century—"

"You don't think they're sick?"

"No! Absolutely not! They're normal people, like you or me."

"Like me? Are you crazy? What they do, it's, it's, it's totally unnatural! *N*, Nature, right? How're we supposed to harmonise with Maãt if we're unnatural?"

"Number one, everything that exists in nature is *by definition* natural. Number two, *N equals Nature* means we need to X-ray the geometry of a thing, how it operates, what it achieves—not rule on whether it *is* natural, since everything is.

"If a thing causes pain and no joy or wisdom, yes, it's pyrite. If it causes joy and wisdom and no pain, it's gold. Figuring out the nature of everything in between—which is almost everything that exists—that's the hard part."

Raptor, with something thick in his mouth. Tasted like pickle juice. "You're telling you think there's something *good* about men, like, you know, doing . . . that?"

"Having sex?"

Raptor curled up his nose.

Moon: "How's anybody's sex life my business unless they're hurting somebody?"

"They *do* hurt people!"

"Some of them, yeah. But so do some heterosexuals. All the time, in fact! And I don't hear you calling for banning straight people—"

"It's not the same thing!"

"Why not?"

"It just isn't!"

"You know how to X-ray when somebody's run outta logic and facts? When they use the word 'just' to defend themselves."

Raptor half-turned to leave. Moon leaned against the counter, opening his hands to soften his body language. "Look, you want a Ting? Or some tea?"

Raptor shook his head.

"I can see you're barely at the edge of even being able to hear me anymore, so I'll keep this ultra-brief. Sometimes our mind is gold, and our heart is lead or pyrite. Sometimes it's the other way around.

"In the Judgement Scene—you know, the painting, where the Scribe Ani's standing in front of Lord Usir? Yinepu has to weigh Ani's heart against the justice feather of Maät.

"But you, right now, when you said 'just,' you'd run out of arguments. Your mind is one way, your heart's another, and you have to weigh them both against the feather.

"A three-way scale, that's a helluva thing to try to operate, transform?

"But when it comes down to turning our backs on someone who cares about us, we'd better be really, really careful when we're running that scale. Especially when someone else's fate hangs in the balance. And Brother Maähotep, he cares about you, young bruh."

Just hearing that: Raptor's skin itched, ants crawling and slime slicking down his face, his chest, his ass.

"Right now, I know you don't wanna hear that. I can dig that. But—"

"Are you telling me that you knew?"

Moon sighed. "Maä's been my best friend for twenty years. We were room-mates for a while. Why wouldn't I know?"

Raptor started to walk out.

"And he shouldn't *hafta* be secret," said Moon, letting him leave, "about something that isn't hurting anybody."

Hit the door. Flew away on his bike.

Downtown. Rice Howard Way. Red brick buildings lining the fancy cobblestone intersection. A stack of rough-hewn boulders looking like an obelisk made by sasquatches.

And a seven-storey parkade.

Hit the brakes on his high-speed flight. Sweating from the heat, heart pistoning like a train. Locked up his bike, ran up the parkade stairwell, walking the last two flights and puffing the final one to the top floor.

No cars up there. Sunday afternoon, and it was just too damn nice out. People were biking and walking, not ACing it in steel boxes on wheels.

Raptor perched himself on the ledge, watching foot traffic seven storeys down.

Gazing at the warbled reflections of Scotia Place's twin gold towers considering themselves, infinitely. Then at the blue glass and steel of Manulife towering above them all.

Put on his headphones, music on shuffle. First song up: Orchestre Baobab's "Dée Moo Wóor." Guitar echoes, bass-thunder like the hammer of Ptah.

Feeling sweat trickling behind his ears, under his pits, down his sides.

Sometime later all the sweat was gone.

Stayed up there past supper time, and he hadn't even had lunch. Hunger he could deal with. Hunger was one of his homies.

A friend he could actually count on.

26.

"I don't know what we're gonna do, Brother Moon," said Jackal.

Raptor'd just walked in on the conversation. And he'd caught him, talking about him behind his back right in front of his face to Brother Moon.

"Hang on, bruh," said the old man, nodding to Raptor and then turning to the customer, a White woman in her thirties with glasses and a pony tail. "What can I getcha?"

"Two Coolios, please. Large."

Evening. Hyper-Market was half-full, but there was steady traffic for coffee slushies. Moon's new drink machines were hopping in the heat wave.

A list of specialty drinks day-glowed from chalk on the menu board. Lupe Latté. Coolio. Ice-T. Ice Cube (bubble tea with cubic tapioca pearls made inside an ice tray). There was no Vanilla Ice.

But you could order a Baaba Maalkshake (made with coconut milk and pineapple) or a Fela (a plantain-chocolate smoothie, and delicious; Moon had had to explain to an embarrassed Ãnkhur why they couldn't name a drink Felatté).

After the woman walked out with her boyfriend and their Coolios, Brother Senwusret made his case.

"My whole thing is, we've been working her, pushing her for weeks. I *thought* she was gonna make it . . . . "

Raptor's stomach flip-flopped. Jackal hadn't been talking about him after all. Relieved. Disappointed.

But Senwusret looked horrified. Like he was ordering someone to walk the plank. Whispered, "The Kush Party's only a week away. Whole thing is, if she can't sing full-out by now . . ."

Thandie. The big-eyed alpha-girl with the bootay and the arctic smile. At last they'd wised up. Good. For a second he'd feared they were talking about 'Noot.

Jackal finally saw Raptor, did a double-take, then turned back to Moon.

"What're we supposed to do? She's expecting to, like, perform a whole set! We can't have the Falcons looking like a buncha chumps! This is our big day!"

Moon: "I was wondering when you brothers were gonna talk to me. I've been hearing this exact same thing for a month from a bunch of Falcons." He sighed. "Okay. I'll talk to her."

"The girl's trouble," said Raptor.

The other three looked at him, then looked back at each other. Phone rang. Moon took it.

"Whoah, whoah, slow down . . . Noot, sister, c'mon . . . no, hey, wait up . . . 'Noot, 'Noot, are you crying?"

Raptor: the burn. Like a lash in a gash.

"No, c'mon. Let *me* talk to him, then. I'll—. Yeah, but you never know—. I'll—Noot!"

"What is it?" said Raptor, once Moon had clicked off.

"Ah, hell." The old man shook his head. "'Noot's dad won't let her perform at the Kush Party."

Three-boy chorus: "What? Why not?"

"But her family's liberal," said Sen. "That's their whole thing."

"Yeah. Cept when it comes to like, dads and daughters."

Man, he knew Maāhotep had her completely pyrited, even defending him, but was she actually quitting just because Raptor'd had the guts to speak the truth?

"So many men from the old country like this," said Moon. "Even the ones who think they're liberal. Think there's only one way to be. When somebody steps out of that, they feel threatened."

Raptor rolled his eyes, but only Moon saw him do it. He knew damn well Moon was talking about him and Maāhotep.

'Noot's father was *wrong.* An intelligent, hard-working daughter could make beautiful music with her voice, and he was gonna stop her?

And Moon was wrong. How was Moon gonna compare doing something great like being a singer to being a Pyrite pervert psycho, a monster in their midst, like a crocodile just below the surface of the Swamps?

Raptor headed up to the roof to check the peregrine falcon roost. July light. Sun still burning above the buildings at 9 PM. But even from the stairwell he could see the chicks and adults were gone.

Took the spade and dustpan and scraped away the birdshit, then sat on the ledge and took an hour watching the sun go down.

◌〜

11 pm. Through his bedroom window, the sky was electric purple.

By lamplight Raptor was re-reading issue #7 of the old Milestone title *The L*A*B*.

Gorgeous painted Mshindo cover and crackling Eric Battle interiors—the one where X-Man, Dreadlocker and the Dark Fantastic find out that the Klandroids had developed new models with dark skin.

"*The Klandroids look like us, now!*" declared X-Man, uniformed in black suit, white shirt, black shades. "Which explains how come Councilman Shakazulu, outta nowhere, up and joined that country club and married that Marsha Brady-looking freak—"

Front door lock rattled. Raptor shut off his light.

"The girl's amazing," said Moon from beyond his door. "And now her father's just gonna yank her like that, one week before the gig?"

"The key is to talk to the maather. She'll convinnice him."

It was his mum. His *mum*. In Moon's place. And it was almost midnight!

"Yeah, but I'm another man. This guy's not gonna let his daughter sing. How's he gonna handle me talking to his wife?"

"Lett me handle it. One Somali sister to anaather."

"'Weelo, uh, you know, I appreciate the offer and everything, and you know I respect you, but from what you've told me about you and Somalis—"

"I cannutt argue with you on thatt one." She sighed. "Lett me . . . lett me go to the maather with Seshat, then. She's not Somali, but . . . she's a social worker, and between thatt and your Laboratory, she has a goodt repootation in the commoonity. The maather will at least listen to Seshat's advices."

From the living room, music. Water running. Pans clanking. Couldn't hear the conversation anymore. Except once, when he heard his mother ask how her son was doing, and Moon told her about Maãhotep.

And she didn't even react.

Clock radio. Bloodshot LED. His mother left at 1:37 AM.

Mind splashing, thrashing, in a bog. Fog murdered his cries for help, and there were no stars, and there was no moon.

If he'd remembered to gold-mind, he could've slowed himself to sleep.

But he didn't.

27.

"Now, everybody, check these outt," said Araweelo, opening up her mystery cardboard crate. Raptor winced: *Check these outt . . .*

The Falcons flocked round her in the Street Laboratory that Thursday night. No one, not even Moon, knew what was inside the box.

Black pyjamas?

No, check that cut: karate *gis*, but with the sleeves tailored Nigerian-style. Cuffs and lapels all glittering in gold hieroglyphic brocade.

And for belts: sashes of gold-black *kente* cloth.

Gasps. *Wows. O-o-h, snap!s.* And one *da-a-a-yum.*

Questions crackled: How'd she find them? Where were they from? Who made them? How much were they gonna hafta pay for them?

"I've workedt with a lot of immigrant women from many commoonities," said Araweelo. "A Ghanaian sister gott the *kente* for us. A Vietnamese sister had a baanch of karate uniforms she couldn't sell. Andt a Salvadoran sister didt the alterations. Oh! Andt the best part!"

She turned the jacket around.

On the back: A giant, gold-on-black falcon, wings spread, talons grasping *shen*-rings, inside the starburst and the words *IN THE NAME OF THE FALCON.* The Alchemist crest Raptor and 'Noot'd designed.

"I convinnicedt a shop to sponsor the Kush Party. This is their contribution."

And they applauded and whooped.

Moon hugged her, and then so did all ten Falcons on the martial arts demonstration team as she handed each one a uniform.

The last two were adult-sized: one for Moon, and one for Maãhotep, the only person who could match Moon in the ring. But Maã wasn't there.

Raptor wasn't on the demo team—performing with Golden Eye was plenty—but he loved the look.

"Da-a-a-yum, boy," said Jackal, "your moms is crazy-connected! She gets stuff done, fuh real! Hey—maybe Golden Eye should go on tour with the demo team, huh? Like our own S1Ws?"

"Now that's what I'm talkin about!"

Inside the Lab filled with Falcon calls, Raptor heard Moon ask his mother, "Any word from 'Noot's mum?"

"Seshat and I hadt a nice chat with her." She shook her head. "I just don't know if we gott through to her. Or if we didt, if she can get through to her husbandt. You know men. They call it pridte."

"I know what *you* call it."

"But I don't want to use thatt kind of language around your school of Falcons."

Laughed and smiled with each other.

Fire, beginning at his feet, racing up his legs . . .

Breathed. Deep, deeper. Deepest. Again.

What are you afraid of?

Of him taking her? Or of her taking him?

Or of them, together, abandoning you?

"Anyway," said his mum, "now itt's in her handts."

The Street Laboratory's front door clanged open. A skinny woman stormed in, too much make-up and too-wild eyes. Her daughter at her side, a younger copy of herself: Thandie.

Oh, no.

The woman, at Moon: "Who the *hell* do you think you are?"

The room crisped into silence.

Thandie stood behind her mother, giant eyes blazing like jailhouse searchlights on a bunch of escapees about to get shot.

"Mrs. Braithwaite," said Brother Moon, "we already went through all this the other day for about four hours—"

"My daughter," snapped the woman, helmeted in a bright red hat, the kind of thing Raptor'd seen Caribbean people wear to church, "is not some dog you can just have put down because she won't perform tricks to your satisfaction!"

Araweelo: "Whatt are you implyingk?"

The woman glanced to her daughter, who whispered something to her.

"Oh, ri-i-i-ight," she sneered. Spanking each word: "The *mother* of the *boy* whose *gangsta rap group's* got a *starring role* in this little *concert* of yours! The boy who's *living* with you, Mr. Man! And you—what kind of mother hands her teenaged boy over to some bizarre—"

Araweelo: "Now you listen to me!"

Raptor'd heart smacked against his ribs.

"Don't you dare castt your asper-a-sions on me or on this man! If your headt is so sick with such perver-a-sions, maybe it's *you* who's the sicko—"

"Now you listen to me, Miss Africa—"

"—and too bad for you your doughter cannutt sing! Boo hoo! This isn't *American Idol*! Go live outt your dreams some aather way!"

Moon: "'Weelo—"

"—think you can get away with this, Mr. Cult Leader, you got another thing coming! I know a-a-a-all about you and your dirty little secrets—I don't care what nonsense is on YouTube!"

Even Thandie looked embarrassed. But she was just a kite in a thunderstorm.

"And forget about this bush party concert! I'm calling the police, the mayor, the media—everybody! You hear me? You're *done*!"

"You crossed the line, lady," said Moon. "You wanna abuse me? Fine. Go ahead. I've taken a hell of a lot worse. But you start threatening my kids and their months—"

"Oh, they're *your* kids, are they now? You hear that, kids? Man thinks he's your father! Wonder how all your parents're gonna feel when they—"

"You're trespassing. Get off this property now!"

"Oh, I'm going," she said, yanking her daughter with her. "I know your type. You're nothing but a new Black Hitler!"

Eyebrows round the room twisted into *WTF*?

"Are you some kinda nutjob?" said Raptor, his chest dynamited open. "Off your meds or something? You don't have a freaking clue in your head what you're talking about!"

Her eyes, wild, on him. "You SHUT your mouth, boy! I'm trying to save you! And you, Mr. Man, one day, you mark my words—" (her arm was a staff, her finger the spearhead aimed at Moon) "—this whole place of yours is gonna BURN!"

Stampeded out with Thandie, almost ran down *Sbai* Seshat who was just coming in.

The room. Silent. As a crypt.

"O-*ka*-a-a-y," said Seshat. "That sounded bad."

28.

Friday morning.

Slow-mo:

EVERLAST

yellow letters on black

chain links, steel glinting, metallically crunching. . .

swinging back from the bottom of his left foot. . .

—fluid, left foot pivoting down, toes 3 o'clock—

—in peripheral, EVERLAST swinging back for the counter-attack—

—body-springs uncoiling in the hips first—

—right ankle rising, arcing, hunting—

STRIKING *EVERLAST* where its ear would be

jumping its whole black leather body up on the chain

and right foot grasping floor, pushing him forward, swinging left elbow into EVERLAST's ribs . . .

Raptor, not even stopping to wipe sweat, racking up for another twenty front-re-verse round-houses combos, this time starting right, ending left . . .

Friday evening. Final rehearsal.

Senwusret scratching, Raptor rhyming, Jackal double-timing, Golden Eye shining.

But the duet of rhyme and song was silent.

No phone call. No Facebook. No email. No text.

No 'Noot.

On they went, teeth without smiles.

29.

"Weren't they terrific, folks?" said Councilman Brothers, his voice echoing over the intersection of *Khair-em-Sokar* and 95th Street.

It was only 3:30 PM, event was just ninety minutes old, and there already musta been damn close to six hundred people.

"I mean, *amazing* young people! Give em another round of applause!"

The martial arts team, black uniforms glinting gold from cuffs and crests, actually *step-danced* off the stage to extra loud applause.

Turn-out was way better than anyone'd had a right to expect. Sun was undiluted Saturday afternoon glory, and not even radar could find a cloud to complain of.

Raptor had plenty on his mind that wasn't sunshine. No 'Noot, still the lurking threat of Maāhotep, and then the fact that with all the Kush Party posters and ads up with pictures of Golden Eye, he and Jackal were like a coupla carnival ducks just waiting to get lit up by Marley and Lexus, the psycho murderers on release—

Stop. Breathe. . .

What is It *doing back in the Swamps? I just got* It *out of there* . . .

Hated using anything from Maā, but desperate times . . .

"And that kind of excellence, that's what you see when young people get the proper support from community leaders and civic leaders."

Alderman Gary Brothers was smiling, almost laughing. But from what Raptor saw, Brothers really meant. The politician slid a pale hand through his grey, straight hair, an *I can't believe it!* gesture.

Nobody was there specifically to hear Brothers speak, but with an election only four months away, the politician wasn't gonna sleep on any microphone time he could grab.

"That's why I, and the mayor, and the entire City Council, have taken such an interest and worked hard to provide funding and support for this remarkable Street Falcons programme."

Sbai Seshat, at the edge of the stage. Beaming at the turn-out, at the sunshine, at the city councillor whose second campaign (first successful one) she'd managed.

"That's why," said Brothers, "I helped arrange flying lessons for these teenagers, and got them municipally-owned space from a derelict building for their 'Street Laboratory,' and employment grants and job training, so they could truly unlock their potential!"

Seshat, who was always geo, dramatically clapped above her head, wiring her own applause through the crowd to amplify it.

"Thank you, thank you," said Brothers. "We know that Somali youth, Ethiopian and Eritrean youth, Rwandan youth, Sudanese youth, coming from such diverse cultures and languages and religions—"

Raptor had to give it to the man: he evidently knew Africa wasn't just one big jungle country full of gorillas and guerrillas.

"—bring a wealth of talent that with support, can help them become fabulously productive and successful members of our community!"

He hyped himself and the mayor for a while longer, but even Raptor knew it was all in the game.

"And hey, right there, folks, remember all those young martial arts action-stars? Well that's their teacher, right there!" Pointed at Moon near the stage. "You all saw it in that YouTube video! C'mon, I know you did. The man is practically Bruce Lee! He's—"

Some Falcon on the demo team shouted from the other side of the stage.

Brothers: "I'm being told I should've said he's like, uh, Mooser Powell? No, sorry . . . Musa. Someone important. Anyway—"

"So, why are we throwing the Kush Party?" Moon said at the mic, letting the echo sink in, like the sunshine.

"118th Ave was a dangerous place," he said. "People used to be afraid of being mugged down here. Or knifed. They called the city 'Stabmonton' for a while, remember that? Cuzza 107th Ave and this avenue right here.

"Then people started getting shot. A lot. Surprised nobody started calling it 'Leadmonton.'"

The crowd loved that one. Alderman Brothers' mouth smiled, but his eyes were moths under streetlights. Couldn't write *that* one on tourist brochures.

"They called this place, our home, 'the worst neighbourhood in the entire city.' Is that fair? Is that right?"

"No! NO!"

"When you live under somebody else's terms, well . . . you're terminal. When someone else defines you, he's limiting you. *Define*. As in *finite*."

"So we, these young martial artists, the people who arranged this whole day, who brought together all the vendors and the NGOs in all the booths, we're the Alchemists of Kush.

"Once upon a time when all these Nilotic people came to this neighbourhood, somebody figured out they should rename it all 'Kush.'"

Seshat: "Speak it!"

Falcons: "Transform, Brother Moon!"

Moon: "Now we're blessing all the sections of Kush with new names. Like this avenue. *Khair-em-Sokar*. Means, 'Path of Sokar,' one of the falcon gods of Kemet, the Blackland, or Land of the Blacks. What you call 'Ancient Egypt.'

"Self-definition precedes self-determination, you dig? Choose your own name, reframe yourself, you can remake yourself, replace your old self and elevate your new self—"

"*Geo-METCH-rical!*"

"*Trans-FORM it!*"

"We, my fellow Alchemist adults, and the youth known as the Street Falcons, we're leading by example—"

(and on every beat, *uh huhs* and *amens*)

"Building hope . . . with our own hands . . . For the people of Kush . . . Showing how to replace rot . . . and decay . . . with beauty . . . and life! Replace the sounds of cursing and fighting . . . with music and singing! And for our young people . . . replacing *nothing-to-do* with *can't-even-find-time-for-it-all!*"

Applause. Into it, pointedly, Moon said: "Replace . . ."

Falcons: "—and elevate!"

Moon: "Replace—"

"—*and elevate!*"

"REPLACE—"

"—*AND ELEVATE!*"

Applause like an ocean crashing, not just from the Falcons, but from everyone.

And why not? Plenty of them'd heard of E-Town's "Black Belt Jones" or "Morpheus X," but this was their first time seeing him. Local brother made good, with disciplined, uniformed, polite young people at his command? An easy sell even to people who were down to their last seven bucks and change.

So much better than a wild child or two or three hundred teenagers tearing up shit and turning party-goers and even pedestrians into threatened species.

Jackal elbowed Raptor, chinned towards a bunch of sisters pointing up at Moon, eyes and smiles glowing.

"Hope your moms aint seein that right there," joked Jackal.

Raptor laughed. He wasn't worried. He knew Moon was no ho. And he got that his mother needed a man. And with Moon, she'd levelled up about a thousand times from the bad old days of Doctor Liberia.

How far his mum and Moon'd gone along in their relationship, he wasn't sure. Far as he knew, they hadn't even kissed. Which in itself was weird.

Which one of them was more worried? And about what? How *he'd* take it? They didn't hafta to worry about that—

He laughed out loud.

Jackal: "What?"

"Nothing, nothing. Just thinking about something."

Of-freaking-*course* they needed to worry, with the way he always took things. Probably both didn't want him strapping on a dynamite vest for the next Christmas dinner.

A new thing, being able to laugh at himself. Felt good. Musta learned that from Jackal . . .

"Jackal, you know you're my best friend, right?"

Jackal turned a huge smile on him, his dreadlocks dragging over his shoulders as he turned.

Jackal: "Course, son! Obviously! Who else could put up witcha?"

Raptor smiled, clapped Jackal on the back.

Last year he'd've been insulted. Now, with a brother like Jackal, he didn't even have to hear back the words, *You're my best friend, too.*

Course, Jackal'd told him that many times before, but even so. With Jackal for back-up, he was shedding scars like a snake shedding skin, on account of outgrowing the old one.

Tonight. He'd tell Moon and his mum tonight.

But first . . . damn it. . .

Still no 'Noot.

30.

"On mic number two," blasted Raptor, "that's the Geometrical Jester, the Mogadishu Minister, the bombastical-fantastical Black Jackal!"

—*applause, cheers*—

"On the twin Tech 1200s, that's the Wax-Attacker, the Sonic Sentinel, the mixer and the fixer, DJ *Senwusret*—"

Sen scratched left I, I, I, I'm a, scratched right *fair, fair, fair, fair*-PHARAOH on his left Tech 1200, and got the cheers he deserved.

"And I'm another YouTube brother some of you might know—" (clapping and laughter) "—the lyrical lion, the Son of the Sphinx, the electrical MC, the sinister Supreme Raptor."

His voice: bassing through space . . . the crowd's cheering, searing treble.

"And now! For our second number! Straight out of *The Book of the Golden Falcon*! The story of you! Me! And all of us! Hit it, Sen!"

The beat smacked hard, drum-thunder, flashes of high-frequency kora lightning, with a doom-voice from the old *Spiderman* cartoon sampled inside it:

> *Who is this flying boy? What right has he to interfere in my conquest of the universe? I will destroy him!*

Both MCs hit the chorus:

> *Who am I? Who am I?*
> *Who am I? Call me Hru-u-u-u!*

The Supreme Raptor led the charge:

> *Who am I? Call me Hru, falcon-headed—where are we headed?*
> *How about Kemet? Lemme instruct you in the ancient ways intended*
> *I have befriended . . . the righteous, defended . . . the righteous*
> *I might just reunite us and transcend with all the righteous*

The Black Jackal went on the attack:

> *I'm-descending-with lightning in my hands and wings upon my back*
> *I never attack but I defend the innocent Wanderers—I conjure*
> *The spirits, the spirits, the spirits of my ancestors*
> *And rally my brothers and sisters, the righteous resistors*

Both MCs united:

> *Uniting . . . and fighting . . . to free our holy homeland*
> *Called Kemet, the Black Land—reclaiming our own land*
> *A lifetime . . . ago, this sacred place of ours flourished*
> *Ruled by my father, Lord Usir . . . he taught, he nourished*

—*glorifying* in the moment, seeing his mother wailing and cheering, and not one damn *bit* embarrassed—

The Black Jackal, his mic a golden hammer:

> *He lifted up his people with-knowledge, righteousness and mastery*
> *With his wife, Lady Aset, as powerful as he*
> *He brought his gold to all the world, returned to Kemet and my mother*
> *But competing for his power . . . was his destructive brother*

And the Raptor rapped on:

> *The general, the warlord . . . Set the Destroyer*
> *He butchered . . . my father . . . to be the sole controller*
> *Monster, betrayer, killer and enslaver*
> *One day someone would rise up . . . to lead us as our saviour*

And then the MCs hit the chorus, ripped into the crowd like a tide sucking beach walkers out to sea:

> *Who am I? Who am I? Who am I? Call me Hru-u-u-u!*

Offstage, applause still going after their fifth and final song, and all three brothers were backslapping and hugging—even Raptor.

Jackal: "Damn, kid, tolja! Tolja this was gon be just like Chappelle's *Block Party!*"

Senwusret: "Seriously geo! Blew shit up like *Blackhawk Down!*"

Loved it. Like he was flying past Jupiter and onto the next gas giant.

But he felt the ice of Saturn's rings like gravel in the face. Their set was supposed to've been *six* songs, ending with guest vocals by 'Noot.

31.

The sun: turning the whole scene tropical. *Kushitic.* Only things missing were palm trees and an ocean view.

But the sky . . . a blue, intense perfection. The pain-joy heart constriction of unrequited love.

Police barricades blocking traffic from 117th and 119th Aves on the south and north, and 97th and 94th Streets on the west and east.

Parents clutching babies and toddlers and piloting them in carriages through the occupying festival army.

Food kiosks blessing the air with the meat-fat-salt succulence of smoke and steam rising from roasting goat, beef *sbeso* and jerk chicken.

Boyfriends buying ice cream cones for girlfriends, then buying themselves neo-Ethiopian cones, flatbread *injera* smuggling *atekilt aletcha wot* and *doro wat*, and if they weren't careful, dribbling dark-stewed chicken and curried, buttered vegetables all over their over-sized white shirts.

Little kids running, ducking, darting round and between adult legs and among the NGO pavilions where the people of Kush window-shopped for services and ideologies. Social services, churches, mosques, the drivers of the Africentric school initiative, and the year-old SomaCASS, the Somali-Canadian Autism Support Society.

Ting, slushies, ginger beer, condensation dripping off glass bottles like sweet sweat. No beer gardens.

Handbills plastered on streetlight poles:

> *I Drink from the River of Life,*
> *and Will Not Drown*
> *in the Swamps of Death*

Africentric t-shirts selling and donned on the spot. The "Pirates of Somalia" number earning fat stacks of green-faced queens and a few pink-faced Kings for streetseller Wa-Wa and present partner Raptor and absent partner 'Noot.

A Rwandan band seizing the stage, two men in faux-lion and –leopard-fur headdresses and flares on their calves and wrists, acrobatting jumps and slides, bell-rings on their ankles jangling every stomp. Neo-Soul singer Krystle Dos Santos lighting up the crowd, sequelled by the dancehall stylee of Oozeela.

And by 6:30 PM and another couple of martial arts demos, the sun hours away touching rooftops . . .

And Raptor: hunting the crowd with falcon eyes, scanning everywhere for two crazy Somali killers his age, seeking inside the noise his permanent silence.

Maybe even *they* weren't Leadite enough to show up here. Too public.

But *khetiuta* as insane as they were? They slithered with snakes just as full of *isfet* as they were. *Khetiuta* looking to make names for themselves, who didn't know shit about cause and effect, or that every time they aimed the barrel, it stared back at them. And men too stupid to know that were dangerous beyond measure.

32.

"Oh, shit, Rap! Rap!"

Jackal grabbed Raptor. Calgary's Sudanese fusion band Taharqa kept playing. "It's 'Noot!"

Gold-black checkered *hijab* in place, the girl was crowd-wedging straight at them.

Raptor: relieved she was there. Terrified of what she was gonna say. What was he sposta do? Smile? Laugh? Cry?

Then she was there, crowd-crushed against him.

Cupping her hand, yelling up at him, "Can we talk?"

Nodded. Jackal eye-flaring at him: *This one's all yours, bruh.*

Behind the music-muffling, west-gazing bandstand.

"Raptor, I'm really upset with you."

He chewed his mouth. Not knowing what else to say, he said, "I know."

"But do you even know why?"

Already, it was on. So much for his fantasy of a make-up session of holding her hand for five unbroken seconds away from the eyes of the crowd and the entire worldwide Muslim *umma*.

"'Noot, you think you know about these people, but you don't. They—"

"Who's Brother Maã ever hurt, huh? You? Someone else in the Street Falcons?"

"'The absence of evidence is not the same thing as the evidence of absence.'"

'Noot: "Oh, by that token, how do I know you're not a murderer? Or an alien?" Him: grimacing. "What happened to 'innocent until proven guilty?'"

"Do you wait until a crocodile eats your children before you say, 'Maybe that crocodile is a threat?'"

"Raptor, *everybody* is potentially a threat! That's what makes us even human!"

"*Pyrites* are threats! Pretending to be one thing when they're actually something else, *after* something else!"

"Maybe you should study your scrolls a little more closely—"

"Oh, I know my scrolls—"

"Then you oughta go back to square one, the Resurrection Scroll, and the Catechism of the Three Metals. Eighty percent of people are Leadite. Ten percent are Gold, the Nubians. And ten percent are Pyrite—"

"You're proving my point—"

"But the geometry, Raptor!" She held out her hands, squaring air. "Eighty, plus ten, plus ten! You ever even think about that? U-universal?"

"What?"

"Nubians! People who've alchemised part of their own lead into true and living gold. But not all of it! Cuz nobody ever—"

"That's not what—"

"—*nobody* gets rid of all their lead, completely! And nobody can ever even get rid of *any* of their pyrite—"

"'Noot, you're—"

"Let me finish, Raptor!"

He shut up.

"Best you can even hope for is just cutting the amount of time you spend *behaving* pyrite, cut it to less than ten percent of the time! But you never stop being able to lie to others. Or yourself!"

His mouth opened, but silence poured down from his brain, filled it up. He shut his yap.

"Didn't transform that one before, didja?"

"Who told you that?" he swaggered. "Maãhotep?"

"I transformed it myself."

"Listen, 'Noot—"

"You've hurt one of our teachers, Raptor. Badly. Not to mention stoking gossip in our Laboratory—"

"I don't understand you! How can you, as a Muslim—"

"That again? *La ilaha il-Allah.* 'There is—'"

"'—no god but God,' I know, I know—"

"I'm not God. It's not for me to condemn Maãhotep. But he's a good man. He helps people! I saw your booklist on the Alchemy blog. You love telling people about all these great African writers—well, what about Langston Hughes and Alice Walker? Or James Baldwin? Are you gonna condemn them, too? Just throw away everything they've ever done—"

"If they've hurt people, then—"

"When you have proof Maãhotep has hurt people, talk to me!"

Raptor closed his teeth.

"But if you even want me to be your friend, I am telling you right now, I cannot be cool with this, the way you're acting, sowing division in the Golden Fortress and hating on someone I respect and care about like an uncle!"

Behind stage, faces turning towards them. The two teens moved off, found privacy behind a tent tarp. Music was still bassing loud, but nobody was watching them.

"I don't get you," she said. "You always seemed so . . . so hurt. And then every once in a while you'd flash this part of yourself that wasn't so sad and angry. I just wanted to get to know *that* Raptor.

"But this other one? The one that could, just-like-*that*—" (finger-snap) "—turn his back on Brother Maãhotep? Your teacher? Your lawyer? I mean . . . I don'know, Raptor. That's just . . ."

Raptor's head: swirling. Like trying to fly in a hurricane.

Her threat: *If you want me to be your friend . . .*

Tell her Fine. I don't need you. Don't flatter yourself. Think I care what you think?

Raptor, whispering: "Okay."

"What?" she said, eyes crinkled, protesting his quiet against the music's boom.

"I said okay." Trying not to sound like he was begging. "I'll . . . wait. For proof."

"And you'll stop all your talk? All your whispering behind Brother Maä's back until you have something definitive?"

Nodded low, chin almost touching chest.

Shock in her voice: "All right, then." Like even though she'd given it one last shot, she'd assumed she was gonna lose.

'Noot, softly: "You still wanna perform 'The Emerald Song'?"

"But, but our set . . . it's over."

Smiling. "I already talked it over with Brother Moon and Spurs of John Ware. They'll let us come onstage during their set. Just make sure you actually even just listen to your own lyrics for once, okay?"

Took everything he had not to rip her off the street and hug her right into the air.

33.

During the applause tailgating the sixth song by Spurs of John Ware, bass player/ lead vocalist Onyx Cowboy drew 'Noot and Golden Eye onstage. More cheers. Crowd loved the Spurs' spaghetti-funk, and it was just about to get rapped *up*.

Raptor: breath stuck in his throat. They'd never rehearsed with live musicians, let alone performed with any.

Jackal slapped him on the back, muting his mic. "Roll with it, dude. Be just like the Roots!"

Onyx Cowboy, heating the stage with his bass. Drummer Mill-Dread rumbling and clicketty-clattering her drums into blood-thumping intensity. Electric banjoist Matoxy Sexapeequin giving Golden Eye the melody that Sister Yibemnoot needed for launch:

> *Chased by priests and gen'rals*
> *It's more precious than em'ralds*
> *Yet the woman working at the mill stone*
> *Holds such jewels inside her soul*
>
> *Irrepla-a-a-aceable*
> *Unmista-a-a-akable*
> *It's the prince-of-all*
> *Invi-i-i-incibl-l-l-le*
>
> *It's wisdom*
> *Wisdom*
> *Wisdom. . .*
> *Wisdo-o-o-om!*

Jackal sliding in:

> *I've got some words stored up*
> *That I have got to-say-to-my-son*
> *Some people's lives are done*
> *Before they've even begun . . .*

'Noot, just too damned beautiful, and seeing her singing in that vast space, somehow these thousands of people were only an idea, a sparkling desert, and she and him were alone up there, joined by their microphones and their music . . .

(almost missed his verse)

> *You could lose your mind, in time*
> *Denying all of your crimes*
> *Re-defining all-of-your crimes*
> *Or maybe crying over-your-crimes*

Together, while 'Noot overdubbed them with wails and *Wisdoms*:

> *But if you truly listen*
> *And-then destroy your superstition*
> *You can glisten in the shining*
> *Glorious truth-of-my-golden rhymes*

Written this months ago, but now, listening like 'Noot'd warned him to, each line cut his gums.

He and Jackal, a verse each, then synergising on the third:

> *Do you waste your time conniving?*
> *Do you waste your time depriving?*
> *Are you raging, overdriving*
> *When your spirit should be thriving?*

> *Are you dismissing people*
> *That you're really missing?*
> *Or are you giving in your living*
> *Forgiven and forgiving?*

> *Cuz sometimes Hell is whatcha make it*
> *A Golden Mind, you just cannot fake it*
> *Your gold is waiting-for-you-to take it*
> *Don't-shake-it-or-break-it, just . . . remake it!*

Spurs of John Ware, amplifying their sonic storm, and 'Noot swing in like she was riding lightning:

> *Irrepla-a-a-aceable*
> *Unmista-a-a-akable*
> *It's the prince-of-all*
> *Invi-i-i-incibl-l-l-le . . .*

34.

The set was over, and Moon took the stage:

"Kot-TAM!"

TAM-TAM-TAM-TAM-tam-tam . . .

"That was the most amazing thing I've seen in the last ten years! You with me?"

Cheers, howls, wails and *likkashots* and *Bo-bo-bo!s* . . .

"Spurs of John Ware, Golden Eye, they're all amazing. But that young sister, Yibemnoot . . . *geomet*rical, am I right?"

Spurs of John Ware was still on stage, playing low and giving Moon a soundtrack while he speechified, like he was the ancient god Garvey igniting millions.

"Voice like that . . . like a young Shirley Bassey . . . You all know the song 'Goldfinger'? Yeah, that's the one . . .

"'Cept that sister was tragic . . . Didn't even want people knowing she was a sister. Imagine: all that success . . . trying to hide all that pain and all that *self*.

"Not *this* sister. Am I right?"

Let the cheering blaze at the end of every phrase.

"'Slike the universe stayed up late on a Saturday night to give that voice another chance at happiness!"

Cheers, and into every pause fell more cheers.

"Still have more amazement coming up. Somali band Mogadishu . . ."

"Ethiopian singer Haimanot Brehanu . . ."

"Hip hop super group Politic Live . . ."

"And reggae superstars Souljah . . . *Fyah!*"

"But first up—I gotta say, is this night amazing or what . . . ?"

"When we work together, what can't we do?"

"Fact is, seeing all of you here like this, like an army, or better yet, the kind of construction force that built the pyramids . . ."

Raptor, wondering, was Moon gonna drop his line, same thing he said every time someone mentioned the pyramids?

Moon: "And don't be buying any of that propaganda that the pyramids were built by slaves—"

Raptor, mouthing the words along with Moon, making 'Noot laugh.

"—aint a single legit historian in the world who'll tell you slaves built the pyramids—they were a paid workforce! You look like them! And like the man who designed the original, Imhotep! Ready to take on a major project. Am I right? ARE YOU WITH ME?"

Massive cheering—

"See that kiosk for the Africentric School Initiative? Over there, in front of Habesha Restaurant. The Alchemists, the Street Falcons—we support that . . .

"We need a school to help our kids succeed so they can become scientists, doctors, engineers, entrepreneurs . . .

"Cuz we don't think a grade of fifty-nine percent is good enough for our kids, even if these teachers do! ARE YOU WITH ME?"

Thunder . . .

Asked everyone to sign the school's contact list, donate whatever they could, and come to a meeting scheduled for the end of August.

Thanked the mayor and Alderman Brothers, and all the sponsors and NGOs, then made it clear, it was actually the people of Kush who made the event possible.

"Kush belongs to you! It used to be a swamp. But by working together, we have drained that Swamp . . .

"And we're on our way to raising up some pyramids!"

THUNDER . . .

10:30 PM. Sun'd already been gone half an hour. Sky was cobalt embedded with diamonds.

"Which leads us to our special surprise right now . . ."

Falcons in the crowd pulled away tarps from what most people must've assumed was a barrier.

Hands, ropes, yanking, an overhead pulley.

Raising a tower tapering to an elongated pyramid.

Up it went, silhouetted against the sky, two storeys tall upright, taller than all the low buildings around it.

An obelisk.

Then its architect, the man named Maãhotep, stepped forward to flick the switch.

Its sides lit up with LED hieroglyphics, golden light gleaming in the darkness.

"TransFORMED!" said Moon, and as one Kush howled and screamed.

35.

The killers were there.

Raptor saw them: Marley and Lexus, crocodiles slithering through the crowd. Red bandanas, incisor eyes, facial scars as victory medals from jailhouse butchery and rape.

The obelisk beaming. Souljah Fyah electrifying five thousand at midnight mass. And the cops that before were everywhere were nowhere.

Jackal, silking up three stage-struck girls. Raptor spun him by the shoulder, pointed straight at the murderers. Jackal's eyes went frosty.

Couldn't find Brother Moon. Couldn't find Sbai Seshat and Jackal couldn't find *Sbai* Maāhotep. So it was on them.

Grabbed shirt-seller Brother Wa-Wa and their four toughest fighters, none of them from the martial arts demo team. Nobody had weapons. Moon'd taught them: your enemy could transform your weapon into your own death, so rely on yourself.

But Raptor. He had his fang. Had it since his neighbour'd helped him build the box in the base of his bed when he was thirteen.

In the concert noise, cell phones were useless. They could text, but that meant taking their eyes off their targets. Jackal handed them each four glowsticks. Two yellows: in position. Two reds: emergency.

The seven of them filtered into the crowd, radar primed for red bandanas. The plan was . . . what was the plan? Surround them. Watch them. And if those *khetiuta* made a move against Moon or Jackal or Raptor, put their marrow on the asphalt.

Sliding among sweaty, reggae-drunk partiers. Concert bass from two-storey speakers beating almost heavier than their own hearts.

Two yellows in one hand. One Falcon not too close, not too far. In position. Up only three seconds, then down.

A second hand, two yellows.

A third.

Still no Moon. No cops.

Onstage: Souljah Fyah's Sista J sang, locks swinging and metronoming the crowd while joyful melody bent brains with bitter lyrics:

> *Everyone says you're bad for me, but I don't cyare*
> *See you running around on me on the town*
> *Everyone says you're bad company, but I don't cyare*
> *Cuz I'm always happy when you're around*

Fourth hand up.

The fifth—

Jackal and Raptor, closing in behind the murderers.

If they weren't in a crowd they'd be in kicking distance. Not close enough for *wing chun* phone booth fighting, and not close enough for *Sanuces-Ryu* grappling.

His fang, ready in his pocket, hungry.

Hunt me, you worthless muthafuckas?

Shoulders, spine on fire, but palms sweating blood—

Turn around—

Heart jack hammering both ears—

Time to die—

Bandana #1 turned to face him—

Raptor, on the edge of the crowd, bending over a metal crowd barrier that looked like an old headboard.

Ropey puke dangling from his mouth and nose.

Jackal, rubbing his back as he came up for air. "Dude! *Dude!* Y'okay?"

Somebody handed him a water bottle. Sipped. Swished. Spat. Sipped and swallowed.

Looked at his hands.

Shaking.

Could've buried a blade in the esophagus of some harmless brother cold-lamping with his homey on a Saturday night street party in Kush.

All of them, locking eyes.

Intense: relief, then shame-disgust.

Dying of thirst, then drinking your own piss, just to survive.

Who is the Destroyer?

Before he could change his mind, left the Kush Party, found a storm vent. Knelt and dropped his butterfly knife down into the sewage coursing below. Couldn't even hear the splash.

36.

Sunday morning. Above the street. The Palace of the Moon.

Sunlight streaming golden through curtain-breaks, dust motes twinkling, turning to stars.

His mother, curled up on the couch, a cat. Snuggled in blankets.

Sitting beside her, edge of couch, his own hip and rump nuzzled next to her belly.

They'd all gotten here late, almost 4 AM, dawn's first verses written red on sky's eastern scroll. Moon'd insisted she take the bed and he'd take the couch. She'd refused. Back and forth ten times.

Raptor'd finally said, "Brother Moon, you can't win against my mum. Just go to sleep."

Morning time: Moon, padding down the hallway, into the kitchen. Smiled at Raptor, eyes extra soft towards his mother.

She woke, yawning and stretching so big it was funny, a cartoon lioness. They'd already set the table, piled it with pancakes, butter, syrup, fruit, free-range turkey links. Sweet steam twirled up from table. And they all sat and served themselves.

Mum, happy and free. Moon, same.

Him, ashamed and so damn grateful he could cry.

"Look, just wanted to say, I know," said Raptor.

Eyes on him.

"I know how you feel about each other."

Forks clinked on plates. Jaws refused to close.

"And, y'know, I'm fine with it. Fact, I'm happy."

Their astonished faces. He smiled, sharing his own sunrise. "You've got my blessing."

Moon, shaking his head. "I . . . I don'know what to say . . ."

Araweelo, getting up and clutching her boy and kissing his cheeks over and over. "Then don't say anything!"

Raptor, his mum still hanging onto him, shuffled to the stereo and hit Shuffle. First song up: jangly bass, strutting drums, Motown style. "100 Yard Dash." Raphael Saadiq.

Spent the whole morning eating, dancing, drinking tea and talking and laughing about whatever they felt like.

37.

Strolling mid-afternoon, free from the Hyper-Market.

Blazing sun and crazy-named new beverages meant blossoming business, enough to pay for the new staff member and every weekend off for Moon.

The three of them, walking, smiling, nodding, whassupping and dropping *Nub-Wmet-Ānkh* to anybody who knew what time it was.

Announcing their presence for all of Kush to see and bless.

Rap, no earphones, but his internal soundtrack rolling pure Senegalese gold: Orchestre Baobab's "Dée Moo Wóor." And just like in the video, strutting and strolling in hot summer sunshine like the world was one giant welcome.

And then the red tabloid newspaper box, and the headline:

Somali body count hits 7

Coins into slot. Crowding round.

Far west side of Kush, a body found in a synagogue's Dumpster, of all places, by a homeless man scrounging for food. Stabbed *and* shot, but no blood on the scene. Junked there, while Kush had been jamming reggae beyond midnight.

Seventh one in seven months.

Leadmonton indeed.

38.

After the shock, after supper at Habesha, after silently feeding ducks and loons in the landscaped lake of Hawrelak Park.

Trying to forget and failing.

Watching the stars whisper into existence.

Moon sailed them in his shining gold-black Sunfire back to Araweelo's walk-up, Al Hambra. Pulled up in front, on the street. Walked up the sidewalk—

"What the FUCK is going on here?"

All three spun.

Parking lot: shambling towards them, jacket and tie on despite the summer night-heat, disaster in wing tips and lifts.

Doctor Liberia.

Moon, both hands out: the reassuring *take it easy, fella* gesture, but Raptor decoded it. A defense posture, ready to transform ribs into lung-cutters.

"Jacob!" cried Araweelo. "What are you *doing* here?"

Almost on them, and the fumes rippling off his body like a force field, eyes so red even street lights couldn't hide it—

"*I'M* asking the fucking questions, you goddamn whore—"

Liberia's hands burst into fists—

—and then he was doubled over, then swishing back up and his head snapping right and he was on the walk-up's lawn like two sacks of shit stuffed in a suit.

Raptor overtop him, replanting his talons on the grass, standing just outside of grabbing range, panting.

His mother, clutching her hand over her mouth.

Moon, collecting the man's tooth and mangled glasses.

One of them cell-phoned 9-11.

A few curtains opened, shut again just as quick.

39.

Flying, whirling, streaking among Jupiter's rings and moons and above its massive *Ujat.*

The bloody hurricane, bigger than three earths, reaching out into space like a giant lamprey mouth, and sucking him down into storm, darkness, and invincible gravity.

ASSAULT
ON THE
GOLDEN
FORTRESS

Eight
Righteousness
& Mastery

The Book of Then

1.

I STAYED OUT IN THERE IN THE WILDERNESS. I DIDN'T GO BACK TO THE COM-pound. With the trees I brought down, I built a new nest, almost a warren, one even foolish crocodiles couldn't penetrate.

I needed to stay close to my work, live in it, sleep in it, without interruption in my sacred labours.

Draining the Swamps of Death.

When I slept, my Shining Eye showed me the path. The River Eternal flowed from high up in the cradle, past Ta-Seti, born in mountains among living jade and emerald.

But the miseries of the occupied Blackland, the filth and pain seeping into the River, turned it choking-thick and deathly. By the time the poisoned River reached the Savage Lands, its waters curdled into the Swamps of Death, vile and bubbling.

I'd set the waters free to find the Great Green Sea beyond the Savage Lands. Because if waters move where they desire, they're free.

And in that freedom, they can purify themselves and become a source of life.

2.

"I'm astonished," said Master Jehu, surveying my work.

It was fogged-out sunrise three months into my labours. He stood on the bank above me. "And just one man."

I was up to my waist in the Swamp, sweating, mud-caked, scaled with leaves. My hands were armoured gloves of callus. I was covered in bruises, cuts, and gashes, glorious in my rubies of crusting blood. Breathing deeply from my morning work.

I was light and free.

"Master, I'd like to request help now."

"Good," he said, smiling. "I thought it best to wait until you asked."

I bowed. "Thank you, Master."

"I've kept your project secret. Nobody except Yinepu knows you're out here. But when the youths find out what you're attempting—what you're doing—they'll be lining up to fill your work-gangs."

I smiled, looked up at a gnarl-footed trunk on the bank. I'd shorn off its trunk my first day. I glanced at leaves and lily pads swimming past me.

Just a sunrise before, this entire region was submerged up to my heart in rancid, murderous, scumthick sludge.

Now I'd smashed the dams of muck of filth and turned the wound into a vein. Waters flowed around my hips, found the gate I'd cut and the cascade beyond, fell to bubbling rapids down below.

3.

At moonrise, Master Jehu returned. He was afraid.

He said, "War's coming."

We ascended through the night-mists, him as ibis, me as falcon, back to the compound I had not seen in a lifetime.

I've been sending rangers out into the Savage Lands to assess the strength of General Set. One after another has returned with news: He knows about our compound and sees us as a threat to everything he clutches. He's planning to annihilate us, if need be by burning down the Savage Lands and making it a desert.

But why? I asked. *Since before I was born, why this mission of destruction? What threat could we possibly pose to him?*

Anyone who shows he can survive outside the realm of Set, proves it can be done. That another, better world is possible . . . there is no greater threat to a tyrant than this truth.

From on my wave of wind, I looked below to see campfires inside our compound's walls.

What's your plan, Master?

Your mother wants to—

My MOTHER?

Yes, your mother—

But I . . . she's—

My son, I healed your mother, don't you remember? With your brother Yinepu assisting me in her anointing. You were there with us, wrapped in shadows! After I'd returned her to life, she raged at me and claimed I was your captor and you my slave.

I couldn't see, Master, when I was wrapped in shadows of such depth. I could barely hear . . . I thought I'd dreamed it all.

No. Your mother is alive.

So all these months, she's been in the compound with you?

Yes, my son. Come see her!

I . . . but after what I did to her—

Come!

Down we soared. I became a shadow. Master Jehu, understanding, let me.

I perched on the wall. My mother—returned to my life a second time—could not or did not see me. She argued with Master Jehu, angrily as ever.

"We've scored victories, but my forces are isolated, hiding in pockets." She stabbed her finger at the ground. "This war's coming to us sooner than my oracles foresaw. I need your children. Now."

"What?"

With her hand she swept across the sleeping areas of our compound, now two dozen times the size when Yin and I had laid its first bricks. Hundreds of youth and children slept here, unaware of my mother's plans for them.

"We need armourers," she said. "Weapons-makers. Soldiers. Sorceresses. With the power of the Measurer behind us . . . *that's* what we need to tip the balance!"

"You mean to snap the balance in two," said the Master. "To smash a measuring-rod into two killing-spikes."

She aimed a finger in his face. "I informed you, Jehu, as a courtesy. I need neither your permission nor approval."

She uttered words-of-power, and in moments, the hundreds of the Master's pupils assembled in perfect regimentation.

Each held a pike, or a knife, or a rock.

But their eyes were closed.

"What've you done," he yelled, "to my children?"

"Prepared them."

"Prepared them to be slaughtered? To be trampled under the feet of stampeding men with swords? To suck knives into their throats, and arrows into their lungs? To scream themselves to death?" He stamped forward and swept up his arms like a *ka*. "*I'm* training them to civilise the world!"

"You're a sad, lonely, pathetic, crazy old wizard." She sneered. "How long has it been since you've been with a woman? Hm?" She laughed hatefully.

"Listen, dreamer, hiding in the Savage Lands, afraid—who's going to build this world of yours after Set's men have ripped through your orphans like boars feasting on chicks? Have you thought of that? At least my way, they've got a chance!"

"A chance to serve your revenge." He clutched the golden chain that circled round his neck. I saw his chest drawing air. "You think I'm blind? I've seen the wastelands left by soldiers in the villages, the devastated crops and knackered beasts, the starving, sobbing orphans, everywhere Set's armies have been and gone . . . and all those towns and farm-homes in the hinterlands that offered food and rest to Set's forces rather than be murdered by them.

"I've seen what's left of *those* people, their lands, their animals. Their children. So tell me, Sorceress . . . who was the Destroyer *then*?"

Who was the Destroyer?

I fluttered down from the compound wall, became a man again, revealed myself from shadow for the wall of sleeping children waiting for my mother's march to war.

And my mother saw me.

I'd begged the gods—when once I'd cursed them—for a second chance, to erase the crime I'd done, to strip me of my sin.

And now I faced my mother.

Me, the son who'd murdered her, and she, a murderer of a multitude beyond measure.

Neither of us spoke. We didn't move towards each other. We did not embrace or cry.

Ten million things that could have been were strewn in space between us, that two nights of knives and fire had killed three lifetimes ago.

I offered, "Milady."

"Jehu's . . . *apprentice.*"

"Mother," I tried again.

"Hru," she accepted.

"Please . . . I know you want to avenge my father. That you want to stop my uncle. I'm asking you . . . begging you, to join me in a mission that's bigger than . . . than even defeating the General.

"We've both seen—I've seen, to my shame—how much easier it is to destroy than to create. I'm asking you to help me finish what I've started. I'm draining the Swamps of Death."

"What?"

She stood, staring. I waited, silent.

"You're—you're serious? You. The entire Swamps?"

"Yes."

"Are you—" she sputtered. She turned to the Master. "What've you done to him? How've you twisted him like this?"

"You haven't seen what he's done already, by strength of arms and will alone. By himself he's transformed a field that used to be up to his chest in water. Now it's down to his loins."

She was stunned. And silent.

"Mother, help me," I said. "Without the Swamps poisoning the Savage Lands, giving monsters home to swarm and breed and slaughter, enslaving children with curséd water, providing Set a quagmire he can always hide in and keep anyone from mounting an attack against him, he'll rule forever. You know that this is true."

"He's coming anyway," she said to me finally. "No matter what your plans are. And you know *this* is true."

"Either way, we fight to kill," I told her. "Only in one way do we fight to live."

4.

It was not yet dawn. The final stars glittered, a spine of light on the indigo skin of Noot.

I was sitting beside Yin inside his ring of sleeping jackals when he woke.

He looked afraid—not of what I could do, but of what I would say.

"Thank you," I told him, "for saving my mother's life."

Hugging him tightly, my cheeks and nose wet, I felt his breath escaping his chest raggedly, in clouds of pain, released up into the night.

He asked me about where I'd been and what I'd done. I told him.

He looked at me in awe. "You're so different, Hru."

"What do you mean?"

"You, you look so much older. Taller. And you don't talk the same. You sound just like, well . . . . "

"What?"

"Like the Master."

I thought about that.

"I'm sorry," he said, "about my father. And yours."

I understood the question he didn't speak. "Yin, you will always be my brother."

5.

"Over here," yelled Yinepu. "We need ten diggers here, and another twenty over with Hru. Who's going where?"

We were the foremen of the labours.

It was the fourth week of the compact between my Master and my mother. Master Jehu let her teach our school her arts of war, on condition she used her vast and secret lexicon-of-power to teach us arts of healing and creation.

Master Jehu instructed a measuring magic I'd never known existed, a number code revealing all the known and unknown lines inside the universe, how they converged, how one group of lines could teach us of many others. He called this magic *geometry.*

With it, we elevated grunting, slashing, heaving and shoveling to a number art that revealed Maät in every segment of the world, letting us transform the low into the high.

We felled dead trees by thousands. We grew the channel, deepened it, directed it through lower lands and on towards the Great Green Sea.

Our tools were shining metal, hatchet-heads and spades, scimitars and shovels, forged from Master Jehu's fire-magic and hammered true by four apprentices of mine, sturdy boys named Duamutef and Hāpi, Imset and Qebehsunuef.

They armed us all so that the work that sheared our bones went faster, this *geomancy* that remade the world.

Some waters we diverted to the sandlands, where trickles from the Swamps of Death could do no harm, indeed, where power of the sun-fired sand could kill the water's curse, and with the flowing silt and mud, transform the orange zone of death into loam-fields where one day—one day—new life would grow abundant and eternal.

6.

And on the eighth week of training soldiers and geomancers, the water of the poison-bowl where I'd begun my work had sunk so low that we now stood inside a valley, and at the bottom, beside where dark-clean water now flowed swiftly, there was an entrance to a cavern beckoning me.

I called my mother and my brother.

We descended. Inside, stalactites and stalagmites, great monster's fangs, guarded throat beyond. We slipped among them down towards the heart.

With my Shining Eye we walked in darkness to the belly of the cave, found the cedar-wood vessel sunken there by weight of bolted pyrite bas reliefs.

With trembling hands but strength of hundred-and-a-hundred moons' anticipation and rehearsal, my mother pressed her fingertips against the pyrite-ingot seals that kept the lid shut tight, turned them molten, let them boil away, flaring yellow in the dark, dripping down to kiss the floor.

Together we hefted the cover.

Inside, my father's skull stared back at us.

And my mother wept.

7.

It took four days for Yinepu and me to retrieve the pieces of my father that Yinepu had found for her, embalmed and sealed inside her secret, hidden shrines across the Blackland and the Savage Lands.

My father's killers, fearing she would find him and revivify him, must have smashed apart the metal seals they placed, and carved him like a sacrifice, scattered him like dung, believing no one could unite the many into one.

Without Yinepu, she never would have found them all.

The penultimate piece retrieved had been my father's manhood, which, said Destroyer's soldiers captured by my mother and persuaded into testimony, had been thrown into Eternal River where a fish had gulped it down and swum away. Even that one, Yin had located, undecomposed inside the fish that had choked to death.

The only body-chunk they'd left, resealed inside the box, was the one we'd found, the final one. The skull.

With the gold my four *Mesnitu* blacksmiths smelted and kept liquid, and with the guidance of Master Jehu in our circle, we descended to the sacred cavern, aligned the severed members, skull and trunk, welded them together with our molten gold and obsidian words-of-power.

And he rose.

Black-skinned, eyes rimmed golden, the Great Instructor, the Lord of Limits, the Being Beautiful.

And the cavern floor birthed a throne of turquoise shining from ten thousand years of darkness.

And he sat upon it.

My father!

Return, he Instructed, *to world of tears in righteousness and mastery, to make stand those who weep, to reveal those who hide their faces and to lift up those who sink down, so all the world might rise nearer to Supreme.*

My mother asked us to leave.

8.

Master Jehu and Yinepu and I walked together through the night, dazzled by what we'd been privileged to behold.

When we saw the compound just ahead, Master Jehu smiled, faraway. "I knew your father when he was just a child."

He shocked me yet again. I was angry—yet another secret? But as he taught us many times, *The truth is like the sun: with the same rays a bringer of life and yet a champion of death . . . The time to know will come when it is right.*

"I was there when he met your mother," he said. "And I was there the day of his return, and the night of his final banquet."

I steadied myself, drained the anger of my swamp. "Master, when he was little, what was my father like?"

Yin, too, was excited to know more about the man he'd spent so many years to reconstruct and resurrect.

Master Jehu's eye erupted with an arrowhead and shaft. A spear gashed through his chest.

I whirled, dodged the hammer aiming for my skull, saw the mace which broke my Master's spine and sent him plunging to the muck.

"Murder!" I shouted, and then let Fang announce himself. I cleaved necks from shoulders, thighs from calves, turned skulls into halves.

"Go!" I told Yinepu. "Protect the children!"

He ran inside.

More murderers erupted from the shadows, surrounding me and casting mesh upon me, gagging me so I that couldn't speak my words-of-power.

They clubbed me till I heard my own bones snap, and when I buckled, I sank to sand and roots and rocks and saw the severed heads of seven jackals on the soil, and everything went dark—

And then men dragged me like a netful of fishes, hefted me and dumped me to the grass. My elbows and wrists were bound, my gag tightened, my face pressing into the ground. My nostrils drank the stench of shit and piss, and burning-smoke of wood and meat.

The heavy footsteps thudded through the mud and matted reeds, stopped behind me.

"So you're him, huh?"

I'd never heard his voice before, but I knew at once just who he was. Just as I'd never been stabbed, but still I'd know a knifeblade if a knife slipped between my ribs to steal my life.

I wrenched my head to glimpse his face, but he was silhouetted by the bright inferno of our compound crackling to its death.

All I could make out was the outline of his war-helmet, the square-cropped upright ears of an ant-eater. Or the blunted horns of an arch-devil.

He growled, "So who do you think *I am*?"

He walked closer. Kicked my thighs open.

He knelt behind me—I felt his kneecaps between mine.

I tried to get up, tried to fight, tried to scream, but the gag shackled my words and his men clutched my ankles.

"Who *am* I? Huh? Who *am* I?"

He yelled, howled, laughed, screamed, raged while bucking, while cutting me, while gouging me, while bleeding me, while defiling me, while ruining me.

"Say my name!" he screamed. "*Say my name! SAY MY NAME!*"

The Book of Now

1.

A CAGED BIRD.

Raptor, in A & D, at the Remand Centre.

Jail.

Statisticalised.

He'd told himself long ago he'd never let anybody enslave him again.

But here he was.

Cold darkness, steel clanging echoes, and the stench of the holding cell: stovepot stewing Lysol, cheese slices, and diarrhea.

Wouldn't be having visitors at the Remand Centre. The Ream. That's what they called it, and he knew why. Everybody knew why.

No visitors except a lawyer, cuz now it was all space-age. Video visits from offsite. So you couldn't even *smell* your loved ones.

Knew the stories. Heard em all. Guys who ended up dead in their cells. Human excrement attacks—psychos filling up potato chip bags or milk cartons or pop bottles with piss and shit, placing them just under the cell doors of inmates and stomping them or *bombing* prisoners with em.

"And these fuckers have AIDS, man," whoever'd told him about it had said. "Their fuckin shit's full of it!"

Not even guards were safe. They got *bombed*, too. And shanked. And stomped. And choked.

Scanning the cell. Remembering . . .

Some scarred-up Hispanic guys. Bandidos? MS-13s, the Salvadorans from LA? Over there, Asian Syndicate? Some Punjabis—Millwoods Mafia? Cree dudes . . . Alberta Warriors, Redd Alert? A couple of patois-dripping yahd-bwois: North End Jamaicans?

No way of knowing who was connected, or if all those gangs even really existed or were just the typical bullshit that all wannabe gangstas—wiggers, Brown wiggers, even Black wiggers—ate up like Cream of Wheat.

Mangled truth or outright lies with better flow and more hype than anything by Lil Jon or Young Jeezy. Or even NWA.

But those swastikas were no joke.

Two skinheads, both taller than he was, one thick-necked, the other with grey eyes so pale they were almost all white except for the pupils.

Somebody behind him whispered: "White Boy Posse."

Somebody answered it: "Aint they like the farm team an shit for the Hell's Angels?"

And on their arms . . .

With his Shining Eye, he saw it there before him, the crest he'd designed with 'Noot, burnished gold beaming sunrise, a falcon grasping two shen-rings in its talons.

But on the skinheads across the holding cell, a tattoo on each like an armband: an eagle grasping a hooked cross inside a circle.

Straight outta the Righteousness & Mastery Scroll, the Cosmological Alchemy: he was an electron. They were antielectrons.

All they had to do was touch, and they would annihilate each other.

Standing on the LRT platform, Central Station, cuz his bike had a flat. Been borrowing Jackal's bus pass for a couple of days, but he'd left it in his locker at Centre High.

Thought about never-minding it and boarding anyway, but decided to hoof it back the three blocks.

Vaulting up the stairs, when the guard yelled at him to stop. He did. Guard questioned him, demanded, Show me your pass. He tried to tell him. Guard said, You're coming with me. No, I'm not coming with you. Already told you.

You're coming with me—

The thick-necked Nazi. Muttering to his partner, loudly: "Lookit all these fuckin mud people in here."

The one with the white eyes: "Like fuckin *Lord of the Rings*."

Heads cranked, but nobody moved. The balls on these assholes. Like grenades.

Two sentences into the cell, and the Nazis already punking everybody.

Flew up the stairs, LRT plasticop chasing him. Ran right into a real one. And not just any one.

Heard about him from a whole buncha kids. Even saw him once before: looked just like that crybaby nutcase doughboy racist on FOX.

Jackal's joy-riding friends'd taken beat-downs from him. One ended up in the hospital.

Constable Babyface.

Thick Neck and White Eyes closed on a guy. Maybe Lebanese. Called him "Osama"—big biceps and angry eyes. But somebody with nobody.

Blood fists flashed, head hitting cell floor. Thick Neck put one foot on the kid's chest, leaned in, and the kid went *whoof* when all the air came out.

Kid knew better than to scream or beg for help—not that he could do either one.

Finished, the Nazis turned 270 degrees. Eyefucking everybody in sight.

If they touched him, or if they tried to—

They would both die.

Off where the security cameras didn't point, Babyface'd punched him in the jaw. Raptor went down and training sent the knife-edge of his foot into the cop's balls.

Babyface's baton slashed—

And again.

And again, and again.

Finally hauled him to the cruiser.

While Raptor was in the back seat, the cop took out his Taser.

"Better start rapping for me now, homey, or I'll hafta use this on your ass. Or up it."

Exploded: "Think I'm afraid of some fucking retard Lead-Head like you?"

—agony spiking under his fingernails, nailing through his bones and gouging into his eye sockets—body arching like a branch before snapping—

Collapsing, cuffed, into the back seat . . .

"That's for mouthing off to the police," said Babyface. "And this one's for canning me."

—*lightning*—

Thick Neck and White Eyes took down another Arab. Nobody stepped in.

Knew they'd come for him. Only a matter of time. Surprised they hadn't done it yet.

Knew from training he'd have maybe one second to fix the outcome. Can't grapple two at once, so he had to strike.

Stomp feet or thigh-front, which nobody ever expected. Gouge eyes, then crush throat. Second one, no choice but to improvise. If anybody helped him, he might survive. But nobody would.

White Boy Posse freaks. The year before, some of them'd gotten busted with three hundred grand in cash, half a mill in coke, and a shitload of guns and swords. Kot-tam. *Swords?* Those White boys were psycho. Jeffery *Dahmer* psycho.

Knew that killing even a Nazi psychopath about to kill him would win him a life sentence. And unlike Marley and Lexus, he'd be killing when he was already eighteen, past protection of the Young Offenders Act.

So, he sobbed to himself, the end of his scroll was already written. Best he could do now was paint in some details.

At the station, cops checked his record. Nothing.

Cuz he'd never gotten caught.

Wiil Waal Abdi, the smiling twenty-year-old who'd seemed so grown up when Raphael was just a kid moving into Al Hambra with his mum.

Name meant "Crazy Boy" (or add in *Abdi* for Crazy Boy Slave, since racist Arabs had imposed the common surname/slurname). But he wasn't crazy. He was nice. Saw Raptor sitting on the lawn outside Al Hambra after school one time.

"Whatcha reading, little man?" he said, Somali accent channeling a vibe he'd probably looped from some 50 Cent CDs.

Raphael showed him the *Static* comic Mr. Jack'd given him.

"Static, huh? Betchu causin all kinda static your own lil self!" And every time after that, the man called him Static. Didn't know why Wiil Waal liked him, but he did. And Raphael liked the nickname and the man who gave it to him.

Coupla weeks and five *whassup-Static!*s later, Wiil Waal even gave him a few bucks to go buy some more issues, which he finally found in a Wee Book Inn somewhere among stacks of *Juggs* and *Biker* and the store's overfluffy mascot cat.

Once during winter he forgot his apartment keys. Couldn't even get through the front door into the stairwell. Shivering out on the front step like a bird that forgot to fly south. Wiil Waal let him come up to his apartment, and they played Xbox on a plasma screen and ate delivery pizza from Rosebowl. Rap felt like Richie Rich.

Raphael's mother was furious at Wiil Waal, yelling at him in Somali and calling him a "typical Somali low-life."

But Wiil Waal didn't care, and neither did he. His mother was never there when he got home from school anyway, and Wiil Waal was usually only getting outta bed by then. So Wiil Waal's crib became Raptor's after-school care centre.

It was the only after-school care in the city where the music was mostly NWA. Wiil Waal had all their CDs, and a pristine vinyl of *Efil4Zaggin*, even though he didn't own a record player.

One time Wiil Waal saw some of Raphael's drawings. They were crude back then, but the twenty-year-old gave him mad props and paid him twenty bucks to draw him a picture of NWA, including Ice Cube, the first one to leave the band and build a solo career.

Raphael would've used his commission to buy a battered copy of Lee's & Buscema's *How to Draw Comics the Marvel Way* from Wee Book Inn, but Wiil Waal bought if for him when they went for a drive, and within weeks his skills leapt years.

One day Wiil Waal asked Raphael to store some stuff for him. Just a few small sandwich bags for a week. Easy. And pinned twenty bucks on him for his work.

Within a couple of months of Raphael providing weekly mini-storage, Wiil Waal asked him to keep more than a baggy or two. He helped him build a stealth stash in his box-spring. Big enough for what Wiil Waal called bricks, darkgreen and Saran-Wrapped.

They went out for milkshakes and burgers at Burger Baron down 118th Ave to celebrate his promotion. Amazing. Outta nowhere, he had an older brother, a friend, and a job.

He only sipped at the cash, but even back then, it ran out quickly. So four years later—like during his end-of-inventory night when Jackal'd driven up in Nuke's stolen car—he sometimes sentineled an unclaimed corner in Kush, diming out what was left after Wiil Waal was long gone and the police had seized the man's Xbox, his plasma and everything else.

A week after Burger Baron burgers, Wiil Waal musta gone outta town, cuz when Raphael tried returning some NWA CDs after school on a Monday, Wiil Waal didn't answer the door even after five minutes of knocking. And it was the same the next day.

The day after that he saw Wiil Waal's face on the cover of the *Sun*.

Statisticalised.

Police'd searched him, cheering like hillbillies when they unrolled his socks.

"Whoah, lookit these!" said one, figuring he'd found two dozen joints.

But they were scrolls, Resurrection Scrolls, rolled and taped just like the ones Brother Moon'd put into his and Jackal's hands back when they were still mentally dead.

But what if he'd been packing his butterfly knife when Babyface grabbed him? Would he be dead now?

After the Kush Party, after almost gutting an innocent man, he knew the only knives he'd ever use again were his hands.

The Nazis were working their way through the crowd. And still nobody'd stood up to them.

Maybe *none* of these guys was gangsta.

Babyface'd Tasered him. Filled him with electricity. Maybe he really was Static now. Thought made him smile: projecting blue fire from his hands and exploding those skinheads' heads like eggs in a microwave.

Muscles twitched. Jaw clenched.

If nobody else was gonna do it, he would.

Jackal, long ago: Why would Moon risk his life for two strangers, especially against two strapped stone-cold killers?

Finally he could transform it: Because sometimes you're just so pissed at seeing people get shit on, cuz it reminds you of how much you got shit on, that you will totally fuck up anybody who steps to you or even near you and maybe even get yourself killed, just so you never have to say, *I stood on the shore, in the mud, surrounded by reeds, doing nothing, while watching crocodiles in the Swamps snapping through kids' skulls and swallowing their brains.*

Tapped guys who'd be on the Nazis' hitlist but also looked like maybe they could fight. Found seven, of seven different colours.

In the corner, whispering—*conspiring*, like he'd learned from Brother Moon's etymology: *breathing together.*

Explained they were all next unless they stood together.

One guy, desperately sucking down his near-tears, finally just said, "Shit, man, I'ont know how to fight!"

Some people woulda been disgusted, but he knew what this guy was feeling.

Put a hand on Near-Tear's shoulder. Guy didn't shrug it off, either.

"You don't *hafta* know how," the Supreme Raptor told him and his new coalition. "Just kick em or stomp em as hard as you can, anywhere you can, especially if they're on the floor."

Raptor's eight turned to the centre of the cell.

Time: ice. Dripping. Dripping.

Even against eight, these skinheads would be hard-core, and probably half his own insta-crew would bolt and the other half would crack.

So he was probably going to die that night.

Alone.

Who loved him?

When his dad sent him and his mother ahead to escape along the Nile, he must've known he was gonna die.

And that was a man he'd never said more to than *goo-goo gaa-gaa.*

His right foot took the first step.

Who would miss him when he was dead? Who loved him?

Jackal, no question. And 'Noot—she didn't love him, but she cared. His mother— maybe before he would've bullshitted and said she didn't, but he knew she did.

Moon.

Two steps in, and the Nazis were turning towards them.

Hit him like sleet: until Moon, no man who'd ever known him had loved him.

Of course father sacrificed himself, but for a baby. His dad hadn't really known him, not the him he'd become.

Yeah, Wiil Waal found him useful, even liked him—he truly believed that. But Wiil Waal also used him, put him in danger.

Three steps and the Nazis were already advancing on them. Felt, like he had Daredevil's radar, two of his own crew peeling away.

Seventeen years old before he met Moon. Seventeen years before any man had loved him.

Falcon and pigeons flying straight into eagles, and the ice was melting faster.

Sounded crazy, those words, like a kot-tam R&B Lead-headed bullshit love ballad, songs so shallow they couldn't hold a raindrop, cuz they never said anything bizarre or made anyone uncomfortable or asked twisted questions.

But what was love if it wasn't bizarre or didn't make you uncomfortable or force you to ask twisted questions?

Eight steps and thick Neck and White Eyes and swastikas like whirling buzzsaws mounted on their foreheads, and it was time to kill and die.

2.

The C.O. led him down the hall. Felt like a tunnel, a flesh tunnel, throbbing him forward.

Mud blocked his senses. In his ears: foot-echoes like sloshing through mud. Nose turned the air to smoke over piss. The guard's hand on his arm: ooze. Gravel.

No wounds, no blood, not even the first punch thrown, because the guards—

—trying to ram down a breath to stabilise his gyroscoping mind—

Stopping, guard holding him up.

Standing on the other side of the portal, an emissary from the land of the living. The man who'd gotten him out.

A trick? A kot-tam Pyrite scam to make him grateful, make him lower his guard?

Shuffling forward, legs jellying with each step.

Tripping, falling forward, and the man caught him, and trying to climb up and away from his saviour turned into holding onto him and then grinding down his teeth so hard they hurt, just to keep the screams inside.

But he couldn't stop the shudders.

A wary hand. On his shoulder.

When Raptor didn't let go, Maãhotep dropped his briefcase and hugged him tight with both arms.

Driving Kushward, south from 186th Avenue. Didn't even know there was city this far north. Practically the arctic. Expected polar bears.

First week of September, two in the morning, and enough stars above the empty freeway for every one of his ancestors.

Maãhotep's ride ran so smooth it felt like gliding. From the front seat, the Infiniti smelled like fancy coffee and cleanliness.

Back seat: Moon. His mother. She'd hugged him out. Never'd seen her like that. Furious, happy, relieved, giddy. Moon faked calm, tried to be reassuring, but Raptor could tell he was furious. Plotting. He could almost see a sword in his Master's hand.

But both kept quiet so Maãhotep could continue interviewing his client.

Raptor answered every one of Maãhotep's questions, but Maãhotep asked him only about the case.

3.

"Damn, boy, locked up with Nazis? Fuh real?" said Jackal, magnetised.

The two brothers sat drinking hot chocolate around Moon's kitchen table. Jackal'd insisted on coming over at 8:30 on a Saturday morning. Moon and Araweelo'd said it was okay, since they hadn't slept, anyway.

So while Raptor answered Jackal's questions, the adults sat in the living room to break from Raptor's case and talk about Moon's upcoming Wednesday night national cable news interview about the proposed Africentric school.

"Those boys are crazy," whispered Jackal. "Shit, all a buncha dial-a-doping meth-heads, transform? High school drop-outs. Mosta those fools grew up in townhouses across from Safeway with lowlife 'uncles' coming over to fuck em while their moms were drunk—"

Raptor turned death-ray eyes on him.

Jackal shut up, then said, "Bruh, I'm just glad you're okay."

A knock at the door. Raptor must've looked scared, like he was expecting cops or Nazis to break it down.

Jackal: "Chill . . . it's probably just 'Noot. Told her to meet me here."

Raptor ran to open it.

She flung her arms around his neck, tippy-toed up to press her cheek and ear against his. Crushed her tears there. They smelled like apple juice.

He started to say her name and she closed his lips with her own.

Sheet lightning, flaring across the skies of his eyes.

This wasn't pain at all.

From a million miles away, a voice:

Da-a-a-a-yum!

Both broke away, mortified, glimpsing Jackal jumping back, also mortified.

<h1 style="text-align:center">4.</h1>

The Street Laboratory, that afternoon. Five of the streetest Street Falcons clapped Raptor on the back like returning from lock-up meant he'd just earned his black belt or Master's degree or something.

Shook their hands off like rats. "Don't even *think* that shit!"

Their eyes widened. Room went quiet. If *Raptor* was swearing, he meant *bidness.*

"All that wack 'graduation' shit is just a played-out Pyrite trap! Why else you think these *khetiuta* want us hearing it a million times on every CD? While they're making billions?"

Jackal replaced-elevated the subject to an all-styles martial arts tournament coming up. Across the room, 'Noot went back to talking with Moon and Seshat. Logistics for their next-Monday demonstration at City Hall.

"Don't get me wrong," said Seshat to Moon, "but you know this'll cost us, right?"

'Noot: "What does it cost us *not* to do it?"

Both adults fell silent, smile-frowning.

Raptor, watching her over there. Proud.

Kept glancing at each other since that kiss.

But neither knew what to say.

Her, a *muhajabah,* and him . . .

Couldn't get her out of his mind.

S, Simultaneous: felt like laughing and crying at the same time.

Baton bruises were still yelling across his body, and the thought of next Monday's rally made him want to sidekick everything in the universe or hide away in a cave. Or both.

But *kot-tam.* 'Noot. She tasted just like a Red Delicious.

5.

"The woman's unhinged," said Seshat.

Sunday night. While Raptor did his Social Studies homework at the kitchen table, Seshat held a battle-briefing with Moon. Moon poured her more tea while she sat across from him on the couch.

"Ever since we had to fire her daughter from the Kush Party, woman's been wearing war paint instead of mascara."

"Aw, c'mon, Seshat, really? She had her chance to throw down some craziness. Probably just gonna go away now."

"Brother, I've known the woman since we were in high school. She's not just some drama queen. *She's Waiting to Exhale* meets *The Shining*."

"You're saying she's gonna throw away my clothes, burn my car and put an axe in my chest?"

"You're laughing, but it's not funny. She's left ten crazy messages on my machine. She's saying she's gonna go after all of us: in the community, in the media, mess up our situation with City Hall . . . and you heard her, she practically threatened to burn down your store."

"What, you think she actually meant that?"

Raptor glanced up for the answer. Saw Seshat, tilting her head and shrugging.

Moon: "So what do you recommend?"

Again, tilting and shrugging.

"Let's just hope she's not at the rally tomorrow."

Nodding. Gravely.

6.

"How many more of our young students, scholars, children, have to have their heads beaten in by the police?" yelled Brother Moon, amping his call-and-response groove.

Four hundred people between him and City Hall's reflecting pool shouted back: *"How many?"*

"How long these Destroyers gonna keep electrocuting our people with Tasers?" *"How long?"*

"How come these Destroyers think they have a right to abuse us and misuse us?" *"How come?"*

Uniformed cops, flanking the reflecting pool. Not like a phalanx. More like stragglers.

City Hall's security armed with walkie-talkies and armoured in ill-fitting polyester uniforms glanced nervously everywhere.

Civilian "peace officers." Looked like highway cops outta some American TV show. Fronting, trying to look hard, but nobody was even window-shopping.

Beyond them, camera-men grabbed crowd shots or got "streeter" interviews, ignoring Moon at the podium.

Same image on the hundreds of pre-rally posters was on their placards: Constable Babyface.

Someone'd cell-phone photoed his picture, but the blurry low-rez made his face even more disturbing. Not a man anymore. A storm.

Raptor and Jackal, standing on the side, pumping their fists, cheering every time Moon dropped a verbal bomb. Raptor, pointing to his favourite placard: *Spank Babyface*. Both of them laughed.

A White dude in a windbreaker and a thick mustache. Standing close to the boys, listening to the speeches or looking for somebody.

Raptor, low to Jackal: "What do you think he's doing here? He one of those anarchists or whatever?"

Jackal: "Naw. Too clean. Watch this."

Soon as the man crossed their path and they were just beyond his peripheral vision, Jackal said quickly, "Constable?"

Dude stopped and turned without thinking—maybe half a second—then cranked his face like he was about to make something up.

"Just checking, officer," said Jackal.

The man moved off, grinding his jaw. Jackal and Raptor fist-bumped and laughed.

"—and this one vicious, disgraceful, low-life cop, Mr. Babyface—" railed Moon.

"*Speak it!*"

"*Oh, no, he didn't!*"

"*Go on and tell it, bruh!*"

"He's out here, running wild like a mad dog, biting and snapping and barking and howling, assaulting our young people! He took our young brother, the Supreme Raptor—you all know him from YouTube and the Kush Party, I believe—"

—cheers—

"Officer Babyface brutally punched him in the jaw over nothing! And when our brother defended himself, this same deviant, despicable Destroyer Tasered him, Tasered an unarmed eighteen-year-old youth!"

—boos—

Raptor, loving Moon's rap, wishing he'd taken Moon's offer to speak.

But he wasn't ready. Sweating all weekend just thinking about coming here. Figured the cops were gonna beat em all down, throw em all in jail. And how was Brother Maãhotep gonna spring the entire Laboratory?

"Don't be thinking this is all about Mr. Babyface," said Moon at the mic. "Cuz you know and I know . . . these storm troopers and rent-a-cops in malls and the LRT . . . are harassing our people three hundred and sixty-five days a year . . . insteada solving crimes against us . . . Am I right?"

"Yes sir!"

"Am I right?"

"Right on, Brother Moon!"

"Tell it!"

"We have Somali men getting gunned down like it's hunting season, and what are the police doing about it?"

"Nothing!"

"That's right. Nothing. But you know who else I blame for all this?"

"Who?"

"You know else who I blame?"

"Who?

"You want me to tell you?"

"Tell us!"

"Each . . . and every one . . . of you."

"Speak it!"

"I blame you!"

"Tell it!"

"I blame you! Because you let these Destroyers come into our community! And run wild like wolves! *Ripping* us apart—I said *ripping* us apart—until the streets are slippery with our blood! You let these Destroyers, killing our Somali men, get away with it. You do!"

"Tell em!"

"And then what you *think* these Destroyer cops gon do . . . after they witness that disgraceful behaviour? They kno-o-ow we aint gonna protect our own! Defend our own! So they come in . . . swinging, shooting, and electrocuting!"

—applause—

"They did it to *me*! Beat my legs and Tasered me to the ground! Just last year . . . when I was doing their job for em! And now . . . they do the exact same evil deal to my young Falcon! Electrocuting *him*, too!"

—boos, curses, *shame-on-thems*—

"Who the hell these Destroyers think they are? The electric company?"

—laughter, applause—

"Maybe their problem is, *rope's* just too damned expensive these days."

—*laughter, applause, cheers*—

"But we got our brother out. Because we've got one of the best legal minds in the city on our side—" (cheers) "—and meanwhile, they're releasing killers, actual *killers*, back on the street! The exact same ones I turned into breadsticks like you saw on YouTube—"

—*laughter, cheers*—

"And let me tell you! All of you, all of everybody! If these Destroyers . . . inside the Somali community . . . if these Destroyers inside the police . . . if they think they can attack us and get away with it anymore . . . let me say it, it's a new day dawning!"

—CHEERS—

"Falcons! Assemble!"

Twenty Falcons double-marched it up the stairs and flanked Brother Moon, flicked their coats off into the hands of other waiting Falcons, revealing their martial arts uniforms.

Suddenly every TV camera there was aimed at the front.

Moon: "Ready!"

Ten feet behind the podium, twenty bodies clanked into attack stance. Raptor saw a camera-man grinning like it was Christmas morning. A security guard next to him looked like he'd just shit his Fruit of the Looms.

"Strike!"

Twenty right fists—sleeve-snapping strikes sounding like the bolt action of a shotgun.

"Strike!" Twenty left fists, hitting air the same second—

"Strike!" Twenty right feet at the end of sidekicks—

"Strike!" Twenty left—

"Transform!" Twenty two-punch combos, twenty frontkick-roundhouse explosions, twenty axe-head elbows slamming down onto twenty invisible skulls, twenty voices crying out, "*HAI*!"

"Transformed!"

Crowd screaming, cameras spinning, cops on the perimeter lining up, security jabbering into walkie-talkies.

Raptor: mind-whirling, fire and ice. If those cops moved in, what were they gonna do? Did the cops have snipers up on any of the rooftops around the Square?

Brother Moon: "And we don't just want Babyface disciplined.

"We don't just want him fired.

"We don't just want all the Babyfaces fired and thrown *under* the jail.

"And we don't just want an end to police brutality.

"What *do* we want?"

"*Justice!*"

"What do we want?"

"*Justice!*"

"When do we want it?"

All Falcons, on cue: "*FOREVER!*"

"As of today," said Moon to the crowd, "we are filing suit . . . against Constable Babyface . . . and the Edmonton Police Service . . . for fifteen million dollars."

Hollers, cheers, applause like cannon-fire—

Raptor, stopping dead: Huh? Why didn't Moon tell him? What about all of Babyface's other victims? Was this gonna be a class action suit?

Saw Seshat and Maāhotep. Faces: beige. Looking at each other like they were in a speeding car headed into a Mack truck, and their driver was whacked out on meth.

Ninety minutes later. Up at the Palace of the Moon. Seshat and Maãhotep burst in. Seething.

Raptor got up to head to his room. Moon told him, "Stay. This affects you."

"You're damn right it affects him!" said Maãhotep.

Seshat: "You can't just, just not even *discuss* something of this magnitude with us, Moon, and then go ahead and announce it to the world during a rally!"

"How'm I supposed to do my job and get taken seriously," said the lawyer, "if you're blind-siding me on the six o'clock news?"

"I just got off a twenty-minute phone blast from Alderman Brothers!" said Seshat. "This could cost us everything—the job grants, City amenities access, the *Street Laboratory itself*—"

Moon: "Guess he's not much of a friend, then—"

"Who said he was a friend? Who needs friends? We've got a million *friends* who won't lift a finger for us! Brothers was an *ally*! The man delivered!"

"Listen—"

"No, Moon, you listen! You cost us and you napalmed *my* bridges. And for what?"

"Maybe we even would've gone for this," said Maãhotep, "but for you to just unilaterally spring this on us in a public forum, no less, when none of us is ready, when we haven't even X-rayed it . . . and what if we can't do this? Then we look weak and disorganised! And you know what happens then!"

Seeing someone talk to Moon like this—even Seshat and Maãhotep—it rocked Raptor. Why wasn't he hitting back? Was he just rope-a-doping? Exhausting them?

But Moon's eyes were all wrong. Like he was seeing something none of them could see.

Raptor's guts: bright ash, angry red coals.

"—and in light of today's performance," said Seshat, "you should seriously re-think that interview tomorrow—"

"Agreed," snapped Maãhotep.

Seshat: "The Africentric school's got plenty of very capable advocates—"

Moon's eyes blinked into darkness. "Oh, I'm *doing* that interview."

7.

"Oh, snuh-*ap*!" barked Jackal at the Street Laboratory's TV.

Sbai Seshat shushed him.

"Yeah, but you hear what this ho just—"

Glared. "Excuse me?"

"I mean—this heavily mistaken lady—"

"We're trying to watch!" chirped Sister Ānkhur.

Jackal grimaced and shut up.

A dozen or so Falcons, magnetised by the battle on-screen. Raptor: feeling like he was at the Roman Coliseum. Within smelling-distance of his warrior friend raising shield and swinging mace, fighting for his life on the bloody dirt.

And any time the Pyrites who ran the death-ring wanted to finish making their point, they could just send in eight or eighty gladiators, plus an elephant and a couple of lions.

The national cable news host was some middle-aged blonde woman Raptor'd never heard of. Had a nailed-on sneer that broke off the top half of her face from the bottom. A crack in a vase.

In the weeks leading up to this night, Moon'd been calling her "that Nancy Grace wannabe." Seshat just called her "Nancy Graceless."

Three other guests—a couple of academics and a "concerned parent"—joined Brother Moon by satellite link-up, and another one shared the host's Toronto studio.

But the Moon vs. Host firefight barely left a second for the rest of the guests to launch a single word.

> HOST
>
> *—Mr. Ani, as head of the Street Falcons gang—*

> YIMUNHOTEP ANI
>
> *Appalling. We're not a gang—*

> HOST
>
> *You are called the "Street Falcons," are you not? Certainly sounds like a gang name—*

> YIMUNHOTEP ANI
>
> *Our football team's called the Eskimos, and not one of them is Inuit—*

Jackal: "Kaboom!" Seshat smiled—at Moon or at Jackal, Raptor couldn't tell.

The host linked back to the actual topic. But Raptor figured since she'd planted her poison seed, she was coming back soon enough to water it.

> HOST
>
> *Mr. Ani, how can you justify asking tax-payers to pay for a school that would exclude White students from attending?*

> YIMUNHOTEP ANI
>
> *You should fire your whole research staff. We haven't said one word about excluding anybody—*

HOST

Really? So you'd be wide open to mainstream children?

YIMUNHOTEP ANI

"Mainstream." Of course. Completely in favour of that. Long overdue. White students have been the victims of Eurocentric education for the entire history of this country—

HOST

So you want to replace one bias for another?

YIMUNHOTEP ANI

If you think one school could ever replace this entire country's worth of bias, all of corporate media's worth of bias, I'd say you need to enroll in a course on reality—

HOST

But that's the result, isn't it? Fragmenting the community on race lines? How comfortable would mainstream students even be in a school where—

YIMUNHOTEP ANI

Comfortable? How many minutes in your entire career have you devoted to whether our children are comfortable in your schools? Ten? One? Zero?

HOST

Isn't it that type of thinking that's the problem? "Our" kids versus "your" kids? Isn't it one of your African proverbs that it takes an entire village to raise a child—

YIMUNHOTEP ANI

Then why are your village schools failing kids from our village so badly? Maybe "It takes a whole village to depress a child."

HOST

What about family responsibility? Personal responsibility? If all these children care about is the latest gangster rap album or finding ways to make their pants sag even lower, how is that the school system's fault?

"Ho, you did not just say that!"
    Sister Seshat's words.

Whole room turned to look at her.

Jackal smirked.

"Brother Jackal," said the *Sbai*, "when you're right, you're right."

YIMUNHOTEP ANI

What about government responsibility? We pay taxes! These schools have been failing our kids for generations! Unless, what, you think they're failing because they're genetically inferior—

HOST

Doesn't take long for you to play the race card—

YIMUNHOTEP ANI

—otherwise why're our kids disproportionately doing poorly? Supposedly—

HOST

—but really, on this issue, when are you not—

YIMUNHOTEP ANI

—everyone in this country believes in a free market and competition and all that, so maybe if we have our own school, that'll force the public system to step up, compete with us, and do a better job—

HOST

Why should the taxpayer trust you, or anyone with some sort of racial agenda, to operate a—

YIMUNHOTEP ANI

The proof is in the pudding on racial agendas, namely our kids failing and you not caring. So it's your racial agenda. We'd rather not be in the position to have no choice but to set up a school. It's a huge expenditure of labour, resources—

HOST

So what's your motive, then? Profiting from the children?

YIMUNHOTEP ANI

Profit? Are you for real? Unlike the public system, we actually care about African kids—and not in some do-goodery, liberal, 'aren't I a saviour' way about helping poor-little-pagan-babies in some so-called African village in some unnamed country—

HOST
You're quite hostile. Is that the kind of attitude teachers should—

YIMUNHOTEP ANI
—trying to help real kids, right here, right now, and if some people don't want us to have our own schools, then step up and fix your own.

HOST
In the meantime you're urging segregation as the solution—

YIMUNHOTEP ANI
Evidently you don't know history or you wouldn't even ask that question! That's not what segregation means—

CONCERNED PARENT
And that's the problem right there, Mary, is that this is turning back the clock to the 1950s—

YIMUNHOTEP ANI
Words have meanings! You don't even know the meaning of the word, but you're throwing it around like—

HOST
Go ahead, Mr. Listerveldt—

CONCERNED PARENT
—in the American South, where the races were separated, and why would anybody in their right mind want to—

YIMUNHOTEP ANI
—segregation means somebody tells you you can't go here, or live there, or take that job—

HOST
Mr. Ani, you said we need to attend to the meanings of words, but my producer is telling me, he's just looked it up, Googled the meaning, I mean, of segregation, and it's, yeah—here it is, from Wikipedia, and you can't tell me that's the government—

CONCERNED PARENT
Ha ha, exactly—

Raptor: "What's that even supposed to *mean*?"

HOST
—quote: the separation of different racial groups in daily life, such as eating in a restaurant, drinking from a water fountain, using a washroom, attending school, going to the movies, or in the rental or purchase of a home. Segregation may be mandated by law or exist through social norms—

YIMUNHOTEP ANI
We're not talking about passing any laws, and nobody's gonna be denied entrance to or be forced to go to this school on the basis of race, so why are we even—

HOST
It's not my definition, Mr. Ani—

YIMUNHOTEP ANI
Right, right, your wiki-research staff. So when you leave work tonight, are you going to your home, or your producer's home? Is that segregation? No, it's separation—

HOST
So you're a separatist, then? A Black separatist?

"*A-a-a-a-aw!*" wailed the group, like they'd just seen a b-baller throw an elbow into somebody's eye when the ref wasn't looking. Raptor had to fight not to kick in the TV screen.

YIMUNHOTEP ANI
Let's talk real separatism! Just in Edmonton Public Schools alone, you've got a Science Alternative school, a so-called Traditional School, a performing arts school, a Waldorf school, a Canadian Studies school, Army Cadets school, a Hebrew Bilingual school, Distance Learning school and a Music school. Two dance schools, two Aboriginal heritage, three International Spanish Academy, three all-girls' schools, three "arts core" schools. Four—

HOST
All open to everyone, of any background—

YIMUNHOTEP ANI

Even the girls' schools? Four Sports Alternative, four Ukrainian, four Arabic bilingual, four Academic Alternative, five German bilingual, seven Home Schooling schools, seven Christian, seven Advanced Placement—

HOST

Congratulations, Mr. Ani, on your ability to memorise long lists—

YIMUNHOTEP ANI

—almost done—nine pre-Advanced Placement, twelve Mandarin bilingual and eighteen French Immersion. And that doesn't include the Catholic schools, and there're ninety-six of them in this city alone, none of them private—all of them paid for by all taxpayers!

HOST

But you don't have to be Catholic to attend!

YIMUNHOTEP ANI

Yeah, but non-Catholics can't teach at Catholic schools, right? That's legalised religious employment discrimination right there. And if you're a gay Catholic who's out, then you're really out, as in fired—

HOST

The Charter of Rights and Freedoms grants freedom of religion, but it doesn't say a word about racial separatism—

YIMUNHOTEP ANI

That's the fourth time you've said that, and the fourth time I've told you our school would be open to everyone, so please stop deceiving—

HOST

So you say now, but how do we know two years from now—

YIMUNHOTEP ANI

Then let's talk about Catholic schools which've been running here more than a century. Almost a hundred tax-paid schools just in this town alone, which's gotta be at least a thousand across the country, and probably way higher. You're accusing us of doing something, something nefarious before we've even got one school—

HOST
Nobody's accusing you of any—

YIMUNHOTEP ANI
—and meanwhile the Catholic Church has had how many pedophile priests? And residential school abuse scandals for horribly abusing First Nations children for generations? And you want to go after us? For one school? And we haven't even started it yet?

HOST
So to get this school of yours, step one is throwing the Catholics under the bus. What's your next tactic? Anti-semitism?

YIMUNHOTEP ANI
I can't believe you just—

HOST
Professor Sanford, how do you think—

PROFESSOR SANFORD
Well, I—

YIMUNHOTEP ANI
—demand you take back that vicious, utterly misleading smear—

HOST
Please, you've had plenty of time to talk, please don't try to silence the women on this panel—

YIMUNHOTEP ANI
I'm not gonna get shut up after you try to libel me—

HOST
It was only a hypothetical—

YIMUNHOTEP ANI
—a completely misleading, manipulative—

HOST
Misleading? What about the anti-White rhetoric all over your Street Falcons web pages? Calling White people "devils"—

YIMUNHOTEP ANI

That is a total lie! We never use the word "devil"—we talk about Destroyers, but Destroyers can be—

HOST

A rose by any other name. But you admit you're anti-White—

YIMUNHOTEP ANI

We're not anti-White and we're not pro-Black! We're anti-destructivity and pro-creativity! It's not about race. It's about deeds. Action. All we want is to build justice, prosperity and beauty for all human—

HOST

Isn't this really an attempt to set up some sort of Black Liberation Theology madrassa?

YIMUNHOTEP ANI

First, there's nothing wrong with Black Liberation Theology, whatever you think it is, because you obviously don't know what you're talking about if you think it's something bad. Second, how could I be any kind of theologian? I'm an atheist—

Raptor's peripheral: Seshat. Jaw open. Irises shrunk. He wondered, *What's the problem?*

YIMUNHOTEP ANI

—this is obviously, text-book discriminatory. It's about your fears. Fears of African people. Why should we pay for your bigotry and your pathology?

Seshat got up from the circle of chairs, yanked out her phone.

While everyone else was compass-needled TV-north, Raptor watched Seshat punching keys, shoulders hunched, eyes glassy.

"Brother Maã, it's me . . . Yeah, yeah, that's why I'm calling. Can you meet? . . . Say, eight o'clock? . . . Exactly. Fires're burning. Got maybe a day to put em out—"

Saw Raptor staring at her. Moved further out of earshot, out of view.

He didn't know where it was coming from, but the crackling hurt his ears, the ash burned his nostrils, and the smell of charred human meat turned his gut to roiling.

8.

"The Fortress is burning," said Seshat.

Had her arms crossed, leaning back in her chair at Moon's kitchen table. Raptor listened from the couch.

"All right." Moon sighed. "Let's hear it."

Wednesday evening. Data Salvation Laboratories was closed for the night, and two Falcon teens whose pay was topped up by youth employment grants were running the Hyper-Market.

Seshat, fingers against the table: *tap-tap-tap-tap*. "I've gotten probably forty calls about your atheist comment, and that's just from people who had my number."

"So?"

"'So'?" said Seshat.

"'So'?"

Maãhotep, the ever-put-together brother, wasn't put-together. Jacket off, tie off, shirt sleeves rolled up. Under the table, a toenail poked out of a new hole in one of Maã's socks.

"So you had to know," said Maã, "how any kind of atheism reference would affect the Somalis backing the Africentric school project—"

"That school was never supposed to be religious!"

"Doesn't matter, Moon!" said Seshat. "They were holding out hope they could steer it that way, or, or, or maybe just have some kind of, I don'know, school chapel or prayer time set aside, but with you talking like that—"

"Brother Moon never said he *wasn't* an atheist!"

All eyes clicked on Raptor. Wasn't like him to leap in when the elders were in a war *shenu*, but was he just supposed to let them beat on him like that?

Moon said, "*Thank you.*"

"And you never said you weren't a Muslim, either," said Maã.

Seshat: "And you know damn well most of those Somalis, especially whenever they saw you rockin a *kufi*, just assumed you were—"

Moon: "So because they assumed—"

"Don'even try that! They're saying you lied to them, and it doesn't matter what the reality is now."

"Before," said Maã, "they could tell themselves our Kemetic imagery was just for fun, just Africentric history. Now they're saying we're pagan idolators!"

"Right. The pagan atheist. Maã, you're a Muslim. Can't you—"

Maã's glare froze Moon's words mid air. They dropped to the table, shattered.

Raptor's skin scorched. What'd he mean? That Somalis knew Maã was . . . was a . . .

But he hadn't told anyone, and Maã sure as hell hadn't been broadcasting that around other Muslims, so—

"And it gets worse," said Seshat. "Our City funding's gone."

Moon swallowed hard, like he was suddenly extremely thirsty.

"Alderman Brothers told me he fought to save it, but—"

"But who knows?" said Maā. "City's going to the polls in weeks, and he practically had you muralled all over his electoral yacht. And now with the Somali vote distancing itself from you—"

"It's really that serious with the Somalis?"

"Yes!" said Seshat. "Are you listening? Are you hearing me about City funding? That means the job grants are gone! And so's the Street Laboratory!"

"Then we sue them!" said Moon.

"On what basis?" said Maā.

"You're the lawyer!"

"That's right. And I'd be going up against the best firms that a million tax-payers can hire—"

Down the stairwell, the door clicked and clacked. Footsteps, running up. Araweelo. Her eyes were grim.

Flashing Maā and Seshat a quick hello, she ran over to kiss her son on the cheek before pulling Moon aside to his PC.

Everyone pretended not to be eavesdropping, but they all were. Glancing instead of staring.

Moon studied the paper screen stonily, then drooped his head.

Araweelo crushed herself against Moon. He held her limply, then walked to the window.

"Moon," said Seshat, "what?"

Araweelo nodded them over. Onscreen, the blog of a Toronto right-wing wolverine columnist.

Bottom line: after the national interview with Moon, the columnist'd gotten emails from "unnamed sources" in E-Town and in Minneapolis that'd "filled him in" on Moon's "history of trouble making," including taking part in dozens of "violent protests" like the one in Edmonton that week, of "suspicious activity with minors" and preaching "black liberation theology" and "black supremacy."

But the best was saved for last.

More unnamed sources said that when Moon lived in Minneapolis, the "unstable extremist" had been locked up in a mental hospital and forced to receive electroshock therapy.

What the *fuck?*

9.

Seshat croaked out, "Who're these 'unnamed sources?' Who would've done this?"

Maā asked, "Katrina?"

"You both knew her," said Moon from the window, into the silence. "My ex is a crazy, vindictive piece of work, but . . . even her, naw. Naw. I don't think she even knew. Too wrapped up in her new man."

Seshat: "Then who?"

"Who knows? Cops?"

Maã: "Yes, but medical records—"

"I don'know!" He turned at them. "What're you implying?"

"Moon—"

"We're in the Savage Lands, and Destroyers are everywhere! That's our life! That's our fate!"

"Moon, all I meant was—"

"And we can't even slip up once. Not once!" Eyes wild. "Cuz even if some're sleeping, the rest aren't. 'Murderous knives and fingers cruel.'"

Turned back to the window. Raptor, still as stone. Araweelo, wiping mascara from her cheeks.

Is it true? thought Raptor. *And if it isn't, then why isn't he saying anything?*

"Well," said Moon, as if he'd been mind-reading, "obviously *you* wanna know, 'Weelo, Rap. This bullshit about being locked up in a mental hospital is complete lies."

"That," said Maã, "we *will* sue for."

Raptor breathed out for the first time since finishing the article.

"But yeah," said Moon, "I got electro-convulsive therapy."

Raptor gasped.

It was small, and he caught himself, but it was out and he knew Moon'd heard him. All he could say was, "Why?"

"I told you about how, how . . . how when my wife left, I was basically destroyed. Fell into a huge depression. She wouldn't let me see our kids . . . threatened to lie to the judge and tell her I'd—"

He cleared his throat.

"And her new man, he was a lawyer, so . . .

"I couldn't work. Lost my job. Basically rotting in the apartment I rented after she forced me out. Was just about to get evicted. Anti-depressants seriously messed me up. The juice was the only thing that saved me."

Chuckled, coldly. "Well, that and Brother Maã. He flew down, helped me get it together."

Raptor looked to *Sbai* Seshat. She must've read *You knew?* in his eyes because all she did was nod.

"So. Now you know," said Moon. Slouching. "Guess . . . guess you'll need some time to think about this, huh?"

Araweelo rushed forward but stopped when she saw him stiffen.

"No, Moon, of course nott! I know your mindt . . . and your heart!" It came out *of chorus* and *your harrit*, but everyone knew what she meant.

"Naw, 'Weelo," rasped Moon. "You need to take your time. You have the right." He chinned towards Raptor. "You too, young brother."

Raptor, straightening up. "I've already had more than a year, Brother Moon. I know who you are."

Moon smiled sadly, nodded without agreeing.

But the truth was, Raptor *was* afraid of him now.

10.

"Man, what is up with you and 'Noot?"

Two hours later in the Hyper-Market, Sister Sentwaset working evening shift, and Jackal was sitting at the computer carrel next to Raptor's. Both were rocking the online *Vengeance of Serious Sam* MMO.

"What?" grumbled Raptor.

He was *trying* to machine gun phalanxes of evil mummies and take down two fire-breathing sphinxes without getting his own ass blown off. Trying to replace-elevate his mind outta the swamps he'd been sinking into for days. Now Jackal wanted to drag him down again?

"Seriously, dude," went Jackal on again, "what is your problem? What's a girl gotta do? She planted one right on you—"

"Jeez, quiet, all right?"

"Why're you avoiding her? She's not a library book you can just check out and check back in and get back anytime you want. She's more like, like, like a *match*book, y'know . . . you like rip off one match, get a coupla sparks, but if you gotta rub it more than once—"

"Please, no more similes—I can't take it."

"Man, you can dodge, but you can't duck."

"Seriously," said Raptor. He shot his last rocket-propelled grenade into the man-lion's mouth, which exploded. The Sphinx became a giant, flaming skull and ribcage, crashing to the sand. "Anyway, listen . . . what do you think about Moon's . . . y'know—"

Jackal didn't stop joysticking. Just corner-glanced Raptor long enough to shoot a *cut-the-shit*.

"If you're asking," said Jackal, "it's cuz you already know what you think, and you're hoping I agree. And quit changing the subject—"

"Naw, naw, maybe I'm hoping you can convince me otherwise. Persuade me."

"You? The mighty Rap-Tor? Since when do *you* listen to anybody?"

"Damn, Jackal, this's hard enough—"

"Okay, okay. What's got you?"

Raptor explained his reaction to the blog, which'd been linked to from all over the internet. On the Falcons blog, everyone formed a defensive shenu around the teacher, but email traffic, he knew, was more varied. Far less sure. Some of it . . .

He told Jackal the truth: all his years running from one refugee camp to the next, then fleeing to E-Town, and finding men like his Somali neighbour Wiil Waal and Doctor Liberia, from one end of the planet to the next: adults either destroying themselves or destroying everyone around them.

Was it really so impossible that Moon was . . . well . . .

"Dude," said Jackal, shredding a scimitar-wielding Hyksos cavalry charge with hyper-boomerangs, "if Brother Moon's crazy, then I gotta level up some crazy, transform? So, what, you're afraid of him, now?"

"No," he whispered. "I mean, I thought I was. But maybe, maybe it's worse."

Jackal actually put his controller down, swiveled to face Raptor. "What?"

"I don'know."

"What? You're, you're disgusted? You look down on him? You're ashamed of him?"

Raptor: feeling his eyes flaring under the X-rays.

Jackal, leaning forward. Quietly: "What if he was getting, like, chemo? Or a heart transplant?"

That threw him. He shook his head.

"*So what* if dude got depressed? Who wouldn't be? Shit, Moon doesn't even *touch* drugs, booze, doesn't mess around . . . how many people you know like that?"

"Out there you got rich Leadites drinking thousand-dollar bottles of Cristal, politicians snorting coke, all of em boning hoes like hoes're being phased out—and all Brother Moon needed was some electrons to get by? And that's sposta be bad or suh'm?"

Jackal leaned back. "Shit, sign me up! My wife leaves me and accuses me of being a pedophile, just so she can take my kids away? I'll be wetting my own damn finger and sticking it in a socket tomorrow!"

Raptor laughed. They both did. And then Constable Babyface walked in.

"—Mr. Black Panther, not so big now, are ya? Now't yer liberal fuckin friends've dropped ya like a steamin pile a shit?"

Coors-bent as a muhfucka, wagging his sneer right at Moon. Already'd driven the dozen customers outta the Hyper-Market by the time Raptor'd gotten the boss from upstairs. Just the sight of the man stabbed Raptor with the recollection of electrical torture.

"Don't think for a minute," said Moon, "this bullshit isn't gonna be part of suing your ass into the poorhouse!"

Raptor and Jackal, backs against the wall, Sister Sentwaset behind the cash register. Eye-mailing back-and-forth among them: fear.

Just like the night that Jackal and Raptor met Moon. Same block, different fumes, same rage, different cop.

And what could they do? Babyface was one word away from violence. He was a cop, a Destroyer with a pyrite badge. He could kill them all legally and mount their heads on the cop shop wall . . .

Fuck it.

Even if Raptor's heart *was* rupturing towards explosion. This was no time warp. This wasn't a year ago.

Cuz this time, Raptor and Jackal had the back of their Master.

"You're a real smart smart-alec, aintcha?" The thick-necked cop staggered one step to his right. "Thinkya know everything? Pal, you got no idea whatcher up against! Yer, yer, yer goin down!"

Moon: "Babyface, anybody going down, it's you. Last thing I do, Destroyer, I'ma get you, hear me?"

"Blah, blah, *BLA-A-AH!*"

Barking breath so fume-foul Raptor had to wince.

"I already know," said Moon, "you're getting charged with insubordination for Tasering my son and then failing to get medical attention and not properly documenting—".

"*FUCK* your documenting!"

Babyface jabbed a finger close enough to stab Moon in the eye.

Moon didn't budge.

Raptor knew: even with just that one finger Moon coulda jujutsued the big man through the floor tiles into screaming tears. As if Moon's hands were Tasers.

"Better get outta here," said Moon. So frostily, the air coulda fogged white. Thumbed up towards his security camera. "Before I hafta YouTube me breaking your ass off in two for the whole world to see."

Babyface's eyes drained, like he'd just seen his chief and his chief's chief heading straight at him. Practically ran out, his stagger losing half its drunk.

Moon, at the door, yelling down the street: "YO, DESTROYER! Stay the FUCK AWAY FROM *MY KIDS!*"

Through the window, two pedestrians, maybe would've-been customers. Recoiling from Moon back into the night.

Moon. Mortified. Furious. Turned back into the Hyper-Market. Tromped to the rear. Told Sentwaset to close up, that he'd give her a ride home if she needed it.

The two boys looked at each other. Raptor saw a stain in Jackal's eyes. Fear. And maybe shame.

When Raptor stopped shaking and went upstairs, he overheard Moon talking on the phone to Maãhotep.

"It's time . . . I mean, if they're taking it all away anyway . . . yeah, that's right . . . Year ago they Tasered me and beat me, and now I'm dealing with *this* shit? Yeah . . ."

"Yeah, ten million. I like the sound of that."

Raptor: wanting to go to bed, wanting to sleep, wanting to shut it all out when it seemed like everything was roaring into cinders.

Instead he boiled water for tea and put on a Boondocks DVD. Clicked the one that'd made Moon laugh so hard he'd coughed his tea all over himself and Raptor'd had to run get him a towel.

The one where the world's greatest sell-out, Uncle Ruckus, facing a terminal prognosis, received Ronald Reagan in a vision. Reagan revealed to him the only way he'd get into "White Heaven" to meet "White Jesus": *God loves the White man, and if you teach everyone on earth to love White people, you, too, can join us in Heaven.*

They sat drinking tea. Watching the show in laughless silence.

Moon. Slouching. An agèd king, watching war burn through the final planks of his kingdom.

11.

Al Hambra apartment. Evening.

Sitting on the couch, his mum wide-eyed him. Drily: "This is a firstt." It sounded like *furrestt*.

Night off from the Hyper-Market, his homework done, Raptor'd phoned his mother. Asked if he could eat supper at her place. Shocked silence.

Then she offered to cook something up and asked him to hurry over.

Raptor, standing, opening his hands. "Well, I'm just curious."

"In the five years I wass with Jacob, you never once askud me about my 'relationship' with him."

"Well," he said, pacing in front of her, "I'm older now. And I just don'really know what's going on between you two."

"So . . . Moon doesn't . . . ?"

"I think he's trying to balance your privacy, my privacy and his privacy. So he doesn't say much, no."

She licked her lips. Looked at a worn patch on the rug.

"Well . . . we love each other."

Raptor nodded.

"Beyond that, we're . . . taking it slowly. He was hurrett badly, and so was I."

"I know what you said to him, about knowing his mind and heart and all, but—." Raptor's eyes dissected the room for clues on how to proceed. Only found empty food trays from their President's Choice frozen dinners.

"How do you really feel about Brother Moon's . . . mental health? And shock treatment?"

"Itt's calledt ECT," she said softly. She'd worked a year on contract with the inner-city Multicultural Health Brokers Co-op. She had a lock on all the lingo.

"By North American standardts," she said, "your own *father* would've been consideredt bipolar."

Stopped pacing.

"He'dt work like a sandstorm for two weeks, then drop." She stifled a yawn, like she could feel her dead husband's exhaustion herself. "Sometimes a day, sometimes two weeks. I coveredt for him as much as I couldt."

Didn't bother to say, *I had no idea.* That territory between them was still land-mined. Shouldn't've surprised him, really. She always was drawn to men combusting with drama.

"He wass an excellentt man, your father," she said. "Three thingks you should never allow: adultery, addiction, and abuse." He let her list go, then wondered if maybe it wasn't a blind platitude, but a confession. "But affliction? Love . . . calls us to a higher duty."

He mumbled something.

"What's that?"

"I said, 'A righteous labour.' It's from the eighth pledge of the *Nub-Wmet-Ānkh.* Does Brother Moon ever tell you about our teachings ?"

"No, no. Tell me."

"*'By the sunrise, I set my thoughts and words and hands in righteous labour to drain the Swamps of Death and master the elevated lands. I lift my hammer towards the raiders, but I will never harm the Wanderers, and I will raise a Golden Fortress for the orphans of the Savage Lands.'*"

She nodded. "Thoughtts and wordts and handts. And heartt." *Harrit.* "And what about you and this singing girl?"

"What? I don't—"

"A woman can figure out plentty on her own. Almeera, right? Her 'golden name' is Yibemnoott?"

He sniffed appreciatively. "Right. But . . . well, she's Somali—"

"So you think I won't like her."

"No. Well, yeah, but I mean, that's not why I'm . . . ."

He sat down on the couch. Next to her.

"Dating's tough," she said.

Dating advice from his mum? Like watching TV with her when an ad for feminine napkins or condoms came on, and he knew she was probing his face for reactions.

"Even though she's a *muhajabah*," she said, "that doesn't mean she's naïve. Plenty of those girls have hadt boyfriendts."

"Mum, 'Noot's not some kinda—"

"No, no, you're taking me wrong. I just mean . . . you don't have to feel like you're corraaptingk her or something—"

"Because she's already corrupt?"

"No, because she's probably gott enough strength—" ("sta-reng-guth") "—to make her own decisions."

Turned his knees towards hers.

"Her singingk at the Kush Party," she said, "wass beautiful. I wish I couldt do that! Great voice. Great spiritt. You two were greatt up there together!"

He blinked up at her. Couldn't help but smile.

"She's smartt and nice and talentedt. If she treatts you well, thatt's a blessing." She wove her fingers together, rested them in her lap. "But carryingk on a, a forbidden romance . . . ah! There it is in your eyes. Thatt's why all this nervousness.

"I won't lie to you," she said. Put a hand on his knee. He let is stay there. "It's very difficultt. Somali father, uncles, brothers . . . hidingk is no fun.

"And lyingk all the time, it's poison. In a Hindi movie, of course, it's very romantic and dramatic, but—what? Why are you smiling?

"*She* loves Hindi movies, too."

"So—she and I have something else in common. Somali girls who fall for smart, handsome Garang boys."

Looked down, up, down, smiled till he felt it twanging his cheeks. She touched his face softly. Her eyelids: fluttering like butterfly wings.

When he hugged her, she smelled like flowers and oranges.

Phone rang its apartment-buzzer ring. Araweelo picked it up. Raptor heard the tiny voice: "Flower delivery for a Ms., uh, A-ra-weelo . . . Kaultom . . . Farah?"

Buzzed the guy in. Stood, eyes glinting. Nearly giggled. "He's a truly romanatic man!"

At the door, the man repeated her name. She nodded. He reached behind the bouquet and tapped her outstretched hands with an envelope.

"You've been served," he said and scrambled away.

Raptor pounced over to her. Flowerless, she opened the envelope, read her news.

"Mum, what?"

"Doctor Liberia!" She'd never called him that, ever. "He's suing me!"

Two hours later. Maãhotep, sitting on a fold-out chair, legs crossed at the ankles, expensive socks toeing the worn floor.

"Well," he said, "all the money he lent you over the years, he kept records. Cancelled cheques . . . and a ledger. He wants it all back, with interest."

"But that's, that's—"

"And he's suing Moon, too."

Mother and son: "What?"

"Yes," said the lawyer. "Apparently this Jacob Needle came here in the summer and you lit him up, Raptor."

"Yeah, so? He was about to hurt my mother!"

"He's saying Moon corrupted you. That you two, actually, you *three*, had a great relationship until Moon turned you against him and trained you in martial arts so you'd assault him."

"Thatt's complete bullshitt!" said Araweelo. For the first time that night, Maã smiled. But hearing his mother curse wasn't new for Raptor. He'd heard her do it in three languages, many times.

"Surely he caan'tt win on something so aatterly—"

"He doesn't *need* to win." Maã, smile gone, with such exhaustion he actually apologised for it.

"Needle might want to settle, or he might want to bankrupt Moon with legal costs. Right now, everthing else swirling around, Moon's blood is in the water, and the Devourer can smell it a whole Nile away."

12.

Next evening. A dozen pairs of bare feet on the vinyl mats of the Street Laboratory. Assembled not in dojo rows, but in a *shenu*. A smaller class than usual for *Sanuc-es-Ryu*. All of them in their *gis*.

Moon tapped Raptor to lead the warm-up. A surprise. Raptor began the stretches, stumbling over the occasional Japanese phrase but getting most of them.

Never'd been asked to lead the warm-up before. No one had.

Roll-outs across the room and back, and then Brother Moon stepped up to model a combo: wrist-grab reversal, double locked-arm shove-down, single arm-bar flip.

Moon started flipping Senwusret like a pancake, even thought Sen'd put on a good twenty pounds of gym muscle since joining the Falcons, and was solid before that.

"Any questions?"

"Yes."

Everyone turned. What with recent events choking morale like smog blotting sun, no one expected questions. Least of all from Wa-Wa.

"*Sbai*, I'm wondering, and I don'mean any disrespect—"

"Go ahead."

"Well, that combo, it looks so, so complicated. I mean, I was watching this *Muay Thai* YouTube, and . . . like, it's just a couple of knee-strikes and the guy's down."

Moon: "Sometimes you can't afford to break a guy's nose, or you don't want to. I don't teach you to use maximum force. I teach you to use the righteous amount."

"Okay, but . . . if you tryinna save your life, isn't suh'm like *Muay Thai* better?"

Faces twitched. Even people who'd never been schooled at any other *dojo*, *kwoon* or gym knew: you did not question the house art.

Raptor's fingers itched. Wanted to text Wa-Wa to STFU so Moon wouldn't pulverise him just to prove his art's worth. With everything he was under, any second, Moon would have to explode: *Who the fuck do you think you are, Wa-Wa?*

Moon asked everybody to sit down. He stood.

Orbited the *shenu*. On the outside. Behind their skulls.

Talking so softly that anyone on the opposite side had to strain just to hear.

"Whether it's a martial art, a culture, a religion, politics . . . unless it's completely worthless, which one you choose . . . honestly, it doesn't matter much in the end."

Kept walking, kept whispering.

"In fact, not even choosing Alchemy is any guarantee. Not like you can't find successful people who aren't Alchemists."

Raptor scanned the *shenu*: in everyone's eyes and eyebrows, shock.

"It's not so much what you study," continued Moon, "as how you act upon it. Your level. Of *conviction*. And *ambition*. Say it with me. Conviction—"

"CONviction . . ."

"—and *am*bition."

"—and AMbition."

"We teach you to be righteous. And being righteous is the only way to banish *isfet*, and master your own soul so you can rise nearer to the Supreme.

"But take any individual, any country, any religion that achieves greatness, it's because they believe in their destiny. That they *deserve* greatness, that if they only stand up, they'll reveal themselves like the titans of Ramses at Abu-Simbel."

Stopped walking. Right behind Wa-Wa. "Whatever they claim their ideology is, whatever creed they swear to, what *really* counts is their gravity. They've got an organising mission. Makes everything fall into place around their sun. That they've got their own language, so they can talk around outsiders and keep their plans secret, just like we've got Somali or Amharic or Hutu, or, yeah, Falconic. That they've got their own institutions so they can continually transform themselves and the world—*revolution*—so they can gather as much gold as possible without jealous eyes seeing it all."

Raptor saw it in the *shenu*'s eyes: confusion.

Moon maybe didn't see it. So what *did* he see?

"There's one thing some of these ambitious groups have that we can never have. Any ideas?"

Suggestions popped up. As usual, Moon didn't say no to any of them, and no one waited for him to. They did as they practiced: kept offering ideas until he could say yes.

"Camouflage?" suggested 'Noot.

Raptor'd been avoiding her for days, but there she was, wearing her Alchemical *gi*, her matching black *hijab* tucked into its jacket.

"Exactly, Sister 'Noot. The Destroyer's men all carry his mark, like a tattoo: that old anteater. Doesn't seem scary, unless you're an ant, in which case he's gonna destroy your whole civilisation.

"And what about Hru? He and all his people, they all carried the emblem of the Falcon.

"So with those markings, how many of the righteous could ever infiltrate the ranks of the Destroyer?"

What did any of this have to do with *Sanuces-Ryu* versus *Muay Thai*? Moon was rambling. Off on something he'd said one other time, when somebody asked him why some people thrived after oppression but Africans were still suffering in Savage Lands across the world.

But for all he knew, nobody else in the room had a clue about that topic.

Around the *shenu*, faces showed loss: lost the topic, lost their way, lost their Master, and Raptor knew their *sbai* was orbiting less like a planet than a comet, ellipsing way the hell out into interstellar space.

Moon's own eyes: fear.

That he couldn't control his trajectory, that he saw them all receding while he went shooting past them into the deeps and the Oort Cloud beyond.

And angry. That they weren't following him. Or that they couldn't.

"Forget about 'being equal to' and 'as good as'!" Sneering, like he was gonna say what he had to say, regardless. "You think any of these people who reach the top bothered two seconds with that talk? It's loser talk! You wanna win, you focus on getting to the capstone of that pyramid! And we've been losing a long time! You feel me?

"You think, what, Oprah, Mo Ibrahim, Sankara, Maathai, Mandela—you think any of them got down on their knees, begging the Pyrites, 'I'm as good as you! Please, please let me be on the team!'

"Naw, naw! They told them*se-e-elves* 'I *am* gold! True and living gold! And I'm gon shine so bright the whole world will hafta flip on visors!'"

Smacked his hands together. Made Raptor's ears ring.

"Now, I'm not telling you to be a bunch of raving egomaniacs." Started walking again. "Nobody likes a brag-boy. But whether it's one person focused on a golden destiny or an entire people saying it's the chosen one, the elect, the middle kingdom, the master race, the true believers, the greatest country on earth, the hundred-and-forty-four-thousand, whatever, you either see yourself as lead and stay that way, or see yourself as gold and transform into it!"

Moon raked everyone's eyes. His own were quivering. Neck muscles cabled. Sweating like a fever was throttling him.

He looked—it was like something Ānkhur'd said once about her Baptist church: their new minister had "caught fire" but his parishioners hadn't ignited with him. Call-and-response died on call. She liked that minister and never knew why the congregation didn't. She told Raptor with rare somberness, "It was like he was preaching to an empty tabernacle."

The Street Laboratory was silent.

"Forget it," said Moon, defeated. "You want power techniques? You got it. Half of you, strap on pads, partner up. Knees and sidekicks, fifty of each, each side, each partner. Hard as you can!"

13.

At the end of class, 'Noot cornered Raptor and he knew he had no choice.

Alley behind the Street Laboratory. Evening. Both teens stood sweating.

"I thought *I'd* be the reluctant one," she told him.

She told Raptor they had fifteen minutes before her father would show and she had to be at the front door.

Everything was bizarre. Nighttime, in October, and hardly even felt like fall at all. Like late spring. Cool air and warm breeze.

'Noot: "You can't just keep avoiding me like this."

"I know."

"Is it because I'm Muslim?"

Didn't say anything.

"I mean, plenty of Muslim girls have boyfriends," she said, and then pre-emptively. "Not me, understand. But just even friends of mine. And they're just quiet about it. We can just be careful, okay?"

Chewed his lip.

"I mean . . . don't you care about me? Or am I just making an idiot out of myself here?"

Wanted to run away. Forced himself to stay.

Finally he blurted, "Sometimes, when I'm really, y'know, depressed or angry, the only way I can replace-elevate myself out of it is to gold-mind about you."

She gasped a little. Blushed a fragile smile.

"Really?"

"Yeah."

"Like . . . how? I mean, what do you—"

"Not like *that*—"

"No, I didn't mean—"

"I just visualise us . . . talking. Walking together. Me, like, making supper for you—"

"Oh!" she chirped, just like Ānkhur. "That's so sweet . . ."

Would've felt patronised by the word *sweet* except that she'd grabbed his hand.

His heart: pulsing all the way from his ribs to his fingers, beating him like a sockful of billiard balls, pounding like a bass string as thick as his leg, *tha-whump . . . tha-whump . . .*

"What else do you visualise?"

"Just, like, us . . . you know . . ."

"No, what?"

So he told her what he knew he should never have said in thirteen-point-eight billion years.

" . . . married."

Her eyes: double suns on the horizon.

"Rap, I—"

"No, look, don't, I shouldna said that—it was stupid, *I'm* stupid—"

"No, Rap!" Grabbing his other hand so he had to face her. Even while he squirmed not to.

Knew she wanted him to kiss her. And he wanted to.

Would've bolted except that her phone rang.

"Damnit! It's my dad! I'm sorry—"

She ran through the back door and left him by the Dumpster.

14.

Raptor, at home in the Palace of the Moon, raiding the freezer for ice cream. At the back of the freezer, something forgotten and buried. Like golden treasures of Tutankhamen hidden in three millennia of darkness.

Wrapped inside aluminum foil and sealed inside a jar for more than a year, since that apocalyptic thunderstorm and blackout.

The hailstone. The one the size and shape of an egg.

He re-wrapped it, then put it back gently and closed the door.

Eleven PM. Moon was already asleep. That'd never happened before.

Raptor searched the My Pictures folder on Moon's PC, finally found the faces and names he was looking for.

Searched Facebook. Found only one of them.

Of course, the profile photo didn't match her pictures from when she was a kid. She was all grown up now, long braids, dark eyes, gorgeous.

Made a Friend request. Wrote:

> *Dear Sister Kiya, you don't know me, but I'm great friends with Yimunhotep Ani. He's practically a father to me. I know that he and your mother separated a while ago and that there are probably some hard feelings, but he's having a really tough time right now and I'm sure he'd love to hear from you. Please write back to me.*

Stayed up online, reading random sites, cheering himself up with the FAIL blog, writing lyrics, blogging, Facebooking Falcons. Kept checking his inbox to see if Kiya'd written back.

Nothing.

At 3 AM he tried finding her so he could message her again. But he couldn't find her. Double-checked the spelling, but nothing. Surely she hadn't . . . ?

He logged in under his other FB account, Supreme Raptor. Found her on his first search.

She'd blocked him!

15.

Moon was already on the computer when Raptor woke up. Hoped Moon didn't have any operational net-tracking software, revealing Raptor'd been digging in his photos and searching for his ex-step-daughter.

But he wasn't spying on his spy.

"Look at this!" said Moon.

Onscreen: a crude cartoon. Two cops, both with smoking guns, standing over a dead chimp. Caption: "*When Moonkeys attack.*"

"What the hell!" said Raptor.

"Brother Maä sent it," he said. "Someone on the inside leaked it. Freaking cops. Maä said it all goes into the suit."

Moon got up. Hadn't shaven in two days. Shaggy. He hobbled like his back was hurting.

Three hours after Raptor Facebooked Jackal asking him to reach out to Kiya, Jackal wrote back five "words":

WTF? She blocked me 2!

16.

Got home from martial arts—not just warming everyone up but actually leading class, as Moon had asked him—and found Moon asleep on the couch. It was only 10 PM.

Raptor called his mother.

"He's been carryingk two hundredt teenagers," she said. "Who wouldn'tt be exhaustedt? Let him restt."

The TV was still on. Wasn't like Moon, a pathological light-turner-offer and picture-straightener.

A DVD, paused.

Webcam footage of the street peregrines that once lived on the roof.

Raptor unPaused it, FFed. Next was footage from the rocket-cams, springtime at the Strathcona Wilderness Centre. And then from a separate trip, just Moon, Jackal, and Raptor, when they'd gone out to launch three-stage rockets, just the three of them.

Other DVDs were scattered and out of their boxes on the arms of the couch.

The Warrior Within documentary featuring the founder of *Sanuces-Ryu*, Master Musa Powell. *The Motorcycle Diaries. Paradise Now.*

But a ripped *Blackhawk Down?* Moon hated that film.

Books like a Jenga stack on the coffee table: Sun Tzu's *The Art of War*, and books by Mao, Che, Robert Taber, and Anthony James Joes, all on guerrilla warfare.

His mind: a rope of firecrackers. Moon the mental patient, Moon the publicly disgraced leader, Moon the victim of police brutality, doing . . . something . . . he could never take back—

Breathe.

Breathe.

What else? What else?

Other books in the stack, all with multiple book marks: Steven Biko's *I Write What I Like.* Wangari Maathai's *Unbowed.* Benjamin Karim's *Remembering Malcolm.* Claude McKay's *Selected Poems . . .*

Whirling and turning, whipped . . . getting sliced to feathers, bones, and meat in the widening spiral, in the radioactive methane hurricane of millions and millions of years, the *Ujat*, the Great Red Spot, Jupiter's Eye, and he was screaming and couldn't hear his own voice getting ripped away, and roaring below him, a gut bigger than a thousand Earths and surging with a blood-dimmed acid tide, burning, burning the innocent—

—above him, the stars, and a glittering golden chain—

—spoke his words-of-power, renewed his wings and body, hurtling down into the maelstrom of ice and charcoal fogs lit only by lightning, guided by the beam of his Shining Eye—

—there!

—streaking downwards, reaching downwards, clasping, grasping him, falcon finding falconer, and straining hard enough to rip even renewed wings from his back, cleaving up the hurricane tunnel towards the stars—

—and both were reborn among them in the blessed and eternal darkness . . .

Would it be enough, when poison scrolls had yet to be unfurled, and the Devourer of Millions of Souls was swimming upriver to the Holy City . . . to *gorge*?

17.

Friday night, bursting outta the Hyper-Market, barely four minutes before he was sposta be teaching his third class, glancing behind and choking—

Headlights, near-silhouette—right in front of Data Salvation Laboratories, and zero doubt this time—

Lexus and Marley.

(They hadn't seen him.)

Flew to the Street Laboratory, mind blinking back to one of the refugee camps he'd fled—maybe one in Ethiopia?—when they'd had to hide out in the forest, running past the carcasses of burnt cows and limbs and torsos and half-split human skulls. Hiding out there, and bees, bees, bees stinging everyone again and again, and him, just a silently-sobbing eight-year-old, but if he'd cried out even once, militia men would've found them, raped them, butchered them all—

Inside the Street Laboratory, on the mats, twenty students, all of them in gis already.

"Everybody! Shoes, now! The shooters Brother Moon took out? They're standing right in front of the DSL!"

Jackal grabbed him by the right biceps. Quietly: "You sure this time?"

"Sure as a sword in my hand."

Bravado, or flair, or freestyling. He didn't know. But Jackal barked. "Weapons! Only if you're trained!"

Raptor: "Wa-Wa, choose a squad of seven, and take your cell phone!" He pointed to the Lab's back door. "Flank round the back. When you're in position, phone me and hang up after exactly two rings. I'll be on vibrate. We'll be right behind the street-bend, you know, the diagonal? Right in front of Chip Yick Printing. They won't be able to see us."

Everyone in uniform but Raptor. Half of them hefting *kung fu* and *karate* weapons: *sai*, chain-whip, staff, three-section staff, *nunchaku*, sabres, sickles, and a Guan-Do battle-axe.

They split, Wa-Wa's squad down the alley, Raptor's down *Khair-em-Ānkh-Tawy*.

Raptor, in position. His pocket buzzed. Twice.

Both teams stepped out, tightened their vise.

Lexus and Marley.

Surrounded.

Cut off from wherever their car was.

Eyes wild at the black-clad phalanx.

If they were strapped, they didn't even flex.

Looked like they'd just shit themselves.

Raptor walked up, one-leg distance from the two killers, hands empty of everything but the power to take life.

"You ever come back here, we'll find you. And annihilate you."

The Falcons opened a channel, let them run downstreet, hop in a broken-backwindowed Ford Escape and burn the fuck outta there.

Fists and weapons in the air, everyone chanting, greeting and blessing transformed into battle cry: "*Nub-Wmet-Ānkh! Nub-Wmet-Ānkh! NUB-WMET-ĀNKH!*"

When Moon came down and found them there, Raptor and Jackal glanced at each other, gulped, told him what'd happened while all the Falcons fell silent.

Moon's stone face. Almost silver-black beneath the streetlights.

Suddenly shone.

"You . . . my kids . . . my young champions! What you did? It was dangerous, it was foolish, but kot-*tam*, it was brave!"

He glanced downstreet where they'd said the thugs had driven.

"You see that?" he said, pointing at the road like something was on it. "I think they left a trail of shit!"

Everyone laughed.

"Now," he said, smiling, "get those weapons back inside the Street Laboratory before we all get arrested!"

Fifteen minutes later at the Lab. War stories already.

Door opened. Brother Moon. Two big boxes: books, CDs, DVDS, medallions and trinkets. Treasure for everyone like Pharaoh Ahmose rewarding his lieutenants after crushing the *Heka Khasut*. Or maybe just a Kemetic Santa Claus.

Moon, handing out his possessions: "Tonight . . . you all mighta just saved my life."

"Brother Moon," said Wa-Wa, "we've always got your back!"

"Listen, but seriously now, I aint gon live forever. So . . . when it's time for me to go forth by day—"

Raptor didn't like this. The depression, the books and DVDs Moon'd scattered round his place, and now this talk of "going forth by day," which went over the heads of all the newbies.

Clutching their prizes, Wa-Wa, Ānkhur, Senwusret, Joser, Imhotep, Taharqa, Jackal, Raptor and eight others gazed at Brother Moon. Their teacher smiled back. Calm. Faraway. Like he was sitting under an awning, smelling spring flowers on a warm breeze, or walking free of the hospital after a long illness, and heading home.

"So if anything happens to me," he said, "just remember I don't want anybody crying for me. Tell em if they let even one tear drop on my casket, I'm gonna flip open the lid and light em up right there, transform?"

Everyone laughed. Moon said it again. "Transform?"

"Transformed," they all said. But magma flowed through Raptor's intestines.

Araweelo, at the door, with a flat of food: sambusas, rice, stewed vegetables and meat.

"Mum, you *cooked*?" said Raptor.

Smiling: "Smartt ass."

Everyone pulled up the gym mats, swept and washed up, and then dug in. Moon put on music—the Cubano-Senegalese lilt of Orchestre Baobab. Gave 'Weelo cash for the food he'd ordered, pulled her and Raptor aside, away from everyone else's ears and eyes.

"Uh-oh," said Araweelo, joking. But maybe not really.

"Listen, you know, I don't usually mix you two together if I'm talking about things that'll affect the other one. I always talk privately with you one at a time."

Raptor: "Yeah?" Anxiously, as in, just drop the axe already.

"And maybe I should be sticking to that policy, but what with everything—." Took a breath. "Well, look. I love you both. And you both know that. And 'Weelo, it's crazy, you spending all that money on your apartment, by yourself."

"Whatt are you—"

"I'm asking you to move in with us."

Beamed at him, then: "Aboutt bloodty time!"

Hugged him, kissed him on the lips in front of the whole room, but everybody was too busy stuffing their faces.

"Raptor," said Moon, "sorry for blindsiding you like this, but I'm hoping—you okay?"

Released his breath. "I thought you were gonna . . . well, you've been so down, you were giving away all your stuff, you had all those books out—"

"What? What books?"

Awkwardly, in front of his mother, Raptor named them.

Moon laughed. "Your mother just wanted to borrow them, so I pulled them out! What, you thought I was gonna go suicide bomb the cops or something? And I was giving away stuff because—"

"—because you were making room!" Raptor let out a long, loud sigh. "Yeah, *now* I get it." And they all laughed together.

18.

1 AM, and Raptor and Araweelo were driving back from Al Hambra apartment in Moon's borrowed Sunfire packed with Araweelo's belongings. Neither one of them said a word when two fire engines sirened past them down *Khair-em-Ānkh-Tawy.* So what?

But crossing 97th Street, they couldn't deny their terror any more. Same two engines and then a third and a dozen scrambling fighters attacking the inferno: The Hyper-Market. And above it the Palace of the Moon.

Pulled over across the street. Both of them stabbed their cell phones—her calling Moon's cell and Raptor calling the Street Laboratory. Both got Moon's voice. On voicemail.

Lit by raging red and white and yellow, they stood before the furnace, held each other, sobbing.

Nine
Create-Supreme

The Book of Then

1.

As if . . .

As if . . . I'd been chained to a live boar and dropped into the muck and strangling weeds of the Swamp of Death . . . thrashing, bleeding, wailing, drowning—

I remember choking, trying to scream and being unable to, my arms and legs straining, darkness—

. . . mist . . . fog . . . grey light. . .
. . . giant black spiders crawling upside down . . .

. . . cold hands on my burning forehead . . .

2.

I sat upright in the tent, weak. It was dark.

I was dizzy. My eyes were throbbing. Outside, crickets screeched in chorus.

Arrows. A spear. A hammer.

Master Jehu.

My ribs, my throat, my skull . . . ached as my chest heaved and my face slickened.

The tent flap lifted up, fell back in place with her on my side of it.

"Mum?" I blubbered.

"Hru . . . ." She held my head against her breastbone, tucked beneath her chin.

"My son." She sat behind me, rocked me back and forth, one hand on my cheek and another on my shoulder. "At last. You're awake. You were burning up."

Yinepu lifted the flap. His eyes went wide on me.

"Thank gods!" he said.

Ducking back outside, he returned with a gourdful of steaming soup.

My trembling hands accepted it from him. I drank the broth, chewed bits of goat and carrot, lemon and onion, between my soft teeth.

"Thanks," I said between sips.

My mum told him, "Bring the medicines."

3.

At dawn, when I stood—for the first time in a week, my mum said—I asked Yinepu what happened after I was beaten into darkness.

"I went back, like you told me to," he said, "to get all the children. Your mother'd trained them well, so the sentries'd already roused them the moment they saw the raiders approaching. Almost all of them slipped away to our hiding spots."

I leaned on my cane. It was a far cry from Fang, which the raiders must've taken . . . if not that gods-damned Destroyer himself who'd . . . who'd . . . .

I put a hand on my brother's shoulder.

"I'm sorry about your puppies, Yin."

"Me too," he said. "Thanks."

"What'd you, you know . . . ."

"Do with the Master's body?"

"Yeah."

"When it was safe to come out of hiding, I took him. Anointed him, and the children who didn't make it, including some who died in the fire. Wrapped them in linens we had stored in jars in the secret caches.

"We took them down to the sacred cavern, in the outer chambers before your father's throne."

The sun came up. Yin's eyes flared like dark honey, like brown amber.

His voice was small. "We buried them all down there like seeds."

4.

That night, the longest night of the year, my mother convened a war council in the largest tent with the eldest among us.

She unrolled for us the tapestry of combat she'd spent years in weaving.

Finally she said, "Of course, we'll need arms. And armour."

"My protégés," I said, using a word I'd once hear Master Jehu use for Yinepu and me, "will steel all our hands and bodies."

I nodded to them, these young men with clever fingers and manifold scars and burns of labour. "*My Mesnitu*: Duamutef, Hāpi, Qebehsenuef and Imset. They'll work their metal magic to transform us all."

They smiled, nodded back, gave their oath: "By the sunrise, we will."

"We need guardians," said my mother, "for the sacred cavern. So General Set cannot blaspheme against my resurrected Lord."

"There are three young warriors I can think of," said Yin, smiling grimly. "Three of the sneakiest, nastiest, hardest, deadliest boys who ever walked or hunted anywhere in the Savage Lands. Gods-damn, these kids are so dangerous they scare themselves!"

Everyone laughed. I smiled.

"Good, then," said Mum. "I've begun the training of our legion, Jehu's orphans, continued it in their warrens in the wilderness.

"And I've appointed deputies from my secret army I've spent fifteen years assembling, plus three dozen sorceresses and warlocks to continue training Jehu's young miraclists. They're spread out, but our forces number three thousand."

"Three thousand?" Yin's sneer showed shock and fear, not only disgust. "That's it? After fifteen years?"

"Since the war begun a decade and a half ago, Yinepu," spat my mother, "we've lost twice that to the Destroyer! There are limits—"

"My father," I raised my voice, "is the Lord of Limits."

All eyes fell on me.

"Three thousand?" I said. "If it were only three hundred, or three dozen, the task would be the same. You saw what we did with the Swamps. Removed the dams. Set the water in motion. When it gathered speed, nothing could stop it."

I stood up, my head warping the tent's cloth sky.

"It's time," I shouted, "for us to burst the dams!"

My mother and Yinepu looked at me like they'd never seen me before.

Then Yin nodded to my protégé, Qebehsenuef. Master Jehu'd once said he looked like a younger version of me. Something about his nose and his eyes.

Qebehs presented me with a rolled-up hide. I unfurled it.

Shining there, a ray of the sun made solid.

Fang.

"I thought it was . . . " I whispered. "How . . . ?"

"You must've thrown it just before the raiders took you, so they wouldn't get it," said Yin. "One of my pups, Genmi, grabbed it. They put four arrows in him when he was running to find me. By the time he did," said Yinepu, clearing his throat, and again, "he was just blood and fur."

"Gods bless that pup." I put a hand on his forearm.

"I cleaned him, anointed him and wrapped him up, him and my other dogs." He snuffled. "Planted them with all the other kids."

"In the cave of martyrs."

"With your father, and the Master," he said, his eyes like two moons. "Yeah."

Mother snapped: "How long until you can arm and armour all our legions?"

I nodded to my *Mesnitu.* Duamutef answered, "Working at the four secret forges of the Master, we'd need a year."

"We can't wait a year!" said my mother. "If Set could find your compound, he'll soon find the other hidden bands—"

"Didn't anyone hear me? Didn't anyone understand what I just said?"

Again, all eyes were on me. Light flashed into my eyes, not from the torch, but from the golden blade now reunited with my hand. I shook my head.

Fang no longer suited it, now that it was like the beaming sun . . .

Ray.

"It's time," I said, "to smash the dams."

And so began two hundred moons of war.

5.

I attached my mother's martial tapestry to my own loom, wove in colours she had never dreamed.

The first prize we seized with axes, arrows, and blood was a treasury of a thousand talents. Our survivors hauled away the gold to all our blackhouses where the *Mesnitu* alloyed the sacred metal, hammered shining spades and shovels, five thousand times the Labourers in our legion.

And every village of the enslaved we found and freed by force, we planted in each open hand a golden implement, and Instructed them in draining of the Swamps.

They smashed their dams and turned their redlands black, and after exodus of crocodiles, the Eternal River gathered strength on path to Great Green Sea.

6.

In the eighth year of our revolution, our force had grown to fifteen thousand, recruiting as we went by virtue of the golden-alloyed tools we granted.

We held entire regions, intensified and purified the river's flow, reclaimed the souls of all who'd drunk the poisons of the Swamps of Death.

Our ranks brimming, we mounted battles and waged mischief, dividing the Destroyer's thunder-fists into whisper-fingers, slipping among them to take what we desired and leaving only bleeding wounds as payment.

At Min-the-Beautiful, we smashed the gates, descended to the mines to free those in the slaving tombs. They offered us the treasures of their labour, thinking we expected ransom.

None of them believed me when I said, "You cannot buy your freedom, and we cannot give it to you."

I sat beneath an acacia tree, eating salted fish and dates while waiting for the ambassador of this mining nation.

Finally they brought forth their foreman so I could tell him that his men were free to work at their own choice, not under the Destroyer's command, nor under ours.

"Hru?" said their foreman, blinking at me. "Is it really you?"

I almost didn't recognise him. He was older, but the years of slavery had beaten him like the sun would out in the open desert. Upon his chest a vest of welts, upon his legs an apron of scars, and his left eye misted-over like the fog above the Savage Lands.

All those many years ago, when we were running from the night-raiders, he was the fisher who fed us all and taught the rest to harvest from the river.

"Jedu, little brother! What happened to you?"

"Set happened," he said. "The Devourer spat us out into the Swamps of Death . . . and we got separated, and Raiders grabbed us, a few at a time. Some of us, they sent to farms, others to mines. Some . . . some they forced to fight for him."

Crying, he choked out, "I thought . . . Hru, thought I was the only one who survived."

I held him, rocked him, remembering him as he was, a child waist-deep in the river's embrace, hauling fish from nets he'd made from vines, dancing in the river's swirls, singing songs he must've learned since before our men were murdered, songs of longing for a beautiful girl or seeking her forgiveness for a foolish blunder, songs he'd memorised too young to know the meaning of the verses. Like all of us who ran or fought so we might simply live.

I wondered how long it had been since he'd sung about anything.

He cried in my arms, shaking, shuddering. I didn't stop him.

When he cooled, I fed him.

"Yin is still alive, too," I whispered. "And my mother. Maybe she can heal your eye."

"I don't care about the eye!" he said. "Because of what this other eye has lived to see today!"

I smiled, helping him up so I could take him to my mother.

"Hru?"

"Yes?"

"Are you . . . are you the one they call 'The Master of Ten Thousand Spades?' And 'the Golden Blacksmith?'"

I hadn't heard the first of those titles before, but I'd heard the second. I knew that everywhere we severed chains, I gained new names.

7.

We fought. And bled. And died. And killed.

For fifteen years.

Together with the fifteen years that I had been a fugitive, both as my Master's pupil and as my mother's son . . . I'd spent my entire life at war.

8.

And finally our revolution encompassed Behudet, the Forge City, and when we liberated it, we gathered on the bank of the Eternal River, where we gazed across at all the butchers and betrayers of the Blackland, the swarming slaughterers who served the Archfiend, the Usurper, the murderer of the Lord of Limits, the Great Defiler: Set the Destroyer.

The skies roiled with red and purple clouds. Lightning raced, sparks from the hammer of the god Ptah, the original *Mesnit* who'd shaped all things. Thunder echoed from where the hammer struck unto the ends of the universe.

Then the lord of killers emerged from among his men, towering, with massive shoulders, his war-helmet shining pyrite-yellow with its squared-off horns beneath the broken light of sunset.

"You! Boy!" he yelled, his voice competing with the thunder, magnified by decades' hate in heart and untold murders on his hands. "Sparrow-Prince!"

His fools laughed loud enough that we could hear it full across to our side of the river.

I stepped forward, bowmen at my sides, swordsmen beside them, hatcheters and pikesmen outward still.

Behind me, and behind him, our armies shifted anxiously, awaiting order sending them to kill and die in agony.

He shouted, "I knackered your father like an rabbit in a snare! Threw his meat and bones into the dirt like knots of shit!"

His words: like burning winds against my eyes and in my nostrils.

"I chased your bitch-mother out of her own country! Into exile with the forest-mountain savages of Rebarna! Where she fucked and sucked any man who promised her so much as a sharp stick to bring back here to fight me!"

His hyenas, a pack of thousands, cackled a storm.

"I skewered your idiot wizard like a campfire snack," he howled, "and turned your children's camp into a smoking yard of broken bones and bricks.

"And you! I ripped *you* apart like a virgin-bride promised to a lonely elephant!"

Those hyenas, gasping laughter across the river—I smelled the stench of it. Their master had to yell, even with his thunder-voice, above the din.

"So I ask all your trained monkeys over there . . . . Who, among all the peoples of the Savage Lands *or* Blackland, could ever bow to *him*?

"What kind of king could he ever be? A king of cripples? With their asses ripped open? You swarming rats have been nibbling my sandals for fifteen years, and for what? So you could all die here, today, drowned in this river?

"So let me tell all of you over there who are about to die," he said, sweeping his scimitar towards us, his arc of intended massacre, "*I grant you one chance.*

"One chance for me to let you live as my slaves, instead of dying as my sacrifices with open skulls, and your hearts ripped from you and fed to our war-dogs.

"Turn your Sparrow Prince over to me. Now. Or we will exterminate you."

In fifteen years of war, I'd heard fifteen thousand tales of battles, speeches hurled prior to mass-murder, inspiration-harbinger of expiration. I'd studied my Master's Instructions, knew their wisdom-words that were undiminished in their strength from the First Verse of creation.

But the only words I spoke were silent ones, words-of-power I had heard inside the sunrise.

I hefted Ray before me, and marched upon the face of the River Eternal, and did not sink.

And Set spoke thunder, and his flesh unfurled like a bolt of cloth, and his face became a serpent's, and across the water he splashed, and we met at river's centre, uncle and nephew, killers both, to decide the universe's fate.

We struggled, slashed and bit, strangled, gashed, transformed ourselves across a dozen bodies each, seeking butcher's path to victory.

Yet as the hours boiled and the sun fell behind the edge of the world, I could see no means to kill my way towards the Golden Fortress that my Master tasked me to create.

The Destroyer was too battle-strengthened, too learnèd in the arts of death, too belly-forged for me to break his back or bind his limbs and hack them off.

Unless I set a fire that burned the cosmos, I knew I could not defeat him.

So in night's clutches I retreated to an island in the river, and spoke a voice that could've rung from Ptah's own anvil, while holding Ray above me yielding golden light so great the stars went dark.

"I . . . *surrender!*"

My legions raged, "*No, Hru! No! No!*"

Shaking Ray to sky, I shouted at the waters, "I surrender, do you hear me?"

My soldiers screamed. The Destroyer's killers cheered.

"It's what you've waited all these years to hear me say, isn't it? So why wait any longer?

"I *order* you to come take me! I *command* you to meet me a final time!

"Come, Grinder of Bones, Shaker of the Earth, Eater of Old Gods, take from me the priceless prize of my stolen weapon!" I stabbed the sky with Ray. "If you dare!"

Set, returned to shape of man, stood sopping among his troops upon his riverbank. Above his legions' screaming, he yelled up to the sky.

"Do you hear this, gods?

"Do you hear this, all my fighters?

"All you fools who followed this Sparrow-Prince?

"He's a coward! A willing slave! You all heard him—he surrenders! Groveling like an old and ugly whore for moldy bread!

"He wants to give me his weapon in exchange for mercy? I'll take it, and choose myself what to give him in return!"

He waded forth and swam towards me.

And when he was in the deepest waters, I threw Ray towards him, and he caught it easily and laughed in victory before hurrying forth to carve my organs from my spine.

And then thunder burst the water from behind him.

A mouth the width of an infinity of fallen souls smashed through the river's surface.

Waves burst over the Destroyer. He struggled gainst a new and boiling current as the mouth of the invincible Devourer, ten-tusks tall-and-wide and a thousand fangs less one, sucked him towards it.

That mouth slammed down on Set's enchanted pyrite armour, forged in hell's unquenchable flames, unbreakable, and could not cleave his chest from belly.

Set gripped a tusk of the Devourer and heaved, re-opening that monster's mouth, a violation unlike any since the world was born. And with the other hand, he reached for Ray, the mightiest weapon of them all, to gut the beast and win control of Death's own empire.

And then in blackened sky, the moon was born, and descending from it, haloed by a ring of lunar light, was my transfigured Master.

And at his side within his grip, my mother.

She leapt from that embrace, sank into the water, emerged and swam towards the Devourer's mouth, and climbing into it she gripped my uncle's sword-fist, and with her other hand, jailed his mouth so that his words-of-power could not slither to the unseen and eternal worlds.

The vast maw thundered shut, consuming its two prey, and the Devourer sank into the depths of river's darkness.

9.

When I stood at last beside my forces, my generals urged me, "Let us track these bastards to the devil-cliffs and hack their hands from their betraying arms!"

But I remembered hills of horror I had seen, and refused to become the Destroyer.

Those who surrendered, we took in chains. Soon they'd join—even unwillingly—the Labourers who were purifying the Swamps and Savage Lands. Those who fought, we fought and killed.

From the river bank, my Master Jehu, now the Ancestor Jehutí, spoke a final time to all survivors standing. I wanted with my entire spine for him to stay. Yet I knew he could not do so.

"The time to end this war is now." His voice was like the music of the sacred cavern, his blackness perfect, his chest a creche for stars. "So go to heal each other, bearing witness to the sun, while you raise a Golden Fortress for eternity."

He looked at my *Mesnitu*, my brother Yinepu, and then at me. And smiled.

And then ascended to his shining palace in the centre of the secret Silver Desert on the moon.

I was bleeding and exhausted. My bones ached like the earth's after a quake. I faced my legions, found the words I needed, spoke them.

"The sunrise . . . is coming.

"By the sunrise . . . by every sunrise, we must . . . purify the Savage Lands wherever we find them. We must drain the Swamps of Death wherever they are. We must defeat the Destroyer . . . whoever he is.

"We have to find all the lost farms where the children are bent over weeping from slavery and drudgery, and make them stand. We have to find all those people hiding their faces, hiding them for shame of just how low they've been degraded, and the ones hiding their faces because they're afraid of anyone discovering their crimes.

"It's our duty to reveal them both.

"And all those people who've sunk down, the ones in the mines, the ones in the prison caves, the ones exiled to the lowlands by the Great Green Sea . . . we have to lift them up, too."

My people stood silently, like stones.

"Do you hear me?" I shouted again. "We have to lift them up!"

They murmured their agreement, but I wanted more than mere assent.

"If you hear me, let me hear you!"

"We have to lift them up!"

"Let me hear you!"

"We have to lift them up!"

"Let the gods hear you!"

"WE *HAVE TO LIFT THEM UP!*"

10.

And thus the war was over.

I spent the night out on the open desert, crying for my mother.

We were so long apart, then reunited in the worst of times, bound by blood, yet so unbonded.

I remembered being held by her when I was little. I remembered her singing songs to me with stories that meant nothing, but a voice that held the world entire. I remembered sitting beside her at campfire, roasting skewers of meat and plantain, the dipping-oil bubbling-hissing as I held the cooking-meal inside the flame. I remembered her smile when I sang to her. I remembered her kissing both my cheeks again and again until I slept.

I remembered her crying.

The Book of Now

1.

THREE NIGHTS AFTER THE FIRE, IN THE UNIVERSITY HOSPITAL ICU, ANOINTED with mysterious unguents, wrapped in protective linens.

Eighty per cent of his body burned.

Master Yimunhotep Ani.

A living mummy.

2.

Street Falcons and adult Alchemists sat outside the room of Brother Moon around the clock. Some, without even having seen him, couldn't bear at such close distance the thought of his holocaust, and did not return.

But Raptor and Jackal sat or stood, sentinels, unwavering. They had no shifts that needed covering. The Hyper-Market: a black mansion chalked by ashes. If any peregrines had still been roosting on the market's roof, the blaze had driven them away, and their aerie was carbon.

Burned but not destroyed, the Street Laboratory itself was another casualty by person or persons unknown.

In her lamentations, Araweelo Kaultom Farah wandered from station to station in the hospital, seeking answers, finding none.

Fire inspectors inspected, police investigators investigated, but no Alchemist expected answers from the City.

Means, motive, opportunity. . .

Who benefited?

Speculation raged:

Thandie's wacked-out mother, who'd stormed the Street Laboratory to call Moon a "Black Hitler" and scream, "One day, you mark my words—this whole place of yours is gonna burn"?

Lexus and Marley, the Somali killers they'd driven off at point of *sai* and sabre?

Doctor Liberia, drunk out of his fucking mind?

The nazi skinheads from the Remand Centre?

Babyface?

Who was the Destroyer?

And then there was the filth in the media and online, bullshit rants and accusations about Moon succumbing to his own botched arson, torching his own place for the insurance, or torching the Street Laboratory because he was revenging himself upon the City, or because he was trying to frame the cops and make himself a victim . . .

Pyrites.

Raptor got permission from the fire department to go upstairs briefly to bag whatever clothes and other belongings of his he could salvage. Everything reeked of smoke.

Some of it reeked of burnt meat.

Vomitted all over the blackgrey floor.

Sought water from the taps, but of course they didn't work.

Licking away the spew at the corners of his mouth, he spat it all out, wiped lips on sleeve while the fireman who stood nearby looked away.

Insanely, he opened the freezer door, seeking the hailstone ice-egg wrapped in aluminum and sealed inside a jar.

He hid his face from the fireman. Body buckling in silence.

Wiped his nose and cheeks and eyes. Came down the sooted shaft that once had been the stairwell to the Palace of the Moon, now doomed for demolition.

Raptor Deng Garang never returned.

3.

In the hallway outside the burn unit: Araweelo, Jackal, Seshat, Wa-Wa, Ānkhur. Benched.

On facing bench, Raptor, beside 'Noot. No one noticed, but beneath her folded-over jacket on the bench seat, her and Raptor's fingers merged.

Maāhotep strode up, raggedy, unshaven, glasses instead of contacts. Beside him was a much sharper-looking cat, the younger man Raptor'd seen that fateful morning at Maāhotep's.

They weren't holding hands, but when they sat down in the empty space, the younger man briefly rubbed Maā's right shoulder and biceps.

Raptor's gut ripped, burned with magma, but he forced himself to breathe, breathe, *breathe* . . . transforming . . . molten rock . . . into steaming water . . . then cooling it . . .

No one else paid Maā any mind beyond hello and sharing situation reports. Maā leaned forward, his elbows spiking legs just above his knees. His "friend" rubbed his back with his left hand. No one else noticed, or if they did, they acted like they didn't.

Silence.

Maā snapped upright in his seat. "My god!"

323

Seshat: "What is it?"

"I just realised—no one's told Moon's kids!"

"Uh," said 'Noot, "I just sent his step-daughter a Facebook two hours ago—"

"Really? How long've you been in contact with her?"

"Well, so far, not even at all. Raptor and Jackal and I've been trying to reach her since even before the fire. But she just *blocked* them—"

Raptor, bulldozing himself to talk to Maä: "We tried finding his stepson, Ptah, but he's not even on Facebook, at least, not under that name."

Maä's face: like Raptor'd just said he'd been trying to milk a platypus. Turned back to 'Noot. "Has she blocked you?"

"I don't know yet—"

He handed the young woman his X-Fone, asked her what she'd written to Kiya. She logged in, showed him her sent mail. Raptor read it over Maä's shoulder.

Your step-father has been horribly burned in an accident. He probably
won't live. If you want to say goodbye, I suggest you come immediately.

Wasn't true. Moon would not die. *Couldn't.*

Maähotep glanced at 'Noot. "Good lord!"

'Noot looked mortified. "I was so blunt because she'd already even just blocked two attempts to reach her and we didn't know what to do and—"

"No, no, you did the right thing, 'Noot. And hey, look! She took your Friend request! She sent a message—I won't read it, but where's the—okay, under *Info* . . ."

He punched in a number. "Kiya? Is that you? It's Uncle Maä . . . . Right. Yeah, I'm so sorry . . . No, no . . . we don't know . . . nobody knows . . . Yeah, I think—"

Looked over at Araweelo, lowered his voice.

"No, that's right. I wouldn't wait."

Got up, put space between him and Raptor's mum.

"Do you and Ptah have valid passports? Can you make it today? . . . Yes, I know, but . . . do whatever you have to . . . Look, that's not an issue, all right? I'll cover you both . . . No, don't worry about it. Just get here."

Raptor opened his eyes to the lawyer, seeing all the seams in his clothing, seeing missing buttons that weren't yet missing, seeing grey hair that wasn't yet grey. Seeing Maähotep standing beside a river and up to his waist in lotus flowers breathing pollen into the breeze. Seeing Maähotep reaping maize and lighting a fire and making cornmeal pudding for them all while the sun went down and someone played the kora, igniting stars with it.

"Look, everyone," said Raptor, standing and clearing his throat. "Could we . . . could I just suggest . . . that we move down to the cafeteria and step into a *shenu*? I know I could use some Daily Alchemy."

Everyone. Glances. Araweelo and Maähotep's friend looked unsure. Were they expected to leave?

"You're welcome to join us. It isn't hard. Just . . . when I say *Nub-Wmet-Ānkh*, you say it too, all right?"

He introduced himself to Maāhotep's friend, a brother named Gamal.

Shook his hand. And smiled at him.

In a clear space in the caf, standing with 'Noot on one side and Gamal on the other, he suggested something totally unorthodox for Daily Alchemy, but no Nubian standing there complained.

They all held hands.

"By the sunrise, I choose to resurrect myself . . ."

4.

"Geometrically, we're the originals, y'feel me?"

Jackal spat fire, and the crowd caught it, raised it on torches crackling to the sky.

Camera men and photographers digitised the speaker, the people, the zooming and rubbernecking traffic. Cops kept their distance, except the barely-undercovers who stood out like vitiligoed skin.

"We were *there* on Resurrection Day, when Brother Moon was handing out the first scrolls!"

"*Transformed!*"

Beyond a couple of hundred civilians, musta been all two hundred Falcons there, from occasionals and hangers-on to the core fifty and the nine originals who'd transformed up to the Create-Supreme Scroll. Kids whom Moon, Seshat and Maāhotep had taught, fed and fostered—neglected limestone they'd cut, smoothed, polished and placed into their pyramid.

And when Jackal hit it, they were widdit.

"When hardly anybody knew him, we were *there*!"

"*Transformed!*"

5:00 PM, so all the news cameras would be there. Inside the Norwood schoolyard on the busy nexus of 95th Street and *Khair-em-Ānkh-Tawy*, so four directions of drivers would see them.

Three days, three hundred posters, three thousand handbills. Seeds of Sbai Seshat's media training had yielded them this mighty harvest.

"We built Kush with the golden hammers he gave us, cuz we were there! Am I geometrical?"

"*Geometrical!*"

"When he named 107th Avenue *Khair-em-Nubt*, which means the Path of the City of Gold, we were there! When he raised up the Kush Party to replace-elevate us into a better way, *we were there, doing it with him!*"

⌒

"They wanna tell us our man, our warrior, our teacher, our brother," said *Sbai* Seshat, "burned down his own business, his own home, and his own *self*." Mic-booming, Senwusret's system, no longer one but four Optimus Primes. "Y'all b'lee 'at?"

"Naw! No!"

"Boo-oo-ool-shi-i-it!"

"Forget *that!*"

Raptor, surveying everything. Logistics: 'Noot, Ānkhur, Jackal and him. Even press releases and calls with reporters—that'd been Ānkhur.

So now all Raptor had to do was watch the blocks stack up. And revel in *Sbai* Seshat's microphone control. She was always a stepping razor in the Street Laboratory, but out here in front of real crowd, she was a buzzsaw.

"At's right!" she said. "You damn skippy! Whatchall got is a buncha professional liars trying to damage control themselves out of a lawsuit by controlling public opinion!

"Lemme tell ya suh'm: Brother Moon's brilliant. Brother Moon was an electrical engineer before he went into computers. Brother Moon faced gun-toting killers with nothing in his hands but bravery and a talent for fool-smacking!

"So you actually trying to tell me if he wanted to start a fire for insurance, he'd burn up his own self along the way? How you sposta collect insurance if you dead?"

Dropped the D-word, but they gave it up anyway, even if the laughter tasted like bile.

But Raptor knew. Just like that song by Martina Topley-Bird: Moon was too tough to die.

But whoever did this to him . . .

Some were sworn already. *Menfítu*. Soldiers.

And when their proof was iron, they would act.

"How many times," she said, "has the Destroyer come with fire to our homes? In Min-Nefer? In Kigali? In Port-au-Prince? In Darfur? In Philadelphia? In Montreal? Or come with long-fanged metal machines to tear down our homes in Africville! Killing our babies in Soweto! Killing our men in the Audubon! Raping and killing our women in Congo! I said how many times?"

"Too many!"

"*How* many?

"TOO MANY!"

"And how many times we rallied just like this, in the cold, in the gathering dark, saying 'no more' when in our hearts, we all KNEW! That shadowed men. With murderous knives. And fingers cruel. Were coming BACK?

"Coming back cuz we failed to stand up as one with our golden hammers in the air, saying, 'You take one of us, you gon hafta take us ALL!'"

Applause, cheers, howls, and then, ore in a smelter bleeding and breeding gold, someone shouted:

"I *am* Brother Moon!"

Someone else: "*I* am Brother Moon!"

Scattered ones, then a dozen: "*I* am Brother Moon! *I* am Brother Moon!"

And on the mic Seshat said, "I am Aset the Avenger! And I am *Hru!*"

Cops glanced and flexed, cameras aimed and clicked, reporters scribbled and scrambled, and Kushites jumped and cheered:

"I am Hru! I am Hru! I am HRU! *I AM HRU . . .*"

5.

Facing the hurricane, the adult Alchemists were overwhelmed. So the Street Falcons stepped up, held fast.

Step one: securing replacement space for their charred Laboratory.

'Noot block-booked Wednesday evenings at Sprucewood Library a couple of blocks south of *Khair-em-Sokar* on 95th. The meeting room held only thirty people. On that first night they were sixty. But the overflow read books or chilled out on the library's main floor.

Pocket change easily covered the $15 half-day charge. And they knew Raptor was right when he transformed it in the *shenu*:

"The Golden Fortress can't be destroyed. It didn't burn down in the Street Laboratory. Look around you. Whenever two or more of you stand together, you're raising the Golden Fortress right there!"

After Daily Alchemy, they studied the Scrolls together, Originals training middlers and middlers training newbies.

Then they organised fundraising plans for their lawsuits—goods to sell, services to provide, a hall party where 'Noot and Golden Eye would perform. And made a list of organisations to approach for larger training space.

Divided the city into sectors. Glorified each with a golden name: Southern Millwoods transformed into *Swenet* . . . Strathcona, *Saqqara* . . . Muttart and its glass pyramids, Giza . . . Westmount, *Waset* . . . the North Saskatchewan River, the Nile . . .

At leaving-time, instead of the usual *Hotep* or *Nub-Wmet-Ānkh*, one Falcon after another said, "Raise the Shining Place forever."

Outside. To range.

Their revolution: to seek out all the Wanderers in those Savage Lands, to make stand those who wept, to reveal those who hid their faces, and to lift up those who'd sank down, for in so doing, they would all rise nearer to the supreme state of being.

6.

A few hours later. Maãhotep's place, before Raptor and 'Noot headed back to the hospital.

Gamal, putting mugs of hot chocolate and a plate of cinnamon banana bread on the table between the teens who were working on Gamal's and Maã's laptops.

Planning the next rally, locating space, putting out fires.

A YouTube up in the corner of Raptor's screen: a Moon wisdom from sometime around Christmas taken on a shaky mobile phone.

> . . . *we're not a temple. We're a laboratory. Because we're Alchemists. You have to be able to pick up beakers and test tubes and turn on the Bunsen burners and experiment so you can actually learn . . .*

Raptor: "That's not too distracting, is it?"

'Noot, eyes and smile happysad. "Naw, it's comforting." And back to work.

Him, glancing at her screen. Posting to the Falcon blog. A booklist? Damn. Girl was taking over the job Moon'd given *him*.

She clicked POST.

Cover graphics for every book, plus links to buy online. She was good.

Kalakuta Republic by Chris Abani
Aya of Yopougon by Marguerite Abouet
King by Ho Che Anderson
Mindscape by Andrea Hairston
Half of a Yellow Sun by Chimamanda Ngozi Adichie
The Shadow Speaker by Nnedi Okorafor
Palestine by Joe Sacco

"That's golden, 'Noot."

She smiled. "Thanks."

Moon, still revealing wisdom:

> *Yeah, we have you memorise your lessons, but not to turn them into prayers. You memorise em in the same way you learn safety and procedure in any lab. But then you get down to work.*

"Just remembered," said 'Noot, reaching for her bag. Handed him a CD, still wrapped. Orchestre Baobab's *Specialist in All Styles*.

"You're always just even talking about how much you love that song—"

"'Dée Moo Wóor,' right!" He grinned. Tried to step up. "It's so passionate." Hoped he didn't trip down the stairs. "Like me."

She didn't call him on it.

"Thank you, 'Noot!" And he actually reached for her hand. Squeezed it. She smiled at him even when he let go.

Ripped off the CD's wrapping, opened it, looking for lyrics. Never'd found any online, not even after years of looking. Could find any Top 40 Leadite lyrics going back fifty years, but the most romantic love ballad ever performed, if it was written in Wolof? Forget about it.

No lyrics. But a summary:

Ndiouga Dieng gives a memorable performance of Dée Moo Wóor. Over a sparse backing he recalls the nights following the death of his father which he spent contemplating the true meaning of life. He reflects on how life can be disappointing and cruel. The weeping notes of Barthelemy Attisso's lead guitar are a perfect compliment.

'Noot: "Something wrong?"

Leaned back. Pulled on his lip.

"No, no . . . "

Bit into banana bread, sipped hot chocolate. Knew each tasted good, but he was X-raying that paragraph while his comprehension cleaved from the nadir to the zenith.

Moon, urging him on:

We expect you to debate everything. Question it all. Turn it upside down. They're your tools for investigating the universe. Don't hide em away. Use them, all the time. The truth can always be questioned. Only lies die in the light.

Stunning. To think he could've been that far off for that long about that song.

And if he was that wrong about that, what else was he doing or thinking wrong that needed replace-elevate?

And then once you started overturning everything, how were you sposta know when you could stop?

True and living gold. That's what you are. If there is a God, a creator god, or even just something called Universe, no matter what, since matter and energy are neither created nor destroyed but simply repatterned, then they're all part of that divine spark, that Big Bang. Their stuff, their substance, was there 13.8 billion years ago. They're made of "God." Which means, sure, they're God. And therefore so is everyone around you. And therefore so are you.

Gamal came by, cleared the two mugs and the plate of banana bread crumbs. 'Noot, still focused on her own screen.

Maybe if you started acting and thinking and treating yourselves and each other that way, the Golden Fortress would already be here. 'Whatsoever you do to the least of your brothers,' transform?

"Okay, guys." Gamal, putting on his coat. "I'm headed back to the hospital in two. You ready?"

"Yup," said 'Noot, powering down the laptop.

Raptor, shifting posture, faking like he was ready to go.

So for you Christians, God is in the bread. And in the wine. But also in you. And in your enemies. And in pain and joy and defeat and victory and oppression and in justice.

Moon, the online immortal:

So yeah, you can find God everywhere. In everything. That's called panentheism. So if it's true, what're you gonna do about it?

'Noot and Gamal, standing at the door, coats and shoes on.

Raptor, powering down machine and powering up himself. Flipping open note pad, uncapping pen.

Outside, in the car, on the way. Let 'Noot ride shotgun.

Asked Gamal to put in his gift CD, hit track 3.

"Dée Moo Wóor." Still no lyrics, but one paragraph of liner notes and he'd begun a new revolution.

Began scribing: "How far . . . can a falcon . . . fall . . . ?"

What else needed revolution? Today? *Right now*?

Because there might not be much time.

7.

Outside the burn ward. Araweelo, hurrying from the elevator with the two charges she'd shuttled from the airport in Moon's Sunfire.

One: a striking sister, maybe twenty or twenty-one, five-eleven, with beaded braids and cat glasses. Looked like the actress Zoe Saldana. Jackal almost broke his eyes staring so hard.

Even frumped by jet lag, she projected two things: intellect, and pain.

Two: Kiya's brother Ptah, young and serious-looking behind his own glasses, skinny inside his bright yellow windbreaker. His hair wasn't long, but it was pebbly. Needed tending.

Maāhotep embraced Kiya in a long hug, then nodded to her brother without offering even a handshake. "Ptahhotep, you're huge! Do you remember me?"

"Of course I remember you, Uncle Maä," said the fifteen-year-old. His tone was so even it was like it'd been planed. "I haven't seen you for thirty-one months and nine days. How are you this evening?"

Maähotep winced. Tried smiling. Glanced at Raptor, who was puzzling together pieces he hadn't known had ever been a puzzle.

Ptah's hands were fists. But was no violence in them. Only restraint.

"Pete," said his older sister, "these are all Dad's friends."

Ptah, rotating to each one: "You're Jamal, also called Jackal. You're Raphael, also called Raptor. You're Almeera, also called Yibemnoot—I saw your reading list," he monotoned. "I saw all your pictures on Facebook. I've never been to Edmonton before. I've never been on an airplane before. We flew on a DC-10 manufactured by McDonnell-Douglas. Many people are afraid of flying in airplanes but statistically people are more likely to die of heart disease or automobile accidents than from air catastrophes—"

"That's very true, Ptah," said Maä. "Good job. And I'm glad you're here." To Kiya: "Are you . . . ready?"

She looked at the floor. Her beaded braids slipped past her shoulders, drooping.

Raptor, standing: "Your dad's the strongest man I've ever met."

"Take your time," said Maä, smacking Raptor quickly with his eyes. "But not too long. Do you think your brother should . . . ?"

"I'll go first. Can you . . . ?"

Maä nodded.

Why he wasn't on Facebook. Why he didn't shake hands or hug. Why Moon had the skills to chill Jackal's little brother during his freakout. How Moon could point all those Somali families and their committee in the right direction.

Raptor, introducing himself without offering to shake hands. Asking Ptah if he knew about Static. In fact Ptah knew quite literally everything about Static, both comic and cartoon and how they were made, and began reciting it all.

Araweelo went for information from the doctors, having lied from the beginning that she was Moon's common-law wife.

Kiya came out fifteen minutes later. Eyes were red, face was puffy.

Ptah said, "My sister Kiya has a lot of allergies. But it's the fall here so I didn't expect her to have a reaction."

Ten minutes later, Araweelo returned, beiged. Her eyes: empty.

Took Raptor aside, held him close, whispered: "He's conscious now. You haven'tt seen him before, my son. So prepare yourself."

Raptor started to move inside, eager to fill Moon in on "Dée Moo Wóor" and everything they'd accomplished and were about to accomplish while he was getting well.

His mum grabbed his arm. "If you have anything you wantt to say to him, Raptor . . . don'tt waitt."

8.

Washed, socked and smocked in hospital togs, Raptor entered the white sepulcher.

Found his mutilated master.

The fire'd torn him up, melted him back together. Brown lumps, rippled through with white and pink streaks, puckering with blasted-open blisters. A humanoid volcanic eruption.

And that was just the exposed skin.

The sight of him. Raptor's intestines coiled and snapped. Like he'd missed two steps down a staircase.

The unbandaged part of Moon's face, thank god, still a man.

Lived together more than a year. Shared food and books and music and life. And some secrets, but not all.

He'd yearned to tell Moon. Sometimes got close enough to feel his throat bulging, esophagus dilating and tearing to deliver the words and expel their wretched afterbirth.

Yet hadn't Moon also kept things from him?

Why did people do that? Keep their truest selves from the only people who'd earned the right to meet them?

The ninth scroll included *The Man Who Was Weary of Life*. Ballad of a spiritually destroyed man in the civilisational collapse of the Middle Kingdom. Contemplating suicide. And visited by the only one who could understand him.

The *ba*-bird that was one of his own souls.

Heard patiently his every misery, but begged him not to murder himself, to hang his pains on a coat-hook, make offering to the gods and cling to life. Promised, when his real day should come, to guide him to the eternal plains and raise a shining place with him forever.

So which one of them was the *ba* now?

And what could he offer?

He spoke to Moon's uncovered eye.

He was nine.

The camp was in Kenya, but sometimes in his mind it was Chad, or Sudan, or Ethiopia. The birds were huge, maybe buzzards, feasting on trash, and when they found bodies, on them, too.

They'd known each other in one camp when they were five or six, then miraculously had met in Kenya after three years and several exoduses and camps apart from each other.

Wacera, the running, laughing little girl who was raindrops and blossoms and mango in the desert.

The NGO: Jacob's Ladder. The aid worker's name was Seth Apsey, but he didn't make kids call him Mr. Apsey or Bwana Apsey and mostly they didn't even call him *mlungu* because he told them "Just call me Seth—c'mon, say it! Say my name!

That-a-boy!" and gave out candies and chocolates and Laughing Cow cheese in silver-wrapped wedges, which none of them had ever seen or let alone eaten in their brief and brutal lives.

In the locked-boxes of his fabulous tent, Seth held even more wonders, including dried fruit and salted meats and blocks of cheese. The worst of which was called Trappist cheese, which smelled to Raphael like feet, armpits and ass.

"These Jacob's Ladder people," Raptor said to Moon (eyelids fluttering, irises wobbling slowly in a widening gyre) "they were evil."

Tried swallowing, couldn't. Dry-heaved the words.

"They said they were trying to help Darfur refugees. But I wasn't from Darfur. Neither was Wacera, or most of the kids.

"Told the parents they were gonna fly us to Europe for medical attention, that they'd bring the parents on the next flight.

"They told us they were gonna take us all to foster homes in England. But I was there with my mother, and most of those kids had at least one parent. Stealing children . . . those fucking Pyrites!"

Looked at the banks of blinking machines, the sine wave telemetry of Moon's heart.

"When I came here and learned how to use the internet," said Raptor, "I found out six of those bastards'd gotten convicted in Kenya for child abduction, and a bunch of journalists, too, journalists who'd been covering up their crimes for them. Got sentenced to hard labour.

"But the British government, those *khetiuta* leaned hard and on the little old Kenyan government. *Poof!* Every last one those Pyrites got pardoned."

Raphael'd woken up on a sheet inside the barely-lanterned darkness of Seth Apsey's tent. It was the stink that knocked him awake. A big block of Trappist cheese with a hunting knife sticking out of it on a wooden cutting board. Reeked like men trapped together inside a cell for days, sleeping and sweating and pissing and shitting, without relief, in the baking heat.

Head ached like he'd been puking. His asshole hurt like he'd had diarrhea for days. Naked, and smelled of shit and blood.

On the cot, Seth was grunting, tossing sweatdrops from his greasy hair, bucking and shoving his cock into the unconscious limpness of nine-year-old Wacera.

Raphael's blood became lava.

The hunting knife plunged through Seth's ear and into his brain, and his body kept spasm-fucking Wacera as it shuddered to its death.

Pushed the monster's carcass off of Wacera, failed to wake her up, then found his own clothes and hers and dressed them both. Carried Wacera back to where her father slept, crept back in silent sobs to where his mother slept.

"And, and, and," said Raptor, palms into the broken levees of his eyes, smock-sleeve against his nose to staunch the snot.

"In the, the, the morning, when they found that fucker dead . . . . An *mlungu* murdered? We couldn't stay. A, a whole bunch of people just took off to, to wherever."

333

Grabbed tissues, blew his nose twice, three times.

"I never told her," said Raphael. "Or Jackal. Or anyone but you."

Moon's eye, on the unbandaged side of his face. Wide open.

Horror dwelt there.

He'd never let Moon hug him. And now he couldn't hug Moon.

Moon, with his one good hand, gestured.

Raptor took that hand, held onto it for life, saw Moon's eye soften, and he crumpled against the mattress with his head near Moon's knee.

Cried there until a nurse came to tell him he had to leave.

9.

The man was Seshat's friend, but Araweelo'd also worked on his campaign. Raptor'd heard of him, but didn't know a damn thing about provincial politics.

All he knew was that "Brian" was a fifty-something White dude with a greyblack moustache, and he'd been able to pull the paperwork together almost overnight.

"And, yeah, right there and . . . there," said the MLA.

Moon, with Araweelo holding the form for him, weakly signing his name, barely an X.

Seshat and Maāhotep witnessed, each of them clamping jaws and setting eyes.

The hospital wasn't supposed to let this many people in. Even with the special dispensation, Seshat, Maāhotep, 'Noot, Kiya, Ptah, Jackal and Raptor were allowed to enter and remain only for these last few minutes of the ceremony.

Araweelo stood beside Moon in his bed, resplendent. A southern Sudanese red flowered dress with beads and cowrie shells. A red veil.

Kiya, in borrowed, beautiful Muslimina fashion from 'Noot's cousin, since Kiya was a full half-foot taller than 'Noot.

Moon's throat was too damaged for speech. And when the MLA said to kiss the bride, Araweelo leaned down and kissed Moon so gently Raptor wondered whether their lips had even met.

Zero
Peace-Life-Eternal

The Book of Then

1.

MEN AND WOMEN, FIGHTERS ALL, DANCED AND SANG ON THE DAY FOLLOWING the Night of Victory Over the Destroyer.

I remember that morning like it was now.

There was mist pulling away from the kiss of the River Eternal. Spray from oranges and limes, freshly bitten, sparkling on the breeze and in my nose. Hard-boiled eggs, hot-born from cooking water, and callus-handed warriors with too-big fingertips pulling bits of shell from breakfast.

Bread, round and brown, puffing up on hot dome rocks, then flung as discs to outstretched hands. Flutes, lutes, voices. Laughter. Stories of what to do and where to go and how to dance and whom to kiss and how many babies to make when everyone got back at home.

And the sun.

2.

I couldn't dance. And I couldn't sing.

My limbs might've lost their metal, but they hadn't found their water, either. The poetry that had dominated my voice, that fanatical devotion to a cause, had shattered like forge-steel struck one too many times.

When everyone was celebrating, my words would not cavort, not even inside my mind. No longer did they shine like emeralds. They fell from my mouth, stones in sand. Soundless, even, because I couldn't bring myself to talk.

But the Revolution demanded I resume my motion, even though all I craved was sleep and eternity to grieve, to wail for everything we'd lost to win what we had gained.

And I wore yet another title, one I hadn't asked for, manacles, a yoke.

Sun-King Hru.

3.

We constructed boats, sailed the River Eternal to the lowlands, found the city called *Het-Uar*, the capitol of my defeated uncle. Its perimeter of blood-encrusted pikes.

We buried all the thousand skulls and desiccated heads we found upon them.

At the centre of the city lay his pyrite palace.

Maybe there'd been a time when the idea of watching its metal friezes melt, its ramparts burn, its guard-towers implode in the all-consuming flames . . . .

Maybe there'd been a time when such images promised comfort. I'd probably imagined I'd be shouting raging, joyful curses, hurling stones at stone statues of the Destroyer, condemning him millions upon millions of times.

But while my legions danced and sung around the incinerating mansion, hefting all its looted treasures they'd looted back again, the castle's death-smoke burned my eyes and throat, and dried my lips.

4.

We glided on the current to the lowlands, floating next to teeming fishes, their scales flashing in the noon.

Twenty years before I'd seen this place the first time. Unrelenting fog, black spider-trees, cascades of crocodiles, children beating each other to death and drowning in the sludge.

Twenty years before I'd given it a name I later found everyone before me had already known, as if everyone's ear had caught an echo of the tremors from the birth-pangs of the world, as if everybody's noses smelled the same corrupting afterbirth.

The Swamps of Death.

Now, only sunlight and clear water.

I leaned over the prow to look into the water, hoping I'd see a smiling child's face reflecting back to me.

But all I saw there was an old killer, a butcher for whom songs were being sung, from whom prayers were being memorised, for whom ten thousand glorious, poetical, absurd and overbearing titles would never be enough.

5.

We reached our destination. I left my Grand Vizier, my brother Yinepu, in command while I made my pilgrimage alone to descend to Sacred Cavern.

I slipped my way around the stony teeth, plunged ever deeper into darkness, until I found the sparkling ceiling, the house of stars.

And the inner chamber where my father sat upon his turquoise and obsidian throne.

I bid you enter here.

I bowed, and shut my eyes.

And then he spoke again.

You know me. I'm the one who loved you before you were even born.

"Duh-daddy?"

"Hru, come see your father."

His voice was soft as water. No more crashing echo from eternity. No more an underworld-beshadowed god-king. The throne, the cavern, the gold-rimmed eyes . . . they all disappeared to me. He was just a man.

I came to him, an adult, and he waved for me to jump into his lap. And it never occurred to me that I should not. My war-bulged muscles smoothened, my scars melted like footsteps in the riverbank, and beside my ear I suddenly felt the long-ago cut-off single braid of a child.

I stopped myself, but *almost* started sucking my thumb.

In his lap I was the child I'd forgotten ever having been, while he kissed and cuddled me as if decades had never turned to embers.

And then I saw them, over his shoulder, lurking in the shadows and lit by torch-lights, their skin now the total-black of my father's, their eyes rimmed in glittering gold.

I almost screamed.

"Daddy!"

He knew. He nodded like they'd always been there and always would be. My mother. Another woman I didn't know. And my uncle. My hated uncle I'd spent half my life escaping, and the other half trying to kill.

"Daddy, daddy!" I said, clutching his forearm with both my toddler-chubby hands. "Why's he here? He's bad! Don't you know what he did to me and mummy?"

"Son," he said, shushing me, holding the sides of my face so I could see him and only him. "He's here because I want him here."

"But why? He's a very bad man!"

He looked at me sadly, like he'd had millions of years to think about it, and would be pondering it for millions more.

"Hru, the lady beside your mother . . . do you see her?"

"Yes, daddy."

"That's your aunty."

I was shocked. I didn't know I had an aunty. "Mummy never told me about her."

"She's your mother's sister. Aunty Nebt-Het. Your cousin Yinepu's mother."

I didn't feel stupid. I just accepted it the way that children do, even though I'd had twenty years to ask Yin about his mother and never had.

"Your uncle always resented me," said Daddy. "And resentment, bitterness, jealousy . . . those swords are sharp enough to murder even gods. Do you understand?"

I nodded, but I really didn't. Even if I'd been old enough to know what my father meant, I was terrified of my murdering uncle standing right there behind him with his sharpened teeth and dagger eyes, my uncle who'd slaughtered our men, who'd executed my Master, who'd beaten me and knelt behind me, who'd . . .

"He wanted your mother for his wife. But she loved me. So he took her sister for consolation.

"But that made him only despise her. And then when she gave him a son, well, because he couldn't pry his mind from me, he thought everyone else was the same. So his belly burned with one belief: that your cousin was my son, not his."

If I'd been a man and not a boy, I would have asked him the obvious question: *Was he?*

But I wasn't a man, so I didn't.

"So he killed her," said my dad. Behind him, my aunty cried tears of molten gold, which puddled on the dais, gilding it.

"I didn't know it then," he said. "They were journeying the lowlands. He said she'd run away. On my journeys of Instruction, I thought I once saw her from a distance. But it must have been her ka in mournful wandering.

"Your mother never believed his story, but I did. And I was too stupid to listen to her about him.

"Oh, I had great plans, son, vast notions on how to change the world, teach everyone the righteous path, Instruct them in my way, which I knew was *the* way. So I left. I abandoned my wife. And that gave—*I* gave—my brother all the time he needed to—well. To prepare."

He crushed me against him, kissing my head again and again.

"I'm so sorry, son."

I was a boy, but even as a boy I knew the power of those words. Had anyone ever said them to me?

They were a balm on the burns that covered me.

"Here. I have something for you." He reached behind his throne. It was a linen satchel.

"Open it," he said, smiling.

I cupped the contents in my small hands. Tiny gemstones, black and rainbow. Sparkling.

"I'm just glad my Master found you," he said, cupping my cheek.

And again, because I was a child, I didn't ask what he meant, or any of the million questions whose answers a son should seek after learning something like that.

But mostly, I didn't ask because I was again trapped by the terrifying eyes of my uncle. Even here, standing right next to my father in this house of stars, there was fury-hatred erupting from his eyes like pus, like he couldn't wait to start his treachery again, to trap and hack my father again, to drive my mother into exile again, to enslave thousands again, to defile me again—and that if he could, he'd do it all forever and ever, to all men and women and girls and boys, throughout the universe.

"Daddy!" I grabbed his arm even tighter. "Why do you let him stay here with you? Can't you make him go away forever?"

"No," he said. "And son, as difficult as this is for you to understand . . . and you will, one day . . . even if I could, I wouldn't."

He lifted me from his lap, stood me down. Old scars crept back across my body like slugs returning home. Muscles swole like hills born from earthquakes.

I blocked my uncle's murderous glare and aunty's tragic face, and said goodbye to my mother, who smiled at me and blew me a kiss.

"I love you, my son," said one of them. Or both.

"Now . . . return to the world of tears."

6.

At sunrise, all of us sojourners took chalices or bowls or hands, knelt before what was once the Swamps of Death, and drank our fill from the River of Life, the Eternal River that now flowed free from Cradle to the Great Green Sea.

We unfurled our sails and let the winds, like a mother's tender hands, carry us upriver towards the Cradle.

And everywhere we stopped, I planted black and rainbow stones, and maize sprouted, and we feasted, and lotus blossomed, and we made perfumes and balms.

7.

It took us twenty years to raise the Golden Temple that Master Jehu had commissioned me to build.

But finally it stood, glorious in perfect geometry and flawless in its masonry, a sunrise on the earth itself.

When I sat upon my throne, I thought of whom I'd been. A refugee. A ranger in the Savage Lands. An acolyte of a dreaming madman in the wilderness, a visionary, a god-beholder. A killer who decapitated his own mother. An atoning labourer. A general. An avenger of his own father. And a king.

I made laws from that throne, and rendered judgements from it. I ordered men to their deaths while sitting in it. I prayed inside it for righteousness, for justice, and for mercy.

I begged the gods to keep us pure, to keep us dedicated enough to gird and gild our fortress walls, to keep them beaming light out to the world, to keep our fortress gates open for all the orphans running terrified from evil men who hunted them for sport or hate or lust. To keep our gates as open arms for everyone who wept, for those who hid their faces, and for those who'd sunk down.

I prayed to them to keep the Golden Fortress from the claws of wisemen, warlocks, and warriors who'd commission priests to compose poems to the glory of pyrite and coat the fortress walls with it, while keeping all the gold for themselves and their idols.

For the Destroyer never died. He lives forever, at the right shoulder of my father. And he can come at any time, or *be* us if we let him, to rule any palace as his own.

I prayed to them that if that day should ever come, to have the strength to burn our Fortress to the ground.

And then I set to build the Golden Fortress, as ceaselessly as the stars sail the skies, for eternity.

So, Duamutef, Hāpi, Imset and Qebehsunuef, my sons strong and good and loyal. You were there for much of what I've just told you. Is that how you remembered it?

How much of what I said was wrong?

I'm glad you feel that way.

I pray you're right.

The Book of Now

1.

C OLD, DARK, BUT STILL NO SNOW. C LOUDS CHISELED THE STARS FROM THE SKY, and city lights frosted it navy blue.

And on the street, inside yellow *DO NOT CROSS* tape and in front of the Hyper-Market's blackened corpse, flocked Falcons.

Scarves. Toques. Long coats. Puffy jackets.

Gritted teeth. Boiled eyes. Sopping Kleenex.

Gloved hands gripping candles flickering, flickering inside 2L pop bottles cut in half, necks for holders.

Jackal, with a hoist, stood on shoulders of muscled Senwusret. Balanced, leaning on the wall above the still-standing door frame.

Raptor handed him the battery-powered drill and the thick book.

Jackal, deck screws between his lips, taking one at time, drilling the four corners of the yellow-covered tome against the black wall. Raptor, handing him up the wooden laser-etching and one more screw.

And Jackal descended, anointed in soot.

Raptor, gut like magma rupturing into ocean brine. Steam erupting up his gullet, out his nostrils. Eyes floating in sulfuric acid.

Over there, Ãnkhur, Sen next to her, his arm around her. Her head in his chest. Sen's glove smearing across his own eyes, and again.

Raptor, kneeling beside a destroyed wall, four small ceramic jars out of his back-pack. Each one with a face painted on it: a man's. A baboon's. A jackal's. A falcon's.

Placed them and their scrolls inside the ruins.

Sekhmet, the Rwandan girl with French accent, standing in the *shen* and holding her pop-bottle candle, her face above it, and the *hiss* as its flame died, drowned by water droplets, and the light in her face went out, replaced by smoke.

'Noot and Jackal both, not even hiding it. Just blubbering.

And then more moaning, from another three dozen there. Except for one.

And that one standing up, charging into the *shen*.

"Nobody here remembers what Brother Moon said?"

All eyes up and aimed. Him, swinging his face around the shen like a mace.

343

"Nobody? Huh?"

Jackal, softly. "Rap, dude, c'mon . . . . "

Raptor, giving up nothing but a glare.

"What did he *tell* us?"

Behind and above him and the door frame, the wood bearing the laser-etching of Moon's face, and beside it, impaled on four screws with the jackal-god Yinepu on the cover, *Pert-em-Hru*, mis-titled in English, *The Book of the Dead*.

2.

"I know from having overheard some of you young Falcons," said the man at the podium, sunlight streaming bright and cold above him through the high windows, "you're thinking, you're not supposed to cry. Am I right?"

Maãhotep. Again, put-together. A perfectly-pressed dark suit, shining cufflinks. But grey had stolen into his hair, or maybe he'd just stopped dyeing it.

Either way, during the early morning march towards the ceremony, Jackal'd called him—respectfully, affectionately—Old Man Maã. Already other Falcons were calling him that, too.

"Because Brother Moon told you that, right?" said Maã. "He said, apparently, if you cry for me, I'll reach up from the coffin and smack you. Right?"

Somebody somewhere chuckled. Plenty nodded somberly. Some threw on pride, like a suit jacket two sizes too large.

"Well, I'm here to tell you," said Maã, "that's *bull*shit."

Two hundred Falcons ruffled their feathers, and hundreds of other community members shuffled in their seats inside the Africa Centre's gymnasium.

Cursing bad enough—but actually contradicting Brother Moon at his own funeral?

And from Mr. Lawyerman, no less?

He answered their nonverbal objection by ignoring it.

In the first row, Raptor felt his mother's shoulder and hip to his left. Shaking. Shuddering. Not even trying to dam. And on his right, Jackal's eyes on him like fangs.

Jackal nudged him. Raptor, eyes forward, didn't budge.

"They were friends longer'n most of us've been alive," stage-whispered Jackal, but enough for everyone to hear. "Old Man Maã can say what he likes. Transform *that*."

"Thank you, Brother Jackal," said Maã. "Yes. Why *shouldn't* people cry, especially when they've got every right to be sad? Tell me that. When someone they love and admire is gone. Dead. Is there any pain in the world worse than that?

"And you're supposed to act like it doesn't hurt? When you've got agony like a sharpened spear sticking through your spine?"

He gazed at Falcons' faces, one at a time, making sure each one saw him- or herself being seen.

"I've known a few sisters who act like that," said Maã, "but most of the time, as *Sbai* Seshat was reminding me just last night, it's brothers who inflict this, this immiserating idiocy on themselves with this 'I *can't* cry' and 'I don't *feel* sad' nonsense.

"To the point they violate their spirits so much, they end up thinking only two parts of their bodies are *allowed* to feel anything: their fists, and their dicks."

Again, ruffling and shuffling, but less this time.

"If Brother Moon said not to cry," said the old man, his voice sandpapered and bloody, "it was because—and I'm not revealing anything that hasn't come out by now—he *remembered* . . . what it was like . . . being severely depressed . . . when his when his marriage fell apart."

Raptor, at last, put his arm around his mother. Felt her shuddering shake him to his core.

"And he spent a good year alone," said Maã. "A bad year alone, rather. And by his own description, crying, pretty much every night. Brother Moon reached the point where he couldn't leave his own apartment. That's called clinical depression. When the, the *spiritual immune system* is so damn compromised it just can't heal the soul anymore."

More faces, more eyes. And then he locked with Araweelo, and with Raptor.

"He just didn't want anybody falling into that kind of misery, especially not for his sake.

"Personally, he felt humiliated that he'd ever reached that stage. He shouldn't've felt that way, but he did. Nobody wants to feel powerless, but he couldn't forgive himself for it.

"But remember the Triumph Scrolls and the *Nub-Wmet-Ānkh*: '*I will not drown . . .* ' In what?"

Hundreds:

"'*In the Swamps of Death.*'"

Maã: "That doesn't mean simply booze, or drugs, or promiscuity, or television. It means whatever poisons you.

"And that's like what *Sbai* Seshat said: for too many brothers, it's refusing to acknowledge how we really feel. Afraid that if we do, it'll make us soft. Weak. Turn us into punks.

"And the most lead-headed among us so are afraid of the world and of ourselves, we even say crying makes you a bitch."

Let the brittle word shatter against the walls.

"Or a faggot."

Another shocked shatter.

"Because, you know, *they're* supposed to be weak."

Silence, except for the hum and hiss of forced air heating.

"And here you are . . . in the Savage Lands . . . dying of heart disease and cancer in your fifties . . . dying by drinking yourself to death in your forties . . . or dying by booze-crack-or-chronic-induced violence in your twenties!

"Look at those words! A diseased *heart*. Or chronic, *another* way to say an illness that shackles you till the day you die. *Crack*—in your spirit. Some of us carry the Swamps of Death inside us. We turn *ourselves* into Destroyers.

"But crying—at least for a while? That's the way to drain those poison waters.

"Think Hru didn't cry? Think Master Jehu didn't cry? Think Queen Nzingha didn't cry? Think Lumumba or Malcolm X or Sankara didn't cry? Think again."

Maa leaned back from the podium. Straightened his tie. Clamped each cufflink, one at a time. Spoke his last words.

"So be like Hru. And drain those Swamps."

Finally Raptor stepped up to the mic.

"As you all know, I lived with Brother Moon. You know he was like a father to me. But . . . I also know he was like a father to plenty of you. And I don't wanna take that away from any of you by saying, y'know, that he was all mine, like he belonged to me and just me. 'My father.' So maybe we should just call him 'our father.' Transformed?"

"*Transformed.*"

"Then say it with me. Father Moon."

"*Father Moon.*"

"Speak it!"

"*FATHER MOON!*"

"Father Moon . . . was worth more to me than I could ever say. So . . . maybe instead of saying anything else . . . I'm hoping that a few of us could sing something for him, in his honour."

And then, calling up Jackal, Senwusret and 'Noot, the four of them sang Raptor's new lyrics to "Dée Moo Wóor."

> *How far can a young falcon fall*
> *When the hurricane conquers his home:*
> *The palace of moon and sk-y-y?*
>
> *Can he fly in a savaging squall?*
> *Or's he battered gainst mountain and stone*
> *To be shattered and crucifi-i-ed?*
>
> *On ground where the broken all crawl*
> *Releasing their miserable moans*
> *Will he heal or will he be deni-i-ied?*
>
> *Then a falconer answers his call*
> *Weaves his magic of feathers and bones*
> *With his spirit that amplify-i-ies*

And the falconer builds him a wall
Gives him arm he's turned into a throne
Till his miseries all subsi-i-ide

Then he launches his falcon to all
Of the winds of directions known
So renewed, he can soar worldwi-i-ide

The falcon who flies above all
Will never be lost where he's flown
For his falconer dwells insi-i-i-de . . .

3.

Late October. But a warm afternoon.

Three rented buses ferried scores of Falcons out of E-Town, north to Athabasca, east to Amber Valley. Others car-pooled with community members.

Green grasses, yellow leaves. Big sky country and gently-flowing hills, living waves, eternal form.

Old farm on *Sbai* Seshat's family land.

Atop a low rise, Seshat said to the youth, "Here, Maidstone, Breton, and down in John Ware's country and a dozen other places . . . this is where my peoples came a hundred years ago."

Maãhotep and Gamal arrived in a cube truck. Falcons and Alchemists unloaded the pieces of the obelisk, carried them as work gangs up the hill.

Rebuilding them under Maã's guidance as if they were reuniting vertebrae into a spine.

"*By the sunrise, I serve the cause of peace and cause of life,*" they all recited, led by *Sbai* Seshat, the capstone to the *Nub-Wmet-Ānkh*. "*So may we raise the Shining Place eternally.*"

Without a generator granting electricity, the obelisk would never light out there. But Seshat affixed a plaque:

> *A blacksmith of words is a victor in life.*
> *The tongue is the shield and the sword of the Pharaoh.*
> *Speech is the greatest martial art, for no one can overcome the skillful heart . . .*
> *Give your love to the world entire,*
> *For a joyful one is remembered for the ages.*
>
> Pharaoh Kheti III
> *U. 6-9, 314-315*

Sbai Nehet the archer armed her composite bow.

Fired one arrow to the south for the heart of the Nile.

Fired another to the east for the Sun.

Fired a third to the north where suffering turned to fields and mountains of ice.

Fired the final shaft to the west for the millions upon millions of ancestors who'd walked and breathed and laughed and birthed and grieved and come to wisdom and come to death.

Then all of them marched in a vast and silent circle a kilometre in circumference, around the obelisk's hill, a slow and kinesthetic shenu inscribing the obelisk with forever.

4.

Gamal rode back with Seshat on one of the rented school buses. Raptor took his seat in the cube van.

Fields receded past their windows. Highway slid beneath them.

Maãhotep, hands on the wheel.

"Because your mother is legally Moon's widow, we'll be continuing his lawsuits on her behalf as inheritor of his estate. Obviously, it was easier for him to marry her than to, well . . . to adopt you, but you understand—"

"It's okay, Brother Maã. I know how he felt about me. And he knew how I felt about him."

"Okay."

Driving past road-sign, reflecto-green and -white in the headlights: *Edmonton 75 km.*

"Moon'd be proud of you—I'm proud of you—the way you've handled all this organising. You've become quite the activist."

"Thanks."

"I've got something for you. Moon left it with me for safe keeping, in case . . . Anyway, he wanted you to have it. I put it in the glove compartment there for you."

Inside: Moon's carved wooden box. The one he'd opened for him and Jackal during one of their first Alchemical lessons. He hadn't remembered that the box was rubbed with amber, smelled of its citron-cinnamon essence.

Opened it up.

One hunk of lead, and another of pyrite. And Moon's pendant, the cartouche in gold.

Stunned. To see how much he'd grown. Back then he couldn't read the cartouche's hieroglyphics, but now he couldn't *not* read them.

Inside the elongated *shen*-ring. Up top, from leaf to waves, the god whose name meant "the mysterious or unknowable." Below, three characters reading "is satisfied," which also meant "peace."

Yimun Hotep.

He put on his talisman, hanging from its golden chain.

Dark. Pulling into E-Town.

Maãhotep, telling how he and Seshat arranged through a third party to buy the partly-destroyed Street Laboratory from the City "at a fire sale price."

Raptor, smirking, shaking his head. "Ouch." Maã chuckled. They both talked: how they'd rebuild, what they'd change, how they'd raise their Shining Place forever.

Then Maã, without segue: "So, after you finish upgrading, any thoughts on a career direction?"

Raptor gave his answer, smiled seeing how his answer made Maãhotep jump, even trying not to.

"I want to be a public interest lawyer."

5.

That night, *Sbai* Seshat's for dinner. Jackal, Araweelo and Raptor and 'Noot, Ānkhur and Senwusret, Maãhotep and Gamal.

Plus, for their final night in town, Kiya and Ptah.

Dinner. Delicious, but alien to everyone except Seshat and Ānkhur: baked macaroni, collard greens, homemade deep-fried chicken, German potato salad with tofu dogs. Before anyone dug in, glasses raised, and together they said, "May we drink from the River of Life."

Raptor served 'Noot's and his mother's plates. Araweelo was quieter than he'd ever seen her. He kept giving her side hugs. Even—and this was totally new to him—kissed her on the cheek, in front of everyone.

Nobody said anything about it. But each time he kissed her, she looked up and touched his face as softly as if she were cradling a newly-hatched chick.

Dessert: bean pie with marbled butterscotch ice cream, and over coffee and tea, conversation. Philosophical, almost theological.

Because Moon hadn't lived long enough to teach the Originals the Peace-Life-Eternal Scroll, none of them could transform the paradox of the Destroyer's fate in *The Book of the Golden Falcon.*

"Yeah, I mean, fuh real," said Jackal. "Dude killed his own brother. Raped Hru! He was a warlord, he enslaved people. How's that punk end up getting to stand beside Lord Usir in the House of Stars?"

Seshat, leaning back and sipping coffee so pungent it woke Raptor up just smelling it. "Any of you know the Gospel story of the landowner who offered the same wage to everyone? Whether they worked from sunrise or only showed up just before quitting time?"

Ãnkhur knew it, everyone else: blank eyes.

Seshat, in a wide arc: talking rapists and rape survivors, murderers and murder victims, the *Ubuntu* philosophy of *I am we*, even the idea that Set himself had probably been raped in war, or as a child.

"You know, some people set their whole lives on getting payback, and they still never get it. Imagine that—their whole lives, everything they do, for nothing.

"*Years* spent nursing that misery and hate and loss when they should've been nursing sick people, or nursing babies. Transform?"

Maãhotep, snatching from his plate the final crust and crumbles of his bean pie. Nodding worth a thousand words.

"What about us as a people?" said Seshat. "For the Maafa? For the first fifty million taken, and for the billion born into the hell that came? When's *our* payback? Even if we *could* force them to give us reparations, it'd take three planets and ten thousand years. And what about the ancestors already gone?"

"Yeah, *Sbai*," said Jackal, "but forget about reparations for the victims a minute. I'm saying, *rewarding* the guy who committed the crime in the first place?"

Plenty of nodding around the room, and Raptor leapt in: "Exactly! In the tenth ãrit, Set's standing right there, next to the greatest mind in the world, free as free can get, and no shackles on his arms and no sword at his neck?"

"I know. I hear you," said Seshat. "It's disgusting, isn't it? Offensive, that someone so sick and twisted-evil not only doesn't get punished, he gets to be, what, forgiven? Gets to keep his status? Be rewarded by sitting beside the Lord of the Limits forever?"

She wiggled the coffee pot towards Araweelo, who accepted a mugfull. Maã got up. "I'll make tea. Keep going."

Seshat:"The tenth ãrit of *The Book of the Golden Falcon* lays it out straight: the guilty, the guiltiest of history, ain'never gonna get what they deserve."

"What about," said Ãnkhur, singing Marley's melody to Haile Selassie's words:

> *We Africans will fight*
> *If we find it necessary*
> *And we know we shall win*
> *For we are confident*
> *In the victory*
> *Of good over evil*
> *Of good over evil, yeah!*

Kids snapped on it, slid skin at Ãnkhur's smoothness. Seshat: "Where'd y'all learn to slide like that?"

Sen said, "Father Moon." Seshat smiled and went on.

"C'mon, now. You know I'm right. Look at history. How many butchers got butchered? How many super-thieves paid back the people they ripped off and then set the people up in mansions? And how could anybody ever pay you back for taking the life of someone you loved?

"So *Golden Falcon* prepares us. Says, 'Forget payback. Forget 'good triumphs over evil. Ain'gon happen. South Africa after apartheid? Right. Got millions who can't even count on water or electricity.

"So the story shoves our faces right in it: what it takes to turn people into the Destroyer. That if we keep lusting for revenge cuz justice is denied, we will become Destroyers. Probably of everything we believe in and everybody we care about."

The kettle whistled.

Old Man Maã hotted the pot, dropped enough loose leaves into a massive tea ball for everyone around the table.

Tea steeped. They cleared dishes, washed and dried them together, except for Seshat who'd prepared the meal.

6.

Next day. At the airport. Kiya, Raptor, Araweelo, and Raptor.

Raptor, waving goodbye to Ptah without offering him a handshake.

But he held out his collected edition of Static, one of his few possessions that wasn't burned since he'd been transporting it from his mother's place to Moon's on the night of fire.

Hadn't had much choice in clothes for the same reason, until the Falcons got together with some hand-me-overs and a Zeller's gift certificate.

Ptah, shaking his head, trembling. "I have to pay for things I want!"

"It's okay, Pete," soothed Kiya. "When someone gives you a gift, then it's the right thing to do, to take it. You just say thank you."

"Thank you for the gift, Raptor." Took it. Kept away from Raptor's fingers.

"You're welcome." Relieved.

Kiya, looking more like Zoe Saldana than ever now that she was finally smiling, leaned down slightly to hug Raptor.

Wasn't Moon's daughter genetically, but somehow he saw Moon's face in hers, and felt suddenly wrong. Like watching his own sister in a bikini.

Plus, there was 'Noot.

Asked her to stay in touch via Facebook. Promised she would.

"Uncle Maã said you wanted to study Law," said Kiya. "You should think about coming to Minneapolis. There are some great law schools there. Or Howard. I might go there, too."

Shocked at her implication. "Thanks."

"I liked what Seshat said about that story," she said.

"Excuse me?"

Her smile, gone. "I was angry at Moon for such a long time," she said. "My mother lied to me about him. And when I found out she lied, I mean, I guess I'd kinda known for a while . . . but, I just, I felt so stupid and ashamed, it was just easier to stay mad than switch."

He nodded a *been there*.

"Do you think—I mean, I never even wrote back to all the letters he sent me, even after I found them in my mother's closet. Do you think he—"

"He absolutely loved you, Kiya. No question."

She kissed him on the cheek and hugged him tight, and then took her brother and flew away.

"C'mon, Mr. Bootiful," said his mother, and they walked out with her arm round his waist and his round her shoulders.

In the parking lot, inside the car. Engine on, heat flowing.

His mum didn't put the car in the drive.

Raptor finally turned on the stereo. Pharoah Sanders was on the deck. "The Creator Has a Master Plan." Just starting . . . the bells and then the bass line. A long one—display was clicking down from 9:02 . . .

Let that agonising joy ring out in the silent car, while inside his head he wrote out a scroll, crumpled it, and tried again a dozen times while Sanders' tenor sax soared skyward.

Finally.

Didn't have a clue what else to say. Or how to say it.

"Mum . . . " he croaked, "you've lost . . . *so much* . . ."

They crushed each other in their arms, gear shift and CD compartment between them. Ignoring the interference.

When the CD finally shifted to Coltrane's "A Love Supreme," Araweelo put the car in gear, and they drove away.

7.

Snow coming down. Him texting on the highway back into town.

So when they got to Al Hambra, 'Noot was already waiting for him in a heavy coat at the door.

His mother, smiling. Staying in the car while he got out. Said she was "going out for groceries."

He smiled back.

Inside. Sitting, drinking President's Choice cola. And neither saying anything. Till Raptor turned to her.

"It was pretty dumb of me to talk about visualising us married."

"Maybe," she said. "But it was still sweet."

"If we're gonna . . . be boyfriend and girlfriend" (nearly choked on the words) "it's gonna be tough. You know that, right? With your family?"

She sniff-laughed. "You hardly have to tell *me* that."

He chuckled.

"But I'm happy," said 'Noot, "that you want to. You know. Try." She wet her lips. "So what changed?"

"I talked with Brother Moon . . . before he died." Deep breath. "He helped me . . . work through some things."

She didn't ask for an explanation. Just nodded.

"There's this one poem," he said, "in one of the last books Moon was ever reading. He had it bookmarked. I can't remember the whole thing, but . . . . "

"Please!" she said. "Tell me!"

He was lying. He'd memorised the entire poem for her. It was the sonnet "Courage" by Claude McKay. His recitation reached its peak:

> But in the socket-chiseled teeth of strife,
> That gleam in serried files in all the lands,
> We may join hungry, understanding hands,
> And drink our share of ardent love and life.

His heart, shooting thunder up his arteries into his eardrums and his brain.

But he'd been transformed.

The trembling was no longer from terror, but from anticipation.

She touched his hands. He touched her cheek.

She didn't kiss him, and he didn't kiss her.

They kissed each other.

And she tasted like Red Delicious.

8.

Raptor and Jackal, to all the world inseparable, roamed *Khair-em-Nubt* in the light and falling snow, chatting up any young brother or sister they met after disarming them with smiles.

Noted names and faces of everyone who gleamed, and if they ever met again and if the gleam was still there or greater, then they'd grant them Resurrection Scrolls.

In fact that day, they did run into four kids, two sets of siblings, they'd twice before encountered while out "mining." So Raptor and Jackal gave them each a scroll, Jackal joking when he saw their confused faces, "Don'be smoking them, neither!"

One girl, opening up her scroll right there, seeing hieroglyphs and the alphanumeric code beneath the Grand Seal of the Alchemical Order, *oo*ed and said, "Cool!"

Raptor named their website and told them to check out 'Noot's latest reading list (containing the novel he'd been reading, *Allah is Not Obliged*). And then they continued on their way and their labours.

At the Dinka youth club house—barely a hallway with chairs—Raptor grabbed the door handle.

"Fuh real?" said Jackal. "That's great."

Inside, tall, skinny, dark-skinned South Sudanese, not only Dinka but Nuer and Nubian.

Raptor tried out a few phrases in Dinka, chatting up some young men and saying he was available to help tutor younger kids and offer English help to anyone who needed it.

On the street, Jackal said, "Since when do you speak Dinka? That was Dinka, right?'

"My mum's been teaching me."

"Geo, man! Damn, been meaning to tell you. Show you, actually. Found this a few days ago. Doing some etymology for teaching summa these eggs."

Jackal took out his Android, thumbed, showed Raptor:

> Raphael. *Masc. proper name, Biblical archangel (Apocrypha), from L.L., from Gk. Hraphael, from Heb. Rephael, lit. "God has healed" from rapha "he healed" + el "God."*

Raptor looked back up. Didn't know what was on his face. Wasn't even sure what was coursing up and down his spine. But felt it crackling.

Jackal smiled again, big enough to shoot sparks. "You're welcome."

9.

Walked the long distance across *Khair-em-Nubt* and then up to *Khair-em-Ānkh-Tawy.*

Stopped in front of Data Salvation Laboratories.

The DSL'd survived the fire, mostly, and was back open for business, still staffed by the quiet Rwandan brother Hakizimana, still owned by Moon's partners Seshat and Old Man Maä with a third share owned by Moon's estate.

Whoever'd torched the Hyper-Market and the Street Laboratory didn't know about the DSL—or ran out of time to destroy it.

"This is where I got resurrected," said Jackal.

Raptor nodded.

"I love you, JC," he said.

Jackal looked—not embarrassed—but stunned.

"I love you, too, Rap."

They hugged each other, a *shenu* of two.

10.

Moon, Raptor and Jackal. Standing in the glory of a prairie dawn. Birds chirping, cat tails absolutely still in the sweet, cool air.

At the very edge of hearing, first bees of spring: a string-section tuning before a performance.

To the east, a slough: sapphire beneath the sky.

Not a desert, like where so many religions had been born, where mountains and forests couldn't distract the soul from the blatancy of heaven and earth. But its living counterpart, the prairie, its gently rolling sway a tide on the schedule of God's long day.

"Takes a subtle eye to see this," Moon'd told them so many times that they'd started rolling their eyes about it.

In the slough. Tadpoles swimming, dreaming of legs and freedom. On the field, a hare, ears back. Motionless.

Moon, smiled at it all, then even more when he saw the falcon ranging above them.

At a clear patch, they set up their launch pad for their three-stage rockets and set off two, and then the final one.

Raptor: "Seems like a rip-off."

Moon's face: horrified.

Jackal: "You crazy? We did all this work building these things, Brother Moon drives us out here at six in the morning—"

"Wait a second, wait a second! You didn't let me finish! I don't mean this *trip* is a rip. Thanks, Brother Moon. I meant . . ."

Pointed up at the first and second stage rockets, coming down with parachutes. Far lower than the third stage on its slow and downward drift.

Raptor, riffing: "Look at em. I mean, those lower stages did all the work to get the third stage up that high, hit the zenith, take pictures from way up there like it's crashing some angel party, then come back like a hero after the war. Or like a scientist after one of those *eureka* days in the lab. Mr. Third Stage gets all the glory, and what do *they* get?"

Waited for the old man to join with jokes.

But Moon said nothing.

Suddenly, upon the horizon, the sun was born.

Moon's face, gold. His eyes, amber.

They looked up where he was looking, into the sky for that third-stager.

The first- and second-stages were halfway to ground, but they couldn't see the final rocket which had merged with the solar brilliance.

Moon: "Don't worry about them, young bruh. They knew what they were doing."

THE BOOK OF THE GOLDEN FALCON

The First Arit, also called Resurrection

The boy rescues himself and other children from night raiders

¹ The boy awoke upon his reed mat to screams of men in the night. ² Around him, fire thrashed and consumed the grove of trees, and beyond the circle of children, men staggered with arrows in their necks, and sword-gashes in their bellies, and where they fell, the sand drank their blood. ³ The boy screamed for his mother, and his screams rose like smoke to blacken the stars, but his mother did not come.

⁴ And all the children woke, and screamed, for from the chaos came men with murderous knives, and fingers cruel, to slay them all.

⁵ Seeing them screaming, the boy yelled to rally them, and they fell behind him in a line, and with his only utterance of power, turned them into shadows who passed beyond the flames. ⁶ And as shades they waded from the eastern bank through the shallows of the river, found the island in the darkness, and hid in the gullets of caves, where hares dwelled. ⁷ There they stayed as shades until the dawn, when the bats returned, and until night when the bats left again to hunt, and through another rising and another setting of the sun.

⁸ On the third morning, the boy spoke his words-of-power, and the children were made flesh again, and they emerged from the cave to gaze across the river at their smouldering camp, which stank from the burnt meat of men. ⁹ Hyenas laughed there, and vultures frolicked, and tugged again and again to reveal the bones of the slaughtered.

¹⁰ The children were behind him, crying, "May these hunters never gain mastery over us! May we never fall under their knives!" ¹¹ And the boy, fearing for himself and for them, led them across the shallows to the western bank, and from there they crept and fell to stillness among the reeds and lotus, like rabbits when an eagle blots the sun. ¹² And they wandered, lost, afraid, hungry, wounded, and sobbing, past ravaged houses, past bludgeoned bodies, past gutted animals, past burnt crops.

¹³ And the boy looked upon the ruins, and asked, "Who is this Destroyer upon the lands?"

The Second Arit,
also called Revolution

The children are swallowed by the Devourer of Millions of Souls

¹ In the third month of flight and foraging on the west bank of the river, the boy hatched a plan of revolt against the Destroyer and his men of murderous knives and fingers cruel.

² The children gathered the tools of fallen farmers, and sharpened them against rocks, and practiced the way of war until the night when they would rise invincibly like the moon.

³ But the men of murderous knives and fingers cruel fell upon them, butchered the smallest and the slowest, and chased the others to the river before the boy could turn them into shadows.

⁴ Then the Devourer of Millions of Souls rose from the waters, and swallowed the boy and all the survivors in his following. And the terrified murderers fled like hyenas before lions, and the Devourer submerged to the deeps.

⁵ The boy and the children wailed their terror in the stench and darkness of the belly of the Devourer, and they were thrown upon each other like knackered bones in the slaughtering yards.

⁶ And for seven days, the boy grasped at a rotten fang in the monster's mouth, and pulled at it with his every strength, crying in rage until he was weak, until those in his following joined him in his labour for freedom.

⁷ On the seventh day, the fighters broke off the fang, and the Devourer swam up from the depths, and in a rage spat the children upon the mud and reeds before returning to the dark below, while the boy still grasped the monster's sundered tooth.

⁸ The boy was afraid, for he was in a land that he knew not, and yet he felt the curse of the shallows around him, and told the survivors in his following, "Before the sunset, we must find water, food and a hiding place."

⁹ But the children, being in the agony of fear and thirst, drank of the cursed waters. And some choked and died before they fell.

¹⁰ Others staggered from the mire, groaning as they did, scum-armoured, their eyes like the charcoal of a week-old hearth. For the tendrils of the depths had sucked their souls from them, lodged them in the bottom-mud and slime like sunken pots. He called to them, but they heard him not.

¹¹ So it was the boy said, "What Swamps of Death are these!"

¹² And hearing the cackling hunters with their murderous knives and their fingers cruel, he fled, alone, into the night.

The Third Arit,
also called Triumph

The boy meets a second ranger in the Savage Lands

¹ The boy gathered reeds and branches, weaving himself a home hidden among vines, and transformed himself to shadows against the beasts and men who stalked him.

² In the night, he heard the screams of children, and so he slipped from his nest to find those who had fallen from his following.

³ He beheld them drinking from the cursed waters, whereupon the largest attacked those beneath them, and they in turn attacked the smallest, whom they threw into the Swamps of Death to drown.

⁴ The boy cast off his shadows, confronted the brutal congregation, and dragged the

smallest child from the waters where the reeds clutched like hungry fingers. The vicious, swamp-mad children fled, not from the boy-protector's wrath, but from the crocodile legion descending then upon them.

⁵ With the Devourer's sundered fang in both his hands, he cleaved the foremost crocodile's head in two. Yet to wield his weapon so, he'd released the rescued child, whom the other scaled and thrashing fiends then shredded into bone and blood inside their vengeful maws.

⁶ And the boy, abandoned and alone, fled the Swamps of Death, and returned to his nest in darkness.

⁷ When next arose the sun, the boy emerged to forage and to range, and from a distance spied the lifeless march of bound and fettered children by the thousand.

⁸ Witnessing their damnable procession, he saw their brutal guardians break the bones of some for grim amusement before casting dozens into mines of lead and glinting pyrite.

⁹ Still others, chainsmen led to fields so as to join the sun-whipped toil of ten thousand others digging, planting, pulling in the rock and sand and soil.

¹⁰ The last and largest of the lifeless children drank from skins the bondsmen poured out for them, scum-choked filth drawn from the Swamps of Death. And they were handed hatchets, pikes, and daggers, conscripted into soldiering until released by severing of their limbs or lives.

¹¹ And understanding rescue of all these conquered innocents was beyond his means as child with but a single weapon and without allies, he returned to his nest

hungry, and lying down to rest, he wept.

¹² The sun rose, and during his forage he found a batch of eggs. Two were smashed, their insides feasted on by unknown creatures, yet the third egg was whole, and the boy took it for his meal. But in his hands the shell cracked open, and from it pushed a falcon chick, calling *hroo-hroo, hroo-hroo*.

¹³ And so the boy commanded his belly to silence so that he might marvel at the tiny bird, which sank its beak into his finger. And he threw down the eggling bird, about to crush it beneath his foot. But it cried to him, *hroo-hroo, hroo-hroo*.

¹⁴ So in his mercy the boy sucked upon his wound to draw forth blood, which he fed by droplets into the falcon's opened beak.

¹⁵ Then before him was a wild boy with hair mud-plaited like the upright ears of jackals, and seven jackals were behind him as his train. And he declared, "I am Yinepu, apprentice of the Sorceress, the boy who prowls the swamp lands and hunts what he chooses and is not hunted. Who are you, boy who feeds a falcon from his finger, boy who trespasses upon my hunting grounds?"

¹⁶ And before the boy could answer, his falcon called out, *hroo-hroo, hroo-hroo*. And so the boy said, "I am Hru, the boy who revolted against murderers in the night of fire, the boy who stole a fang from the mouth of the Devourer, and with it killed a crocodile in the Swamps of Death to avenge a child, the boy who walks where he will, and fears not jackals or their boys."

¹⁷ And brandishing his captured fang, he retreated from the jackals and their boy until he found his nest, where he fed his falcon with his blood while he went hungry, and beneath a night sky dark without a moon.

The Fourth Arit, also called Ancestor-I

The ancestors send a mentor as a channel for their wisdom

¹ Nights passed and days passed, and the moon grew full, and Hru tended to his falcon chick, suckling it from his finger after foraging for himself. But the two boys in the

Savage Lands were never far from confrontation, stalkers in turn stalked, weakened by their constant fear and rage, while ever more determined to annihilate the other.

² And on the night of greatest moon, the rangers met in darkness, shadowed Hru with monster's fang fastened as a spearhead, and Yinepu with hungry jackals, teeth a-gleaming.

³ And as they ran towards each other poised to render death, between them stepped a man who spoke a word-of-power, and the boys fell silent, and the jackals stilled, and they walked with him until they found the summit of a cliff, whereupon he invoked words of even greater might, and the boys beheld in wonder as the sun was born.

⁴ Around them rose a cry: an academy of baboons chattered praises to the rising Glory. And the man whispered to them, "Fight with each other no more, but learn beside me how to tend a garden, so that you might one day raise up a world."

⁵ And they were dazzled by this man of wondrous magic, whom they then called "Master." At his home he fed and clothed them, welcoming the falcon chick and band of jackals.

⁶ The moon revealed and hid himself once, twice and many times. With lengthening bones and thickening muscles, the rangers grew in craft of making mud-bricks, baking them beneath the sun triumphant, while their Master taught them arts of measurement for the laying of the bricks and the expansion of his house into a larger compound and a garden.

⁷ And the Master said to them, "The ancestors scatter their wisdom like a sower his seeds, and those who would feast must first sweat beneath the sun."

⁸ Foraging for their daily meals, the rangers found abandoned children wandering, mad from drinking water from the Swamps of Death, and they brought them to the Master, who chased the poisons from their bodies with herbs and fruits and words-of-power.

⁹ And watching their Master, Hru tended to his falcon chick, and taught it flight, and Yinepu taught his jackals to be sentinels in the darkness while the compound slept.

¹⁰ So the Rangers and their juniors grew their walls and inside them raised their garden. The Master counted bricks and time to make and cure them, and counted children as they came inside the garden for their labours, and counted days and nights and lessons yet to teach, measuring all so all could be made right and true.

¹¹ Through their raising of the first fortress and their rescue of the lost and weak, while one and two years passed, Hru and Yinepu transmuted rage to calm, and enmity to union, and became brothers.

¹² Children pulled from savagery but not yet civilised challenged Yinepu, demanding, "Where is your vaunted Sorceress, Apprentice? Or are you just like us, a wretched jackal-pup who begs for scraps from madmen?" His belly screamed for him to strike them down, but grasping for the Master's rays, he left the fortress and was gone for days and nights as was his way.

¹³ Hru, who did not know his brother had departed, asked, "Who are you, Master Measurer, who saves children lost in these Savage Lands?" The Master said, "A Measurer once saved me in these lands, who was himself saved in his time by another, and before him too, and ever since the first sunrise. My mission is theirs, for my ancestors and I are one."

¹⁴ In awe of Master's wisdom, Hru asked the Measurer, "Why did the Destroyer kill my father, force my mother to flee, and bring misery upon the land?"

¹⁵ The Master whispered unto him, "The truth is like the sun: with the same rays a bringer of life and yet a champion of death. Sustainer and annihilator, it grows the one plant full and sweet, while it shrivels the other one into crackles. The time to know will come when it is right, but it is not right yet."

The Fifth Arit,

also called Father-Brother-Son

Hru tracks Yinepu to the City of Dogs and learns his origins

¹ When the moon had shrunk and swollen and Yinepu had still not yet returned, the Master sent the ranger Hru with aid of falcon ward to find his comrade, for Hru was eldest of the Measurer's clan, the bravest, most intelligent, the one to whom he'd taught the strongest words-of-power.

² And with those words young Hru traced Yinepu's path by following scent of heart-smoke while the sun was overhead, then slept inside his own-spun shadow while Falcon drank the night with gold and onyx eyes.

³ On second day, the ranger found a town with animals slain and blackened houses sacked and smouldering, where no child played, no father built, no mother ground their grain.

⁴ On third day, Hru and Falcon beheld mounds of severed hands a-swarmed with flies and stench revolting. And Hru said, "Who is this Destroyer, who dismembers thousands, turning fingers, thumbs and palms to hills?"

⁵ Finally on the fifth day, Hru, the boy who revolted against murderers in the night of fire, who stole a fang from the mouth of the Devourer and with it killed a crocodile in the Swamps of Death to avenge a child, who ranged the Savage Lands with only Falcon as his guardian, found a city of brick and stone, where dwelled ten thousand dogs, and one boy Yinepu, who cried while jackals stood their guard.

⁶ "Why did you not return?" asked Hru, to which Yinepu said, "I went to find my teacher-Sorceress, to hunt as she dispatched me for the prizes she does seek. Yet where she is, I do not know."

⁷ Together they left the City of Dogs, and in the night, when shadow-magic of exhausted Hru did fail, a crocodile yearning vengeance for his brother crept towards the sleeping ranger's body.

⁸ Yinepu and his jackals leapt upon the monster, none strong enough to best the beast alone, but as a force united battling it until Yinepu's fingers blinded it. And Hru said, "Truly, you are my brother."

⁹ When they returned, the Master Measurer embraced them, and they told their tales of rescue, to which the Master said, "Now is time for you to learn of the Destroyer."

¹⁰ The Master said, "Thirteen years ago returned Lord Usir, who'd ranged the world to spread his wisdom, to guide and teach the people of the Blackland once again, in justice and in wisdom with his Lady Aset, throne of power, at his side.

¹¹ "At banquet's height, Warmaster Set, with flattery and with guile, bore a present, a glorious pyrite chest, in which he tricked the Lord to lie. Latches fastened, molten metal poured, stilled quickly, and blades chased guests who scattered in the night like chaff from scythe.

¹² "Lady Aset's words-of-power slew a phalanx of the warlord's murderers, but Set's accursed pyrite charms crushed her speech to silence. His soldiers, slick with blood, took Lord Usir's body to the west, and butchered him in the north, sowing sacred members in the swamp, in soil, and in sand. And Lady Aset cried, wandered lost, and swore reckoning.

¹³ "You, Hru, are son to widow Lady Aset and her martyred husband, our Lord Usir. Warmaster Set, who rules our Blackland with wickedness and terror, is your uncle, known to you as the Destroyer.

¹⁴ "And you, Yinepu, Apprentice of the Sorceress, ranger of the Savage Lands, who hunts and is not hunted, jackal-guardian who raises of a Measurer's fortress, you are the Destroyer's son."

The Sixth Arit,
also called Mother-Sister-Daughter

Hru discovers the Sorceress whereafter he sins and suffers greatly

¹ The brother-bond was sundered by the Master's revelation, and Hru retreated to the Savage Lands to find his souls.

² Once-faithful Falcon, ever braver in his flight and ranging ever further, one day flew beyond Hru's vision and did not return by setting of the sun.

³ Hru, fang-wielder, crocodile-slayer, child-rescuer, waited for his ward, but nightsky filled with stars and nothing else. At dawn the young avenger, invoking words-of-power bequeathed to him by Master Measurer's wisdom, transformed himself into a falcon and cleaved the sky.

⁴ Growing weary from his maiden flight but having journeyed far from his community, Hru alighted in the City of Dogs, Yinepu's capitol, drawn by his Eye as honed by Master's mind. There inside a knot of vines upon a throne of onyx sat the one he knew must be Yinepu's Sorceress.

⁵ She called to him, "Falcon, to me," and without choice he fluttered to her, alighting on her arm, and she said, "Precious raptor, do you know me?"

⁶ And though two years had passed since last his eyes beheld her face, and though she was disguised with plaited hair and markings strange, he knew at once she was his mother, Lady Aset, and knowledge of it transformed him back to human shape, which she admired.

⁷ He demanded knowledge of her last two years, and she allowed his impudence an answer, that she'd been rallying an army, training bands of warriors and of warlocks, and tracking all the butchered members of her murdered husband, raising martyr-shrines at each chaotic grave, towards uniting all the sundry limbs by force divine to resurrect the Lord.

⁸ Yet Hru's belly burned with rage, for he discerned that Yinepu's many disappearances for days were to aid this Sorceress, his mother, who'd abandoned him and chose another boy for lessons, words-of-power, protection and a mother's holy love.

⁹ "My son," she said in her defense, "the war with cursed butcher Set divided us. I searched for you and found you not, but never for one heart-chime did I lose the scent of you, my precious child."

¹⁰ And Hru, his heart defiled by pain of lonely years, his spine bound by betrayal's chain, slashed out with monster's stolen fang, and cut off the head of Lady Aset, his own mother.

¹¹ And seeing the abomination of his crime, the doubly-orphaned matricidal boy fled into the labyrinths of dusk.

The Seventh Arit,
also called Replace-Elevate

Master Jehu grants to Hru an amulet

¹ With ranger Yinepu and his jackals, the Master traced the path of Hru unto the City of Dogs.

² He found the fallen Lady Aset, and with apprentice Yinepu and the anointing skills he'd taught to him, uttered secret words-of-power that focused light of Moon to fuse the head and body of the Sorceress to restore her life to her.

³ "Who are you?" she demanded, and he answered, "Master Jehu."

⁴ "I've heard your name, Lord Measurer, as

have all the wanderers of the Savage Lands and far beyond. It's said you harvest children after butchering their parents on the lonely walkways in the darkness. Are you the one who's trapped my son inside enchantments foul of your accursed prison?"

⁵ The apprentice Yinepu was filled with rage at accusations by his former master hurled upon his present one, and so his jackals' hackles raised to greet the battle that his fury signaled.

⁶ But Master Jehu bade him find his calm, like lotus flowers sipping of the morning mists.

⁷ The Master said to her, "In my compound, lost, abandoned children find a home, as was offered me so many years ago, and before that by my master's master, and his, until the time when cosmic egg first splintered and from it emerged the great Original. Your son's imprisoned by enchantments, aye, but not my own."

⁸ And the Sorceress Lady Aset, with Master Jehu and ranger Yinepu, began the journey back to walled community of Measurer and his children.

⁹ But the boy Hru was still not there when they returned. And Master Jehu, waiting for the night, used Moon as Eye to gaze upon the shadowed-blue and darkling world, and found the child trembling on an island in the Swamps of Death.

¹⁰ Descending there, he found the boy Hru and tried to comfort him with news of how he and Yinepu had saved the Lady Aset from the swift decay of death, but Hru, ashamed and stricken, would hear none of it. He cried, "Who was the Destroyer?" And so the Master saw the boy's devotion to Instruction.

¹¹ Using Moon as Eye again, the Master peered inside the shadow of Hru, and found a night of fire inside which children screamed and fled into the darkness; a swath of towns whose citizens were butchered inside blackened, smouldering homes; countless men of murderous knives and fingers cruel he'd met and never met who wished to strip his bones of meat; and the body of a headless mother on the sands beside a throne.

¹² "Your souls dwell here?" asked his Master, and Hru confessed they did. So Master Jehu took from round his neck a chain forged from heart of distant star. Speaking words-of-power, the Master said to Hru to clutch the talisman, whereupon his souls imprisoned slipped the grasp of all their tortures, and ascended to the palace of the rising sun. And Hru was free.

¹³ But Hru, then faltering in his ascent, asked, "Why did Falcon leave me, Master?"

¹⁴ And Master Jehu said to him, "All things meet the wind eventually, my son. For a thousand floods and thirteen thousand triumphs of the moon, I've found and gathered children wandering on these Savage Lands, fed them, held them, taught them, lost and grieved them.

¹⁵ "My souls are weary, and if ever I'm to be Triumphant in the House of Stars among the souls of my departed small ones, you, Hru, must build not my humble compound, but a golden fortress, immortal and invincible, to shine at rising of the sun for all the world to gaze upon in awe."

¹⁶ "How do I begin, my Master?" asked the boy whose spine was yoked with misery of the knowledge of his crime. And Master Jehu answered him, "Remove the rotten reeds and worm-bit wood, and in their stead place gold."

¹⁷ And so it was that young Hru, ranger of the Savage Lands, rescuer of children doomed by crocodiles, murderer of his mother in the City of Dogs, began to carve a channel with the fang of the Devourer to drain the Swamps of Death.

The Eighth Arit,
also called Righteousness & Mastery

The compound falls to war

¹ While Hru recruited all his might to drain the Swamps of Death, Master Jehu's well-trained scouts ranged far to measure strength of gathering hordes of killers, for Set, the lord of war, designed annihilation for his foes.

² Across the Blackland and the Savage Lands, the Lady Aset's fighters hid in nests like cobras did, yet cover would not save them from the ravenous inferno that approached.

³ Uttering words-of-power, the Sorceress instructed Jehu's children to assemble for the coming war and arm themselves, but the Master said to her, "These innocents must not be sacrificed upon the horror-plains of arrows, knives, and screaming butchery, but cultivated, nurtured, so they might generate abundance for the world."

⁴ And the Sorceress said to him, "When the Destroyer's stuffed his belly full with children's hearts, these young ones' sole abundance will be meat-picked bones upon the tortured earth, or are you blind to this, o madman in the marsh?"

⁵ So Master Jehu said to her, "I've seen the wastelands left by soldiers in the villages, the devastated crops and knackered beasts, the starving, sobbing orphans, where the armies of the Warmaster had rested without slaughter. So tell me, Lady Aset, widow of the fallen Lord Usir, Sorceress-bonder of soldier-infants, who in those hinterlands was the Destroyer?"

⁶ And the Lady Aset, her belly burning at the Master's inquiry, fell silent at the sight of Hru the Labourer.

⁷ The two killers, son and mother, gazed upon each other seeing all that might have been that never more could be.

⁸ "Mother Aset," said the Labourer, "these Savage Lands and Swamps of Death afflict the body of our people like a poison. I beg of you: Instruct these children in your secret means, so we might drain these Swamps to clear these lands for habitation, and drive the scale-bound butchers to western lands, and carve a channel straight and true for the Eternal River even here."

⁹ And even Lady Aset, fearing growing chaos brought by men of murderous knives and fingers cruel, heard the truth in her son's words, and took their counsel.

¹⁰ So she Instructed words-of-power to the lost who'd found the Master, and with her son Hru and nephew Yinepu as her two foremen, in righteous labour Jehu's children carved great channels in the loam and then into the sandlands, and in the months while fetid waters sank to earth they gained their mastery.

¹¹ And lying at the bottom of the revealed valley was a cavern at whose centre was the sacred skull of Lord Usir.

¹² And Lady Aset wept.

¹³ So she dispatched her son, transformed into a falcon, to fetch the members of the martyred Lord that Yinepu'd embalmed and she had hidden. He'd ranged across the Blackland and the Savage Lands to find them all, had even found the severed manhood that the oxyrhincus swallowed from the scattering of the Night of Butchering.

¹⁴ When he returned with holy treasure, the Sorceress and Labourer and Anointer Yinepu descended to the cavern to unite the far-flung members. Using gold made molten by the Lady Aset's whispers, the trio, joined by Master Measurer, melded limbs with trunk and then with skull.

¹⁵And in the world of black below, with Lady Aset, son Hru, nephew Yinepu and Master Jehu, the Great Instructor, Lord of Limits, and Being Beautiful, sat upon a throne of turquoise shining from ten thousand years of darkness.

¹⁶ "Return," said he, "to world of tears in righteousness and mastery, to make stand

those who weep, to reveal those who hide their faces and to lift up those who sink down, so all the world might rise nearer to Supreme."

[17] And Lady Aset bade the others to return, so without audience she might commune with her beloved. So the men ascended, found their way in night back towards the compound, where slaughterers with murderous knives and fingers cruel and abominations magical drove a spear through heart of Master Jehu.

[18] Hru and Yinepu battled with the butchers, Hru unleashing Devourer's fang and Yinepu attacking with his jackals, but invaders were well-armoured and well-armed. Hru commanded Yinepu to save the children, and then he fought alone and could not win.

[19] And then the fratricide, the burner of the groves, the devastator of the Blackland, the brother of the father of Hru, Set the general slid from shadows to reveal himself, girded in the squared-horned helmet forged for war.

[20] And with his nephew bound in pyrite fetters, Set defiled him while his soldiers burned the compound into ashes.

The Ninth Arit, also called Create-Supreme

The Contendings of Hru and Set

[1] Inside the ancient cavern, Yinpu embalmed the Master and all the fallen children of the compound, wrapped their limbs in linens, sealed them inside chests and planted them as seeds.

[2] Tending to her shattered son, the Sorceress taught Yinepu all her healing balms and words-of-power, and slowly wounds of Hru's body turned invisible.

[3] Then on the shortest day, Lady Aset strategised with wisest of the orphans of Jehu, who now had grown to adults, Instructing them in medicine of murder she prescribed.

[4] Hru chose his protégés, Duamutef and Hapi, Qebehsenuef and Imset, the blacksmiths four, to turn the skin of orphans into shells and hands to claws.

[5] And so began two hundred moons of war.

[6] The blacksmiths four transformed a liberated cache of gold into a million shining spades, and everywhere the Labourers went, they dug canals to drain the Swamps of Death into the Redlands, so the Eternal River's flow could purify the Savage Lands, and those who'd drunk the poison could then find new life.

[7] The revolution rose in glory, spread its rays, shattering shackles of the weepers so they'd stand, piercing palaces and prisons to reveal the hidden faces, and reaching in the lead and pyrite mines like cables lifting up the many who'd sunk down.

[8] And in fifteenth and final year of massacres and misery, of hiding in the hinterlands and striking in the night, Hru, Wielder of Devouver's Fang, Drainer of the Swamps of Death, Resurrector of the Lord of Limits, met on facing banks of the Eternal River the fratricide and Warmaster, Usurper, Desert-Dweller, and Storm-Bringer, the Great Defiler, Set.

[9] "You, boy, Sparrow-Prince," called the murdering uncle of Hru, while River flowed between two armies tensed to execute each other, "I had your father knackered, chased your mother into exile, lanced your Master, burnt your fortress into embers, and stole and crushed your manhood. Who among the peoples of the Blackland could ever bow to you? You are no king to anything but loss! I'm your better and your master. Yield to me and I will let you slave beside my sandal!"

[10] And Hru, learned in three masters' words-of-power, stilled his belly and his mouth but raised his fang. On the battlers

charged through river to embrace each other in vengeance and in death.

¹¹ Set transformed himself into abomination, a crocodile-man without a heart but with a belly. Hru became a falcon-man, who flew and hurled his spear with Fang upon the head of hated kin. And so the battle churned for days.

¹² And when the sun descended on the third evening of combat, the young insurgent recognised that no matter of his might, he could not defeat the chaos-maker Set, unless he burned the world eternally.

¹³ So he spoke a grim surrender which his warriors heard with terror. Holding spear to stars, he called, "Come, Grinder of Bones, Shaker of the Earth, Eater of Old Gods, take from me my priceless prize of stolen weapon, if you dare!"

¹⁴ And Set, in laughter and in rage, raced forward with his blade to eviscerate his nephew, who handed him his weapon mighty. "Now let the all the lands behold this!" raged Destroyer. "The coward-slave surrenders, groveling for mercy from his Master! And with this captured prize I'll give it to him!"

¹⁵ Then the Devourer of Millions of Souls arose from river's depths to suck Destroyer in its terrible maw of a thousand fangs less one.

¹⁶ But mighty Set was clad in pyrite armour thoroughly unpierceable. He stood on monster's tongue and grabbed two tusks above him, so the beast could not bring shut the trap that had doomed millions.

¹⁷ And on the river's edge appeared the Measurer transfigured, with disc of moon above his head, surrounded by academy of baboons and heralded by an ibis. He whispered to the Sorceress, who heard him well.

¹⁸ And so it was that Lady Set, mother of Hru, Sorceress, Instructor of Yinepu, leader of an army, destroyer of cities, splashed forth to meet her husband's brother in embrace, hurtling so the two fell backwards in the mouth of the Devourer, which shut its jaws, descending to the deeps.

¹⁹ And the Ancestor Jehutí spoke a final time before ascending to the moon: "The time to end this war is now. So go to heal each other, bearing witness to the sun, while you raise a golden fortress for eternity."

²⁰ So Hru the Labourer and Warrior and now the King, alighted on a hill and said unto his battle-mates: "By the sunrise, let us create hope, joy and justice, to make stand those who weep, to reveal those who hide their faces and to lift up those who sink down. In doing so, we will all rise nearer to the Supreme."

The Tenth Arit, also called Peace˜Life˜Eternal

The enthronement of Sun King Hru

¹ Hru and Measurer's orphans found the vanquished general's lead and pyrite palace, and wielding cleansing fire, sent the structure back to earth from which it came.

² Descending to the cavern, Hru communed with Lord Usir and saw upon his father's dais stood his mother, Lady Aset, and behind her, Set, his uncle. His father whispered to him words he shared with no one else, and gave to him a black and shining satchel filled with gemstone seeds. And Hru returned to world of light and brought his

people with him southward to the cradle.

³ Beside Eternal River planted they the gemstone seeds, and from the loam arose a treasury of maize and lotus.

⁴ With Master Yinepu as foremost mason, they hewed stone blocks and squared a base for soaring walls, which blacksmiths four, the adopted sons of Hru, covered then with gold.

⁵ Inside the Golden Fortress sanctuary dwelt the sufferers from two hundred moons of war and more before them, who

dined on golden maize and drank the water from the River of Life.

⁶ The Anointer and Embalmer of Lord Usir, Weigher of Righteousness, Prince of the Divine Court, Vizier of all the Blackland, the Jackal-Man, the venerable Master Yinepu tasked the blacksmiths four, Duamutef and Hāpi, Imset and Qebehsunuef, with the righteous three Maā-Atef-f, Kheri-Beq-f and Hru-Khenti-Maā, to be the Seven Shining Ones to guard the sacred cavern where the body of Lord Usir was the seed for spring for millions upon millions of renewings.

⁷ And so the Hidden Orphan, Ranger of the Savage Lands, Wielder of the Fang of the Devourer, Jehutí's Disciple, Atoning Labourer, Drainer of the Swamps of Death, Vanquisher of the Destroyer, Avenger of Lord Usir, the Falcon-Man and Sun King Hru, enthroned in his great house, the Golden Fortress, then granted laws, bequeathed Instructions, rendered verdicts and gazed upon a hundred thousand risings of the sun.

⁸ And on his final night before ascending to the House of Stars, he blessed Master Jehutí's orphans with a litany of wisdom, concluding through a final verse demanding duty:

⁹ "Protect the Golden Fortress. Grow its walls and ever open keep its gates to welcome vulnerable and powerful alike. But should deceivers ever crust its walls with pyrite, do not rest your hammers and if necessary melt the palace to the ground and start anew, to raise this fortress for the world for all eternity."

FALCONIC GLOSSARY

Starred entries denote the Alphabetical Alchemy

A

A* Africentric: "Africentric means centered on Africa and Africans, our civilisations, sciences, arts, histories, heroes, struggles, pains and triumphs, wherever we are in the world and whenever we exist in time."

Alchemical Alphabet and Numerals: In **Alchemy**, the contemplative associations for each letter of the alphabet and numerals 1 through 9 and ending in 0, used especially in Daily Alchemy.

Alchemists: A secret, Africentric mystical society founded by Cheikh Anta **Diop**. Also called the Alchemical Order, the Alchemical Society, and the Pan-African Order of Alchemy.

Alchemy: The collected mythology, practices, and values of the Alchemists for personal and planetary liberation and transformation.

Alchemy, Daily: For Alchemists, the practice of individual or group reflections and goal-setting through meditation upon the *Nub-Wmet-Ānkh*.

Am-mít: The Eater of Souls at the final judgement. All whose hearts were not "as light as the feather" (see **Maāt**) faced oblivion in the mouth of the crocodile-hippopotamus monster.

Ānkh: 1. "Life." 2. The loop-cross symbol of life; two ankhiu together mean "eternal life." Known around the Mediterranean for thousands of years, the ānkh may have inspired early Christians, until then using the fish as their symbol, to adopt the cross as their icon.

Ārit: "Chapter," especially in *Pert-em-Hru* or *The Book of the Golden Falcon*.

Aset, Lady: Queen of Kemet, wife of Lord Usir, mother of Hru. Called Isis in Greek.

B

B* Build: "To build means to assemble internal or external things into new forms, especially to make that which is beneficial to life."

Ba: In Kemetic religion, one of the human souls, represented as a bird with a human head.

Book of the Dead, the: Misnomer. See Pert-em-Hru.

Book of the Golden Falcon, the: The central modern allegorical text of the Alchemists, written originally in Wolof (possibly by Cheikh Anta Diop) and translated by senior Alchemists into various languages. The story of the passion of Lord Usir, the lamentations of Aset, and the contendings of Hru and Set.

By the sunrise/sunset: Oath, as in "indeed" or "damn straight!"

C

C* Create: "To create means to bring into existence that which did not exist before."

D

D* Divine: "Divine means godly, ideal or perfect, or to foretell the future."

Delta: 1. The northernmost region of the Nile, where the river branches into a triangular pattern like the Greek letter of the same name; the same area, added to the Nile's "stem," is sometimes called "the Lotus." Before being drained, the area was a crocodile-infested swamplands covering hundreds of square kilometres. 2. In mathematics, "change," "difference" or "transformation".

Destroyer, the: 1. Set. 2. Any person whose deeds causes needless suffering of other beings.

Devourer of Millions of Souls, the: See **Am-mít.**

Diop, Cheikh Anta: Senegalese Egyptologist and author of *The African Origin of Civilisation: Myth or Reality?* among many other works. Prior to Martin Bernal's publication of *Black Athena: The Afroasiatic Roots of Classical Civilisation*, Diop's work was the leading text attacking the Whitewashing of Ancient Egypt and asserting its Africanity.

Duamutef: One of the four sons of Hru ("Praises his mother").

E

E* Evolve: "Evolve means growth into new forms because of differences previously not perceived as advantages."

F

F* Family: "Family is genetic relationship, meaning connection of origins, and relationship of deep devotion."

G

G* Geometry: "Geometry is literally the measurement of the Earth, but universally describes shapes and spatial relationships. To build anything of greatness, one must understand forms and relationships, and therefore geometry."

Geometrical: A compliment meaning "exactly," "perfect," or "it all adds up."

Gold: Knowledge, especially that which expands justice, compassion and beauty.

Gold-minding: The Alchemical use hypnosis, self-hypnosis and guided imagery for self-mastery and elevation.

Golden Fortress: See *Nub-Wmet-Ãnkh.*

H

H* Hero: "A hero is one who struggles at great risk, not for personal reward, but to defend the vulnerable and create justice."

Hăpí: 1.The Holy River Nile. 2. One of the four sons of Hru.

Heka Khasut: "Shepherd Kings," also called "foreign dominators" and "the Sea People," but known to Moderns as the Hyksos. After settling in and eventually overwhelming Lower Kemet, these West Asian nomads destroyed the Middle Kingdom. Nisut Ahmose led a revolutionary war expelling them, thereby establishing Dynasty XVIII.

Hotep em maãkheru: "Peace and triumph (to you)."

Hru: Heir to Lord Usir, the Sun-King of Kemet, defeater of Set. His many titles include Hru-Netch-Hri-Yitef-f ("Heru the Avenger of his father") and Hru-sa-Aset-sa-Usir ("Heru, son of Aset, son of Usir").

I

I* Individuality/Intelligence: "Individuality is the possession of unique characteristics and personal perspectives, behaviour, and goals. Intelligence is the geometry of all mental capabilities including internal and external awareness, creativity, analysis, memory, and emotion."

Imhotep: History's first recorded multigenius (ca. 2650-2600 BCE). Architect of the Step Pyramid, the world's first mega-structure. A poet, the true father of medicine, and Grand Vizier under Pharaoh Joser.

Imset: One of the four sons of Hru.

Instructions: Kemetic moral and social teachings, as in *The Instructions of Ptah-Hotep*.

Isfet: Disorder, deceit, chaos, disharmony, temptation, sin.

Iten: The disk of the sun. Claimed by Pharaoh Ikh-en-Iten, the world's first recorded monotheist, as the most visible and dazzling emblem of the One God. Also, Iton and Aton.

J

J* Justice: "Justice is equality of rights and treatment, proportionate compensation for labour and punishment for crime, and compassion and relief for sufferers."

Jehutí: The netjer of wisdom, science, writing, and other mental disciplines. Jehutí's emblem is the ibis (tehu, tekhu), probably because the name "Jehutí" comes from the moon, Jehu, as time-keeper; Jehutí means "The Measurer." The Greek name for Jehutí is Thoth, and Greek mythology's version of Jehutí is Hermes, providing the terms "hermetically sealed" and "Hermetic Tradition" (a secret knowledge system requiring initiation for access).

K

K* Knowledge: "Knowledge is the application of intelligence to information."

Ka: In Kemetic theology, a person's soular "double," depicted as one's coal-black duplicate; the hieroglyph for ka is two upraised arms.

Kemet: "The Black Land," meaning both "of the black soil," and "Land of the Blacks," as in "Black Africa." Indigenous name for Egypt (Gk.=Aigyptos, from Het-Ka-Ptah, or House of the Ka of Ptah).

Khair: "Street" or "King's Road." For E-Town Alchemists, the following roads range between 124th Street on the west 84th Street on the east.

Khair-em-Sokar: 118th Avenue, named for Het-Ka-Sokar ("House of the Ka of Sokar," called Sakkara in Arabic).

Khair-em-Ãnkh-Tawy: 111th Avenue, named for Ãnkh-Tawy ("Life of the Two Lands," another name for Waset, called Thebes in Greek and Luxor in Arabic.)

Khair-em-Nubt: 107th Avenue, named for Nubt ("City of Gold," called Kom Ombo in Coptic).

Kheper: Scarab.

Kheperi: The scarab god, whose androgynous insect counterpart rolls its dung-ball eggsack across the sand as the sun is "rolled" across the sky.

Kheperu: From E.A. Budge: "1. To create, form or fashion; form, phase of being, something evolved, transformation, revolution, evolution; those who become."

Khetiuta: Fiends or devils.

L

L* Liberate: "To liberate is to free those who are unfree."

Laboratory: Any place of Alchemical labour.

Leadite: Any of the eighty per cent of humanity who is easily tricked by the Pyrites into relinquishing his or her gold and thereby dwelling in poverty and ignorance.

M

M* Minister: "A minister is one who ministers. To minister is to care for and serve others."

Maã: Justice; unalterable cosmic law.

Maãkheru: 1. "Triumphant; vindicated." 2. "Resurrected."

Maafa: The European and Arab holocaust in Africa, including Atlantic and Pacific human, the subsequent genocidal military occupations of the continent, and the proxy wars of the neo-colonial period, whose combined death toll exceeds, conservatively, 80 million.

Maãt: 1. "Right, true, straight." 2. The netjer of justice, represented as a woman with a feather (the Maãt feather) suspended above her head.

Manu: Mountain range west of the Holy River Nile.

Medu netjer: "Words divine." Hieroglyphics.

Menfítu: Soldiers.

Meröe: A pyramid-building ancient civilisation of Sudan.

Mesnet: Any Alchemical base of operations (lit., "foundry").

Mesnitu: Blacksmiths, i.e., followers of Hru of Behudet (the Lord of the Forge-City, Edfu).

N

N* Nature: "Nature is the universe, everything it contains, and the way it behaves."

Narmer: Semi-mythical first king in the Archaic Period. He united of the Two Lands in a military victory recorded on the proto-hieroglyphic Narmer's Palette, a bas-relief stone tablet. (Also, "Mena" and "Menes.")

Nebt-het: Sister of Lady Aset, wife of Set, mother of Yinepu. Literally, Lady of the House. Called Nepthys in Greek.

Nefer: Good, happy, beautifully-spoken; divinely beautiful. Plural is neferu.

Netjer: 1. A "god," or the name of a divine aspect, e.g., justice (Maät), industry (Ptah), science (Jehutí), etc. 2. Holy or sacred.

Nile: 1. Hāpi, the largest river in North Africa, and lifeblood of Kemet. 2. In E-Town, the North Saskatchewan River.

Nisut: King.

Nome: A district of ancient Kemet which, in religious terms, had its own twinned region in heaven.

Noot: The sky netjer of Kemet.

Nub-Wmet-Ānkh: 1. Lit, "Gold, fortifications, life." Greeting. 2. "The Golden Fortress of Life" or "the Golden Fortress," an alternate name for the Alchemists. 3. The oath forming the basis of Daily Alchemy, employing the ten Alchemical Numerals.

Nubian: 1. Literally, any member of the Nubian nationality of Sudan, found also in Egypt. 2. The language of the Nubians. 3. An Alchemist; one who has transmuted his Lead into Gold (nub is Ancient Egyptian for "gold," as Nubia was rich in gold).

O

O* Orbit: "To orbit is to circle a body because of its superior mass and gravity, but both orbiter and orbited exert power over each other."

P

P* Power: "Power is the ability to make things happen, meaning to create, build, replace, elevate, degrade, or destroy."

Pert-em-Hru: "The Book of Coming Forth By Day," the Kemetic resurrection manual for the souls of the dead, recorded on papyrus and inserted into the coffins of the dead whose families could afford them.

Pharaoh: Hebrew version of Per-āā, or "Great House." See **Nisut**.

Professor X: Dr. Foday Xaasongaxango, a student of Cheikh Anta Diop and adept in Diop's Shemsu-Hru. Acknowledged as the English translator of The ***Book of the Golden Falcon*** (unofficially credited to Diop), he may have written much or all of it.

Ptah: The netjer of construction, portrayed as a potter. Ptah-worship was centered in Het-Ka-Ptah ("House of the Ka of Ptah"), a name the Greeks turned into Aigyptos and the Anglo-Saxons rendered as Egypt.

Pyrite: 1. Iron sulfide (FeS_2), or "fool's gold." 2. Any of the ten per cent of the human race who deceives and defrauds eighty per cent to control them so as to live in splendour with impunity.

Q

Q* Question: "To question is seek information so as to expand intelligence. Failing to question is to stagnate or destroy intelligence."

Qebehsunuef: One of the four sons of Hru.

R

R* Revolution: "Revolution is revolving or total change internally or externally."

Rā: The eagle-headed netjer, chosen by some priesthoods as the supreme netjer of the universe.

Rebarna: Modern Lebanon and nearby land, known also as Phoenicia or Canaan.

S

S* Simultaneous: "Simultaneous means existence or action of two or more things at the same time."

Savage Lands, the: 1. The Delta, the brutal land of slavery and war, centre of the Destroyer's empire. 2. Symbolically, any place of strife and misery.

Scroll: Any Alchemical document, whether brief enough to be printed and rolled into cigarette size, or large enough to fill chapters.

Set: Brother and murderer of Lord Usir, also called the Destroyer.

Shemsu-Hru: 1. "The Bodyguards (or, Followers) of Hru." 2. The Alchemists.

Shenu or shen-ring: 1. In medu netjer, the rope-line encircling the names of kings and queens. 2. In Alchemy, any group circle, especially for reciting the Daily Alchemy.

Street Falcon: Any member of the E-Town based offshoot of the Alchemist Society.

T

T* Truth: "Truth means that which actually is, as opposed to lies, incorrect beliefs, fantasies or foolishness, and exists independently of thinkers."

Ta-Setí: "The Land of the Bow." Nubia.

Throne, the: A name for Lady Aset.

Transform: 1. Interjection of encouragement. 2. As a verb, a synonym for "understand," as in "Can you transform that?"

Transformed: Interjection meaning "victory," "justified," or simply, "excellent."

Two Lands, the: Ancient name Kemet, the state formed around 3400 BCE by southern king Narmer (Mena) by annexing the northern Delta kingdom.

Two Rangers: Hru and Yinepu, especially before coming under the guidance of Master Jehu.

U

U* Unite/Universal: "To unite is to bring together. Universal means existing throughout the universe, or throughout human affairs."

Ujat: "The Eye of Hru" or Eye of God, the hieroglyph and amulet of a stylised falcon eye. In Kemetic mathematics, its various parts representing fractions ½, ¼, 1/8, 1/16, 1/32 and 1/64, giving a total of 63/64, implying a whole greater than the sum of its parts, and a progression towards infinity. Also spelled *utchat*, *utjat* and *watchet*.

Un-Nefer: Lord Usir following his resurrection, meaning "the beautiful being," "the ever-joyful one," or "the beautiful hare."

Usir, Lord: The mythical founder of pre-historical Kemet who introduced law, agriculture and moral philosophy (the lost Instructions of Lord Usir) in neighbouring countries. Assassinated by his brother Set. With his wife, the Lady Aset, he posthu-mously sired son Hru. In the Duat, Lord Usir discovered the techniques of resurrection and revealed the Wisdom through his son and other mystics. Hru avenged his father to take the throne. Called Osiris in Greek.

V

V* Victory: "Victory means triumph over obstacles or enemies, internal or external."

W

W* Wisdom: "Wisdom is the application of intelligence towards action and justice."

Wanderers: The orphans and other displaced people in the Savage Lands, and a more compassionate term for Leadites.

Waset: Capitol of Kemet in Dynasty XI and most of Dynasty XVIII, except during the Ikh-en-Iten Revolt when the capitol was transferred to Iakhut-et-Iten. The Vatican of the ancient world. Called Thebes in Greek, Al Uqsor in Arabic and Luxor in English.

X

X* X-ray: "X-rays are short wavelengths of electromagnetic radiation produced when high-speed electrons strike solid targets. To X-ray is to look through opaque surfaces to see what is hidden within."

Y

Y* Yam: "A yam is a tuber or root, the base of its plant, rich in sweetness and nutrients. The yam symbolises origins."

Yimun: The hidden netjer ("The Mysterious One" or "The Hidden One"), spelled
variously as Amen, Amon, Amun, Imen and
Imun.

Yinepu: Cousin and ally of Hru, son of Set
and Nebt-Het, Yinepu assists resurrection as
a guide or guardian of the dead. His symbol
is the black jackal. Called Anubis in Greek.

Z

Z* Zenith: "The zenith is the supreme or
highest point in a sphere, opposite of the
nadir."

ANCIENT KUSH

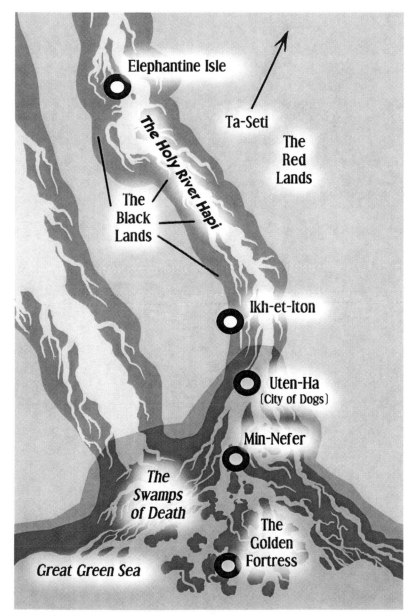

Elephantine Isle

The Holy River Hapi

Ta-Seti

The Red Lands

The Black Lands

Ikh-et-Iton

Uten-Ha
(City of Dogs)

Min-Nefer

The Swamps of Death

The Golden Fortress

Great Green Sea

MODERN KUSH

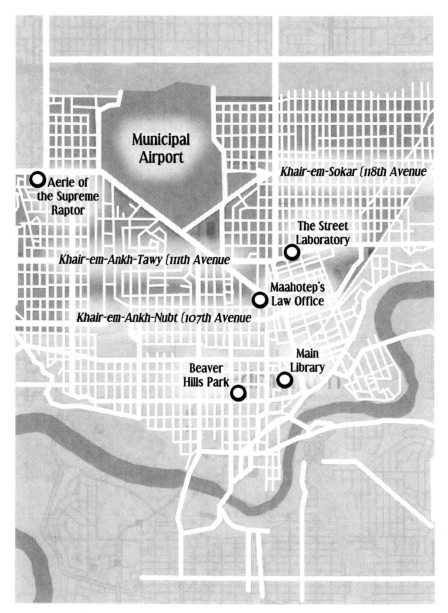

Municipal
Airport

Aerie of
the Supreme
Raptor

Khair-em-Sokar (118th Avenue

The Street
Laboratory

Khair-em-Ankh-Tawy (111th Avenue

Maahotep's
Law Office

Khair-em-Ankh-Nubt (107th Avenue

Main
Library

Beaver
Hills Park

SOURCES FOR FURTHER READING

The ideas that went into this novel were gestating in my mind for more than twenty years. The seeds found soil when I began learning in the late 1980s about the Nation of Gods and Earths, also known as the Five Percenters, and sprouted shoots and leaves when I attended the 1995 Million Man March in Washington, D.C.

Although the story in this novel's "Book of Now" is inspired by the history of the NGE, I can't stress enough that my story is far from a rigid parallel. Some members of the NGE, doubtless, will be offended by this book, and I'd like to assure them that doing so was never my plan.

The richest histories offer endlessly fascinating opportunities for allegories, and I've always loved allegories. I hope that Earths and Gods will take this book the way that some Muslim and Arab readers take Frank Herbert's *Dune* (an allegory for the Arab Revolt in which T.E. Laurence participated)—not as the forensic photograph of a victim, but as the reflection of a face in a rippling pond.

Below is an excerpt from the list of resources that inspired this novel. If you're interested in reading or viewing more about the ideas, personalities, and histories dramatised in *The Alchemists of Kush*, I hope you'll find these sources enriching.

HISTORY OF KEMET

Mario Beatty. *Reflections on Cheikh Anta Diop.* http://www.video.google.com/videoplay?docid=-3434087937070392047#

Martin Bernal. *Black Athena: The Afroasiatic Roots of Classical Civilisation* (*The Fabrication of Ancient Greece* 1785-1985, Volume I). Rutgers University Press, 1991.

Cheikh Anta Diop. *The African Origin of Civilisation: Myth or Reality?* Lawrence Hill Books, 1989.

Shomarka Keita. *Ancient Egypt, Its Neolithic History and its Sudanese & Saharan Connections.* http://www.youtube.com/watch?v=WoeELytDAFo

Richard Poe. *Black Spark, White Fire: Did African Explorers Civilise Ancient Europe?* Prima Lifestyles, 1999.

SUDANESE REFUGEE EXPERIENCES

"The Long Journey: Sudanese Refugees in Mississippi Tell Their Stories." http://www.millsaps.edu/news_events/releases/february/thelongjourney-completecolor.pdf

MYTH, MANHOOD AND EDUCATION

Robert Bly. *Iron John*. Perseus Books, 1990.

Wallis Budge. *Egyptian Religion* [1900]. Citadel Press, 1987. *[I include it here because it contains Plutarch's rendering of the* Passion of Usir, *the* Lamentations of Aset, *and the* Contendings of Set and Hru.*]*

Geoffrey Canada. *Reaching Up for Manhood: Transforming the Lives of Boys in America*. Bacon Press, 1998.

Clyde W. Ford. *The Hero with an African Face: Mythic Wisdom of Traditional Africa*. Bantam, 2000.

Jawanza Kunjufu. *Countering the Conspiracy to Destroy Black Boys*. http://www.youtube.com/watch?v=FhZzIx6aKqw

Joseph E. Marshall and Lonnie Wheeler. *Street Soldier: One Man's Struggle to Save a Generation, One Life at a Time*. VisionLines Publishing, 2000.

THE NATION OF GODS AND EARTHS, AKA THE FIVE PERCENTERS

C'BS Alife Allah. *Journal of Allah's Five Percent*. http://www.allahsfivepercent.blogspot.com

Saladin Quanaah Allah. *ASIA: Allah School in Atlantis*. http://www.atlantisschool.blogspot.com

Wakeel Allah. *In the Name of Allah*. A-Team Publishing, 2009.

Karl Evanzz. *The Judas Factor: The Plot to Kill Malcolm X*. Thunder's Mouth Press, 1993.

Karl Evanzz. *The Messenger: The Rise and Fall of Elijah Muhammad*. Vintage, 2000.

Mattias Gardell. *In the Name of Elijah Muhammad: Louis Farrakhan and the Nation of Islam*. Duke University Press Books, 1996.

Michael Muhammad Knight. *The Five Percenters*. Oneworld, 2008.

Felicia M. Miyakawa. *Five Percenter Rap: God Hop's Music, Message, and Black Muslim Mission*. Indiana University Press, 2005.

Prince-A-Cuba. "Black Gods of the Inner City." http://www.geocities.com/dre_wali/blackgods.htm

Ted Swedenburg. "Islam in the Mix: Lessons of the Five Percent." http://www.comp.uark.edu/~tsweden/5per.html

The Music of
THE ALCHEMISTS OF KUSH

I've been a lover of a wide range of music my entire life, perhaps largely because of my mother's diverse tastes. I grew especially to love the synergy of music and story I found in television and movies, and how some writers (especially Alan Moore in his landmark series Watchmen) could invoke music in a silent medium to comment upon their stories.

Like many writers, while I write, I play music constantly to inspire me. Sometimes the songs of my work-time soundtrack find themselves embedded in the stories themselves. So even when the narrative demanded that readers couldn't know most of those selections (as with Shrinking the Heroes), music has been part of every novel and screenplay I've ever written.

The Alchemists of Kush contains reference to what I think is the largest number of songs in any of my published or yet-to-be-published manuscripts. Thanks to the linkability of ebooks (and typed urls in paper books), I can actually, finally, connect readers directly with music I love, and hopefully help musicians to sell a few mp3s and even some albums.

So please visit the music page of ministerfaust.com for videos of most of the songs in this book, plus purchase-links for each album. And I'd love to hear from you about your reactions to these songs, especially if these artists are new to you.

ABOUT
MINISTER FAUST

Minister Faust is a writer. When he was 17 he wrote and directed his first play, the science fiction drama *The Undiscovered Country*, in Montreal. He has written and performed sketch comedy for *The 11:02 Show* and *Gordon's Big Bald Head* at the Edmonton International Fringe Festival, and video game content for BioWare and Maxis.

In addition to having written advertising copy, he's an award-winning print journalist who's published scores of articles for publications including *The Globe and Mail*, *i09*, Greg Tate's *Coon Bidness*, and *Adventure Rocketship*. He's an award-winning radio journalist who hosted *Africentric Radio* (originally *The Terrordome*), Canada's then longest-running Africentric current affairs program (1991 – 2012).

As a radio and print journalist, Minister Faust went as far as the 1995 Million Man March in Washington, DC and to the Ain-al-Hilweh Palestinian refugee camp in southern Lebanon to collect stories and hear directly from people living and making history. He also worked in television, including as a judge on two seasons of the ground-breaking reality show *The 3-Day Novel Contest*, and co-hosted and associate-produced the final season of the live national daily *HelpTV*. He's taught print journalism to youth writers, and radio interview technique to community broadcasters.

As a member of E-Town's anti-fascist movement in 1990, Minister Faust and other youth marched on a Nazi skinhead gang house, the hub at that time for a series of violent assaults. Confronted there by skinheads with guns, Minister Faust held them back with nothing but the power of his words. Thus began a speaking career that has taken him across Canada and before crowds in the tens of thousands for workers, multiculturalism, and peace. He also teaches public speaking and delivered the TEDx presentation "The Cure for Death By Small-Talk" which has been watched by almost three quarters of a million people.

Having taught English Literature in E-Town junior high and high schools for a decade, Minister Faust later worked as a mentor and trainer for the Keshotu Leadership Academy, an Africentric organisation whose manual he wrote. He's also taught creative writing for Alberta's YouthWrite, at Clarion West in Seattle, and Shared Worlds in Spartanburg, South Carolina; presented at the Science Fiction Research Association Conference in Detroit, at Georgia Tech and at California State University at Los Angeles Eagle Con on Africentric science fiction and fantasy, and at the University of Illinois at Urbana-Champaign Writing Another Future conference on eschatology in Parliament-Funkadelic. He was the writer in residence at for the English and Film Studies Department of the University of Alberta (2014-2015).

Minister Faust currently hosts the podcast MF GALAXY on pop culture, politics, Africentricity, and writers on the craft and business of writing. His many guests have included Wayne Arthurson (*Fall from Grace*), Molefi Kete Asante (*Afrocentricity*), Martin Bernal (*Black Athena*), Chuck D., (*Fear of a Black Planet*), Ernest Dickerson (*Juice*), Tananarive Due (*My Soul to Keep*), Maria Dunn (*Piece by Piece*), Brandon Easton (*Agent Carter*), Karl Evanzz (*The Judas Factor: The Plot to Kill Malcolm X*), Antony Q. Farrell (*The Office*), Sylvia Feketekuty (*Mass Effect 3*), Tom Fontana (*Oz*), Rick Green (*Four on the Floor*), Andrea Hairston (*Will Do Magic for Small Change*), Faith Erin Hicks (*The Nameless City*), Nalo Hopkinson (*Brown Girl in the Ring*), Reginald Hudlin (*Black Panther*), N.K. Jemisin (*The Killing Moon*), Joy Lusco Kecken (*Homicide*), Michael Parenti (*The Assassination of Julius Caesar*), Eden Robinson (*Monkey Beach*), Gil Scott-Heron (*Winter in America*), Charles Saunders (*Imaro*), Robert J. Sawyer (*Quantum Night*), David Simon (*The Wire*), Jay Turner (*Army of Two: The Devil's Cartel*), Kenneth T. Williams (*Thunderstick*), and. Gene Luen Yang (*American Born Chinese*). The show provides subscribers-only bonus content featuring craft and business advice by famous, successful writers in every field.

A maverick novelist determined to push the frontiers, Minister Faust is the author of the critically acclaimed *The Coyote Kings, Book One: Space-Age Bachelor Pad*, and the Kindred Award-winning *Shrinking the Heroes*. He refers to his sub-genre of writing as Imhotep-Hop—an Africentric literature that draws from myriad ancient African civilisations, explores present realities, and imagines a future in which people struggle not only for justice, but for the stars.

He lives in Edmonton with his wife and daughters.

ACKNOWLEDGEMENTS

Thanks to the many people who gave me information and/or resources critical to the formation of *The Alchemists of Kush*:

The Alberta Foundation for the Arts for its generous financial support.

Saladin Quanaah Allah for his encouragement of the aims of this project.

Anonymous posters at Rapdict.org for their perspectives on the gangs of E-Town, particularly their comments about neo-Nazis, some of which I've given to Jackal.

The first readers of the manuscript including Wayne Arthurson, Nadir Bellahmer, Daniel Roy, Ken Williamson, and Marlon Wilson, for their feedback and encouragement.

Buk Arop, for providing research on the Dinka language, and information about the lives of South Sudanese in E-Town, and for voicing Rap Garang in the book teaser.

Nadir Bellahmer for creating original music for one of the book's promotional videos, and Politic Live and Souljah Fyah for allowing me to use their music for other promotional videos.

Martin Bernal (*maaxeru-em-hetep*) and Richard Poe for conversations regarding Kemetic history.

John Chan, for introducing me to Iron John and other works by Robert Bly.

Mark Cherrington, for providing information on the path of arrestees through police custody and the Edmonton Remand Centre.

Ben Coxworth, for excellent shooting and editing of a promotional video for the book.

Ejaz Farouk, for his helpful insights about youth culture in E-Town.

Faduma Bunule (former owner of Kulmiye Family Restaurant) and her daughter and niece, for their insights into Somali women's experiences in Canada and specifically in E-Town.

Mohammed Maie and Liban "Li-One" Farah for telling me their perspectives on the lives of Somali-Canadian boys and men.

Jibril Yassin for promotional video production and editing, for voicing JC for the book teaser, and for lending his face to JC for one of the book's wallpapers.

Fiona Yates for proofreading the manuscript.

My wife and daughters for giving me the best reasons to celebrate life and engage the beautiful struggle for a better world.

Ultimately, all praise is due to the Supreme.

MORE FAUST

Visit ministerfaust.com

Join his community of Facebook:
facebook.com/MinisterFaustBooks

Follow him on Twitter @ministerfaust

Watch his YouTube channel:
youtube.com/user/MinisterFaust

Read his blog, THE BRO-LOG:
ministerfaust.blogspot.com

Susbscribe to his podcast MF Galaxy:
mfgalaxy.com

Support his podcast via Patreon:
patreon.com/mfgalaxy

CPSIA information can be obtained
at www.ICGtesting.com
Printed in the USA
LVOW08s0831150617

538226LV00002B/8/P